SANCTUARY WITH KINGS
TEMPTING MONSTERS
BOOK III

KATHRYN MOON

D1736926

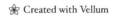

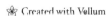

FOREWORD AND CONTENT INFORMATION

Thank you so much for returning to the Tempting Monsters universe! For a complete list of content information *please* check out kathrynmoon.com/books but there are some pertinent details below!

This is a why choose monster romance and includes mf, mmf, mfmmm, and mm content.

Note on Medieval Mythology: I am the first to admit that I play fast and loose with old myths, but since I know Arthurian legend is so beloved I'll go ahead and defend myself a tad. There are versions of the myths that are popular, but there are many older and lesser known as well. I promise I did research, although I did still make my own adjustments in spots.

Content Warnings Include:

Murder - off page discussion and on page action

Violence - strangulation, gore, magical violence (all in scenes of action and conflict)

Trauma - there's a theme of nightmares presenting past trauma in a non-literal and more symbolic way, they are not graphic but they are meant to be menacing and if you would like to avoid those scenes in particular they are all in italics. Light suicidal ideation in early parts of the book.

More CWs at kathrynmoon.com/books

CONTENTS

to salmon, honored sponsor of this book

PROLOGUE

The prickle of my patron's stare scratched at my breasts as the beautiful bodies surged against me, rolling me between them. I'd had plenty of guests who preferred to watch my work rather than partake of it themselves. Some as high and mighty as you might find on thrones or behind pulpits. I'd always enjoyed their strained energy, their desperate refusal. They sought to deny themselves pleasure, but they didn't understand their own habit. The denial was the source for them, and it fed my own hunger and craving every bit as much as the grunting, gasping, sweating figures who touched me with enthusiasm and demand.

But not this man. There was no warmth from his stare, no need and no denial. He watched for some other purpose, studied with some other goal.

It should've warned me, but I was busy feasting.

The *néktar* was rich from the two men on the bed with me. They were *other*, like I was, although not in any way I could perceive.

A mouth lowered to my breath, kiss almost vicious, and I arched with a cry, pressing my ass to the hips fitted behind me. They held me close, their frenzied need like clouds of perfume in the air. I gasped, swallowing it by the lungful, my skin stroked with the ripples of rising sexual pleasure. My ambrosia. My *néktar*. A richer drink than wine, a stronger meal than a king's roast.

In my body, release was a wave, a sweeping, curling,

I

retreating motion. But in my soul, it was a sudden flood, a cascading rush into the hollow of my belly. If I was starving, I might be sated, soothed by the fresh supply of pleasure.

Whoring was clever work for one of Hedone's daughters, and I was never starving.

A golden hand gripped my throat, drawing me back like a bowstring, and the man behind me bellowed as he reached his finish. I laughed as his hand squeezed a little too tightly, my head soaking in the surplus of rapture. My breath was gifted back to me as the lovely young man pounding into my cunt cried out, falling into me, sending the pile of us to heavy, soft sheets.

It was a beautiful drowning. I would sleep for hours until it settled into my bones. I would glow brightly and dazzle eyes for days. I smiled, reaching drowsy hands to my companions, petting them with sweet gratitude.

Out of the corner of my eye, the shadow of my third guest rose from his seat.

"She'll do very well. Collect her."

I giggled at the words, and the man at my back groaned, shoving me to the side, the younger man still catching his breath.

"Quickly," the cool voice ordered. "Before she recovers."

I was drunk and vulnerable in my satisfaction. My hands were limp as someone covered my face with fabric, thrusting a coarse bag over my head. I scratched weakly at the hand that wrestled my arms behind my back.

And still I laughed, cried, trembled in the wake of my traitorous guests' pleasure.

I was trapped, though I didn't yet know what kind of cage had fallen down around me in my foolish naïveté. Only that I was of a kind to survive.

I didn't know that survival would not be a blessing.

And so, centuries passed...

1.
FREEDOM
AND STARVATION

"Fancy a fuck, luv?"

"Give us a wink."

"I'll see you right, mi'lord."

The pretty birds of the evening fluttered on the corner in front of me, skirts swishing up to reveal the wares on offer.

"She's costin' us punters," one of the women hissed as the pack of merry men passed our little huddle.

I hunched and ducked my head, turning my back to the group.

"She's no more trouble than a mouse."

"She looks ill. They'll think we're the same."

I licked my lips, torn and chapped as they were, and they stung in the wake. My hands were numb. My feet too. The street wavered and slid side to side in my vision.

I was *starving*. A fathomless hunger that dug a pit deeper than my frail form could hold.

But I was free.

Maggie sighed, and her shadow loomed and lurched across the cobblestones as she crossed to my little corner of the alley.

"Dolly..." she started.

"I heard them," I rasped, looking up at last.

Maggie had found me. After the fire. After the house cracked. After I'd run screaming into the night, taken my first breath of a world I didn't recognize, found myself *free* of Birsha's shackles.

"I'll get you sometin' to eat. Just go back to the flat, why don' you?" Maggie said gently.

I'd heard the women whispering to each other. Maggie found broken birds, tried to nurse us, mend us. She'd bring me half a pie at dawn and comb my hair and pat my back. It wouldn't fill the massive void inside of me, the twisted, corrupted hollow of craving, rotted and wrong after centuries in the worst company, the darkest pleasures.

"I'll find work," I whispered, stumbling away from the street lamp. The light did me no favors. The other women were right—I'd looked weak and ill the night I escaped, and it'd only gotten worse in the weeks of my freedom.

Pleasure on the streets was cheap and brief, perfunctory. There was no joy in the minutes of grunting and pumping from the human men who stumbled out of pubs and gaming hells. As crooked as the meals Birsha delivered to me had been, they were the appetites and satisfactions of far greater creatures than human men.

I trailed in my path away from the whores who'd taken me in, away from the bright corner of safety, into the darker shadows. Someone would find me. I may not take a coin out of the exchange, but at least it might feed me a little. The night was muggy and foul, but a chill had started to eat away the feeling in my fingers and toes weeks ago, my blood sluggish.

A blessed woman, wasting to nothing but hunger for pleasure.

Pleasure made me sick now. I was a perversion of the woman I ought to have been. Centuries in the cold, barren cage of Birsha's grip had bled me dry.

The wheels of a carriage clicked and ground over the stone street, hooves clopping to a stop, a still groomsman sitting high and silent like a sentry. I kept my eyes ahead on the swimming darkness, but stopped to let the gentlemen have a look at me. He would move away soon. I was not a tempting sight.

Except the door opened silently, a white glove extending out, a silver coin pinched between thick fingers.

"Come into the carriage, and there's another," a low voice offered.

Two silver coins and I might buy my passage to the grave, I thought, blinking at the coin as it tipped and shivered in my eyes. No, it was me that was tilting and weaving and trembling.

"Come out, and you'll only need the one, mi'lord," I answered.

His voice grunted and the hand withdrew and the door closed softly. It would drive away again, which was good, because the men who paid too much often asked too much in return. I started to move, to almost fall forward into motion again, when the door opened fully.

Out stepped a mountain of a man, dressed in gleaming black and shining white. I looked up, but it made me dizzy, contorting the handsome face and setting the liquidy dark eyes spinning until I ducked my head again. He was too big, too beautiful. I backed away, but one of those pristine white gloves reached for me.

"There's better fare down the road," I gasped, twisting out of the way.

The hand clenched on air and then opened again, held out flat in invitation. "Not ones who need so much as you."

I blinked and froze. He was the most alluring trap, his voice thick and low and sweet, like a tongue lapping over my weak pulse, trying to bring it back to life again. He was even more perfect than the pair Birsha had drugged me with centuries ago when I was a spoiled and innocent child. And I was *starving*. Dying, probably, although it might take years more of this withering life before it was over.

His other hand lifted, still holding the silver coin. "Take it, at the very least."

The coin would buy me food, but it wouldn't feed me. No matter what this man wanted from me, I had survived worse already.

My hand shook as I reached for his, my skin dirty and ruining his perfect white gloves with one touch. His grip was gentle, and it was strange to be touched so.

"Come closer," he said.

I swallowed, and my throat scratched itself, dry and aching. My steps were unsteady, and his arm circled around my shoulders, a shelter or a cage, but his warmth soaked through my thin rags of clothing.

"You look tired," he whispered.

Does he mean to kill me? I wondered.

But he bent, and I had to lean back into the strong arm behind me. He dropped the hand he held in order to cup my face, soft white kid leather stroking at my cheek as he tipped my face up. His face was less clear to me than ever as he ducked down, features all blurring strangely. I shut my eyes and found full and heavy lips covering mine, thick breath rushing over my numb face.

The kiss was chaste, barely more than a press, but the power that came with it was like dropping an anchor into my belly, the weight sinking and sinking, measuring the real distance and depth of my hunger.

I gasped and my hands flew up, eyes opening into a confusing cross of visions. The face in my grip did not match the man looking down at me.

"No!" I breathed, but I was swaying, my legs weak, my starvation pleading a new demand for *more* of this man. But he was not a man.

Two brows furrowed, one human and handsome, the other dark and powerful and familiar.

"Forgive me, daughter of Hedone," the low voice rumbled.

And then his hand rose up to smother my scream, bringing with it a heady, dizzying scent that blotted out the world.

࿇

I WOKE, MY HEAD HEAVY, AND MY HANDS TIGHTENED BENEATH me. In their grip they found velvet, so thick and lush and soft that I moaned, rubbing the fabric between my fingers. I turned my head, and the pillow beneath me gave way sweetly, silk cool against my cheek.

My breath caught, a whimper stifled in my chest. I smelled foul, and I only knew as much because the air around me was thick and redolent with lavender and rose and gardenia. I was in the softest bed I was sure I'd ever known. I opened my eyes and shut them again, gasping.

Decadence.

I sat up, eyes squeezed shut, and tried to make myself let go of the velvet blanket draped over me.

"Move slowly," a gentle voice offered, a woman's. "I promise you're safe."

I forced my eyes open again and searched the glittering, gleaming, and lush surroundings. A woman sat on the foot of the bed, pretty and pale, her gaze milky and absent. In the corner of the room, another figure moved, and this time I hissed, scrambling backwards. My strength faltered at the perfect cushion behind me, a mountain of pillows offering me *comfort*.

But the man, the *monster* in the corner of the room, was familiar. The basilisk. He'd never touched me, but he'd been there in Birsha's lair—more than once, from what I could recall. He was tall, with black horns curling high, and he wore a pair of black spectacles that hid his gaze.

"She recognizes me," the basilisk said.

The woman sighed. "I told you."

"I'm *not* leaving you alone with her," he growled, arms crossing over his chest.

And it took me a moment to realize he was speaking to the woman, as if *I* were the threat in the room.

There were bouquets in every corner, works of art on the walls, golden filigree frames, chandeliers dripping with crystals.

"My name is Lillian. I'm human," the woman offered. "And that is Marius. He is—"

"I know what he is," I said, my voice croaking.

Lillian dipped her head. "He is *not* a danger to you."

"Unless you are a danger to *her*," Marius warned in a low snarl.

And the woman, the human woman, sighed in amused acceptance, her lips quirking. She was blind, I realized, watching her stare move aimlessly. And he was *protective* of her. Was she his to torment? Except she wore an elegant yet simple dress, and she had color in her cheeks, and there was...a hint of satisfaction in the air coming from her. I sat up again, scooting down the bed, and my lips fell open, trying to catch the taste.

They were lovers. And it was a sweeter flavor than I'd known in...

"We have a bath prepared for you," Lillian said. "And there will be food. Anything you'd like. For now, I have this."

She lifted a delicate cup on a small plate, both painted and touched with gold. A dense and delicious fragrance floated to me from the cup, and my mouth watered.

"What is it?" I asked.

"Chocolate," Lillian said, with a secretive smile. "When Asterion told us what you'd need to recover, this was the first thing I thought of."

The space between us was vast, all dense and soft bedding for me to climb over, but neither the woman nor the basilisk so much as twitched in my direction.

"What do you want with me?" I asked.

"Birsha's house has fallen," the basilisk said. My body contracted on itself at his name. "You're here to be kept safe."

"Until he rebuilds," I said.

Lillian set the cup aside and twisted toward me, shaking her head. "No. No, not that at all. Until he is *defeated*. You are here to...rest and recover, and to be sure that no harm comes to you. From Birsha or anyone else."

"Asterion is coming," the basilisk said.

I wanted to run to the window at my left, throw myself out into the night, escape. I wanted to burrow down into the deep bed, cry into the velvet, smother myself with the down pillows.

I held still, and the heavy footsteps approached the door.

I knew who he was. Asterion. The minotaur. A legend of my mother's world. An infrequent visitor to The Seven Veils.

He knocked once and the basilisk opened the door, dwarfed immediately by the figure who stepped inside.

He was not wearing his human disguise now, but I recognized the full, dark gaze that had found me in the street. His horns were broad, tipped with gold, and his jaw was massive and squared. Those plush lips had pressed to mine. He was dressed in human gentlemen's clothing, his massive chest stretching the seams of fine fabrics. He was potent and beautiful, powerful and pristine. Just the sight of him was a little kernel of relief to my starvation. My mouth watered and I swallowed hard.

Birsha had never sold me to either of these men, but I'd seen them come and go, Asterion especially in recent months. He bowed now at the waist, his broad shoulders blocking out the room as I stared.

"I apologize for the deception. I don't fault you your caution, my lady. I only wanted to get you off the streets before one of Birsha's men found you."

"Asterion has offered his house to the women who escaped The Seven Veils," Lillian murmured, but I couldn't tear my gaze from the minotaur.

"You were there," I said, glancing briefly at the basilisk to include him.

"An unfortunate part of my role as spy," Asterion said, straightening but ducking his eyes to the floor.

There was a pause of silence and then the basilisk, Marius, cleared his throat. "Temporary necessity."

Lillian snorted. It was a sound of humor and skepticism, but with a sweetness to it that was rare to my ears. Everything, *everyone* in the room was a heady flood on my senses, a buffet of pleasantness so rich, it became indulgence.

"What do you want?" I asked the minotaur.

"For you to rest. To eat. To recover," he said. "That is all."

It was *impossible*.

"Leave us," Lillian said to the men. "We will start with the chocolate."

Asterion seemed almost to flee the room, his steps quick and heavy, but Marius remained the stubborn sentry for several moments.

"I know you're still there," Lillian said with a dry smile.

He twitched slightly in my direction. "If you harm her, I will eat you."

It ought to have frightened me, but the threat was nothing but the promise of an ending.

"Go, Marius," Lillian laughed, and the sound was clear and lovely. I shut my eyes to soak it in. Even the clip of the basilisk's footsteps made a curious kind of music as he paced away. "Here now, drink this."

Fabric swished and whispered, and the bed dipped. But I wasn't scared of the pretty human woman with the tender voice. I wanted to throw myself into her arms, steal all her quiet joy and make it my own. She pressed warm porcelain into my shaking hands, and I opened my eyes just enough to raise it to my lips.

The chocolate was dark and divine, thick and rich. It was bitter, sweet, and salty all at once. I let it sit in my mouth, warming me from the taste alone, and my eyes filled with tears. As I swallowed, I started to weep.

2.
FEASTING FOR
THE SENSES

Lillian hummed a song as she bathed me, her dulcet melody soothing against my ragged whimpers and sniffles. We'd already wasted one round of perfectly scalding hot water just rinsing the grime off of me, and now the tub was full of bubbles, the water silky and fragrant. Candles burned around the room, like mythical blooms on golden stems.

I settled in the water eventually, growing drowsy. My hair was washed and combed, my skin scrubbed clean. Lillian and I finished the pot of chocolate, and then I had an entire plate of tender sandwiches on thick bread to myself.

"Asterion says you are something more than human," Lillian murmured.

My stomach was full, and the edge of my hunger had been dulled by something other than a monster's gruesome pleasure for the first time in centuries.

I studied Lillian. She was healthy, happy, safe, and in the company of a basilisk.

"Birsha kept me because I could survive more than human women," I said, not wanting to tell her the truth.

My mother was a goddess. It meant less than nothing. It was why I'd been collected, and it'd done me no favors.

"And you gain strength from pleasure?" she asked.

Hedonism.

"Yes," I answered. The luxurious bedroom, the spectacular bed, even this bath, were all fresh flavors to my deprived hunger, shocking and unfamiliar. The *chocolate* had been exceptional though, a better meal than I'd known in far too long.

I'd been Birsha's toy to pass around, a bright magnet to bring in powerful clients, and cruelty in pleasure was as poisonous as it was filling.

"We will keep you safe," Lillian murmured, running the comb once more through my hair, the tines scratching gently at my scalp. A tiny lick of a taste to soothe me.

"You belong to the pair of them?" I asked.

Would they make me their toy now too? It would feed me. And perhaps, if they treated me as they did Lillian, there might not be pain.

Lillian laughed. "Only Marius. And he belongs to me too," she added in a conspiratorial whisper. "Let's get you to bed."

Then the minotaur meant to have me. Fatten me up with food and good care first, perhaps bring me back to life a bit, make me a better bed partner.

Water sluiced, and Lillian lifted an enormous sheet of thick linen, smooth and cool, for me to dry myself with. There was a mirror in the bathroom, tall and wide, and I was a pale sliver of bones in the reflection, swaddled in fabric. Next came a silk dress, too exquisite and pristine to be touched, but Lillian fumbled it over my head and then I helped her dress me, lace around my collar, cascading silver fabric stroking over my shriveled breasts and bony hips.

"I think wanting to spoil you with gowns and art is all well and good, but we'd better make a priority to feed you *food* too," Lillian said, after her hands had met my stark ribs.

Birsha had fed me slop, dreadful and bitter or entirely flavorless, anything to starve me and keep me alive at the same time.

"Come here," she said, and she guided us both to the bathroom counter. "There are perfumes. Creams. All sorts of nonsense. Help yourself. I'm going to send for some soup."

There were bottles of cut crystal, jars painted with flowers, little glass compacts of powders. And I was alone—alone in candlelight and steam and perfume.

The room was decadent and ornate, lavish. The tile was smooth and cool, and there were a pair of fur-lined slippers waiting at the counter. And I was still starving. My toes slid into the slippers, and I stifled a moan at the brush of feathery-soft fur against my bruised and calloused feet. I lifted a bottle to my nose and sighed at the gasp of ambergris and vanilla. A jar contained a floral cream that smoothed over my skin like butter.

The creature in the mirror was not a face I recognized, skin sallow and paper-thin on pronounced bones, eyes red and surrounded by shadow. My nails were ragged, hair dully pale. Months of thin snacking on human men from the streets of London had nearly finished what Birsha had started.

I took one of the delicate bottles, pulled out a jeweled stopper, and traced a line of perfume across my throat. Orchid, musk, and ambergris. My eyes stung.

The minotaur knew what he was doing, knew more than he ought to. He was whetting my palate, feeding my starved senses with all the gentlest forms of pleasure.

What I didn't understand was why he didn't make use of the far simpler and less costly method of feeding me. He could fuck me. I would enjoy it; that was my unfortunate nature—provided the person using me was finding pleasure, so must I. And he was a powerful creature, all strength and vitality, so I would probably be fed within a few tries.

So what was this game of pretty objects and delicious sweets? What was the point of offering a starving woman beautiful crumbs?

FOR TWO DAYS, I SLEPT IN SHORT BUT HEAVY BURSTS. Another woman, a blonde with pursed lips and precise movements, brought mugs of broth and plates of buttery, crumbling muffins. In the morning, I woke to music playing, not too near but clear enough for me to hear. Next, the sound of birds and the warm breeze of an *open* window, a precious luxury. During the night, a low and gentle voice—the minotaur—recited poetry from outside of the cracked bedroom door.

It continued as I turned in the silk and velvet, my body

begging for sleep, my mind waking in the old pattern Birsha had trained me in. Four hours of rest at a time. Not a minute more.

Asterion and the house and the music and the food nourished me in scant nibbles.

But it didn't hurt.

I left the bathroom during my next waking and found Lillian waiting for me at a table set with a richer meal than I'd been served so far. Lillian's head turned in my direction, and my slippers scuffed against the thick carpet.

"I want to take you down to the orangery today, before you grow sick of the same surroundings," she said.

"That's not likely to happen so soon," I admitted.

The window by the bed had been opened again, and the sun was streaking through thin curtains. The room was hazy and pink and smelled of the world outside and the breakfast waiting under the tray.

Lillian smiled. "We could go for a walk in the woods on the property, but I'm sure Marius and Asterion will insist on chaperoning. Their company depends on your acceptance."

It was a baffling offer. That I should be allowed outside. That I could refuse the monster's right to guard me. I didn't comment, taking my seat instead and holding my breath as I lifted the lid on the tray. It didn't stop the scents of fat and salt, a tang of lemon, rich fish, and my mouth watered immediately. The plate was a work of art, spiraling dribbles of sauce, roses of radishes, sprinkles of herbs. I lifted my fork with a quaking hand as Lillian continued to speak.

"Asterion worries someone may come looking for you. And Marius worries I'll trip, I suppose," she said, drily.

"He worries I am mad from my time with Birsha," I said. I pressed my fork down into an egg and marveled as vibrant orange yolk spilled over the white plate. I lifted the fork to my tongue and withheld my whimper.

"Are you?" Lillian asked. I glanced at her and her eyebrows were lifted, but her expression was as serene as ever.

She was lovely and quiet, and a strange part of me wanted to slide myself against her, find a way into her apparent peace and claim it for myself.

"I don't know," I said. "I feel as if I'm dreaming, but I forgot how to dream of beautiful things more than a hundred years ago."

Lillian's breath caught, and then she exhaled slowly. "This is real. We will refill your well."

I cut my food into tiny bites, resting each one on my tongue as Lillian poured me a cup of chocolate, her motions measured and careful.

"You were not in The Seven Veils," I said, watching her as I chewed. One drop added to the well with every bite.

"No, I was taken in by another house. One that sought to offer women...the choice, I suppose," she said, shrugging. "I was introduced to Marius there. And he's always been invested in my freedom to choose as well."

It was a gentle defense of her monster. Did she know he'd been a guest of The Seven Veils too? Did she know I'd never touched him? Neither one of us dug further, and Lillian made silence companionable.

I hadn't left the bedroom yet, and Lillian helped me into a loose gown before taking my arm and guiding me out into the hall. There was a balcony that overlooked a large gallery on my left and a few more doors scattered down the hall ahead of us. Downstairs, a young woman with black hair crossed the tile, her arms wrapped around herself. She lifted her face, glancing up at the last moment, her steps faltering as our eyes met.

"Where are we?" I asked, stopping in place.

The woman blinked at me, her lips parting briefly, and then she hurried ahead. I didn't know her name, but I knew her face.

"Grace House," Lillian said. "It belongs to Asterion, but he's given it to the women who escaped from The Seven Veils when it fell. To recover, rest. Simply a home until we know you'll all be safe in the future."

Was she telling the truth, or was this simply a gilded cage to hold us until Birsha returned? I stared at the massive doors in the great hall, the light of the world calling from outside towering windows. I could run. I could return to the streets, escape London altogether. Steal one bejeweled perfume bottle

15

and find myself passage to some barren, remote place where I might starve to death in peace.

But Birsha would not want me fed with cups of chocolate and rich sauces; he wouldn't allow me to rest my head on feather pillows and sleep until I couldn't stand not to wake. He certainly wouldn't allow me to be guarded by a patient blind woman whose arm linked so loosely with mine that even in my shabby state, I could've shoved her away and run.

Lillian seemed to know my own mind, or she understood a slight shift forward as I made my decision, because we walked together again without a word. Grace House was grand and open, although less glittering and lush than the bedroom I'd been set up in. It had the masculine strength of its owner, with dark marble pillars and simple lines. Lillian led a slow path through a well-stocked library, a parlor, a music room, and out to the southern edge of the house, where sunlight raged through glass and the sharp, fresh scent of oranges cut through every other sense.

Lillian released my arm as we crossed the threshold, and I gaped up at the trees growing inside, branches heavy-laden.

"Bring me an orange?" Lillian called back to me, counting her steps to a small table at the center of the room, where cushioned seats waited for us.

Orchids bloomed in ornate pots, carefully sheltered in the shade of the trees. Fat green leaves ate the generous sunlight that spilled over blue and white tiled floors, cut into small triangles and twisted to make shifting patterns. I closed my eyes for a moment, let the morsel of beauty soak into my blood, and then went to the nearest branch, helping myself to a small burden of oranges.

Lillian's face was upturned, a vessel for light to warm, and she smiled with her eyes closed as I joined her at the table and pressed an orange into her small palm.

Her thumb cut into the flesh of the orange and she started a spiraling peel. Someone had tidied my nails while I slept, and I copied her motions. Took in the spray of sharp citrus in the air, the waft of the scent, the velvety pith against the skin of my thumb.

Suddenly, I understood. I'd been made to survive only on what brought me pain and thrilled another.

The bed and the clothes, the perfume and bath, and the food I was fed now was for no one's pleasure but my own. I lifted the orange to my face and sucked in a deep breath, squeezing it in my fist as I fought to bury the scream in my chest.

3.
HOW LONG?

A week passed. I gained weight and found that sating physical hunger with the feasts set on small tables in my bedroom did offer some relief from the soul-deep gnawing that still plagued me.

Lillian came and went. Marius had a house in the city that they were staying in. I considered telling her that I didn't need her company, or for her to guard me, whatever her purpose was, but the truth was I liked her. I liked not being alone.

And I preferred her to the other, colder woman who left me meals, brought me clothes, and stared speculatively at me out of the corner of her pretty blue eyes.

Still, there were improbable hours where I was left alone, the bedroom door unlocked, the window open, as if I were still free. I wandered a gallery filled to the brim with landscapes and heroic figures and women swooning in the embraces of beasts or on velvet settees. I drank tea and nibbled on pastries in the orangery. I stood outside the door of the library and listened to the quiet conversations of the women who'd survived, whose crying I heard sometimes from my open window, who stopped to stare at me and then ducked their heads and skirted away.

I learned Grace House one room at a time, from the kitchens to the attics, spying and snooping, never prevented from opening a door.

And then one day, after Lillian had left, with an offer to wander the grounds the next day—Marius included—I heard his voice.

The minotaur.

"He's on the continent, hiding somewhere, reinforcing his houses there. Digging his claws out of England has just allowed him to tighten his grip elsewhere."

Birsha.

"I don't particularly care where he is or what he's doing, provided it isn't here," a tart, clipped voice answered—the blonde woman. "There are more women to find, Asterion."

"Conall and Byron are searching now," Asterion answered calmly.

I'd been inside this room before, the minotaur's office. What I'd found had been reassuring—letters discussing Birsha's whereabouts, efforts to create a network of allies opposing him, simple bills and business correspondence mixed in. Lillian was right—I *was* being protected here.

"Byron is meant to be guarding us. You're meant to be searching," the woman answered. "Not reading poetry in the hall at all hours of the night."

"Isabel—"

"This house is for *them*."

"This house is my property." There was a low chuckle in the words.

I pressed myself to the wall, peering into the cracked door, but only saw the shelves laden with curious objects, a collection of treasures from an endless lifetime.

"I know that," the woman, Isabel, answered, taking a breath and tempering her tone. "But when you opened Grace House to these women, you did say they would not be disturbed by your kind."

A chair creaked with effort, and the minotaur sighed. "I did, you're right. But she requires a different kind of care to recover. *She's* different."

"So you said." Sour again.

"Don't take that tone. Not when it comes to her. She survived no less than any of the others," Asterion said, voice lowering to a rumble like thunder.

They were speaking of me.

"I'm not saying otherwise, and I don't..." There was a rustle of fabric, pacing footsteps. "I don't argue that she should receive that care, but does it have to be *here*, disrupting the peace of all the others?"

Asterion snorted roughly. "Is my reading so bad?"

"You are here, and they know it," Isabel snapped. "You are standing outside of their bedrooms, and they can hear you. Hear your footsteps. See your shadow. It's not what you promised them. Byron, at least—"

"Yes, Byron remains out of doors and lets you treat him as a hound," Asterion answered, his own voice rising to match hers. "I wear my disguise—"

"It doesn't matter, they *know*," Isabel cried out. "It's rather obvious when it comes to you. You are..."

Silence rang.

"I am what?"

"*Beastly*."

My fingers dug into the wall, my eyes wide. I did not breathe as shock took over every impulse in my body. I was afraid for this woman, and I also wanted to *be* her in all her careless bravery, and I wanted to open the door wide and tell her how absurd she was. The minotaur was beautiful. Perhaps beastly too, but not in the way that cruel, sharp voice implied.

"Snoop." The word slipped into my ear, rasping softly.

I let out a sharp cry, my heart starting again with a shock as I spun in place. A wild white grin beamed down at me, surrounded by bright coppery hair. My hand clapped over my heart and behind me, from the office, footsteps ran closer. The man in front of me, the one who'd caught me listening through open doors, was wickedly sensuous, with eyes the shade of the sunlight cast through leaves in the orangery and long sweeps of red hair gleaming under candlelight. He didn't stop grinning at me, two pink scars slashing through his handsome face on one cheek, a third, smaller one on the opposite eyebrow.

"Conall," Asterion said, flat and hard. "You're not meant to—"

"Come in, I know. But you see, I'm incorrigible, so it's not my fault," Conall answered.

He was bursting to the seams with humor and joy. The wink

of his eye promised either howls of laughter or pleasure. The gloss of his hair promised softness to the touch. This man was deliciousness on my tongue, a heat that built the longer I stood in the force of it.

"Get in here," Asterion rumbled, and he made no mention of me or of my spying. Perhaps he'd known I stood there all along.

Conall held the door open, bouncing dark eyebrows on his brow. I glanced inside of the dark, close room, then back to the hall behind him. His nearness made my mouth water. The scent of pipe smoke and flesh engulfed him, like he'd spent hours in a bawdy house. I stepped in front of him, and the hair on the back of my neck rose in understanding. He was a predator.

I didn't mind.

"How much did you hear?" Isabel asked me, her arms crossed over her chest, chin held high. She was exceptionally beautiful, I thought, and I looked to Asterion next to see how she affected him. But he was staring at me.

And he was wearing that human disguise again, rugged and handsome and huge, with dark curls and large, liquid eyes, like the cups of chocolate I'd been guzzling all week. They were a lovely pair, if not for the fact that their mutual dislike was fairly tangible and set my teeth on edge.

"I don't know," I admitted. "Plenty about me."

Isabel's lips pressed flat, so I continued.

"You don't mind my being here, but you don't like that I'm the reason Asterion is here. And perhaps Marius too?" I guessed.

"Good ol' Isabel. Happy to accept the generosity of monsters, as long as she doesn't have to look us in the eye," Conall said softly, circling around me and helping himself to one of the large leather chairs in front of Asterion's desk.

Isabel's face reddened, and she shot a glare at Conall before marching past me to the door. "Just remember what you promised," she said in parting.

Asterion sighed, and his steps were heavy as he returned to his desk.

"She's rotten," Conall muttered.

"To us. But not to the women who need her," Asterion said. "That's what matters."

I considered Isabel's cool treatment of me so far, but either she resented my bringing the monsters into the house or she resented that I wasn't human. Either way, it didn't seem worth mentioning, and Conall didn't give me time to do so.

"I don't see how she can object to you looking like that," Conall continued, waving a careless bare hand at Asterion's disguise. He flashed me a smirk. "Isn't he pretty?"

"I don't object to either of his appearances," I said.

Asterion sat heavily in his chair, and Conall's eyes tightened slightly. "Don't you? That's nice." He turned to Asterion again. "Isn't that nice, Ast? And after all, what are you doing that's so objectionable but paying for fine meals and all the little baubles and dresses the women seem to need?"

Asterion was staring at me, his hands raised, in white gloves. "Do you mind if I...?"

Oh, the gloves served as his disguise. I shook my head, and they were removed. He sighed, flexing his fists, and leaned back in his chair, shoulders broader than before, horns polished and shining by lamplight.

"I'm reading poetry," Asterion said, relaxing into his seat.

Conall barked out a laugh. "Well, never mind then, your taste in poetry is maudlin at best."

I found myself stepping slowly closer. It was Conall, probably, the vibrancy of him making me crave what I was afraid to take. Or it was Asterion's velvety gaze watching me as he smoothed a large hand around his massive jaw.

"You read the poetry for me," I said.

Asterion ducked his head. "You can ask for anything you like, and I'll be sure you receive it. But I thought it might...be worth a little."

Conall observed us, growing quiet in his seat, still too, dangerously watchful.

"How did you know what I was?" I asked Asterion, now at the edge of his desk, pinned between their two stares.

"Your mother was kind to me once," Asterion said. "I see...I see her touch in you. I knew you as soon as I saw you in that house. I swore to myself I would find a way to set you free."

"Am I free?" I asked.

"Yes," Asterion said, brow furrowing and jaw shifting. His ears looked soft. His bullish features were gentled by his human mother's blood, eyes more keen and aware, face less elongated, but yes, I supposed he was beastly. Even in his human disguise, he was huge and powerful. However, I didn't understand Isabel's objection.

"Because you did drug me to bring me here," I pointed out.

Behind me, Conall chuckled. Asterion's head ducked, sharply tipped horns tilted in my direction. "I did. You were..."

"Dying," I said, nodding, strangely relieved when his gaze lifted to mine again.

"In truth, I would...not want you to leave," Asterion said softly, and the words seemed to wrap around me like the velvet bedding. "Birsha needs one of your kind in his houses. As long as you are out of his reach, and others are safe, he will not be able to rebuild here. But you *are* free."

"Even to return to him?" I asked.

Conall growled at my back, and my spine prickled. Asterion's eyes widened until there was a thin ring of white around the dark. "Do you want—?"

I stopped him, needing to hear the answer first. "Please tell me the truth."

I didn't want to return to Birsha, but I wanted to know the terms of my rescue. Was I a tool to be withheld from an enemy? Or was I *free*?

"Asterion," Conall warned.

"If it is your desire to return to Birsha...I will not prevent it," Asterion said, the corners of his broad mouth turning down.

I released a rush of breath, stumbling back, finding the second chair and falling into it.

"You don't want to go back," Conall said, studying me.

"*Never*," I pressed out.

Both men sighed, Asterion sinking into his giant throne of a seat, Conall rising up out of his. I glanced at him and blinked at the sight of a shaggy red tail swishing out the back of his coat tails. I'd never seen a werewolf who kept any features of his other self, but I'd heard of one, a muttered curse in Birsha's dark parlors.

The Red Wolf.

The bane of some of the were clans, ones who sought to rule themselves outside of the laws that kept monsters safe from human discovery.

Conall returned, two glasses in one hand, one in the other. He passed one to Asterion and one to me.

"The poetry? Does it help?" he asked, sliding back into his seat, stretching out long legs, the end of his tail draped over the arm of the chair.

It's like being offered a single grain of salt, I thought.

But I'd just been reassured of my absolute free will in this house, and unlike Isabel, I would not return that blessing with an insult.

"A little," I said.

Conall beamed. "Then allow me to try my own hand."

"Conall," Asterion groaned.

The Red Wolf sat up in the chair and cleared his throat.

"Come rede me, dame, come tell me, dame,
'My dame come tell me truly,
'What length o' graith, when weel ca'd hame,
'Will sair a woman duly?
The carlin clew her wanton tail,
Her wanton tail sae ready —
I learn'd a sang in Annadale,
Nine inch will please a lady. —"

It was bawdy humor, in an old, rich accent that reminded me of a time before Birsha. It was Conall grinning and flashing sharp canines, and Asterion's eyes rolling while he lifted a hand to cover his groan.

My face stretched, a curl of warmth in my belly cutting through the endless hunger, and a strange sound escaped my lips —laughter, bubbling up from some place inside of me that I thought had shriveled away long ago.

"Shh, there's two more verses," Conall said, winking at me.

4.
A CHANGE OF PACE

L illian kept her promise of a journey around Asterion's estate. As if to prove the minotaur's offer of my freedom, I was provided with a horse.

"Pigeon takes good care of me," Lillian said, leaning forward in her seat to stroke her own horse's neck. At a respectful distance behind us, Marius followed on a dark stallion.

I could flee now. Marius might follow me, but his attachment to his human lover was obvious, and I didn't think he would abandon her alone in the woods, even if it wasn't as isolated as it first appeared. There was another man somewhere in the shadows of the trees, watching us or guarding us.

We were in the late throes of summer, the sun setting earlier but the humid warmth remaining, bringing in frequent storms. Even today, the sky threatened rain on the way. The mare I rode was not as steady as Lillian's Pigeon, bored with our sedate pace and pulling on the reins, but she was sturdy and brilliantly white, and she'd snatched the apple I'd offered in my palm with a greed I admired.

"Horses are good judges of character," I said. Guinevere, my own mount for the day, didn't seem to know what to make of me, and I didn't blame her.

"You're not scared of them, are you?" Lillian asked.

I glanced over my shoulder at her and found her face lifted and eyes closed. Behind her, Marius followed us like a shadow.

"Horses?"

She smiled slightly. "Sorry, no, my thoughts drifted. The monsters. We assumed you would be, like the other women."

"Oh. No. I was never scared of...of a monster simply for their nature. Only that I might be taken back to Birsha," I said. Lillian hummed, and Marius must've been listening because he rode closer, catching up to her.

"How long were you trapped by him?" he asked.

I turned my back on the lovers, soaking up the view of the woods instead. There was a glitter of water somewhere ahead of us. "How long has he had a house here in England?"

"Over two centuries," Marius answered.

"That long," I replied.

Lillian's breath hitched and I licked my lips, trying and failing not to recall the sounds of the house, my cage, being built above the cellar where I was kept. I struggled my way through memory back to the present. The wind was picking up, and we would need to return to the house soon or get caught in the storm.

"I had a lover who was an incubus for a short time," I said, although I'd been young at the time and considered the decades a lifetime together. "We suited each other's hungers, but not each other's hearts. I went back to whoring after that. And then left again when I fell in love with a demon, although that was an even briefer affair."

"How...how long—" Lillian started, her voice airy.

"Do you know the legend of King Arthur?" I asked. Behind me, Marius scoffed.

"You *knew* him?" Lillian squawked.

"I'm not *that* old," I answered, teasing.

"He didn't exist," Marius parried. "Not the way the stories tell it. He was based off many men, kings and warriors alike."

We reached the water, a small pond, and I let Guinevere help herself to a drink.

"I am less than a millenia old but more than half," I said, shrugging. "I knew the poet who wrote Arthur's name in The Book of Aneirin, though he swore he heard the legend from a fae."

"How did Birsha find you?" Marius asked, his brow furrowed behind his glasses.

Guinevere puffed and skittered away from the water. On the rippling surface, clouds compacted into darker shapes.

"I was working in a brothel. I enjoyed my reputation too much, grew lazy and careless, stayed too long. I was very popular. Even King Charles called me to his bed after hearing rumors." I found my lips curling at the memory of the frazzled, straining man beneath me, wrung out from pleasure. "They called me Volupta, the name my mother took for the Romans, the name she brought here. I even posed for a statue of her. I am sure I was not the first whore Birsha thought might be one of my mother's daughters, but I didn't know to hide myself from a man like him. He hired me, offered me bait, and I gave myself away like a fool."

I'd woken in the bare, cold place Birsha designed to strip joy from me, and for many years—a shameful, piling number—I'd imagined I would either find my way into his favor or out of his grip. I hadn't. Not until dark roots tore through the stone walls that night months ago, until they'd ripped the gated door from its old hinges and I'd run screaming into the night.

Run, *run*, run.

"It's true then, that your mother is a...a goddess?" Lillian asked.

"I think so," I said. "She was an actress when she gave birth to me, traveling through London. She left me with whores, and they raised me by day, and by night I...dreamed of my mother."

Of golden fingers combing through my hair, and her voice telling me stories of gods who quibbled over romances and pride, of men who defied the laws of the world above and below, of monsters and the many myths that made them.

"Do you know if she still walks this world?" Marius asked.

"I've never met her while awake. And it's been centuries since she reached into my sleep." I squeezed my thighs around the belly of Guinevere—it was a silly name for a horse, a woman wrestled over by lovers and kings. She let out a soft cry of relief, and her hooves struck their ground with eager force, propelling us through the woods, over logs and on a sharper path than the designed one that wound decoratively over the grounds.

No golden fingers soothed through my hair while I lay on

moldy blankets and ate bitter gruel. No gentle stories murmured in my ear as I recovered in silk-lined rooms and forced a smile to my face in the hopes it might grant me mercy.

My mother left me in that cage. No one came. No brave men defied Birsha's law. No gods struck lightning through the floor to liberate me.

Guinevere bolted through the woods, but it wasn't freedom we sought together. The sound of the thunder growling overhead mingled with her hoofbeats, my pounding heart. The glitter of Grace House, the lamps lit at the broad entry and at the foot of the large staircase that led to the door, were a beacon.

I wanted...shelter.

A carriage approached the door as I came stampeding closer, and I pulled Guinevere's reins hard, grass giving way to pebbles that skittered as we reared to a sudden stop.

The carriage horses jumped away from Guinevere, the coachman calling out to them. And from the body of the carriage, throwing open the door I faced, came the giant figure of Asterion in his human disguise. I jumped down from my saddle as he stopped in place, a frown creasing the handsome human expression that hid the truth of him.

"Is everything all right?"

Asterion leaned back as I marched toward him, as if he might be scared of me, as if I had the ability to overpower him.

I snatched at his gloves, ripping them from his fingers and dropping them to the ground. I stared up at him as the disguise unraveled, replacing the handsome man with the beautiful monster. He was an entire head taller than me, but when I reached up and clasped his broad jaw in my hands, he bowed, reined to my command.

No man, no god, no mother had come to my rescue.

This monster had.

"Thank you," I murmured.

Thick russet lashes blinked in confusion, and Asterion's dark eyes crossed as I leaned in, pressing my small mouth to his wide bottom lip. A cold wet drop of rain struck the back of my neck, and then massive arms surrounded my back, barely holding.

Sheltering.

I pulled away and stared at him again, waited for those arms to tighten, for the mouth to press and demand. Instead, the heavy lashes batted.

"Tell me your name," Asterion murmured.

Hadn't I? Hadn't he asked Lillian? But names were important, and this minotaur would want mine granted freely.

"Evanthia," I said.

More rain landed, faster and sharper now, cutting into my hair.

Asterion's lips curled and he whispered my name, nodding. "*Théa*, goddess. Come inside now. This storm looks unforgiving."

THE MINOTAUR DID NOT PRESS CLOSER. HE DIDN'T TAKE MY arm and lead me to a bed or a floor. He didn't even offer what we both must know I needed to *truly* recover. We sat across from one another at a small table in my suite, Marius and Lillian on either side, and ate *dinner*.

I tried to put the words on my tongue. I'd been a whore, a courtesan, a seductress, and a lover so many times in my life, in so many variations, but I was at a loss now. Had I forgotten how to invite passion during my time in Birsha's cage, too used to being a tool or a toy to be broken?

The table was small to fit into my quarters and Asterion made it appear even more so, his broad frame hunched toward his plate. He dragged little bites of roasted duck through a green sauce and lifted it on a fine silver fork to his mouth. It was almost comical. He had the body of a beast, as Isabel had called it, but the manners of a diminutive debutante.

"Do the young women staying here cook these meals?" I asked.

Asterion shook his head slowly, the gold on his horns glinting with the candlelight. "I gave the house elves glamoured aprons. Don't tell Isabel." His lashes shrouded his high cheeks as he glanced down.

"You give her too much power in your own house," Marius said, his fine jaw raised high.

"I have many houses," Asterion murmured, continuing to eat.

31

"And Isabel is earnest in her care of the women. That's all that matters."

As if the mention of her name could conjure her, a sharp, ringing voice called from downstairs. "No, you're not to be here!"

Asterion sighed and set down his fork without so much as a clink of sound. He was so gentle with every object and person around him, I wondered how he'd ever managed to convince Birsha to let him into The Seven Veils.

"Excuse me while I handle Conall," Asterion said.

I sat up straighter at the mention of the Red Wolf. I'd learned a little about him from Lillian. He was considered a king of *all* werewolves rather than a single pack, and never belonged to any of the houses that catered human flesh to monster's sexual appetites. He hated Birsha's influence over other werewolves, which had brought him to helping Asterion. She also mentioned that Marius found him tiresome and ill-mannered.

I'd only spent a little time in his company, but he'd been like a wick of flame, alluring and lively. His smile promised trouble and his stare called to my heartbeat, coaxing it to quicken the blood in my veins.

"He's too tolerant," Marius said as Asterion paced to the door.

"Maybe," Lillian said, her lips curling. "Or maybe you're a snob."

The basilisk laughed softly, a hiss in the sound. He leaned back in his chair and for the moment, I was forgotten as he stared at the other woman. "In my defense, I keep the best company in my own home." Lillian hummed and took a bite of food, and I swear I saw the snake's cheeks flush. "*Our* home."

"I've had enough," Isabel snapped from the hall.

"I have important information," Conall drolled. "What am I supposed to do? Send pigeons?"

"You're supposed to stay *outside* of the house."

"*His* house."

"Yes. My house, which is under *her* rule, Conall. You know this."

I rose from my chair, Marius mirroring me, and stepped aside so I could peer out the open door to watch the trio.

Conall and Asterion both easily towered over Isabel, but her spine was straight and her chin was high as she glared up at them. I knew she didn't like me, didn't like my presence in the house and the fact that it brought Asterion and Marius inside, but I did admire her bravery against these powerful beings.

"Birsha's men are looking for this house. They suspect we have her now. The wards are up, but you know sooner or later, they'll find a crack," Conall said to Asterion, and there was no wild play in his tone or his hard expression now.

Asterion sighed, and Isabel's hands clenched. "I told you," she hissed.

"They will not get in," Asterion said slowly.

"Ast—"

"They will, and when they do, I know exactly where you'll be —protecting *her*. Not the others. And I'm sure Birsha's men know the same," Isabel said.

"If we lose the divinity—" Asterion started, and the word and its heavy meaning sent a shiver down my back. It'd been a *long* time since anyone had called me that.

"It's bad enough that you come and go. That *he* does," Isabel said, pointing into my room. She glanced in briefly and caught my eye, and the spite on her face was tucked away as she blinked at me. "And now you can't keep your *dog* out of the house," she added, turning the glare back to Conall.

My eyes widened and Conall growled in answer, baring fangs.

"Isabel," Asterion warned.

She carried on, undaunted, "But he's *right*. Eventually, Birsha's men will hammer at this house long enough. Or they'll find a spy, even a woman—a possibility you all are extremely blind to—and someone will get hurt. I've heard you say it: you're spread too thin."

I licked my lips and gave up any pretense of not being a part of the conversation. It was *about* me. I reached the door and stopped as they turned their attention toward me.

"Please, don't worry—" Asterion started.

"Was the house in danger before I arrived?" I asked, gripping the handle of the door just to hold myself steady.

Conall and Asterion glanced at one another, and it was

Conall who spoke first. "Birsha can find new whores easily enough. You are rare."

"*No,*" Isabel answered me, more direct and honest, her arms crossing over her chest. "We have guards. Ones who stay *outside,* but there's been no threat."

I nodded and turned to Asterion, whose brow was already furrowed. He'd taken his glamoured gloves off before dinner and hadn't put them back on to enter the hallway.

"I should leave," I said.

"No," he answered without pause.

"The other women—they're afraid of me too, aren't they?" I asked next.

Isabel's lips pursed. "Only that you bring them to the house," she said, glancing at Asterion and Conall.

"You *must* stay safe," Asterion pressed, inching toward me, still too gentle to reach out and clutch me.

"We could...take her to Wales," Conall said, and he smiled for the first time, winking at me, a sizzle of attraction answering the glance.

"They're not ready," Asterion said to him.

"Laszlo's no slouch. And since *darling* Isabel can't stand the sight of us, you and I might come and go from there. We have a few other names we can call to London to fill our spots. And there's nothing out there. Less of Birsha's lot to hunt her, easier to hear news of strangers in the area. Easier to see them coming too."

"And the danger of traveling? Of taking her back out into the open now that we know they are searching for her with us?" Asterion asked.

"But it would be a danger only to me, instead of to all the women here, wouldn't it?" I asked.

Asterion's nostrils flared and he exhaled roughly. "A danger to you may amount to a danger to many others in the long run."

"We can take her together," Conall said. "Not on the train, but in a carriage. Private, quiet, and as fast as we can manage."

"It would take days by carriage," Asterion said.

"But less risk of being seen."

"The women here need *peace,*" Isabel urged.

"So too, does she," Asterion answered her sharply, clearly at the end of his patience.

I shook my head and drew his eye. "No more peace. It doesn't cure me." *We both know what I really require*, I wanted to say, but my tongue grew dry and the words wouldn't leave my head.

Asterion studied me for a long moment, Conall shifting restlessly, Isabel tense and determined. He sighed at last and shook his head. "Very well. Rest tonight and tomorrow. We'll have a long journey ahead of us on Saturday."

5.
PROPOSITIONS
AND PARTINGS

"**M**onsters can be very high-handed," Lillian murmured as I packed an outrageous amount of clothing—more than I'd certainly had time to wear while staying in Grace House.

I wasn't sure why Lillian had come to the house today. She was free of her duties in chaperoning me now. But she sat on the bed, reminding me to take the robe, the perfumes, the dresses, all the silly little things Asterion had delivered into my keeping.

"I'm sure there's somewhere else you might go. Not so far from here," she added, her hands fidgeting in her lap.

"Do you not trust Asterion?" I asked.

Lillian shrugged. "Oh, I don't know. Marius does, and he doesn't like or trust very many people at all. But he respects Asterion, and I'm sure he'll keep you safe."

"I'd leave on my own, but I..." I paused and Lillian's head tipped, waiting patiently for me to finish.

I could start over. Maybe not in London while Birsha was searching for me. But if I took the clothes and perfumes and even some of the art that Asterion had filled these rooms with, I could sell them all and I'd have the money to run away and start over.

"I don't want to," I admitted, a faint laugh escaping on a sigh.

A knock rapped on the door, but Marius entered without waiting for us to answer. "Isabel's making arguments about luncheon, but she won't speak to me."

Lillian sighed and picked up her cane from the bed. "I'll

speak with her. You'd think she'd warm up now that she's getting her way."

"She's cold-blooded, and I almost say that with respect," Marius answered.

He caught Lillian by the elbow as she moved toward the doorway, pressing his lips to her temple and then slipping a whisper into her ear before she left.

It was the first time I was alone with the basilisk, and even with his dark glasses hiding his deadly gaze, the force of his stare was almost tangible.

"I can offer you my protection," he said, sudden and rigid.

I paused, my hands still gripped around the silk of a gown. "Your protection?"

"I can ward my own house. Asterion may come and go as he pleases. You wouldn't have to...run off to some rubble in the wilds of Wales."

I opened my mouth but found I didn't have a simple answer ready. "Why offer this?"

"Lillian likes you," Marius said, sighing and sitting down in a chair. He was elegantly handsome, but there was a pristine quality to his good looks that left me cold. "She hasn't had the opportunity of many friends in life."

Suddenly, Lillian's objections to Asterion leaving with me made a bittersweet sense. "Oh," I said, sitting down on the edge of the bed.

"I am just as capable as the minotaur of providing you with luxury," Marius said, shrugging.

I licked my lips. They were still healing, and I found myself nibbling at the scratched skin while I thought.

"Would you fuck me?" I asked.

Marius stiffened and hissed. "What?"

"I am *starving*," I whispered, closing my eyes. "And it isn't something fine meals and lovely dresses will fix. Or friendship, as much as that is precious to me too."

There was a long stretch of quiet. "You need *pleasure*. And I don't think either of us would find that together."

I swallowed hard and opened my eyes, nodding at Marius. "I wouldn't want to hurt Lillian—please don't think I asked lightly."

"You asked to make your point," Marius said, dipping his head in acknowledgement. "But you're better off making your case elsewhere."

"I don't want to put Lillian at risk by staying in London, either," I said, and Marius relaxed at last. "So you can tell her I refused the offer she bid you to make."

The basilisk laughed. "I'll have my pride suitably bruised when I tell her." He was quiet, watching as I returned to the work of packing. He cleared his throat and spoke again. "You don't smell of desire."

I startled. "Should I?"

"Asterion won't touch you until you do. I doubt even the wolf would, though he's hardly the most noble of us," Marius said.

"I take pleasure when others do," I said, frowning.

"Yes, that's why you were so useful to Birsha, of course. A powerful lodestone of pleasure in a house that tormented so many. But Asterion is not the selfish sort, and I don't think more force will heal you in the long run."

I stared at him, lost in the words, the way they made me into something mythical and yet stripped me down to a tool who'd been picked up by the hands of a madman. Where was I in the words? Where had I been for centuries? Surely not the creature locked in the cold, bare cell. Perhaps there was another version of me who'd been left on that soft bed in the high-end brothel so many years ago, who went on in her patterns and pleasures.

Lillian rejoined us in a moment, and I turned back to my packing, staring at objects that were called mine by a man who'd plucked me off the street and determined I should not die.

"I've failed to persuade her, I'm afraid," Marius murmured to Lillian.

She sighed and crossed to me, slowing her steps until her outstretched hand found my arm.

"Then I hope we have cause to meet again in the future," Lillian said to me. "Sometime when there's more to talk about than this war."

THERE WAS NOTHING DECADENT, PLEASURABLE, OR HEDONISTIC about a rushed journey by carriage. Asterion did his best for me. There were warming pans, dense cushions, and fur blankets. But there was no lovely bed to fall into at night, and no controlling the ruts and jogs of the roads we traveled on.

My hunger had never abated, but my treatment at Grace House had tethered its straining urgency.

Being locked alone in the carriage day in and out had withered those restraints and let the carving, clawing, gnawing sensation grow stronger again. Through the curtain over the window, hills gathered and villages passed at a distance. I tensed and braced against the bucking of the carriage like I might a client, and I wished for company. Conall and Asterion were taking turns driving the carriage themselves, our only stops long enough to grab warm, sparse meals and a change of horses.

I was growing desperate after two days, bored and miserable and starving for touch, wondering when we might stop again and how hard it would be to convince Conall and Asterion to let me steal a meal from an eager tavern boy, when the carriage slowed and boots thunked on the ground outside of the door. I held my breath, waiting for Asterion to call to me through the wall of the carriage, considering still what Marius had said about the minotaur's intentions with me, when knuckles rapped and the door opened.

There was nothing like the sudden gust of fresh air flooding the cabin of the carriage to make it clear how stale and stagnant and sour it had grown in the days we'd traveled already. Asterion leaned against the door, and even though it was a beautiful glamour he wore with his gloves, exhaustion still wove through the magic in dark circles around red eyes.

"Conall's sending me in," Asterion rasped.

I assumed he meant whatever coaching inn we'd reached, until he glanced inside to the cushions across from mine, swaying so heavily, I thought he might fall to the floor. But he clutched at the top of the door to steady himself and looked at me with those flat, human eyes.

I shuffled to the far corner, and Asterion groaned as he heaved himself inside, shaking the body of the carriage as he tipped and landed on the seat. The door remained hanging open, the toe of Asterion's boots just peeking out. I stretched and caught the handle just as Conall called the horses into motion, and Asterion's toes slipped inside as I shut the door. His breath sawed in his chest, body crunched awkwardly in the carriage, but as I leaned toward him he stiffened, red eyes slitted.

"You don't have to—" he started, but he sighed as I pulled one glove free from his cold hand, and then the other, removing the glamour. His horns dug into the upholstered ceiling and his eyes slid shut in relief.

"I prefer this view of you," I reminded him.

He huffed, broad nostrils flaring, and then sat up just long enough to lift my feet from the floor and pull them into his lap. "This journey has been difficult for you."

My eyebrows rose as his thick fingers tugged on the laces of my boots, pulling them loose and freeing my feet.

"Easier for me than you, I think," I said. And then Asterion's fingers dug into the soles of my foot and my breath caught in my throat.

He hummed, a low, rumbling note. "I've been tired before, and I'll recover quickly."

I stared at him, his eyes closed as he worked his hands into tender, aching spots on my feet, sending that tugging sensation up my leg and deeper into my core.

"I might recover quickly too...with the right treatment," I whispered.

Asterion puffed air through his nose again, an expression of doubt I was coming to learn from him.

I sat up, pulling my foot from his grasp, but he only moved onto the other boot. "Do you assume I'm broken beyond repair, then?"

"No."

My jaw worked and I waited for more, but Asterion didn't tease me and tempt me like Conall. He just worked gently and thoroughly at my stiff feet, and this time when I didn't pull away his hands moved up to my ankle, rolling the joint, stretching and twisting, then higher up to knead at my calf.

It did feel good, better than a whiff of fine perfume, almost as good as the cups of thick chocolate. But while he soothed and stretched and dug knots out of the muscle of one leg, the rest of me tightened. It didn't matter what Marius told me of Asterion, or what the minotaur showed me of himself. I waited.

I waited for force, for his grip on my leg to bruise, nails to dig, for him to drag me to him.

His hand slid down my calf, around my ankle, and then a quick squeeze on my foot.

"You'll claim your recovery when you're ready," Asterion rumbled.

His eyes were shut, his body stretched and lax on the bench, legs spread wide and head tucked into the corner. I chewed over his words, over the aching hollow in my belly, my toes curling and flexing, the warmth of his hands still soaked into my skin.

He didn't stir as I pulled my feet down from his lap, or when my skirts whispered and slid, or even when the cushion by his head dented under my fist. The carriage bounced on the road and I wavered, standing over the dozing minotaur, studying his peaceful, slack expression.

When I'm ready? The suggestion didn't make sense, as if I weren't quaking with need, as if I hadn't withered away, as if I had time to wait to be *ready* to recover.

Asterion rumbled as I braced my knee next to his hip on the bench, golden lashes fluttering up from his cheeks.

"*Théa?*"

"Please," I whispered, settling myself over his lap, grasping his face in trembling hands.

He blinked again and the carriage rocked, forcing our bodies to jostle together. Those fanned lashes fluttered, and the buttons of his coat scraped against the belly of my gown with his deep breath.

"Take what you need," he said so softly I barely heard the words under the rattle of the carriage. His hand lifted to brace against my back but not to haul me closer, just to keep me steady on his lap.

Isn't this enough? I wanted to cry. *Can't you help, take the rest?* I trembled on his lap, still waiting for force, *needing* it, until a flicker of *néktar* twined through the air between us, thin and shy.

I brushed my thumbs over his cheeks, back and forth, and the wisp of pleasure tightened to a thread. His pleasure, not mine, but sweet and curious and something for me to grasp onto.

"Tell me...what you like about this," I murmured, curious as to why such a simple touch might offer any *nektar* for me.

Asterion's hand soothed up and down my back once, stilling at the base of my spine, and I thought he might ignore my question.

When his voice rose, it was dark and low, a private speech just for my ears. "I like the weight of you on my lap, light but steady. I like that you take my gloves off, demand to see me as I am. Your hands are warm, and they don't hesitate when they reach to touch me."

I stroked my hands down to his throat, and the muscles flexed as he sighed out a breath and swallowed.

"You don't frighten me," I said. It was not quite true. I was afraid of what I expected from him, from any man or monster, but he'd never offered any proof to my fears.

"Good."

Still, he didn't pull me closer, shift himself between my thighs. I leaned in, rested my chest to his, wrapped my arms around his neck and rested my cheek on his shoulder. His other arm joined the first, draping around my back.

He sighed again, and on his breath came more *nektar*, richer than a cheap alleyway fuck with a human, sweeter too. The clawing softened to a pleading, but Asterion's offerings didn't dwindle in the minutes that passed.

My eyes stung and my throat tightened and my chest was sore. I wanted to bite at Asterion's warm, soft skin, to tear my way inside of him, as if I might hide my hollow places inside of his.

His chest rolled beneath me, another massive inhale and rushing exhale that warmed my left shoulder and cascaded down my back. Clarity was brief and sweet—Asterion would *not* hurt me. I thought I might learn to trust him even better than I trusted myself.

"Hold on, it's getting bumpy!" Conall's voice called from outside.

Finally, Asterion's arm tightened around my waist. With the first rut in the road, the simple fit of our bodies became something stronger, a slight grind as we jostled on the seat. The dense ridge of Asterion's cock pressed into the cushion of skirts and between my legs. He bit off his grunt but I didn't bother to hide my sigh, letting it stroke his throat. When his arm tried to loosen, I tightened my thighs, scooting closer. Even if I could not make myself take more from Asterion and he would not claim it from me, the road would make something of this closeness between us.

My lips parted as we bounced over the pockmarked road, my brow furrowing as I studied the perfunctory grind and bounce of our hips and the slow flickers of heat that collected in my core. Asterion's skin was warm against my tongue, the velvety bristles of his fur pricking in one direction, silk in another, and suddenly I realized I was kissing his throat, sucking his flesh. Asterion's chest swelled for a moment, his arm squeezing, and then a long and rough groan melted into my ear.

"We should—I should—"

Asterion's breaths came quicker, and with them the *néktar*, sweet and syrupy, gathering on my tongue and sliding down to coat my cavernous hunger. I thought his stuttering words would call a stop to my feasting on his skin, but now that I was drinking him down I couldn't bear the thought of going hungry again.

I sat up only to take his face back in my hands, turn his mouth to mine, and nibble my way across his full bottom lip, an amused puff of breath stroking over my cheeks in my path. I reached the left corner, and Asterion's horns thunked against the back of the carriage as he pulled away, but when he leaned forward again, it was to press his mouth to my throat, tongue snaking out and caressing over my pulse, down into the crooked collar of my dress.

The *néktar* was so heady it made me dizzy, swaying into his arms, arching into his tongue. His pleasure at holding me, tasting me; my own at the slick, hot swipe of his tongue, the pressure of his thickening cock between my legs. I shivered and he nuzzled into my shoulder. The base of his horn was in front of my eye and I caught it with my hand, steering his mouth up to my jaw. He chuckled and pressed a damp, chaste kiss to the corner, his mouth so broad it touched the lobe of my ear too.

I didn't know what to take next, didn't even know if there needed to be more or if I could survive on this, over and over again, all the rest of the way to wherever it was we were going.

And then suddenly the carriage's jostling wasn't bumps but the sudden rearing of horses, and Conall cried out from above.

"Asterion! We have trouble!"

The arm around my waist gripped, and I gasped as Asterion hunched and twisted, pushing me onto the bench in the same motion that he vacated it. His nose pressed to my cheek with a sharp intake of breath as the carriage jerked again.

"Stay here," Asterion said, his voice ragged.

He lurched toward the door, leaping out before the wheels had stopped their turning, jogging alongside and slamming it shut. Behind him, the sky darkened to a hazy shade of rust, threatening shadows lurching through the outlines of a dark wood, sharp and jagged screams swooping overhead.

I reached for the handle of the door, my heart still galloping with the momentum of the halted carriage, the rush of fresh *nèktar*, and the sudden warning of danger. I was torn between throwing myself out of the trap of the carriage, chasing after Asterion and attaching myself to his side; or holding the door shut tight until I heard the safe promise of his now familiar voice again.

A horrible screech circled above, the sound of glass shattering and bones breaking. Ice scratched down my back and scorching bile rose up my throat at the harpy's call. My fingers clawed into the cushions, sweated around the metal handle. Birsha's allies had found me.

They would drag me back to him, push me into stone and straw and grime, push me into the hands of whatever beast had paid to use me.

Steal me away from the warm, gentle frame of Asterion's protection, and the first tease of true *nèktar* I'd tasted in so many decades.

Asterion and Conall were shouting to one another, their

voices circling the carriage, the horses crying out in warning. The curtains shrouded the view of the woods and the road, and with the sun sinking, there were no hints from my hiding place.

I didn't want to hide. I didn't want to see the faces coming for me. If I ran into the shadows again, would I find the same strange sanctuary I'd found with the whores on the streets of London? I forced my fingers to loosen from the edge of the bench, ignored their trembling as I reached for the curtain, the way they flinched before shoving the fabric aside.

Tree roots were surging up from the ground, the carriage jerking as they tangled through the wheels.

"Get the horses loose, I'll handle the crow," Conall barked, passing the window I stared out of. His storming pace faltered as he glanced at me through the glass. The scar over his cheek shone stark and red, and he had the same dark circles under his eyes as Asterion. He dipped his head to me and dove into motion again, shoulders rolling and face stretching into a snarl.

A shadow followed his loping steps, and I wasn't sure if I was imagining its own set of eyes or if my terror was playing tricks on my mind. Was Birsha there in the dark, watching me? My face reflected back at me in the glass, eyes too wide and pale, and I let the curtain fall back in place, sliding down to the floor of the carriage, bracing my hands against either wall.

A low roar—*Asterion!*—thundered at my back, hooves stomped, and something was thrown down so heavily that it shook the ground and the walls and the glass windows and perhaps even the sky. The harpy screeched and the horses screamed, and I joined them, keening on the floor of the carriage, useless and frightened. Too afraid to run, to wipe away the hot streaks of tears coursing down my face or to press my hands to my chest and try and calm my heart.

I didn't want to go back. I didn't want to starve and suffer and be lonely again. I should've slid quietly into Marius and Lillian's home, nibbled on luxury. But in truth, now that I'd tasted what Asterion might offer, I didn't want nibbles either.

The worst came true, and the carriage door yanked open, tipping me forward. A brutal hand grasped my arm and dragged me along the floor. And if I would be stolen back, I would fight.

I screamed, joining Asterion's roar—too far away now to save me, and no sweet snarls from Conall—and twisted on the floor, kicking my bare feet out and bracing them on either side of the door. A ghoul screamed back at me, the memory of a man's face twisted in endless horror, blood crusted down his dislocated jaw, over his throat and into the white collar of his torn shirt. He pulled so hard on my arm it yanked me upward, and I bent my knees and braced those too, slapping my hand against the roof.

The ghoul would tear my arm from my shoulder, or he would pull the carriage and me down on top of him, or he would drag me screaming and weeping out at last—I didn't know, but I would hold on for every second until the next worse thing did happen, because I *did not* want to go back there.

I was not a lodestone or a tool or a body to sleeve a monster's pleasure. I was a woman, and I wanted to live again!

Asterion's roar made my hand above my head weak, but it didn't matter because I didn't have to hold on. He stampeded into the ghoul, body bent forward, bright gold-tipped horns catching a last low beam of sunlight before they pierced the dusty, rotted chest of the ghoul and ripped it away from me. I fell backwards onto my ass as Asterion stomped out of view, but I scrambled up just as quickly. If I was going to be attacked, I wanted to be in reach of the minotaur.

I fell out of the carriage, clutching the door handle with my good hand—the other was numb from being pulled—and stared in disgusted relief as Asterion stomped down on the ghoul's head. Conall came running from my right, crowding close and only pausing when I flinched in instinct.

"You need to get her to the castle."

"And if they are waiting there?"

"Then Laszlo ought to be picking his teeth with their bones by the time you arrive."

Asterion's shoulders were heaving and gore dripped down his horns. I twisted, grabbing the discarded white gloves on the floor of the carriage, kicked into the corner. I grabbed them and Conall paused me, scooping my already bruising wrist up from my side and testing my arm carefully.

"I'll be fine," I said, although I was already mourning that my fresh *néktar* from kissing Asterion would be used to heal the sprain of my arm.

"Be careful," Conall said with the rare solemnity I'd seen so little of from him. His hand was bloodied, but it didn't stop him from wrapping it around the back of my neck and drawing me closer, his lips pressing to my forehead. "Did you get any sleep?" he asked, turning to Asterion.

Asterion grunted, his back to me, the ghoul under his hooves. He jerked as I reached up to his shoulder, ducked his head and tried to twist away from me. I pulled an absurdly ornate hand-kerchief from my skirt pocket, white with a pretty lace border and yellow primroses in each corner. I rose to my tiptoes and used it to clean his horn, the gold smeared but not lost completely.

"Don't let him fall right off the horse," Conall said to me. "The two of you should make it by morning if you ride straight there. I'll clean this up and track our route to make sure there aren't more coming before I join you."

"The Wyrm isn't far from here," Asterion answered, taking the enchanted gloves I passed him and tipping his head to let me clean his other horn. "He might help you, but it'll cost."

"I'll consider it. Just get her to safety."

Asterion puffed, and this time it was a slightly offended sound.

"Thank you," I whispered, brushing Asterion's warm, brown cheek before it vanished in the glamour.

"Don't thank me yet. Not until we've reached the castle, *théa*."

Asterion shepherded me to the horses and lifted me onto the back of a massive brown steed, following me up and surrounding me with his warmth.

"Fast and safe," Conall called.

"Burn them all," Asterion answered, and then he squeezed the steady horse into a quick canter.

We were more than a mile away before I realized all the finery and frippery was left with the wreckage. It was a sad waste of beauty, but I wrapped my hand around Asterion's tense forearm and found I couldn't care.

6.
THE HIDDEN CASTLE

I was not asleep as the sun rose, but also not awake enough to react properly if there was any danger. Asterion was heavy against my back, his breath steady on my shoulder, and the air was sharp and cold in this strange forest we plodded through, but his heat served as a comforting blanket.

Shadows loomed ahead, wrapped in mist, a dark tower rising against the blue-gray dawn. The air in this wood was heavy and made the hairs on my arm stand on end.

"Asterion," I murmured.

He hummed, the arm hanging at his side sliding up my thigh to wrap around my waist. "We're close now."

"Are these woods enchanted?"

"The castle was built with stones from the fae realms, and its inhabitants are collectors, and... Well, you'll see. A little magic soaks into the woods," Asterion said. He shifted behind me, groaning slightly as he stretched, and then slid and dropped off the horse. He walked stiffly alongside me and the horse, his hand resting on my thigh as we traveled. "We're safe this close to the castle. We've made it, *théa*."

And like the spark of a match, a bright orange glow appeared in the black shadows of the castle.

Without having to carry Asterion's weight, the horse picked up its pace, perhaps sensing shelter and a meal ahead of us. In contrast, I felt as though I might slip sideways into nothing without the minotaur as my anchor.

49

The lit torch in the distance bloomed as we approached but didn't move to meet us. The mist slid away with a twisting breeze and the road rose, a figure appearing in the light. It was a monster and a man, with golden wings and russet feathers and hair, and what looked like twin orbs of fire staring out at us. He was dressed in old-fashioned clothing, better suited to centuries ago, before I'd been captured by Birsha, and he wore no shoes on his large furred feet, white claws piercing the earth as he watched us. A tail whipped slowly behind them, three long, bronzed feathers undulating in the air.

When the stone walls of the castle gates were close enough to block out the dawn, I realized this monster didn't have fire for eyes, only a prim pair of golden spectacles on his distinguished hooked nose that reflected the light of his torch.

"He isn't ready. I told you it would take more time," the creature called to us.

Asterion didn't answer, just continued our shuffle until we had to stop, blocked from crossing under the broad stone archway.

"Laszlo Bladewing, allow me to introduce Evanthia," Asterion said, his words heavy and his body hunched and tired. "Daughter of Hedone. Evanthia, this is the Western King of the Clouds."

A gryphon, I realized, my slow and sluggish thought piecing his details together.

"A divinity," Laszlo echoed my thoughts, peering at me with his head tilted.

"She seeks sanctuary," Asterion said.

I blinked at the words, swallowed, and hoped my tongue might find a response when my brain could not.

"I see," Laszlo said, continuing to stare at me. "Come in, then."

Asterion and the horse I sat on remained still for a long moment as Laszlo turned his wings to us, too weary to finish the final stretch of our journey. I tried to slide off, but my legs were stiffened in place and Asterion startled at my jerk, bracing me and stomping into motion.

The castle was broad walls and round columns of mortared stone. Long windows tapered to peaks stacked high, and a few small nests rested in their corners, birds already crying at dawn. High grass lawns and overrun gardens stretched out at either side of the gravel drive, and I turned to stare at a distant pack of animals grazing in the grasses. Sheep and goats, I realized blearily.

"You'd better leave the horse," Laszlo said wryly, glancing back at us.

Asterion managed to scoop me up, and I groaned and wrapped my arms around his broad shoulders, too relieved to protest when he didn't set me down. I didn't mind being carried in this particular pair of strong arms.

From the mist of the lawn, a wispy shadow figure appeared, catching the horse by the reins and leading it away as we stepped after the gryphon into the mouth of the castle.

Cradled by Asterion, warm again from his chest, it was a struggle to keep my eyes open. I fought the urge to drop into sleep, studying the details of our surroundings. I'd expected the castle to be as bare inside as it was out, but the walls were cluttered with tapestries and fine, mismatched furniture was arranged in an almost cramped fashion.

Collectors, Asterion had called the residents of this castle, and so it was obvious—collections from all eras and histories of time, precious and strange items on every surface.

"You'll want to wash and eat," Laszlo noted.

"We want nothing but to sleep for now," Asterion answered, his words slurring.

The gryphon murmured an answer, but the fog in my head grew too thick to make out the arrangements of walls, let alone of words, and I tucked my face into Asterion's shoulder and let the steady plodding pace of his steps lull me. We twisted up a circular staircase, dragged down halls, until finally the hinges of a door squeaked in promise.

"Will this do for you both?" Laszlo asked.

I didn't raise my head or wait for Asterion's answer before speaking, "Yes."

We could've been placed in a barn stall, for all I cared. I wanted to lie down and I wanted to sleep and I wanted the protection and heat of Asterion's body with me. That was all.

A few more steps, and the door shut behind us. I opened one eye long enough to see the spread of a dusty quilt and the rise of pillows, and then we were landing in them together, sharing a relieved groan. My legs stretched out at last but Asterion's arms remained around me, holding me to his chest, his thudding heartbeat in my ears.

And at last, I was asleep.

⚘

WARM MUSCLE SPREAD BENEATH ME, STRONG FINGERS DIGGING into my back, down to my ass, to my spread thighs. I squirmed and found pressure between my legs, thick and dense. Sound rumbled under my cheek, and a wave of *néktar* washed over my weak body, soaking into my skin and offering just enough strength for me to chase more.

My lips parted on a pant as I started to rock, my brow furrowing at the sore burn in my thighs, but there was another heat in my core, sweeter and sustaining, and I craved the offering from the latter. Hands squeezed the flesh of my ass and I whimpered, using their strength to push down harder against the muffled ridge pressed into my core. They released me and traveled upward, and I gasped, finding flesh at my lips, bristled fur, and a long tendon of muscle.

Asterion.

My eyelids were heavy, my heartbeat slow, and I wasn't confident that this moment wasn't a dream. At least I might dream of pleasure and *néktar*.

Thick fingers moved to the buttons on the back of my dress, and cool air licked at the nape of my neck as the fabric parted.

I was barely awake, chasing the hunger that'd plagued me for so long, but those were conscious, intentional fingers, brushing over my spine, plucking carefully at buttons that ought to have been too delicate for Asterion's touch.

Fabric gaped, and I whimpered at my sore muscles and the

need pooling in my core, and then again as I was turned onto my back. I blinked and the room was dark, curtained, the shadow of Asterion rising above me startling and huge as he peeled my dress off my arms and waist, scooping my hips up to drag it down over my legs, past my stockinged feet.

My boots had been abandoned in the carriage, and I was now dressed only in a thin slip.

And then Asterion was unbuttoning the placket of his pants, and it was too dark to see his cock properly, and I was too exhausted to reach for him. *Finally*, I thought, but my body stiffened in expectation, stretched and splayed.

He didn't lift my skirt, didn't bare my sex to his eyes and cock. He didn't use his weight to pin me down, but his hips sank beautifully against mine, the fine silk a kiss of a barrier between us.

And when he surged, I moaned, my eyes falling shut and muscles surrendering gratefully. He ground his cock into my sex, groaned with me at the friction, at how quickly the silk grew damp and clung to our skin. His lips pressed to my forehead and I reached up to his waist, guided him closer, noted how the tip of his cock pooled slippery heat onto my belly.

My body would strain to take him, the massive length and girth of his monstrous cock, although my mother's gifts offered strange secrets in that regard. My thighs burned as they stretched to cradle his hips, and Asterion's panting breaths fluffed my hair as he mimed the act of sex through our delicate barrier. The pressure was beautiful, and the restraint left me loose and easy, soft and receiving to his nudges and bucks.

And every breath was thick with *néktar*. I gulped the air, gasped for more, breaths sawing in our silent union.

I kissed Asterion's throat, sucked his skin, and reveled in the wave of pleasure. A dense weight of warm flesh was pressing between my thighs, against the cheeks of my ass, and it swelled and tightened. His balls, I realized, and he was growing close to his finish. I wanted to say sweet things to him, tease him, slide the silk away and guide him to my opening.

But he was right. Marius was right, too. There were still pricks of fear, open scratches on my heart. And this gift was a bucket of clean crystalline cool water after lifetimes of a burning parched throat in the desert. It was enough for now, and it was only a drop in the deeply drained well of my strength.

Asterion's arms slid beneath my limp back, embracing and clasping me to him, a ragged set of grunts falling from his lips, and an urgent spike of *néktar* jabbing into me and making me cry out with shocked joy.

Asterion bellowed, and he spilled over my belly and chest, soaked the slip and my skin and still further down to the quilt. The hot release bled up to my breasts, kissing at my peaked nipples, and his motions stuttered and trembled and quaked above me, his weight pressing down.

I'd always met Birsha's clients' releases with them, could not prevent myself, and every moment had been a personal betrayal, my mother's gift transformed to a curse.

This was not. It was relief. I might not have met my own finish without Asterion, too tired and too lost in my head, but he threw us there together, and I wept and clutched his back and went spinning into the oblivion with a terrified gratitude.

The power was startling and incredible, not a bucket but a flood, my breath stolen as my hunger from so many years caved under the pressure of our shared pleasure, earnest and delighted for one another. Shy too, a bashful profanity.

My mouth latched to Asterion's throat, my cries muffled, the spill of his release sticking the slip to my skin, to his still clothed chest as I once again tried to find my way inside of this man.

The room swayed and another wave of *néktar* struck at me hard, dizzying my head, proving I was not sated—I needed more. I squirmed in Asterion's hold, tore the skirt of the slip, and we both moaned as flesh kissed. And again, his strength rushed at me, filling me, feeding me.

And this time, I could not withstand its force. I'd been starved and then feasted. My blood was heavy and drunk with fresh energy, and it swam unevenly in my veins. I swooned into nothing, into Asterion's arms perhaps, although I'd hardly left them, and soft lips brushed my forehead as I sank back into the slumber I'd barely risen from.

MY EYES WERE DRY WHEN I WOKE AGAIN, AND MY FLESH FELT strange, almost swollen. I was heavy, as if my bones had been filled with lead. I was naked, tucked under sheets and the quilt, and I knew without looking that I was alone. Asterion was not in the bed, not in the room, and I wondered for a moment if he had ever been, or if I'd imagined the exquisite yet wordless experience in the haze of my slumber.

But as I sat up, I knew the truth—I felt wonderful. Bleary from sleep, but brighter, cleaner, fuller. I brushed a hand over my cheek and my skin was smoother. My fingers trailed down and found my lips less withered.

There was a savory, meaty fragrance in the air, and I rubbed at my face, waking my eyes, and searched the room. It was large, and the view out the window was of the long, green roll of the woods beyond the castle walls. It was not quite as cluttered as the hall we'd entered, but still full of the odd arrangements and decorations and mismatch of styles. The bed was broad, and the quilt spread over me was actually four separate pieces stitched together. The floor was layered with carpets from one rounded wall by the window to the squared one at the door. A small table was set with lidded plates of food, and a large copper basin waited with steaming water by a small fire in the fireplace.

Asterion was missing. My dress was lying over a chair, but I knew at a glance that the chemise folded and waiting with it was not the one he had soaked with his release. My mouth watered at the recollection, and the salty, musky taste of his skin was refreshed on my tongue.

For the first time in a long time, the hunger that hounded me most was physical, my stomach growling. My limbs were clumsy and stiff as I slid off the mattress, moving to the soft chemise, and I found a thick robe and a pair of velvet slippers waiting in the pile.

I touched my belly and imagined the heavy press of Asterion's cock there. My skin was slightly sticky, but I thought he might've tried to wipe me clean when he'd tucked me in. I had a vague memory his hands stroking over my body for a long time. I wanted to find the minotaur, drag him back into this dreamy, strange quiet, and learn the flavor of his cock, of the pleasure he might find on my tongue. But food and a real bath would suit the flesh and bone part of me first. I would attend to one hunger, and then the other.

7.
THE KING
OF DREAMS

There was a wardrobe in the bedroom, full of strange assortments of clothing, and while I found old boned corsets and stiff cotton stays, there was nothing that matched the garments from the trunks still with the carriage. Instead I found a long, loose, black velvet gown and a quilted red vest.

Fed, scrubbed clean in water that never grew any foggier, no matter the dust and grime from the road it cleaned from me, and fully dressed, I helped myself to wandering the castle.

I expected to find servants cleaning rooms or coming and going—surely someone other than Asterion had attended to my food and bath—but at most, I might've seen their shadows passing out of the corners of my eyes. The tower I'd slept in led down to a squared balcony that overlooked a broad hall, flags and tapestries and weapons and art dressing every wall. I paused, listening for male voices, and heard none. This castle was even quieter than Grace House and oddly empty, in spite of all the varied decoration. I circled the balcony, peered inside of neglected bedrooms and sitting rooms, offices where books stacked wildly over shelves and tables and carpeted floors, and even a small antechamber where all the instruments and chairs were arranged as if a band might suddenly appear to play music for a crowd waiting below. But all was silent.

I followed the narrow, twisting staircase down to the main floor, the slippers silent over patchworked carpets, and held my breath, waiting for some sign of life. Was I alone now in this castle? Had I slept for years and years in all my exhaustion and found myself the sole occupant?

I paused at the center of the open room, closed my eyes, and wondered at the pinch of loneliness that squeezed my heart, and also the rare lightness in my shoulders.

And then a door opened, and the distant soft beat of waves reached my ears.

I opened my eyes again and traced the sound with my steps, found a long diagonal corridor at the corner of the hall, and caught a flash of gold near the end. I passed more rooms, enormous dining halls with enough settings for feasts, gaming dens with cards still resting on the tables, little parlors with papered walls and delicate cabinets. Finally, at the end of the corridor I reached the open door, pausing at the threshold to take in the first room to make any kind of sense since I'd left the bedroom. And yet somehow less too.

It was meant to be a library, walls high and lined with shelves and trinkets. But there was a small round table in the center with a single chair and a single place setting. A desk sat to the right side of the room, an open book on its surface and a still steaming cup of tea waiting. At the left end of the room was a fireplace surrounded by a couch and pair of armchairs. The one at the far end was twisted toward the fire and had a blanket draped over the arm. Opposite me, broad windows and a large door opened onto a terrace that overlooked a wide, empty horizon, a line of gray traced across the bottom, the sound of waves still far, but closer here.

It was a room for a single occupant. A single dinner setting, a single cup of tea, a single chair used of a set. A solitary gryphon standing alone on a stone terrace, overlooking a sea that should not have existed in the middle of the woods in Wales.

All at once, I knew Asterion was gone from this castle. A soft pang struck me at the same moment as a whisper of relief. He'd touched me, fed me at last, and then vanished. I craved more, but it was also almost proof of my freedom—of his too.

The gryphon turned, strolling back to the open door, and paused briefly as he caught sight of me.

"Asterion left to retrieve the Red Wolf," Laszlo announced to me as he entered the room. He moved to his desk, to his cup of tea, as if there were no more to say or for me to wonder about.

But there was the sound of waves in the heart of the woods.

"Where does this room exist?" I asked.

Asterion had left me with a stranger, but I knew better than to think he would do so lightly. He trusted this King of Clouds, this gryphon. And while Laszlo watched me with a bright golden stare through a pair of spectacles I doubt he needed, it was the brush of curiosity rather than the glare of intent.

"It's Hywel's dreaming." Which said nothing, really. I glanced at him, and his head tipped. "This is not just my home. Hywel sleeps below the castle. He dreams. Those dreams seep into the stone."

"And if I stepped onto the terrace?" I asked, wondering what Hywel was, and where he slept. It was a pretty, sloping name, with a breathy 'h' that led to a falling 'oh-well.' Old Welsh, I thought.

"You would smell the sea, see it. If you leapt from the edge, you would crash onto the rocks."

My steps were slow, leading to the terrace, brine on the air, the sharp tang in my nose. "And if I walked out front of the castle and around the lawn?"

"You would be surrounded by the forest of Gwydir."

An unexpected smile curled my lips, a sudden laugh rising from my chest. My eyes did not sting, but my vision blurred. *Magic.* Real magic—the wild kind that'd already started fading and dying away even when I was just a girl, the stories myths and legends were made of.

I glanced around the room and wondered at the books on the shelves, the trinkets. How old was this castle? How old was the collection tucked away here?

I was still smiling when I looked back to the gryphon and found him staring openly in return, expression locked away but not predatory.

"Does he dream of card games?" I asked.

"Losing Lodam and Karnöffel," Laszlo said. Outside, the clouds burst apart, allowing sunlight to cut through and glint off the delicate feathers that framed his temples and jaw.

I laughed again, my hands clapping together. "I haven't played Karnöffel since..." I caught my breath, my chest tightening, and shook my head. "So long. And the nook upstairs with the instruments?"

Laszlo was quiet, and watchful and he dipped his head slowly. "Sometimes of balls. The shadows you'll see, they are his dreamers. At a feast, they will crowd the halls and there will be a roar of conversation, but not many words to make out. He obliges the castle by maintaining enough to take care of cleaning."

"And of baths and meals?" I wondered.

Laszlo shrugged. "If you've bathed and been fed, then yes, the dreamers have found you. There are many who are quite independent. But most only come and go as his thoughts turn."

Where is he? What is he? I wondered again.

But Laszlo was turning his face down to the open book, lifting the teacup from the saucer and taking a sip. He had dark talons at the ends of his fingers, and he had to hold the painted porcelain carefully.

"If you need something, think of it, look away. It might be there when you look back," he murmured, more to the book than to me.

I stared at the gryphon for a silent moment before realizing I'd been dismissed, or at least that he had no intention of carrying on further conversation. He turned a page of his book and I stepped back, hesitating between turning to the door and the terrace.

"May I...explore?"

Laszlo looked up from the page, the heavy black of his pupils devouring the yellow iris as he stared at me. Behind his head, his full, fan-like tail feathers waved at me flirtatiously. "Asterion tells me you are free to do as you please."

His name recalled the minotaur's weight above me, between my thighs, and I savored the warmth that spiraled through me.

Laszlo's head tipped. "I suppose, should you wish to keep the sanctuary of the castle, you had better stay within the border walls. Beyond that..." He shrugged, one massive and elegant golden wing rustling with the act.

I wanted to touch those feathers, let their blade edges stroke against my fingers, but I wasn't sure my granted freedom extended that far. The temptation of the terrace was strong, but Laszlo sat at his desk with a forceful air of solitude. I would come back when the room wasn't occupied, but for now, there was another kernel of information that intrigued me.

Hywel sleeps below the castle.

From the first short set of stairs that led down, I found a kitchen, with several blurry shadow figures darting out of corners, and a fragrant loaf steaming fresh on the counter. I watched them work for a moment, the way the figures vanished as they crossed beams of sunlight from the narrow high windows and then reappeared on the other side. Their hands stirring pots were the most detailed part of them, almost solid, while they faded to nothing at their backs and faces.

The next set of stairs led down to a well-stocked cellar. I remembered the fields of grains and vegetables we passed where sheep and goats grazed, and I wondered if the shadows also tended those, if Laszlo really knew how many there were, working in quiet gaps of shade to keep the castle running.

A narrow corridor faced me at the opposite end of the cellar, and I grabbed one of the torches lit along the walls and approached slowly. There was no sign of light or life inside, and the walls were bare. I hesitated at the threshold, a queasy chill circling low in my gut. The wall was cool and rough against my palm, but the light of the torch made the space appear endless.

I can turn back, I promised myself. And Laszlo had said the only risk was outside of the castle. My slippers provided a soft, reassuring whisper as I ventured in, and the floor was slightly tilted, making every step heavier.

I haven't been this alone in centuries. The thought thrilled me. The corridor was dark and bare, but there were no growls in the distance, no pacing footsteps from a cell nearby, no whimpering cries through the walls. I was alone, in a strange castle, with harmless shadows and a reticent gryphon. I was free—to leave, to stay, to explore.

At last, I reached a branch in the corridor, a glimmer of soft blue light from the left, a glow of more torches from the right. I stopped at the left branch where the floor continued to slope gently downward, and a ripple of bright water shone. A bathing pool, possibly even with a hot spring source, based on the mineral whiff in the air.

The right branch was a steeper, twisting staircase. A warmer, deeper fragrance rose from those steps, earth and smoke and sharp metal.

I turned right, holding my torch in a slightly trembling hand, steadying my swooping nerves with my hand on the wall. The walls cracked open near the bottom, dropping back, and the cavern I walked into was grander and greater than the main hall of the castle and filled with even more curious objects. More than the whole castle combined, I suspected. At the far end, a crack in the stone broke open to the sea and sky, the same view as the terrace.

And there, in the heart of the cavern, surrounded by treasures, I found Hywel, King of Dreams. My heart soared at the sight of the enormous sleeping dragon, his long, curled red body reminiscent of a cat, broad jaw resting on taloned feet and piles of velvet. He sucked in a breath and his back, taller than me or even Asterion, rose and fell with a heavy sigh. His breath warmed the room, a fresh scorch in the air. He rumbled with a drowsy purr, and the stone floor, layered with heavy carpets and littered with pillows, shook with the sound. His nostrils flared and his scales rippled, and I thought—hoped, anticipated giddily —that he might wake.

He continued to slumber. And with his sleep, the air thickened and my eyes fell shut, lips parting and curling up.

He was having a good dream. Something sweet and simple, but he was powerful and massive. A dragon's version of "sweet and simple" offered me *so much*. I moaned at the way *néktar* curled through the air, licked at my skin. My steps stumbled forward and I scrambled, finding a vase to hold the torch I'd been carrying, before I followed the siren call to the dragon.

His scales appeared matte and dull at first, until I reached him and found that they were only dusty. I brushed my sleeve over one palm-sized scale high on his shoulder, as high as I could reach, and it came away gleaming and clean, ruby red with a little crack of opalescent white.

His enormous face was right by my hip. If he opened his jaw, I could climb inside. I would be a morsel to him. I would have to climb him, tucking my toes between his heavy, leathery lips in order to sit atop his snout. His head was ridged along the center, and protective horns sprouted over his skull. He was exquisite, and his dreams made my body heavy and loose. I found a silk skirt in the pile he used as a pillow, and pulled it free with only a little struggle.

"You're beautiful," I murmured to the sleeping dragon. "But you need a little tidying up."

I used the silk to wipe away the dust on the part of his snout by my hip, worked my way over to the ridge, and circled it around one of the smaller horns.

Hywel rumbled again, and the sound shook through me, deep into my bones, a stunning vibration that drew a gasp from my lips. Heat pooled in my core, and I gripped the horn to keep from swooning as *nēktar* flooded through my blood like a fire eating through a room with a freshly opened window. I sat down heavily on the thick leg behind me, marveling as I stared up at the enormous jeweled head.

A sigh of pleasure from the dragon, and it was as if I'd feasted on flesh for a week. My head was clearer, my body warmer, and my heart *hurt* from what a relief it was.

"Thank you for that. In exchange, I will clean you up," I whispered. "You deserve to shine again, dreaming or not."

8.
OVERDUE
NIGHTMARES

I paused on the threshold of the large room, glancing at the table where Laszlo sat alone, one chair and one setting for his dinner. I looked away, thinking hard, and then back again, and found him staring at the sudden addition of another seat and setting.

His head turned to me and he blinked, but he said nothing. No protest. No hello.

I'd spent the better part of three days climbing over a sleeping dragon, dusting off scales and sucking up *néktar*. I knew now how much strength I'd lost, how much of my own mind, because it was returning to me one deep, sleeping sigh at a time.

If Laszlo knew or cared where I spent my days, he'd said nothing, and I'd scavenged my meals from the ever-occupied kitchens.

Three days of a one-sided conversation with a slumbering beast the size of a modest house had been soothing, but also hollow. I'd been raw and empty when Asterion found me, and Lillian's company was a balm I hadn't understood how to value, but I missed it now.

"I thought Asterion and Conall would've returned by now," I said, not risking asking for an invitation to dine when I thought there was a small chance he would refuse. I needed to hear another person's voice in my ear, regardless if it was welcoming or not.

"They won't lead enemies here," Laszlo said, watching my

approach. "And Asterion has always been overly cautious when it comes to a woman's safety."

I sat down in the chair across from him, lifted the lid on my plate, and a beautiful meal waited, still steaming. Laszlo picked up his fork and knife and then paused, lowering his hands and staring at me with wide eyes.

"You found Hywel." There was a sharp edge to the words, and I wasn't sure if it was rebuke or surprise.

"I did. I've been dusting him off."

Laszlo's wings stirred, a few tiny feathers floating into the air. "Did he wake?"

His stare was fixed to me, and I couldn't tear my own away. "No."

Laszlo relaxed slightly and returned to his meal, breaking the frozen gaze that had trapped me so I could do the same. "There is a wax he liked applied after he returned from flying. I will find it...if you'd like to—"

"Yes," I said, nodding, my fists clenching around the silverware.

Laszlo was quiet, only an occasional kiss of feathers brushing, barely a scratch from the dinnerware. When I watched him, his eyes were down, but I could've sworn I felt the prick of his stare again when I looked away.

"Hywel has always had a...romantic temperament. His dreams must offer you some relief," Laszlo said, speaking again finally when the awkwardness of our silence had finally melted away.

My cheeks warmed. "I don't know what he dreams of, but he's very powerful."

Laszlo chuckled, but then cleared the sound away before I could appreciate its warmth. "Do you speak to him? He will sense you."

I nodded again, thinking of the praises I'd laid down of his beauty, my occasional gasps of gratitude as he'd shed strength for me to soak up. I stared around the large room, at every solitary station. The desk, the chair by the fire, this dining table.

"How did you come to be in this castle with Hywel?" I asked.

Was Laszlo here to guard Hywel or was he here waiting for Hywel to awaken?

Laszlo set down his fork and knife, and I noticed that his plate was mostly cleared. He'd already been eating when I arrived. I realized with a pinch of hurt that he would rise and leave me here now that he was done.

But first he said, "The castle is our home."

The meaning struck me immediately. Laszlo was not a guard or a friend or simply someone waiting for a dragon to awaken again. Laszlo was Hywel's lover, alone in this vast castle with the company of shadows as the dragon dreamed.

He rose from his chair and I opened my mouth, not sure what would come out, a plea for him to stay—I grew antsy every day spent alone; how had Laszlo survived so long like this?—or an apology for my uncomfortable conversation, but he wasn't fleeing from me. A distant creak and bang heralded an arrival, and I too rose from my seat, the chair skidding back suddenly.

Laszlo rounded the table and offered me his arm, his wings widening. The air around him was powdery, scented of tea and musk, and the shelter of the wing was warm, a few feathers barely grazing my hair braided at my back.

"It's the wolf," Laszlo murmured, stiffening at my side as the approaching steps stomped in an uneven pace.

Sure enough, Conall called out, "Well, Laz, where are you hiding?"

Laszlo didn't bother answering because a moment later, the doors to the room were thrown open. A breeze carried in fresh air as if it had clung to Conall and his long, red locks and heavy coat. He grinned at the pair of us, his eyes holding to Laszlo a little longer. "Finally. Friendly faces." His head tipped, and then he winked at me. "Well, one friendly face at least. Ah, and dinner. Good, I'm famished."

"I've just finished," Laszlo said, gesturing toward his seat. "I'll leave you bo—"

"You'll do no such thing," Conall scoffed, but he didn't hesitate to take Laszlo's seat, where a fresh plate of food was waiting for him. "Sit down and make conversation, or I'll pluck your feathers out while your back is turned."

67

Laszlo's arm tensed under my hand—it was stronger and thicker than I expected, his careful suiting disguising the power of him—but he sighed and another chair appeared at the table, as well as a crystal decanter and three glasses.

"Asterion returned to London," Conall said before lifting the quail on his plate with his fingers and groaning as he took a bite.

"Did you expect otherwise?" Laszlo asked, pulling out my chair for me first.

"Noble bastard," Conall breathed, and he and Laszlo exchanged a brief glance of amused frustration. "Thank fuck Hywel still dreams of good cooks," Conall moaned around another bite.

"He's having an inspired week," Laszlo said with a dip of his head, pouring himself a glass of claret. He looked to me next, decanter hovering over the glass. I nodded and he poured for me, but he passed Conall the bottle to serve himself.

There was a curious tension between the two men. They were familiar enough with one another for Conall to pick at Laszlo, but companionable in their pattern too. I tried not to be too obvious about watching them, but I wasn't sure they'd care either way.

"Have you been terribly bored, *mo chroí*?" Conall asked, but he was pouring his drink, and both Laszlo and I glanced at one another, Laszlo's cheeks coloring slightly. I knew *mo chroí*—"moh kree" as it sounded—was an old Gaelic endearment for "my heart," but I didn't know which of us he meant. Indeed, when he looked up again, his eyes bounced between us with a mischievous glint, leaving the question intentionally unanswered. "Hywel's no closer to waking?"

"I received a few words from him yesterday," Laszlo said, "but I think he was still dreaming."

I'd spent most of yesterday down in the cavern with Hywel, even napping with him, and I wondered when Laszlo had visited the dragon, since I'd never seen him there.

Conall's gaze steadied on me at last. "You look lovely tonight. Have you been reading her poetry, Laz?" Conall asked with false delicacy.

Laszlo's brow furrowed. "Poetry?"

I laughed and shook my head. "I am feeling much improved."

"Good," Conall said brightly. "But we mustn't grow lazy with your recovery. I'm sure you'd benefit from a great deal *more* pleasure still."

There was no mistake in the words and their meaning. Where Asterion was careful to the point of withholding, Conall had all but made a direct offer. If I wanted pleasure, he would grant it. Laszlo's stare moved slowly between us, and I savored the heat of a blush that rinsed over my cheeks and chest.

"Thank you for your concern," I said, dipping my head.

Conall grinned, sharp canines gleaming in his wicked smile.

Laszlo tried to leave again after Conall and I had finished eating, but the wolf was wily and charming, and instead we found ourselves around the fire. I'd started on the opposite end of the couch as Conall, but somewhere after a third glass of wine I realized I'd been coaxed to his side, my head resting on his lap and long fingers stroking through my hair and down my arm, the wide collar of the gown I wore pushed down to bare one shoulder. His touch was hot and teasing, provocative without being explicit, and the wine left me relaxed.

Laszlo watched us from his armchair and Conall's touch soothed me, tying my tongue and keeping me from offering the gryphon a more comfortable seat with us on the couch.

Shadows started to wander through the room, an indistinct murmur of conversation, a few words of passion muttered by the fire, and my eyes drifted shut on the silhouette of lovers embracing on the carpet.

There was no fireplace burning my cheeks, only the deep black of being underground without a window. The cushion beneath my side was not dense velvet and Conall's strong thigh, but the prickle and stench of moldering straw. The air was cold enough for me to see my breath, and the taste of it was stagnant and sour on my tongue.

My cell. Birsha's dungeon.

Thump. A step. A drag of flesh over stone. Thump.

My heart stuttered in my chest. I opened my mouth to cry out, and my throat screamed, sore and dry. My belly gaped and my muscles withered in my limbs, too weak to even protest as I tried to sit up. I remained limp, helpless, heartbeat picking up and then dropping away again with every heavy booted step on stone.

Thump.

Thump.

Thump.

I'd heard them coming, known them by the slow, expectant pace, by the snarls they drew up from the other cells. There were no snarls now. I was alone, defenseless, and abandoned, waiting for the next of my visitors to finally make their way to the door, to my pile of straw, to my purchased body.

Thump.

Thump.

Thump.

"No," I whimpered, trying to twist, to crawl away.

Thump. Shhhh.

I sobbed, managed a flail, and outside of my cell the endless, impossible step stuttered.

"No!" I cried out.

Thump. Shh, now—

I screamed, a sudden strength bolting through me, and then I was falling.

"Damn!"

The word snapped out, breathless, just as I hit hard against the floor, my elbow cracking through carpet into stone.

"Evanthia! Are you all right?!"

I screamed again, scrambling away, but already the world was righting itself in front of me. Not black and cold and stale, but warmly lit and elaborately colorful, the carpet underneath my bruised body soft. And it was not one of Birsha's clients hovering over me, but a wide-eyed and pale Conall, his hands held out in front of him, hovering in their reach for me.

"Forgive me," he gasped out, and then he grasped my shoulders. They rattled in his hold as he knelt in front of me. We were on the balconied square above the great hall of the castle. I'd been dreaming, locked in a nightmare, although it was close enough to a memory, a pattern I'd lived out night after night.

"Con—Con—"

"Shh," he said, the whisper dragging a shudder through me, the sound matching the dragging of a tail over stone, or an uneven footstep. "You fell asleep. I thought you'd want your bed."

I was here in the castle. Conall was in front of me. I was not in my cell.

I threw myself into Conall's chest and he sighed, gathering warm arms around my back. "There you are, *mo chroí*. You're safe. I have you."

My skirts were tangled around my legs, and I couldn't latch myself to Conall the way I wanted, but he managed to scoop me up from the floor. My elbow throbbed, and I pressed my whimper into the wool shoulder of his vest. He'd abandoned his coat somewhere, and my hands gripped at the muscles of his arms through the thinner cotton of his shirt.

The nightmare had sapped some of the strength I'd found from Hywel's dreams, and I was now queasy from dinner or wine, with a dull stab prodding in my head. Conall's steps were quicker, steadier, but I flinched with each one, the sound of his boots on the floor a faster echo of the memory I'd been trapped in.

"My-my room is—"

"Shh. Laszlo told me, and I can...smell your path through the halls," Conall murmured, hiking me more securely against his chest.

I found silken strands of hair as one of my hands stroked up his back, and I locked them in my fist. Conall smelled of sweat and horse, and something deeper and fresher as I sucked a breath of his skin in. Goosebumps raised against my cheek, and his arm around my legs tightened, hand clenching on my hip. But it was the hip I'd landed on, and I hissed and tensed, flinching at his grip against my bruise. We'd reached my room, and Conall all but ran for my bed, setting me down quickly, yanking himself and his hair out of my hold with a brief wince

He stared down at me, startled and disturbed, brow furrowed. "I didn't mean to frighten you."

"It was a nightmare," I said, shaking my head, but my legs were drawing in close to my chest as he towered over me.

He stepped back, swallowing hard, and glanced around the room. There was a fire already burning in the grate, and the moon winked its thin smile through the tall window.

"You should rest," he said, taking another step back.

For a moment, as he'd carried me, I'd wanted to devour his skin. Earlier, as he'd twirled a strand of my hair around his fingers, I'd set my mind to dragging him into bed with me. I may not have been starving, but I recalled the ache and wave of Asterion between my thighs, the joy of sex, and I knew Conall would be an eager lover.

Not now. His steps were too heavy. My left side was jolted and bruised from falling. I didn't want to be touched, didn't want a larger body pinning me down.

I nodded and he gusted out a breath, jolting forward and grasping me by the back of my neck before I could tear myself away. But his kiss on my brow was gentle and grazing, and we both sighed as he held there briefly.

"You need some sunshine tomorrow," Conall murmured, pulling away, his thumb stroking my cheek once. "Sleep."

It was on my tongue to call him back, but he was too fast, out the door before I could draw the words out.

9.
GIVE CHASE

I slept fitfully, my own heartbeat as it slowed too reminiscent of the thumping steps from the past. It wasn't until the birds roosting in the trees outside of my window woke and broke the silence that I was able to fall asleep properly.

Nightmares swarmed quickly. The dark prod of a stare, the tight grip around my ankle ready to drag, the sharp pinch and burn of a bite on my skin.

Conall shook me awake again, holding still at the foot of the bed as I sat up with a gasp and a strangled cry.

"No more nightmares for you, *mo chroí*. Up you get."

I blinked at the wolf. I'd never seen him properly by daylight. He was like the burning wick of a flame at night, glowing and lighting up a room, but in the sunlight from my window there was a softer quality, and it shook the bleak grip of my dreams out of my head.

"Good morning," I rasped.

"Good afternoon," Conall corrected. He was grinning, but there was a tightness around his eyes.

I licked my lips, and those spring green eyes watched the motion. "Last night wasn't your fault."

Conall blinked, his grin and the tension both disappearing. He sat heavily down at the corner of the bed. "I should've woken you."

I shook my head. "Memories were bound to catch up to me. I've been clawing for my life since I escaped that house."

"You're safe now," Conall said, words growling slightly.

I nodded, a fragile smile curling my lips. "I'm learning that. But if I'm not starving and running and hiding..."

Conall's head tipped. "It gives you time to think."

"To remember." I swallowed around the bitter word.

Conall turned his face to the door, eyes narrowing and jaw clenching. A moment later, a breath gusted out of his chest and his head shook, brilliant red hair catching and tossing the sunlight along its length. His laughter was rough and bitter. "I usually leave the heroic feelings to Asterion and the others, but you seem to draw out the impulse to hunt for shining armor."

I shoved the tangled blankets away from me, and Conall's eyes slid back to my body with an entirely ignoble graze over my breasts. "I would think armor is fairly ungainly."

At last, the wolf seemed to recover himself, a bright, feral grin on his lips. "Oh trust me, *mo chroí*, I move much better without it." I hummed and stifled my laugh, and Conall braced his hands on either side of my calves. "In fact, I am at my best out of clothing altogether."

My heart swelled in my chest, and my eyes watered and I shut them quickly, before he might misunderstand the tears. "I don't doubt that," I said on a shaky sigh.

"Hmm...what are you thinking right now, Evanthia?" Conall asked, one hand stroking my calf, gentle scratches from his claws teasing my skin.

I smiled and opened my eyes and watched the worry flicker over his beautiful face. "I missed seduction. And flirting."

Conall barked out a laugh. "Yes, I suppose Asterion and Laszlo aren't the best candidates when it comes to flirtation and seduction."

My gaze slid away as I recalled the stroke and press of Asterion's cock through silk. But that hadn't been seduction so much as a dreamy necessity. I still wondered why he'd done it and then vanished before I could really thank him. Was he only worried about my hunger, or was there any selfish enjoyment on his side?

"Don't take it personally that he didn't return," Conall said, ducking his head to catch my eye, winking at me. "If anything, it's a testament to how badly he wants to be here." I bit my lip, considering a question, but Conall continued on before I could sort it out. "Now. I promised you sunshine today, and in spite of the odds, Wales listened. Or perhaps Hywel caught a whiff of it, who knows with him. Eat something and then join me outside."

"You're a bit managing," I pointed out.

Conall laughed again, rising from the bed and shrugging. "Most don't notice. But yes. And on that note..." He trailed off, eyes taking another languid study of me, smile sharpening. "Don't dress. It's warm out, and you won't want it for what I have planned."

My eyebrows rose, but he just turned on his heel and strode to the door, sliding his hands in his pockets.

"If it's a seducer you need, *mo chroí*, I'm the beast for you," he threw over his shoulder.

My heart kicked with nerves, but the heat pooling low in my core throbbed in agreement.

THERE WAS NO SIGN OF LASZLO WHEN I FINISHED MY MEAL, and the castle was silent aside from Conall's pacing in the great hall. I leaned over the balcony to watch him flit from one object to the next, chuckling at a tapestry of hunters cornered by monstrous wolves, picking up a book and flipping carelessly through its pages.

"Are you coming down?" he called without turning to look up at me.

"What are your plans for me?" I asked, resting my elbows on the bannister.

Conall spun around, flashing me a grin. "In general? Or this afternoon?"

"I *know* your general plans," I answered, and he laughed.

"This afternoon we are going outside to play," he said, the words far too innocent.

Play was a very unspecific word, but every meaning of it was so unrelated to my recent experiences that I realized I didn't care. I hurried to the stairs, and Conall met me at the bottom. I'd put on a robe after all because the interior of the castle remained cool, and I held it shut with my arms around my waist, but Conall simply threw his own arm over my shoulder, a comforting weight and heat.

"What will we play?" I asked as he led us to the large, heavy doors.

"We need to get your blood pumping again, *mo chroí*," Conall said, voice light. "I've a mind to make you chase me."

"Chase *you*? Not the other way around?"

Conall scoffed, but he tensed slightly at my side. "Too easy."

"What if I'm a good runner?" I asked.

"I'm better," Conall said, the taunt clear. "And you have a very...distinct scent," he added, clearing his throat.

Conall released me, shouldering hard at the doors, groaning with their protestations. I winced against the sunlight and raised my hand to shield my eyes. He was right—it was warm out, surprisingly so for this late in the season.

"What do I smell like?" I asked, stumbling out into the light.

I'd found a good pair of slippers with leather soles, and they shielded my feet from the gravel of the drive, but it was only a few steps to reach the grass.

I was busy adjusting to the light, blinking at the wild gardens and short fields that circled the castle, marveling at the sight of a butterfly floating over the wall to feast on wildflowers. Suddenly, Conall was at my back, claws pricking the heavy robe that draped over my hips. My hair was braided back, and his nose stroked against my throat, breath hot and quick.

"Overripe fruit," Conall rasped into my skin, tugging me back to feel the press of his tall form, the way his hips fit to mine, his chest curving into my back. "Young wine." His words took on a growl as I shivered in his grip, and his hands flattened and slid forward, shamelessly covering my sex, curving his grip to the shape of me. My mouth opened on a silent moan, and he continued. "Melting sugar." He stroked me through the night-dress, one hand scooping down between my thighs to press cotton into the lips of my sex, then sliding away to let the other do the same. "Wet pussy."

I gasped, my breath heaving. My body swooned forward as Conall released me, my back cold even under the glare of the sun. My cheeks were burning and my legs trembled. Conall was *potent*, alarmingly so. I'd forgotten fear as he'd snarled into my ear, nightmares flitting away, and I recalled a dozen hungers I'd lost in the years of Birsha's grip—the quaking need of a lover's teeth in my flesh, not bracing for the stretch of a cock but gaping in anticipation, thirsting for sweat and cum on my tongue.

I jolted as starched cotton struck the ground, spun and found Conall wrestling out of his shirt. He had bright, fire-red hair glinting on his chest, down to circle around his dark belly button, the color deepening as it reached the waistband of his pants. His hair swung forward as he bent, unbuttoning his trousers and dropping them unceremoniously.

I stepped back, partly shocked and partly in need of a better view. Conall was broad and tightly packed with muscle, chest carved and thighs thick. He was elegant and wild at the same time, hair dense and almost furred down his thighs. His cock was half hard, the tip a little sharper than a man's, the base slightly swollen. I'd fucked werewolves in the past, been fucked by them in captivity. I knew the pleasure of a knot—the dense muscle that swelled at the base of a werewolf's cock during arousal—and also the trap it became as it locked a cock inside of me. I tore my stare away and then paused at the swooshing beat of a bright red tail kicking behind Conall's back.

"I told you I move better undressed," Conall said, words light, cock already calming.

I swallowed hard, wondering if he was waiting for me to undress too, or if he would pounce and tear my robe and nightdress from my body.

He did neither, flashing me a quick, easy smile, and then turning and darting toward a shadowy orchard grove. "Chase me or not. Up to you!"

His tail swished as he ran, and I laughed at the sight of him, pert ass clenched, hair floating and bouncing.

"And when I catch you?" I called.

Conall vanished behind a tree. "That's up to you too."

He reappeared, darting behind another tree. Soon he'd reach the far corner of the castle and be out of view entirely. And I would not be able to follow my nose, as he could.

I huffed and shrugged the robe off, leaving it in the pile of clothing, and then fisted the wide skirt of my nightdress to lift it up.

In truth, I was not a good runner. After a couple centuries trapped, I wasn't sure what I was in any regard, but athleticism had certainly been abandoned. My legs burned as I moved them, and all of Hywel's borrowed strength could not transform my neglected body completely. I was weak, and my breath sawed in my lungs, and Conall paused and watched me, grinning as I struggled to gain ground. But I didn't stop. I tripped over dropped apples and tree roots and caught my skirt on low branches, and my hair slipped loose of its tie. The sun scratched over my milk-pale arms and chest, until a blotchy, bright red flush of exertion took its place.

I lost Conall around the corner of the castle and found myself in a wheat crop, the bright gold stunning, the bristles tickling my calves and my palms as I trailed them over their tops. I left my slippers in the dirt, and my smile stretched as my toes dug into the earth. My heart was pounding, too fast and too hard, but it wasn't from fear. I lifted my face up and stared into the sun until tears streaked down my aching cheeks.

From a distance, a howl called, beckoning me back to the chase.

I gasped, and ran.

Conall's red hair peeked around another stone wall and then he raced ahead of me, laughing and leaping through the wheat field, tail whipping dust into the air. The ground was hard beneath my feet, but steady too, cool and giving. My arms cranked and my legs quaked with every pounding step, and *néktar* —my own, entirely—coiled through me.

Conall reappeared and vanished, slowed when my lungs refused to catch breath and I had to stop, darted again when I lunged forward. I could see the sweat glittering on his back as we turned another corner into a meadow, a few oak trees littered around the wide yard, horses grazing and eyeing us warily at a distance.

My knees were shaking, my ankles sore, and my hair had come loose and tangled itself eagerly, sticking to the sweat on my back. Conall stopped under the shade of an oak, staring at me, gaze glowing. His cock was hard again, his own chest flushed.

He arched his head back, and my hands gripped my own tired thighs at the sight of the flexing, stretching muscle. My eyelids fluttered shut at the call of his howl, a deeper sound than I expected, aching and answering in my galloping chest. I blinked my eyes open again, caught his stare, and lifted the hem of my nightdress. It clung to the sweat on my skin, peeled away, and immediately the sunlight stroked me, kissed and licked at parts of me it hadn't touched in centuries. My head fell back, lips parted as I panted, and the nightdress dropped into the grass.

"Evanthia."

He croaked my name out, too far away for me to hear more than a broken whisper.

Something cracked in my chest, bloomed, and then clawed its way up my throat. My mouth rounded and I let out the howl, the scream sharp and ragged. The sound carried a dense weight with it and I swayed in place, dizzy. I laughed as *néktar* flickered through me.

Conall had started toward me, but when I straightened and gazed back, the furrow on his brow smoothed and he twisted away, running again. I chased him, watching his legs stretch and work, matching my stride to his. A glimmer of sweat trailed down his back, and my mouth watered. He glanced over his shoulder at me, grinning, then jogged for a beat, and let me see the rise and swollen red of his cock.

I ignored the warning tremble of my legs, the pinch and stab in my gut, the endless pressure in my chest. I ran harder.

Conall howled, and I chorused with him, my own weaker with my short breath, but it carried along with his all the same.

He was slowing—we were getting too close to the horses, and one was starting to stomp its foot in warning—and when he turned, I followed the curve, pumped my arms and legs, and let out a scream of effort.

Conall spun to face me, knees bending and arms outstretched to catch me. I leapt, throwing myself into his chest, and he braced us both, landing on the ground and rolling, our legs tangling together. I caught his hair in my fist, and he snarled as I

79

pulled hard on it. My back hit the earth and then arched up, and I pushed my breasts to Conall's face.

"I won," I gasped out.

Conall huffed and growled, but his mouth devoured my offering. *Néktar* was a storm above us, rushing through me, and Conall's bite was gentle, his tongue swirling and lips suckling on my breast. I wrestled beneath him until my legs were unpinned, gulping down air, my body throbbing with exhaustion, with arousal. I rolled my hips up into Conall's lightly-furred stomach, a trail of short red hairs traveling down his belly, and my breath stuttered.

"Feast," I ordered, and it was a command for both of us. I pushed at Conall's head and he laughed, sitting up and fighting my grip long enough to grin at me.

"Gladly."

My thighs were spread, body a blatant invitation, and I loosened one hand from his hair, shoving it back into the earth as his ferocious mouth dove between my legs. I howled again as Conall's tongue swept against me, gasped as he sucked sweat from the hollow of my hips, bucked into his lips as they kissed chastely at my clit.

"Overripe fruit," he whispered, circling his tongue around my clit. "Young wine," he added, swiping over my folds. "Melted sugar," he said, kissing the darker curls. And then his thumbs stretched me open, claws pricking carefully, and his tongue thrust inside of me. I moaned, fucked myself onto the too-short but perfectly slick length prodding inside of me, and Conall's groan vibrated into my core.

"Such a wet pussy," he growled, pulling away.

My eyes squeezed shut, trying to block out the wave of sorrow, to ride the *néktar* and nostalgia, to remember all the sensations I'd lost long ago.

Conall ducked again, sucking and slurping on me, and my cunt throbbed, empty and pleading. I sat up and Conall scowled as I tugged him away from my sex, but he laughed as I pawed and pushed and threw him down to the ground, climbed over his long legs, stroked and scratched at his chest. His hands gripped my hips, and he was lazy, indolent, and luxurious in the grass, his eyes matching their shadows, his hair strikingly bright. The sun struck my back hard, and I moaned at the very sight of him.

I'd known from first glance that Conall was made for hedonism, and he'd drawn out parts of myself that had been buried years ago. I wanted them back. Immediately.

I found his cock, stroked it in my fist, smiled and marveled as his eyes rolled back and his chest heaved with a low moan. He bucked as I sank, and we both froze, mouths open and eyes wide, as his cock pressed inside of me.

The intrusion was sudden and startling, and my legs were tired from running. I was wet from his licking, from my own arousal, and he fit inside of me with a neat and satisfying stretch. I stilled, eyes shut, and tried to push away the looming outlines in my mind, the thumping footsteps that matched my nervous heartbeat.

"*Evanthia.*"

Conall's voice cracked, and I caught my breath. He sat up, arms twisting around my waist, lines creased between his brow, and our chests brushed, our breaths uneven.

He was lodged inside of me, thick and hard and...

I sighed, and his expression relaxed. My clawed hands smoothed and stroked up his back, circling his throat, and his eyelids drooped in lazy, expectant pleasure. I rolled my hips and ducked down, and we groaned together as he stroked inside of me. Our tongues licked at one another, plunging and pressing and retreating as I ground down into his lap, relearning the feeling of a cock inside of me, the safety of arms around my back. His touch was loose, petting gently at my spine and down to squeeze my ass, but his kiss was urgent, teeth starting to nip and breath ragged.

I pushed, my hands around his throat, and he let out a long, dark sound of pleasure as he fell back into the grass.

"Fuck me, *mo chroí.*"

My hands flattened on his chest, my hair dripping forward off my shoulders as I bent to kiss the warm, short curls there. His hands helped my hips lift, the drag of him inside of me slow and thorough, the drop of my weight back down rushing quickly, making us both yelp.

The sound of our voices together, chorusing with the impact and pound of skin, was *néktar*. Conall's heartbeat racing under my palm was *néktar*. The heat of him inside of me, the sharp stretch, was *néktar*.

I'd survived on other people's pleasure, and I'd forgotten how powerful my own was. I swooped my hips, pressed my clit into Conall's body, pulled one of his hands up to my own breast, and chased every drop of thick, sweet ecstasy that fed me.

"You're exquisite," Conall gritted out, his feet bracing against the ground so he could buck up, follow my retreat. "Pretty, wild beast, clawing for more."

My hands scratched his chest, my head thrown back and eyes tipped blindly to the sky. Conall howled, his grip tightening, saving my tired body from the effort and using his strength to fuck us both. He pulled hard on my nipple, tugging me closer, and scrunched in on himself, snarling lips wet and begging for my tit.

I arched and gave myself to his mouth, moaning and rocking, grinding, divinely lost to sensation. The grass and wildflowers swayed with us, bowed as I moaned, brushed my shoulders and thighs. Conall's hair was silk in my grip, twining around my fists as I steered him to my other breast, immediately mourning the loss of the first, crying out with the victory of the tugging pull between my thighs.

"More, *harder*," I pleaded, scratching down his spine.

He turned us, not pressing me down with his weight but twisting us in a tangle together, drawing one of my thighs high around his waist. His knot pressed to my opening, but he didn't force his way in, and I flinched at the thought of asking him to. I wanted this, the motion of him driving into me, the teasing tip of his cock licking me from inside as he drew out.

We rutted and rolled, wrestling to get closer, kissing with savage strokes and bites when there was nowhere further to go. Grass cut my skin, claws marked my hips, and Conall gasped into my mouth.

He threw me down to the ground, reared high, and reached between us, pinching one nipple and rubbing at my clit, and I was already screaming before I realized his intention. I came, clutching his cock, my first honest orgasm in centuries, stunned and almost frightened by the force, by the taste of my own relief.

And then Conall was pressed to me, chest to chest, hip to hip, even our ankles tangled, and he groaned into my ear as he snapped his hips and bucked through his release, the pleasure more familiar to me from an outside source. Our arms grappled around each other, squeezing tight enough to steal our breath.

Conall's kiss was tentative, his cock still spurting, hips jerking, even as he pecked and pressed and nuzzled his mouth to mine. I sucked on his bottom lip, soothed my hand through his hair, and he shivered to a stop, sagging on top of me, turning us to our sides again.

The grass around us was trampled, a smooth, hard bed beneath our unraveling bodies while we caught our breath. More kisses came, brief, sweet creatures after the frenzy, apologies and reassurance, mutually given. I gripped at Conall's shoulder blades as he started to pull away, and he pressed a slow line across my shoulder with his mouth.

"A feast, *mo chroí*," he whispered. "I'm not done yet."

I let him go, and his mouth slithered down my chest, savoring my breasts until I whimpered, licking down my belly, returning slowly to the place I'd pushed him before. He kissed across my hips, and I gathered his hair gently in my hands, closed my eyes, and let the sun burn my cheeks.

"What do I smell like with you on my skin?" I murmured.

"The same, but better," Conall rasped, and then his mouth served itself between my thighs, my body too sated to do more than enjoy his patient kisses.

10.
THE DREAMERS'
BALL

Candlelight flickered, a halo around my face reflected in the mirror. My lips were painted red, cheeks stained to force color back into my skin. The papered walls behind me were crumbling, soot and smoke caressing the ceiling, crawling ever closer. Nibbling orange fire wove and snapped, working its way down the walls.

My fingers pressed to my face, forcing my cheeks to swell, my lips to stretch, trying to remember the shape of a smile. The burning room was dressed in crystal and velvet, worn carpets, and silk drapes. I did not want to go back to the cell, and so I must learn to smile.

My teeth shone in the mirror and my painted lips cracked, a coppery flavor of blood seeping slowly to my tongue. My eyes stung. The room was on fire, but I must sit and smile. A client would come.

My cheeks hurt. My jaw ground. My eyes were dripping tears from the smoke. My lip was bleeding, the red a good match for the paint it wore.

Smile. A client would come. If I smiled, I could stay in this room.

Fire ate down the walls. Smoke flooded and swirled over my head. My face burnt with the effort, and the expression in the mirror was horror, too much gum, too many tears.

Smile wide, smile bright.

Better here than down in the dark. Better burning cheeks and cracking teeth and bleeding lips.

I tipped my head, tried to force a sound from the frozen face in the mirror, a tinkling laugh. But it was the crackle of wallpaper crumbling, plaster splitting, ash raining down to hiss against my tear tracks.

Smile, Evanthia.

I sat up from the nightmare, sucking down lungfuls of clean, sharp air, my window open to the sound of birds. My cheeks were sore, my lip pulled strangely, and a whine escaped me as I slapped my hands to my face, pushing away the grimacing smile that stared back at me in horror in the small mirror across the room. I flattened my hands over my face and screamed into my palms, teeth clenched, body trembling.

The soft creak of the door opening was buried under my cry. My fingernails dug into my forehead and temples, clawed hands fighting the sudden violent urge to peel this face away, tear away the smile I'd worn to try and placate Birsha and the beasts he hired to keep us in line.

Cool fingers slipped under my palms, and I jolted but didn't release myself. Claws skimmed against my skin, not scratching, just wedging themselves against my cheeks, a gentle force pulling my hands away.

It was Laszlo, not Conall, staring down at me, solemn and quiet as ever. The sight of him took my breath away, silenced my scream in an instant. He was gilded and beautiful, every hair and feather capturing the sunlight. He gathered my tense hands and pressed them down into my lap before reaching up once more. His thumbs pressed to my cheekbones and then stroked down firmly, loosening my jaw and leaving my lips parted. They moved up to my forehead, circling over the spot, spreading down to my temples, over my jaw again. One determined and careful touch at a time, he erased the strain of my forced smiling, a wordless treatment. I swallowed as he stroked down from my jaw and over my throat. He extended his fingers, keeping his claws away, finding muscles I'd forgotten and soothing them calm again.

My breathing was still ragged, still recovering from the clog and scratch of the smoke in the nightmare, and Laszlo seemed unnaturally still by comparison, a bronze statue of a man. His heavy wings were a gleaming backdrop, blocking out the room and the mirror. He smelled like tea and something clean and sweet. I wanted to arch into him, but he was sapping me of all the tension and strength that had seized me from the dream, his hands now circling and dragging down my arms.

My lips shut, not torn and chapped but smooth at last, and his eyes stared down at my lap as he massaged my hands out of their painful claw.

"Laszlo," I rasped.

"I brought you the wax for Hywel's scales," he said.

It'd been a few days since Laszlo and I had discussed Hywel. A few days of racing around the castle with Conall until I was sore and breathless, sharply alive and desperate for touch, wrestling the man down into the grass with me, grappling at muscle and skin, biting my moans off around his shoulder and throat. We took dinner with Laszlo, and Conall continued to tease the gryphon as he pawed and petted me in front of the fire.

I hadn't fallen asleep in front of them again, but Conall never followed me to my bed at night. I considered issuing the invitation the first night, after our wild union in the meadow, but I'd lost the nerve. The game of chase stirred me up enough to take what I craved, but the quiet of evening left me too self-conscious.

And the nightmares came back. Old details and memories warped by the vulnerability of an unconscious mind, my time in Birsha's cage resurfacing with precise horror.

Laszlo reached up to my face again and I flinched instinctively, but he didn't retreat, just slid his claws into my hair. My breath caught and my eyes slid shut as he combed through my strands.

"I haven't visited him recently," I murmured.

"A few days is nothing to a sleeping dragon," Laszlo answered softly. "The werewolf's strength isn't sticking to you."

My eyes flashed open, startled at the idea that Laszlo could read so much, *knew* so much. But he was right, and I shook my head slowly. "The nightmares seem to...unravel it all over night."

That first afternoon, I'd assumed the pleasure Conall and I had found together would surge through me, that I would start to catch up with my deprivation at last. Instead, I had dreamt of cuffs around my wrists and ankles that seemed to tighten endlessly, cutting through my flesh and bone, down into my soul. I'd woken drained and exhausted.

Laszlo hummed, fingers twisting at the nape of my neck,

untangling a few strands. His presence in my bedroom was both startling and soothing. Conall was all flesh and feeling, flirtatious and energetic. Even Asterion was steady and tangible. Laszlo was touching me now, but his gaze left me studied under a glass, his caresses as intellectual as they were comforting.

"I'll visit Hywel today," I said, although there was a tension in the way Laszlo spoke of his slumbering lover that left me uncertain as to what he really wanted me to do.

Laszlo just leaned back, wings shifting to reveal a large porcelain jar sitting on the bed by my calves. "Hywel never has nightmares."

I puffed out a breath, my brow furrowing as I muttered under my breath. "Lucky him."

Laszlo echoed my puff, made it sound more elegant than I had managed, and slid off the bed, heading for the door. "Give him some suggestions. He might share his dreams with you."

❦

HYWEL WAS STRETCHED OUT ON HIS SIDE, ONE FRONT LEG extended out of the cave entrance, his belly displayed, softly pink and streaked with white. His long tail was stretched around the cavern, a few tables of treasures now knocked over, gold spilling over carpets.

He liked being touched here. My cheeks were flushed and *néktar* was heavy in the air, and there was a leathery seam near his hind quarters, where twin cock heads were parting the fold, threatening to emerge. The seam had been almost invisible when I started my work, but it'd grown swollen over the hours of me rubbing my hands and cloth over the dragon's long stomach. I was curious—the tip of one cock was the size of my *head*—but it was crossing a line that didn't feel right either for Laszlo's or Hywel's sakes to go and investigate further.

Instead, I kept my eyes forward on the pattern of the longer, smoother scales, and spoke to the dragon.

"I remember a party I attended. It was midsummer in Dublin. The fae attended, wearing the most absurd attempts at glamours. But the mead was rich that year, and there were only a few of us who noticed their presence. I ended up spread out in a fairy ring outside of the city." My breath caught as the dragon rumbled in drowsy approval. "Mm, yes. Hands and mouth and everything else full. Every inch of me kissed. I was chased out of town the next afternoon, but I couldn't walk straight, and..."

I laughed, but the sound hiccuped in my strangling throat. My legs were weak, but it wasn't from the sweet memory. I sank to my knees, the waxed cloth dragging over scales, my cheeks pressing to the heat of Hywel's chest.

"I did fight him. For years," I whispered, eyes welling, recalling the sting of the smoke in my nightmare. "Sometimes decades. I escaped...briefly. I beat my palms bloody against doors and screamed until I couldn't speak for weeks."

Hywel was sleeping, silent now, his chest nudging against my shoulder as he breathed. But it was a relief to speak. Laszlo told me I should offer Hywel suggestions, but instead I found myself confessing. I turned my head, let his scale burn against my lips as I spoke, the words barbed, biting and scratching as they were pulled up from my chest.

"The truth is, I also spent days or weeks or years or decades trying to please them. Smiling. Smiling through every horrible moment, every bite and scratch and bruise. There were better meals. A softer bed. If I could hide how much I hated them, how sick I made myself smiling...it helped a little."

Except it hadn't really, it'd just been a change in the torment. Better accommodations, hating myself more. A meal with flavor that I threw up more often than not.

"I managed once for more than forty years. I stole a dinner knife, and I kept it hidden for six years, wondering if I would be brave enough to use it. On myself. On one of them." The more I spoke, the easier the words flowed. "And then...there was a girl who needed it more than me. Who wouldn't have survived another visit from her client. She killed him, and I was so...so *jealous*," I hissed, digging my fingers into a seam between scales. "So proud too."

A tear dripped from my jaw and slid quickly over Hywel's polished scales.

"But part of me thought...*always* thought that my mother

would interfere. That someone would come. And not two hundred years later," I gasped out, pulling my hands away, clenching my fists against the rising tide of pressure that rose up in my chest, threatening to crack me open. I pressed my tight hands into my thighs and arched my chest, waiting for the need for air to force me to draw a breath. It came gusting into my lungs, swaying me, chest heaving.

We will have vengeance, pretty morsel.

My hand slapped against Hywel's side, the weight of the words a great pound in my head that nearly toppled me. But his voice wasn't painful. It was stone and silk. It swarmed me, cradling me even as it bore down. I blinked and found one opalescent eye open and gazing back at me.

"Hywel?" I whispered, shocked by the sight of his stare, slow to realize how much he had heard, what he had answered with just a handful of words.

Vengeance. It sounded tender and deadly at the same time.

A pink film of flesh covered the gleaming gaze, narrow black pupil shrinking to a slit, and then a heavy red leathery lid slid shut, Hywel sighing heavily. Behind me, steps echoed on stone, gold coins skidding down the steps.

"Evie," Conall called, his voice unexpectedly loud and boisterous in this massive space I'd come to find almost reverent and holy. "Come up to dinner. We have...surprise guests."

Hywel had woken. Only for a moment, or he simply didn't want Conall to see him so. He'd heard my confessions. He'd made a vow.

We will have vengeance.

"Evie?" Conall said, gentler, closer.

I didn't want him to touch Hywel, to come admire the dragon I had no right to feel so possessive over. Not when I knew perfectly well he did not belong to me.

I rose up, swaying and lurching away from Hywel, and Conall caught me by my elbows, his gaze studying the dragon over my shoulder.

"Are you all right?" he asked, frowning and glancing between us.

I pressed my hands to his chest, pushing him back toward the steps, his gaze sharpening on me at my force.

"Fine. Just...just lost track of time down here."

Beyond Hywel's long leg, out over the dreaming sea, the sun was setting.

Conall relaxed slightly, moving his arm to slide around my waist, to turn his back on Hywel and guide me to the stairs. "Meanwhile, I suffered every minute without you," Conall said, drawling the words, clearly teasing. I flinched. He was joking, but the notion of him suffering was...bitterly laughable, made me want to snarl at him.

He stopped suddenly, turning to me, the joke falling dead between us. "Forgive me, that was a stupid thing to say. I was *bored* today. And I missed running with you."

I understood Conall when he was flirting, joking. I was *overwhelmed* by him when he was earnest. I was potently aware of the dragon still spilling across the room. Of what Conall might've heard me say as he came down the stairs. Of Hywel perhaps still being awake.

"You...you mentioned guests?"

Conall's frown flickered briefly, and then he smoothed his expression into an easy smile. My heart heaved in my chest, the false smile unsettling me, past and present, nightmare and reality swirling together.

"Sort of. Come up with me?"

I nodded, but Conall remained still for a moment. His gaze slid back to Hywel, and his arm tightened around my waist, tugging me against his chest.

"When Hywel wakes, Birsha will have real cause to fear this battle he's been so eager to wage," Conall said, voice low and growling gently. His arm around my waist sank low on my hips, hand barely squeezing at my ass, his hips pressing into mine.

Vengeance.

"And you, *mo chroí*, will have a world at your feet."

I shivered at the words, not understanding the way they touched my skin, sank low in my belly, throbbed in my core. Conall grinned at last, sharp and a little hungry, honest too. He leaned in, pressing us explicitly together. His hair swarmed my vision, blocking out my view of Hywel, my heart racing at the idea of the dragon seeing Conall hold me so close.

"I can't wait to see what you claim for yourself," he snarled in my ear.

I gasped, my breasts brushing against his chest, and his fingers tightened on my ass. I wanted to shift in place, open my thighs to him, wanted him to take us down to the floor and rut me, sudden and rough. I wanted Hywel to watch, to wake.

"Come," Conall said, pulling away too suddenly, leaving me stumbling along at his side as we climbed the stairs. "We have a ball to attend."

⚜

Conall led me into the great hall of the castle, my steps slowing in wonder as music bounced and curled around every pillar and rafter, echoing against stone and glittering mirrors. Shadow figures spun and parted, stepped in unison, circled and bowed. I shrank back, the force of muddled voices loud and shocking after so many months of hiding away, only coming out in London in late hours, on dark streets.

"We were overdue a festivity."

I twisted and found Laszlo on my right, his eyes skimming over the imaginary crowd, hands tucked behind his back under the curtain of his wings. His gaze flicked to mine, bright yellow and sharp.

"Hywel held them off, gave you time to adjust."

There was no reason for my face to go hot at the mention of the dragon, and I tucked my left cheek against my shoulder, watching the dancers.

"Dance with me, Evie," Conall said, bumping his hip to mine.

"I'm not dressed for a ball," I said, lifting my limp, utilitarian skirt up and letting it drop down. Dust from Hywel's cavern billowed off the fabric.

Conall laughed. "They don't care. I certainly don't. Don't let Laszlo's life as a monk infect you. Come and enjoy yourself."

Laszlo's feathers barely ruffled at the jab, his chin lifting, and

Conall didn't wait for me to agree, just swept me up in his arms and spun me out to the dance floor. I was clumsy at first, my steps wooden. I'd forgotten how to be a dance partner, how to settle in someone's arms and let them lead me. Even my sex with Conall was often wrestling for control, battling for pleasure.

We cut through clouds of shadow, the dreaming figures taking no notice of us as we made a messy path through their crowd. The music twisted and reshaped itself, violins crying and sawing through new melodies, moving away from a ballroom and into the rowdy drum and skip of a village square. I laughed as Conall dragged me into a leaping, jigging nonsense of movement, and his answering grin was as bright as sunlight. Candles spun around my head, and I curved into his grasp.

"We'll work up our appetites, *mo chroí*," Conall gasped out. I didn't know if he meant food or fucking, and I didn't care.

Conall's wildness reminded me of who I was before Birsha caught me in the brothel, laid a baited web and snared me for centuries. It wasn't possible to let go of those painful years, but his joyous revelry dragged me through them, back to *life* and *joy*. Not careless pleasure but *determined* delight.

"You and I would've gotten into a great deal of trouble when I was younger," I mused, breathless. The music was settling, and Conall was grasping me tightly as he had down in Hywel's hoard.

"We *will* get into trouble, Evie," Conall said, spinning me slowly, rocking our hips to music, coaching my fumbling feet to follow his.

"And...and if I don't want trouble?" I asked, chest heaving. My gaze fixed over his shoulder as we turned, dizzy from the floating shadows that passed us, searching around the edge of the room.

Conall didn't hesitate. "Wickedness, then. Pleasure." His hand around my waist tightened. "Together, with others. You can have everything you want, feasting and lusting and celebration."

I found Laszlo in the archway of the corridor that would lead to his little sanctuary of a room, away from the revelry. But he was watching me and Conall, and for the first time, I read his expression clearly. The crease between his brows, the crooked purse of his lips, the craving and sorrow in his gaze.

"We'll keep you safe, *mo chroí*."

The music was catching its breath, and Laszlo's wings were hunching closer, his chest just starting to turn away.

"Wait!" I called.

Conall stepped back and Laszlo's gaze struck mine. I glanced at the werewolf, but his smile was mellow, knowing, and I returned my focus to Laszlo quickly.

I'd been seductive once, alluring. I could've tipped my head at the correct degree, slanted my gaze, and a man across the room would've crawled to me on his knees. But that woman had been crushed, crumbled down to dust, and I didn't know if I could have her back, if she could be rebuilt. If she was even who I wanted to be now.

"You have to dance with me too," I said, the words only just audible under the din of the dreamers.

Conall opened our stance, facing Laszlo too, as the gryphon glanced between us. He opened his mouth and I knew at once, my shoulders drooping, that he would refuse.

"Be a gentleman, Laz," Conall goaded. He lifted my hand and extended it toward the watching gryphon.

Laszlo's eyes rolled and I flashed a quick, grateful smile at Conall, who turned on his heel and bent to kiss the back of my hand, as elegant as a courtier. Laszlo joined us, and he didn't storm through the shadows as Conall had, but politely waited for them to pass, even dipping his head once in acknowledgement of a greeting.

"Thank you," I said as Conall passed Laszlo my hand.

Laszlo's grip was as firm and tender as it had been when he'd stroked the tension and tremors out of me.

"Join me in the dining hall when you're done. If Hywel will dream us a party, we ought to be courteous enough to enjoy it," Conall said.

Laszlo sighed, but Conall didn't wait for an answer, leaving us. Laszlo stepped closer, his arm bracing my waist gently. He stepped and my body followed instinctively, the movements unfamiliar but his leading was elegant and calm in comparison with the storm of dancing Conall had led me through.

"He is...*young*," Laszlo remarked, turning us, his gaze glancing over Conall.

I laughed at that summation and nodded. "He is." It made me ache, actually. I didn't know how old Conall was, how long he would live, but I knew he was young compared to me, to Laszlo and Hywel and Asterion.

"He exhausts you?" I asked.

Laszlo frowned at that, his stare drifting up and around the room. I didn't know how long it had been since he'd danced, but he did so beautifully. The more I relaxed in his hold, the more graceful I found my own movement.

"He seeks to draw out an energy in me that I find it easier to reserve. He doesn't understand patience the way that I do."

I let my own eyes slip away, thinking over the statement, understanding it. Conall was drawing that energy out of me too, but it was restorative, vital for me. He left me breathless, but also breathing more deeply than I had in decades. But Laszlo was not a creature who needed hedonism and ecstasy to survive. And Hywel, his partner, was asleep. Had been as long as I'd been captive. Longer.

"So many misunderstand immortality," I murmured, drawing Laszlo's eyes back to me. "They think it means time passes faster, that days are minutes and years are days and we rush through our lives. But you cannot change the length of time, or how it stretches around you."

Laszlo's face was slack, yellow gaze bright and open.

"Centuries are long," I said.

"Very," Laszlo said, brow folding in a shared pain.

"Has no one else been here with you?" I asked.

"Visits," Laszlo murmured. "Brief affairs."

You are lonely, I thought, but the words didn't need to be said. Just as Laszlo didn't have to tell me that he understood how long I'd suffered under Birsha.

He took a breath and I stepped closer as his arm banded just a bit tighter, cradled up my spine. His wings pressed to his back, feathers teasing against the back of my hand.

"We will have more years with him awake than I have waited

as he slept," Laszlo said, his quiet voice brushing against my hair. "But you're right—it does not change the length of the years."

Of being alone.

Laszlo was the perfect height for me to rest my head on his shoulder as we danced, to hear the slow and steady thump of his heart under my ear. We sighed together, stepped together, spun slowly in the company of shadows together.

11.
THE DRAGON'S JAWS

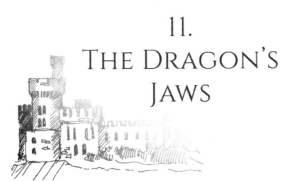

The ball was not a cure for my nightmares.

I dreamt of crowds, wild nights in The Seven Veils, fire burning down the walls. The night I escaped. The night Birsha ran and the house fell, crumbled and torn and burnt to the ground. I dreamt of running through the woods, hiding from the monsters that prowled, that stole the escaping girls for themselves in those strange hours, and instead of the wild living relief I'd felt that night, all I dreamt of was terror.

The ground was hot under my feet, spiraling ash settling in dry grass, but it cooled the deeper into the woods I wandered. The screams at a distance faded, and the air grew heavy. This was not the way I'd run that night. I'd followed the glow of London, hid myself in doorways and gutters until the whores took me in.

This was the woods surrounding the castle, misty and eerie but safe. Up ahead in the dark, a broad and bulky shadow loomed. The castle. Laszlo and Conall, the shadow dreamers. The woods were wet and rich and quiet and the castle waited for me and I was not in London, not running. My steps were heavy, my legs drunk, but there was safety ahead.

And then the shadow shifted. I stilled in the dark as the right side twisted. A bright glow lit, but it was not Laszlo's golden lamp, but a round moon and opal eye, split down the center with a thin pupil.

"Hywel?" I called.

Come here, blodyn bach. **You've wandered far enough for one night.**

"From London to Wales," I mused.

*The dragon rumbled, two eyes now blinking at me in the dark, broad face rising up to stare down at me. **Who feeds you nightmares?***

"My memory," I said. *The woods ran by quickly now, my steps carrying me farther, closer to Hywel, who was no longer shadow but a glowing ember in the night. The grass warmed and softened under my feet, mossy carpet and stones of gold.*

Then my bed will be your respite. Come and sleep in my scales.

What had been distant was now directly in front of me, Hywel's towering form, his bright opal eyes watching me. A tangle of pillows and blankets and clothing sat cradled between his huge legs, and he purred and rumbled as I climbed into the nest.

"I'm glad you are in my dream," *I murmured, curling on my side, stroking one hand over the heavy ridges that ran down his legs.*

His head lowered, breath surrounding me, sweeter than I expected, lavender smoke and summer sun. I'd never fallen asleep in a dream before —it was a funny sort of idea—but it felt like sinking underwater, and my lips curved as I drifted deep into slumber.

৩৵৩

TIME SEEMED TO PASS IN THIS NEW, RESTFUL SLEEP. I COULD feel the hours moving, but there was no disruption, no nightmare or dream, just quiet.

I woke with smooth, warm glass under my hand, my body cradled perfectly in swathes of fabric and goose down pillows. A wet coil stroked around my ankle and calf, warm and silken. I blinked and found that my bed was made of red dragon scales, recently waxed and polished by my own hand. Hywel's cavernous hoard glittered beyond his leg, and every minute or so a great heave of warm air stroked over my body.

Which meant...

I twisted and found the slightly open maw of the King of Dreams poised at my feet. A long, thick, black tongue extended out past the large teeth and fangs to twine around my left leg.

You wake.

I gaped at the massive jaw poised just past my toes, the

spiked dragon chin tucked down against his body, his eyes turned forward and almost crossed to stare down at me.

"I..." I cleared my throat when no words rose to my tongue.

You were sleepwalking, **blodyn bach**.

It'd been a long time since I'd heard any Welsh, but the name he gave me was simple—little flower. The dragon's lips didn't have to move to speak, and his tongue continued to wrap and caress around one leg, teeth the size of my feet bared in what I swore was a smile. If he opened his jaw a little wider, the space offered would be large enough for me to tuck myself inside, crawl down his gullet. My body trembled in hysterical terror at the thought, distracting me from the equally chilling knowledge that I had wandered in my sleeping, down into the dragon's den.

I braced my hands against either of his legs and pushed to sit up. My toes pressed to the rounded thick bottom lip of his jaw and his tongue retreated slightly, just a single loop around my ankle, a slightly damp streak shining on my skin.

"You're awake," I said, stroking his right leg.

Shh, don't tell the others. There was a hint of mischief in his heavy words as they soaked into my head, almost a whispering note.

"Laszlo misses you."

Hywel rumbled, purred, and sighed, a deeper, smokier breath washing over me. *Not for much longer*.

I sighed with him and nodded. Good. After my dance with Laszlo, after sitting between him and Conall at dinner, their knees and thighs brushing against mine, it was almost like betraying my new friend to have this moment of speaking to Hywel.

You've been taking care of me. The black tongue twined again, this time smoothing higher. I stared into the fearsome jaws, the dark red gullet, and marveled at how long that tongue extended, how far back in Hywel's huge mouth it rooted.

"You've given me sanctuary," I answered, eyes flicking up to his, smiling at the picture of his slitted eyes narrowed to study, his flaring nostrils.

I leaned forward, rubbing my palm firmly against the center of his snout, pressing my lips together to withhold my laugh as his eyes crossed and then shut. His tongue unwound from around my knee but then flicked between my legs, batting at the skirt of my nightgown, nudging it up my thighs.

I met a divinity once. A Viking lad. The son of the trickster. He tasted delicious.

I laughed, and my eyes fixed once more on those huge teeth, so close to my own flesh. "How did you meet him?"

He snuck into my hoard to steal my treasure.

"And so you ate him?"

I licked him head to toe...and when we were satisfied, then I ate him.

I licked my own lips, my breath stuttering in my chest, and glanced down at the black tongue that stroked the inside of one thigh and then the other.

"Is that what you're planning to do with me?" I asked, my voice a little too high, but breathless too.

Hywel shook and the whole room rattled and trembled and laughed with him, gold and books and jewels jangling in their cases, his grin broadening.

I would like to taste you, **blodyn bach**, he answered, his tongue sliding higher, rubbing and looping near the top of my right thigh. His tongue squeezed, and I fell back on my elbows with a gasp. *But I should like to feed you, not myself.*

My head fell back, a moan trapped in my throat, my eyes squeezing shut. I'd served and enjoyed many a monster in my lifetime, but never a *dragon*.

"I'm...I'm not sure I could reciprocate," I managed, biting my lip.

Hywel laughed again, even longer and heavier than before, and I could not restrain my groan as the sound—too low and rich to really ring in my ears—vibrated all around me and through the tongue that teased just shy of my bare sex.

Someday, you might. Perhaps even soon. But no, my dwtty creature, not today.

I opened my mouth to correct him—there was no day that I could spread myself enough for those massive twin heads I'd gotten a glimpse of yesterday—but his tongue slipped loose from around my thigh and then played coyly at my center, petting and pressing to my sex.

"Oh!"

I arched between the dragon's legs, sank down into the blankets and pillows, and shut my eyes against the sight of the enormous open threat of his mouth as he licked me. It was like the dull stroke of a cock spreading itself through my lips, but his tongue was not perfectly smooth; there were little bumps and grooves that teased my tender flesh.

Oh, you are much sweeter than the trickster's son.

I gasped and giggled, eyes flying open. I couldn't see Hywel's eyes like this, collapsed in the nest he'd made me, and his jaw opened wider. I didn't know if his words meant to tease or frighten me, or if he was simply a dragon and appetite was as much a part of his nature as it was mine.

His tongue slid up, over the coarse curls between my legs, tangling into the thin cotton of my nightdress, and I fumbled, pulling the fabric up, wrestling myself out and tossing it beyond his massive taloned feet. I stared at the thick, black length—no, it was a deep red color, like wine or pools of blood—watched it slither and slide, caressing over my belly, revealing a split end that eagerly stretched to cup and rub one breast. Hywel growled or purred, and I panted, trembling hands reaching to stroke his long tongue. It was dense, muscular, twisting in my grip, the forked ends able to pinch and pull my nipple as I cried out, but it was softer and more pliable than an erect cock too. I lifted it from my breast and it grasped and pulled on my hand, slid away again, swiped over my throat, and glided up my jaw.

My lips parted, eyes watching the roping tongue curve and curl over my body, my hips hiking up to push against it. My feet rose, bracing on slippery scales, and then higher, pressing to Hywel's thick lips, toes pricking over the pointed ends of his fearsome fangs on his lower jaw.

"Hywel," I whispered, eyes wide at the picture of his brutal teeth and wicked tongue between my spread legs. I was stretched, exposed, and his breath rushed over me, growing warmer with every purr and growl, rumbling into my toes. The sight was shocking and dangerous. If my foot slipped and his jaw snapped shut, I'd lose a limb.

I ought to have had enough of danger, of threats. But Hywel was petting me with his beautifully elegant tongue, and it was me who was toying with those jaws, who was trying to squirm closer, my heart hammering and my cunt throbbing in the same beat.

One dark forked end of his tongue slid over my bottom lip, and I closed my mouth and my eyes, sucking on the very tip of damp flesh, finding the taste of myself. It felt like a thick finger prodding between my teeth, exploring briefly, and underneath my own flavor was a dark and earthy one. I hummed as the second fork of his tongue skidded around my jaw, and then he pulled free, dragging back down the length of my body.

You are a very tempting morsel, **blodyn bach**.

"If you eat me, you only get to do so once," I warned.

Hywel's laughter came with *néktar*, as much as his over-whelming licks. I was spread between a dragon's legs, left open to his licking tongue, at risk of being gobbled up and forgotten. I was making a dragon *laugh*.

I grinned and stretched my arms over my head, finding his huge feet, stroking the knuckles and down to the claws. I arched my back, and Hywel's tongue made a brief return trip to pluck at my nipples.

Lush, he praised.

"Your tongue is lush," I answered, sighing as it skidded over my belly button and down between my legs again, cleaning away the dew of my arousal, stroking back and forth over my inner thighs, heavy and slick. "Your teeth are beautiful. Your scales are smooth."

I have you to thank for that, he answered, purring. ***And so thank you I shall.***

His tongue seemed to shrink, growing plumper when not stretched, and it prodded and pushed against my pussy, split and stroked on either side. I moaned and rocked into the touch, but I kept my eyes on those sharp bright teeth and the dark gullet beyond.

"Laszlo—Oh! Hywel!" I grunted, twisting, trying to escape the determined grip of the forked tongue pulling my clit from hiding, and he released me with a rumbling chuckle. "Laszlo gave me the wax," I managed.

My mate knows what kind of rare treasures I like to find in my hoard, Hywel murmured, and then returned to tormenting my sex, pulling at my folds, my clit, burrowing at my hole.

I flushed at the words, my mouth opening to ask about Laszlo, about what it meant to be *mates* when you weren't the same species, but then I was blushing and crying out because Hywel's forked tongue was prodding me twofold, at my ass and cunt together. My hands gripped around claws, body instinctively ready to drag myself away, but Hywel just returned to petting and licking between my legs.

I gasped and settled and then moaned as the steady pattern soothed heat through me, built an ache that heated my blood.

I frightened you, he noted.

"Surprised," I admitted, blinking up at him.

His open mouth was beautiful and startling and thrilling, but I missed his gaze. I pushed up again and he reticated once more, tucking his head until we were staring at one another. I rose up on my knees and scooted toward him, his eyes blinking slowly.

"Do it again," I said.

He didn't hesitate, tongue flicking out and down, sliding between my parted thighs, dipping and twisting and pressing to my openings. I sighed and stared up the long, broad bridge of Hywel's snout to the wide-set gemstone gaze studying me. When one fork of his tongue slid into my core, tongue curling to rub more of its length against my clit, I let out a bright cry. My hands flew forward, clutching at the horns sprouting from hard scales to steady myself.

Hywel purred, and the reverberation numbed my gripping fists. He bucked forward, jaw scooping down and catching my knees on his bottom lip, and I yelped as he lifted me up, stretched and spread and balanced at the end of his mouth.

I laughed and then moaned as his forked tongue fucked my channel, dipping and rubbing and licking me from the inside out, while the other half burrowed against my clenching ass, wetting and slicking the nervous muscle.

Let me in, **blodyn bach.** *Give me my feast, and I will give you yours.*

"It's not fair—" I gasped, relaxing and immediately invaded by a squirming tongue. "Not fair that you can talk with your mouth full."

Hywel laughed again, and tears pricked my eyes. His laughter was something like honor. My teasing words were from a woman I'd assumed was buried years ago. I worked myself onto his tongue and let my head fall back, ignoring the heavy sway as he reared his head higher, tipping it up, supping on my body. If his jaw opened suddenly, I would slide in, swallowed whole. My legs trembled and my hands grew slick with sweat as I ground down into his tongue.

Breathe, pretty morsel, Hywel purred.

I breathed and then released a long, keening note, shuddering through my distant terror, my immediate and desperate need for more. His tongue started to plunge, extended length still rubbing against my clit, and I scrambled at the top of his nose. The trembling, rising, terrifying pleasure made me unsteady and weak. His head jerked, tossing backwards. I slipped, shouted, and fell against his scales, kissing and stroking over his broad head, quaking in the long wave of my orgasm as Hywel growled. I was pinned on his tongue, my legs flailing with the electrifying storm rushing through me, and I shook bodily with his laughter, stunned and drowned in *néktar.*

You are right—it would be a waste to eat you only once.

I laughed too, limp and barely clutching to his scales, one leg inside of his mouth, sharp teeth digging gently into the back of my thigh.

Hold tight, he warned, and I managed to grab onto his horned snout as he slowly leaned forward once more, dipped his head down, and settled my head and shoulders back into the makeshift bed he'd offered me.

"Wait," I murmured before he could pull away.

He huffed as I stroked his scales, kissing every inch of him I could reach, rubbing my bare breasts against his upper lip, petting around the edge of his jaw. He helped himself to more licks, slow, studying ones, soothing my still quaking muscles. His eyes were sealed with the milky film layer, and his lids were beating shut, opening slowly and then falling closed again.

"You're going back to sleep?" I asked, frowning slightly, crawling up to drape myself over his snout, ignoring the dig of his horns.

He sighed, hot breath tickling my toes, tongue following and flicking briefly. **Not for long**, he answered, but I suspected his version of long might've been different than mine. **Take care of him.**

I blushed at the words, knowing Hywel meant the gryphon, wondering if Laszlo would be able to let me try or if I would even know how.

"Sweet dreams, my lord," I whispered, stretching up to kiss the single white scale between his eyes.

Hywel purred, and I sighed as the sound dug softly through me, coaxing out aftershocks of pleasure. We settled together, my naked body draped shamelessly over his sturdy face. I traced a thread of white with my fingertip, shivered at a breeze sliding through the open cavern, and let the soak of *néktar* and heady release return me to drowsy darkness.

12.
THE PATIENT LOVER

Feathers brushed over my ass, talons combed through my hair, and I woke with a sharp breath, tea and sweetness in my lungs.

"Forgive my touch," Laszlo rasped. "The pair of you are... exceptionally beautiful."

My eyes opened to find the gryphon already stepping back, although he didn't look away from where I was spread over Hywel's sleeping head like the poorest excuse for a blanket. I pressed my legs together, eyelids fluttering at the tender throb of where I'd been thoroughly licked, and Laszlo dove down, drawing my nightgown up from where I'd dropped it near Hywel's feet.

"If you're not careful, he'll tuck this into the whole bundle and you'll never get it back again," Laszlo said, lips quirking.

"I should've asked you, or—or..."

His eyes widened behind the guard of those glimmering spectacles I wanted to rip away. "Nonsense. Hywell is the territorial one, not me. And if I had wanted you to stay away from him, I would've said so."

His eyes lowered to my breasts, fixed there for a moment, and then skidded away. He drew my nightgown up like a shield. "I knew he would be good for you," he added.

Forgive my touch. I opened my mouth to tell Laszlo he could touch if he wanted to—I was feeling exceptional after a real night's rest and a fresh dose of pleasure for my soul to feast on— but he rushed on.

"Asterion's returned. He and Conall are going mad looking for you. Hywel hid the passageway from them."

It'd been almost two weeks since Asterion had disappeared while I slept, and my wobbling legs as I leapt off Hywel's head had more to do with nerves than weakness.

"He can do that?"

"Dragons know how to guard their treasure," Laszlo said, and his arms had slackened slightly, his gaze roving greedily over me.

Touch me, I thought, stepping over Hywel's leg to stand in front of Laszlo. He studied me, his arms drawn out between us, cotton dangling to the floor. He blinked and then stepped forward, shaking out the nightgown and drawing it over my head. I sighed and slipped my arms into the wide open sleeves. The garment was loose, the collar lace, and it sank low on my chest, my nipples visible through sheer, delicate flowers.

Laszlo cleared his throat and leaned around me, digging into the tangle of fabric. He pulled a long blue tunic out of the bundle, shaking the dust out, brushing the feathered backs of his hands over the embroidery of vines.

"Here. This is...this is one of mine," he said, and he helped me dress in the sheath too, which clung a little around my hips and breasts. A brief flash of smug pride brightened his still features, and he turned away from me.

Behind us, Hywel let out a low, soft growl.

Laszlo snorted. "You can have her back when you wake, you lazy beast," he said, but the words were so tenderly spoken it was clear what he meant. *Wake up. Wake up for me. Wake up for her.*

I recalled Hywel's request too, as he'd returned to dreaming. *Take care of him.* So I slid my arm around Laszlo's, snuggling into his side and the shelter of his wing that stretched, rustling in surprise.

Laszlo led us to the staircase, and this time they curved in a different direction. I'd noticed new doors and branching off halls appear on my path down from the kitchens, knew that Hywel gave the castle and its routes a changeable nature. Perhaps Laszlo had some influence over them too, because as we ascended the twisting staircase, I heard the urgent mutters of two familiar voices.

"You know shortcuts," I said to Laszlo, and I smiled as we passed by a lit torch that offered me the glimpse of him preening.

"It is my home, after all," he said.

The stairs narrowed and Laszlo ushered me ahead of him until we stopped on a small landing, a threadbare tapestry hanging over a narrow opening, daylight pricking through the weave of fabric. Laszlo pulled it aside, and I paused at the sight of Asterion and Conall's pacing figures at the far end of the room. We'd arrived back in the great hall, the fastest and most direct route out of Hywel's hoard.

I slipped out of the opening, Laszlo following and shrouding the secret passage once more.

"You have to make up your mind, Asterion," Conall snapped. "Is she under lock and key, or is she—"

"Of course not, but she's under our *protection*! Which involves knowing where she is!"

"I'm sure, had you *been here*—"

"I'm right here," I called, interrupting the rising voices.

Asterion's knees buckled as he spun, the whites showing around his dark eyes. He still had dust from the road on his trousers, and his collar was pulled open, a tantalizing glimpse of carved muscle swelling against the fabric as he heaved in a sudden breath.

Conall's shoulders sagged and he swept tangled red strands back from his sharp features, offering me a crooked, weary smile. Asterion took one lurching step toward me and then froze as I approached.

"I was napping with Hywel," I said.

Asterion straightened, his gaze lifting over my head to find Laszlo. "He's awake?"

"Not yet," Laszlo answered.

I'd crossed half the hall, but both Asterion and Conall's gaze sharpened on me at the same moment. Asterion's nostrils flared, and Conall's smirk stretched.

Asterion's steps fell backward, inching away from me. "I'm glad to see you well, *théa*. I should...clean up from the road." He bowed, sharp and stiff, and then turned, hooves beating an urgent path toward the stairs.

Conall huffed and shook his head, combing his hand through his hair once more, eyes sliding over me with a thorough curiosity. "Napping, were you?" he asked, flashing fangs in his grin.

My face warmed. "You can both smell him on me, can't you?"

Conall nodded, reaching me, his hands cupping my hips. I glanced over my shoulder and frowned as I found Laszlo missing from the room.

"I'm very curious as to what you and the dragon were doing during your *nap*," Conall teased. He tugged me close, breathing deeply, and then clearing his throat and shaking his head, eyes wide. "*Mo chroí*, is there anywhere on you that dragon *didn't* mark as his?"

"Hush," I said, but a soft laugh escaped with the admonishment.

"Come take a swim with me," Conall said, one hand leaving its spot on my hip to catch my hand.

"So you can wash him off me?" I asked.

Conall hummed and shrugged, turning, but sharing a brief smile with me that admitted I was right. "I won't lie and say the dragon's mark isn't a warning I'm likely to ignore. But I'm not the only one Hywel's warned to steer clear of you," he said, glancing toward where Asterion had vanished.

"I think Asterion's intentions were always precisely to steer clear of me," I said.

"His intentions, perhaps. Not his desires," Conall said, voice low.

WHATEVER ASTERION'S DESIRES WERE, THEY WERE IGNORED. In spite of his concern over my being "missing" when he arrived, he spent the next few days taking great care not to be in the same room as me. I didn't know where he slept, where he ate, where he spent the long hours of any day.

It was not just him. Conall had washed me in the underground pool of the castle, and we still ran together around the castle first thing in the morning until sweat ran down my back and I could not catch my breath, but he no longer tugged me down in the meadow to fuse our skin together and kiss each other breathless.

Asterion hid, Hywel slumbered, and now even Conall had retreated.

I stood at the edge of the terrace, cool wind whipping up from the sea, kissing damp salt against my cheeks, tangling the loose strands of my hair. There was no other exit from the castle but this terrace that reached Hywel's dreaming sea, and the stone steps and bannister hung dangerously over the water, waves crashing against jagged black rocks below.

I heard the click of claws on stone and tipped my head, closing my eyes. Against the fresh bite of salt air came the creamy, sweet whiff of tea.

"You're still having nightmares," Laszlo said, reaching my side.

"I have a great deal to remember. I'm lucky to hold most of it at bay until the night."

"You should not have them *here*."

My eyes blinked open and I turned to find Laszlo's taloned fingers braced against the bannister, his sharp, bright eyes glaring out at the sea. Did he resent its churning, the breath and the gasp of the water the evidence of his still-sleeping lover?

"I do know I'm safe here," I said, puzzled by the urge to offer him reassurance. The peace the castle gifted was incredibly tangible, the weight of a good blanket resting over us all, muffling the existence of the outside world and the troubles that waited there.

Laszlo sighed, eyes turning to glance at me out of their corners. "You misunderstand. You should not be *able* to have nightmares here. Not under Hywel's protection."

I turned back to the sea, my hands matching Laszlo's as they tightened around the stone railing. "I..." My heart pinched in my chest and I swayed forward, hips pressing hard into the barrier that kept me from lurching over into the tumbling, turning water "I lived in a nightmare for a third of my life, Laszlo. I am not sure there is any shield that can hold my mind back from the reckoning now that I am free. Even Hywel."

Laszlo's hand was warm, covering the back of mine, our fingers locking together. "Tell me about the nightmares."

A sudden, bubbling moan slipped free of me and I shook my head, trying to force out the previous night's torment, the changing faces I'd worked so hard to forget, the horrible way the features melted and morphed into one another.

Feathers skidded over my shoulders and Laszlo's arm kissed mine, shoulder to wrists. The wind was forced to rise and curve around us, and it created a hollow space in the shelter of his wings, where my unsteady breaths were louder than the strike of the waves on rocks.

"Laszlo—"

"If there is nothing Hywel or you or I can do to stop them from coming, if you *must* remember, then share them with me," Laszlo said, simple and clear. He bent toward me, and I stared down at our linked fingers. His brow rested against mine, a warm, golden place against my aching head, a gentle clarity that made the moment real and the nightmares that plagued me distant ghosts.

I opened my mouth to refuse, and the edge of Laszlo's spectacles brushed my cheek as he nuzzled his long, arched nose to my smaller one.

"It was real, my dear. It happened," he whispered. I whimpered and pulled my face from his, but only so I could hide it against his shoulder, letting the tears that clawed their way from my eyes soak into the heavy weave of his coat. He continued in my ear, his feathers tangling on strands of my hair. "But the nightmares are not real. We cannot let them add to your already unjust burden."

What was there to be gained by repeating the horrible half-truths? What relief could Laszlo really offer? I spent my nights trapped in horrific looping recollections—why did I have to drag them out with me in the daylight? Except that I already was. Without Conall's distracting pleasure, I was spending more hours than not doing my best to remain still and not think. It wasn't working.

Laszlo didn't embrace me, but we remained pressed side to side, heads bowed as I breathed him in and let the clean, sweet scent of him lull me, lower the fragile walls of cracked glass that tried to contain my turmoil.

"I dreamt of their faces," I murmured into Laszlo's shoulder. He remained still, a pillar for me to press into. "I dreamt of the looks on their faces as they reached the heights of pleasure. The lines carved into their brows and the eyes sealed shut, and the gaping, sl-slathering mouths as they—" I heaved a breath and turned, and Laszlo remained still and solid as I burrowed under his chin.

"They kept changing. Incubus into wyvern into lich into..." I shuddered, my heart working too fast, too hard, my lungs refusing to breathe. "Scales melting into fur, bones crumbling and cracking and eyes— They were all *him*. Birsha." I breathed his name, lifting my chin and staring into the tangled pattern of feathers, wondering if I had conjured new horrors outside of the shelter of the gryphon.

"They weren't," Laszlo said quickly before tensing and falling silent again.

"They were in the nightmare. They might as well have been in truth. I don't blame them. I feared and hated them, but I never... I never blamed them. It was him. It was him then, and him in the nightmare. He was the only true source of the torment."

The truth was, no matter what the monsters who paid for my body wanted to do to me, wanted from me, far fewer took a cruel enjoyment at their finish than the many who found a gusting, broken relief. Some followed their nature, the hunter needing prey to chase. Others' cravings were not so different than those of the human men I'd granted leave to slap or bruise me, knowing it couldn't hurt for long, that sensation was heady and control was even more so.

Rarely did the monsters' intentions match Birsha's. Their relief was self-centered. I was nothing to them, a fleshy tool. It was not forgivable, but their pleasure was usually only physical. When Birsha stepped into a room and saw me, trapped to his bidding, earning him money, earning him reputation, dying in small increments, the *néktar* offered to my appetite was blade-sharp and potently bitter. His pleasure was power. Over me, and over monsters.

"I had to take release with them. Pleasure with them," I admitted softly. "It's...my *nature*. And it was all I had to survive on."

Laszlo heaved in a breath and finally moved, his arms circling around my back, one hand rising to cup the back of my neck in a possessive clasp that was too gentle to be startling.

"Was the pleasure forced on you in the nightmare?" Laszlo asked.

I shook my head against his chest. "No...no, in the nightmare it was as if each face took strength away from me. I could see it in their faces, I could *sense*, it like...like a flavor in the air. But it *stole* from me. And when I woke, he *had* stolen from me. It's not —It shouldn't be—"

I tried to breathe but no air would come, and I leaned back against Laszlo's embrace, my hands fluttering between us, trying to catch the air as if I could press it into myself

"It shouldn't be possible," Laszlo said, frowning down at me. "I agree."

He pressed his hand over my chest, and my eyes widened. My heart stopped its uneven beating, steadying, and my lungs bloomed all at once, a great breath drawn in, clearing away the bound sensation.

"Come inside, my dear," Laszlo said, words so gently coaxing, arms and wings cocooning me and ushering me along with the command.

13.
CUTTING TRUTHS

My chest burned, my stomach cramped, my legs were numb from effort, and my face was split with an enormous grin as I ran through the orchard to the west of the castle.

A growl snarled behind me, closer than the one before, and I yipped and spun as Conall caught me by the waist, swinging my exhausted legs around, feet whipping the seeds off the heads of the tall grasses. Our laughter pressed our chests together, and I squirmed to face him, kicking my legs up to wrap them around his waist. Conall grunted, his hands palming my ass to hold me in place, bright, toothy smile shining up at me.

"You're getting faster," he said, hiking me up, scooping one arm under me and raising his free hand to draw his thumb under my eye. "Still tired, though."

I slung weary arms over his shoulders, clasping one wrist loosely as I tried to catch my breath, ignoring the pleasant stretch of my legs spread around Conall's body. I'd found a pair of kid leather breeches in my closet today and the freedom of movement was delicious, although I wished now for a skirt that would be easier to draw up and out of the way.

"You might remedy that," I said, even though I knew whatever Conall offered would be a temporary reprieve, stolen away again in the night.

His eyes narrowed slightly as he gazed up at my face. "I'm not sure I get the sense I might not be...potent enough for you."

I laughed at the sight of his bottom lip jutting out slightly and ducked my head to clasp it between my own. But before I could reach his mouth, Conall's eyes slid to the side, glancing up at the walls of the castle. He stiffened, and suddenly I was pulled away, set back on my feet, his shoulders straightening.

I twisted, glaring up at the castle, shielding my eyes from the late morning sun, catching a glimpse of a gilded horn ducking out of view. I turned back to Conall, who grimaced, tangling his fingers in his hair as he pushed it back.

"Evie—"

"What are you doing?" I asked, taking a step back, my arms wrapping around my stomach.

Conall sighed, his hands flapping briefly at his sides. "Trying...trying to stay out of a friend's way."

My eyes widened. "Am I a *door* for the pair of you to pass through?"

His cheeks flushed and his shoulders hiked slightly, tucking his head down. "Of course not."

"Asterion is more than capable of avoiding me on his own," I pointed out, turning to shoot another glare up at the window, even though there was no longer any sign of the minotaur. I hoped he was there in the shadows, listening.

"Only because he thinks there would be no place for him at your side," Conall said. "And truth be told, with Hywel's scent, it's possible—"

I raised a hand, and Conall's mouth snapped shut. "Place at my side? It's...it's just sex, Conall! And you're still speaking about me as if...as if these are maneuvers you all decide on, not decisions I make." Conall's head tipped, and my hands clenched to fists. "What?" I snapped.

Conall sighed and stepped closer, pausing as I stiffened. "You're right, of course, but—"

"But?"

He cleared his throat, glanced up at the castle and then back at me, brow furrowing slightly. "You are absolutely welcome to offer your attention, affection, to any of us, *mo chroí*. To all of us. Whatever suits you, of course. But we are also not...simply devices for your relief."

I inhaled sharply and Conall winced, raising his hands at his side. "Asterion is my friend. My interest in you complicates his feelings and vice versa."

My tongue felt large and clumsy in my mouth and I looked away, into the twisting branches of the orchard. My cheeks were burning. Did Conall feel used? Had Asterion touched me the night he left not because he wanted to, but because I'd been all but begging him to in the carriage ride? Had I taken mutual attraction for granted, or—

No. No, I hadn't *imagined* Conall's enthusiasm when touching me. Except it had always come after our game of chase...

"Evanthia?" Conall reached for me.

I tightened my arms, shrinking away just enough to give him pause. "Do you avoid bedding me...spending the night with me, because—"

"No," Conall said, cutting me off, ignoring my tense frame and rushing forward, drawing me into his arms. He huffed out a breath, tucking his chin over my shoulder. "No. You are not the only one with nightmares, *mo chroí*," he whispered. "I become violent. I didn't want to hurt you."

I leaned back at that and Conall straightened, meeting my gaze squarely. "Nightmares?"

He nodded but didn't elaborate. Laszlo was the only one I'd told my nightmares to, and they had come out slowly, whispered as we sipped cups of tea, the door to his lounge locked to offer us privacy.

"Have I been...pushing too much?" I asked.

"No," Conall moaned, drawing me tighter into his chest. He let out a soft, grumbling growl and his hands stroked up and down my back. "Damn the stubborn bull. I'm sorry, Evie. I've been an ass."

He's young, I thought, recalling Laszlo and the weary longing he gazed at Conall with.

"You ask for so little, less than I want to offer," Conall murmured, kissing the side of my head, burrowing his whiskered beard into my hair. "And you're right—Asterion should speak to you."

"He's spoken to you easily enough," I muttered.

Conall laughed. "Not really. Not so much as you think, and not since... Never mind. I'll stop meddling."

There'd been a moment, the start of a rainstorm and Asterion's strong arms around me, when I'd thought he was everything I wanted and needed to heal. But the weeks in the castle had made it clear that nothing would be so simple. I needed Conall's energy, his wildness. I needed Hywel's colossal power. I needed Laszlo's quiet comfort too.

I needed to be wanted, and not from an intangible distance.

"Forgive me," Conall pressed.

I sighed and sagged into his chest briefly, his own tension melting in the embrace. I pulled away after a moment, and his eyes searched my face.

"I suppose flaunting ourselves in full view of a window isn't the most subtle choice," I admitted, stepping back.

Conall's lips pursed. "Evie..."

"I am tired," I continued, offering him a wavering smile. "It's not helping my mood."

"Let's rest here," Conall offered, his hand sliding down my arm to try to tangle our fingers.

I slipped them free and turned toward the castle. "I'll go down to Hywel's hoard. I can't dream there, and I'm nearly done waxing his tail."

I ignored Conall's heavy sigh, his scuffing steps. The moment of running, laughing, the joy of being caught, had snarled and torn during the conversation. It might return tomorrow, and in the meantime I wanted time alone to think.

⚜

I HEAVED MYSELF UP THE STAIRS, FORCING MYSELF TO remember the long, spiraling staircase that Laszlo had taken back up from the hoard to the great hall. Hywel's red scales gleamed in candlelight as I left, and the moon hung low over the sea by the time I was done polishing him. I wasn't sure if the moon was real, if it matched the one outside of the castle, but I'd paused at the opening of the cavern to watch it rise up from the calm waters, silver, bright, and solemn.

I hadn't found much rest in Hywel's company, too busy working through my conversation with Conall. It was easier to argue through my clunky emotions while working. Between polishing Hywel's scales and running with Conall, my limbs were wobbly and weak now, and my stomach snarling in an entirely human hunger.

I must've been thinking of dinner, of the men waiting for me, because it was not the great hall that the stairs turned toward, but Laszlo's study. The scent of rich cream and salted meat and hints of ginger and lemon and thyme reached me first, my mouth watering eagerly. The low voices twining followed quickly, conversation steady and just loud enough for me to make out.

"We have allies in South America, Norway, Russia, all searching for more temples," Asterion said.

"He has no houses in those countries," Laszlo said, and I knew at once who they spoke of, my feet freezing just steps away from the top of the stairs.

"Precisely," Asterion answered. "After Amon and Miss Reed destroyed the temple near Jerusalem, Birsha fled England and ran not for his house in Paris, but south to Crete. Eventually, he resurfaced in Rome. We followed his tracks and found another temple, another group of trapped monsters. We don't know how many of these places he has, how many monsters are sustaining him, but we are certain he keeps them out of reach of the lodestones and his businesses."

The word "lodestone" jerked me out of my shock, and my steps were clumsy, scuffing up the remaining stairs. The voices hushed, and then the wall at the top of the stairs swung open, revealing Laszlo by the light of the fire.

"Ah, there you are. Your dinner is waiting," he said, offering a hand down into the dark.

I grasped it gratefully, climbing out and into his study. Asterion sat stiff and upright at the round table now set for four, while Conall leaned back in his chair, eyes fixed to me.

"Birsha has others...like me?" *Sisters?* I wondered. Surely I hadn't been my mother's only daughter, not with the way Asterion spoke of me.

Asterion pushed back from his seat, standing in place and

watching Laszlo lead me closer. Would he run? Was he *so* determined to avoid me that he'd leave the room and conversation?

No, he only waited for me to take my seat between himself and Laszlo before doing the same.

"He has another Divinity in his Shanghai house, a young man, but he's there of a...voluntary nature at the moment," Conall explained.

"Are you sure?" I asked sharply.

Asterion nodded. "He won't leave, we're certain, although when we're ready to take that house down too, he'll be an ally."

"He has a lover in the house he's determined to protect," Conall said. He was leaning toward me, dinner ignored in favor of stretching out a hand to my legs, waiting for permission to touch.

"And who are the other lodestones?" I asked.

"Succubi, nymphs, creatures of pleasure. You don't need to worry, *théa*, we *will* defeat Birsha and all his houses."

Asterion's shoulders were squared, his eyes on his plate but his body tense and solid. *King of the Labyrinth*. I blinked, sucking in a breath, recalling the vision of Asterion in The Seven Veils, standing square in a hallway as I was dragged back down to the cells, his eyes glaring at me. I'd thought then that he would buy my time, but he must only have been playing his part as spy in the house. I didn't see him again until the night the walls broke and burnt and I ran, screaming till I was hoarse.

And then again on the dark streets of London.

"What happens after you have defeated Birsha?" I asked.

Asterion paused in eating his dinner. "You will be safe. You will—you *are* free to go wherever you like, and—"

"And when the next man or monster rises to take Birsha's place, who collects young men and women, creatures of pleasure, and offers their flesh for sale?"

"That won't—we won't—" Asterion stumbled, glancing at the others.

"Birsha has been bold. He's grabbed his power by the fistfuls, fought off foes and competitors, hoping that he alone could offer what no one else would," Conall said.

I nodded. I'd suspected as much. "And when he falls, those

who did not dare challenge him will have an opportunity to take his place. Perhaps not as boldly. Certainly not on such a large scale to start," I said, cutting my food to tiny pieces, ignoring the snarl of hunger as I thought through the future. "How many of your allies stand with you not because they care about the mistreatment of humans, of women like me, but because they resent being challenged by a man who was human once?"

Conall pulled back into his own seat, reaching for his wine, and Laszlo and Asterion both stared at me.

I continued, "How many are just waiting for Birsha to fall so they can steal for themselves in the reckoning?"

"Several, I imagine," Asterion said in a low velvet tone, drawing my eyes to his. "I will fight them too. And I will not be alone, I promise you that."

I'd been right earlier. There were pieces of Conall, Laszlo, and Hywel that I needed. But I'd been right about Asterion too.

His dark eyes held mine, and there was no doubt when he made me the vow, no shy reluctance, no hiding from me. He was solid and safe and strong, and he would not falter in protecting me for as long as I allowed him to.

"I want to know what is happening," I said gently. "You can shelter me from Birsha's reach, but please don't hide information from me. Not for my sake."

Asterion bowed his head in acknowledgement.

"What are the temples?" I asked.

Asterion settled back in his chair, Conall and Laszlo returning to the meal. "They are how Birsha has survived. He binds monsters, consumes their vital organs, symbols of our strength or power, and casts dark rites that hold those bodies in the last moments of life, sustaining the vitality through the part he's taken into himself."

I grimaced at the description, and Asterion nodded.

"You said the temple near Jerusalem was destroyed. When was this? How long before The Seven Veils fell?"

"His focus was on the Company of Fiends at the time," Conall murmured.

"The what?"

"A theater that hired monsters and humans to perform... sexual acts? Skits?" Asterion looked charming when puzzled.

"Entertainments," Conall drawled, answering for him.

Asterion hummed and nodded. "Sexual performances for an audience of monsters."

My eyes widened. "That exists?"

"Bawdy and pedestrian," Laszlo murmured, drawing our attention. He blinked at me. "I went once, long ago. Not long after Hywel started his slumber."

"Birsha had left it alone in exchange for a cut of the profits, but it was gaining popularity again and he grew impatient. Tried to force it into closing," Asterion said. "Instead, he gained himself more enemies and us more allies."

"According to the sphinx and his family, they destroyed the temple more than a month before The Seven Veils fell," Conall mused. "They started their journey back to England not long after."

The conversation continued on around me and I shut my eyes, trying to mute their voices and the information, digging back in memories I would've rather left buried.

Warm fingers laid heavily over the back of my hand. "Forgive us, we need not speak of him or that place."

I shook the cobwebs from my thoughts and opened my eyes, meeting Asterion's, his gentle focus probing openly now. "I'm fine, I swear it. I was only trying to recall that time."

"You needn't," Asterion continued, but Conall leaned forward, eyes narrowing.

"You think you might remember something significant?"

The vision of The Seven Veils came too easily, superimposing itself over the room we sat in. Red leather wallpaper replaced Laszlo's bookshelves, the fireplace obscured by the memory of the small stage where Birsha had invited clients to sample his wares. Behind me must loom the oversized couches and chairs, and I could almost imagine the creak of the furniture protesting the bodies occupied there. Perhaps it was some effect of Hywel's magic, or maybe my thoughts were never as far from my time trapped there as I wished they were.

"He was always in the front rooms, encouraging the behaviors, encouraging the witnessing," I said, my voice rasping. "He wanted the monsters to see each other."

"Yes," Asterion murmured in agreement. "It was a way to encourage those who might be reticent, who only came because they could not find relief elsewhere, to act abominably."

"He liked to watch you lower yourselves," I said. Asterion only dipped his head in acknowledgement.

"But for months before the fall, he...he was not in his usual pattern. There were weeks none of us saw him at all," I remembered.

"Recovering from his injury from Miss Reed, no doubt," Conall murmured.

"Even when he returned, it was only for brief moments. I'd spent...a few years...behaving myself," I said, the words foul on my tongue, drawing an involuntary heave in my gut, and I pressed my hand over the spot. "I hadn't thought of escape in so long, I'd given up, but...it made me start to wonder again. And then one day, he came to the floor. He was pale, and he brought one of the trolls who guarded the house with him, and "

"They dragged you out of the room," Asterion said, voice low and dark.

I blinked and turned to him, and the silhouette of his horns fit easily into the backdrop of The Seven Veils lounge. He'd been there that night.

Asterion nodded. "Yes, it would fit the timeline. He must've felt the effect of the temple falling. He would not risk losing you too. I am sorry, *théa*," Asterion said, leaning toward me in his chair, drawing my hand beneath his closer. "I am sorry I did nothing then."

"You would've been killed," I said, shrugging.

Asterion's nostrils flared, possibly in offense, or perhaps just strong feeling. I turned my hand in his, and before he could pull away I answered his grip with my own, fiercer than I'd managed the last time he'd been brave enough to touch me.

"They left me underground for the weeks that followed," I said, ignoring Asterion's flinch. "But there was a moment in the hall one night I think he was speaking of me, discussing my transport to Persia."

Asterion sat up straighter at that, turning to Conall. "We hadn't considered he might want somewhere closer to the territory he lost."

"You think he wants to establish a new temple or a new house?" Laszlo asked.

"He would take Evanthia for a house," Conall answered. "Perhaps he's already started one beneath our notice?"

"A house in Persia...a temple in the East Indies." Asterion rose abruptly from the table, turning to the bookshelves. His movement disrupted my twisted vision, setting the room back to rights, and I caught my breath with a sudden inhale.

"The East Indies?" Laszlo asked, head tipping. "You didn't mention—"

"I would rather search every inch of this earth and be wrong a hundred times than miss an opportunity to catch Birsha in his hiding," Asterion said, tugging down a large book, opening it, and scowling at the pages. "Your maps are wildly out of date."

Laszlo rolled his eyes. "Yes, well, it is difficult to keep up with the ambitions of the empire in recent years."

"Centuries," Conall teased, but he only gave Laszlo his attention for a moment, instead turning to me and gentling his tone. "The conversation has put you off your dinner, *mo chroí.*"

"We should leave you—" Asterion started.

"No, I'm fine, I promise," I rushed out, picking up my fork and knife again, forcing myself to take a bite and ignoring the three pairs of eyes watching me as I chewed. Conall was right that I'd lost my appetite in the conversation, but it came back, flavors warming on my tongue.

Asterion continued his hunt for a map, Conall finishing his own meal and joining in the search, their voices lowered now to avoid disturbing me.

"I know..."

I startled in my seat, not surprised that Laszlo remained with me, but shocked by the tentative tone of his voice, the stumble and pause of his words. He cleared his throat, eyes fixed on the door, and I thought he might not speak at all, or even rise and leave.

"I know there is a great deal of life you missed during your time with Birsha," Laszlo said softly, focus sliding in my direction, shoulders tipping toward me. "I don't wish to deprive you of anything, any experience, but please know that this castle is your sanctuary as long as you should wish it."

The castle? I wondered. *Or the men within its walls?*

14.
STUBBORN
MONSTERS

I retched once more into the pot, wincing as bile burnt my throat and stung inside my nose, the stench making my already unsteady insides wobble in warning. I stepped away, turning to the fresh pitcher of water. There was no longer a bowl to pour its contents into, but I used a sheet of linen to wash my face with and a cup to rinse my mouth.

My bed remained at the corner of my vision, vast and threatening. I was exhausted, but I knew better than to expect any relief, not in my own room. Giving into sleep would only tempt another nightmare to come and claim me, and the one lingering at the corners was still too fresh.

I sipped more water, staring at the fire, trying to organize the details of the dream. It hadn't been a memory. I had little contact with Birsha directly, but I remembered those moments with almost perfect clarity. The only obscure parts were his features—features which had been sharp and stark in the nightmare, and now lost once more in the shock of waking.

My hands shook as I grabbed my robe and wrapped it around myself, toes diving into the slippers that sat warming in front of the fire.

I would make my way down to Hywel. I'd find rest there if I didn't...if I didn't find company on the way down.

I paused, my door half-open, and realized that I didn't want to go back to sleep. I didn't want to curl up in Hywel's scales unless he was going to open his eyes and grin with all the terrifying beauty of his dragon's smile. I wanted *company*. I wanted someone to take my hand and pull me into their chest, wanted another body's heat to warm mine. Poetry, whether bawdy or beautiful, would be welcome too.

I had no idea where any of the others slept or if I would be welcome if I appeared in their rooms, but I was halfway down the stairs and realized I didn't have to worry. Conall and Asterion's voices were clear, somewhere downstairs but easily made out.

I took a deep breath, hurrying my steps. Conall would coax Asterion into staying, probably to soothe me. Perhaps I could convince them both to keep me company and offer me comfort.

"You're being an ass."

My steps faltered at Conall's hiss.

"We agreed we would come and go," Asterion answered, his lower, smoother tone just barely clear.

"Fine. You've come. And so I will go."

"She needs you. I've seen the pair of you—"

Conall scoffed. "Oh, I'm well aware you've seen us."

I tiptoed down to the balcony, remaining in the shadowed alcove of the stairs to listen. They were not in the main open space of the great hall, but I recognized the warm flicking firelight of a smaller study than Laszlo's.

"If you spent less time *watching* and more time speaking to her, you'd be less eager to run so quickly," Conall snapped.

"I am not *eager*, don't be absurd. You...you know what I am resisting."

"You can't tell me you plan to go to the East Indies." There was a pause, and then the werewolf cursed.

"I suppose it's not practical," Asterion muttered.

I tipped my head and searched around the castle. It was improbable that I should hear them so clearly, even when there was not a single other sound in the vast space, but the conversation circled me, and I *wanted* to hear it. The castle was *gifting* me the ability to spy, another piece of the strange and wonderful magic of this place.

Asterion cleared his throat and continued. "Still, I will go back to London. Ask who we might reach in the east. Find a witch who can arrange a more immediate communication."

"I could do the same. I am more charming than you," Conall joked, earning a grunt. "Admit to me you're avoiding Evanthia."

"Don't you *want* to stay?" Asterion snapped, a chair screeching its heels over stone. "I can still smell you on her. Barely."

"Of course I do, but not so you can position us about to your liking. To your preferred *avoidance* of the woman. I am... I do want to be what she needs, but I *know* I am not all of it. Not enough all at once," Conall said.

"How often do you still have night terrors?" Asterion asked, losing the snarl of his tone.

"Not as often as she does, I expect. And she has better reason—"

"War haunts us all; even Hunter knows its trauma. No one looks forward to what comes with a rise against Birsha. You're too hard on yourself. You *will* be what she needs. Or...or Hywel, if his intention is sincere."

"Anyone but you?" Conall bit out.

There was a settling quiet. My fingertips traced over the rough edges and grooves of the stone wall.

"I am not the hero," Asterion said, drawing me back to them. "I was created out of punishment, born out of spite, and raised to terrorize."

My brow furrowed. I knew the minotaur's story, trapped in the labyrinth, killing those who threatened the king who'd captured him.

"You've paid your penance," Conall said lightly.

"If Evanthia wants me, she will choose me."

"And *only* you?" Conall asked with a soft growl. Asterion grunted in answer. "Not if you aren't *here*. You are miserable. And a fool."

"And I will leave by first light in the morning," Asterion announced.

Boots stepped over stone, scuffed against carpet, and across the shadows of the floor stretched the shadow of two broad horns. Asterion's steps echoed but the castle played tricks on us both, and his path didn't cross mine, didn't bring him out to the square balcony I hid on.

"I can smell you," Conall said softly, startling me as I held my breath in the dark.

His own shadow appeared on the floor, but he moved steadily to the center of the hall and I tiptoed out of the alcove and to the bannister, the pair of us facing one another, his face lifted toward mine.

"Come down, *mo chroí*," Conall whispered when I refused to speak first.

I found the stairs down and he met me in the dark nook at their base, his gaze turned away, like he was waiting for Asterion to reappear.

"You're leaving," I guessed.

Conall turned to me, tired smile crooked and half-hearted. "I am."

"And if he decides to follow you?"

Conall shook his head. "He wants to stay. *I* want to stay. But I will be sure to return at the first opportunity and Asterion would stall."

"I'm safe here with Laszlo and Hywel," I said, shrugging, not entirely convinced that two men who argued over the right to leave the castle and avoid my company were struggling with themselves so very much. It was one thing to claim noble intentions, but I would've preferred the intention to *remain with me*.

No, that wasn't right. I didn't want their commitment—I'd said as much already. I just needed *néktar* and relief.

Conall didn't answer me, and his eyes glowed spring green in the dark for a moment. He stepped forward, and in spite of my irritation I still wanted to be touched, calmed from the nightmare. I sank into his chest and sighed as his hands slid inside of the robe and stroked up my back through my nightdress.

"You are safe. Unless Birsha somehow rallied all his allies to arrive here, the woods let them through, and Hywel slept through the attack. It's unlikely, but it's not a risk any of us want to gamble. Laszlo is strong, but even he can be outnumbered. Even Asterion can when fighting alone." Conall turned his head, his nose brushing aside my loose strands of hair to graze a kiss against my ear. "You need *us*."

And yet you and Asterion bicker over who will leave me first.

"I should let the dragon's scent linger," Conall murmured, nuzzling down to my jaw, lips plucking along my skin. He stepped closer, hips pressing to mine. "But I hate knowing you're angry with me."

"I'm not angry," I said.

I was...*something*, but my emotions weren't familiar to me lately, didn't match the ones I'd known *before* Birsha. Some days I stood at the edge of hysteria, a scream clawing in my throat, a wild violence racing through me. Other days, the only thing that got me out of bed was not wanting to fall back into a nightmare.

"You look tired," Conall continued, nosing into my hair, palms circling over my back. "I could take you back to bed."

"No," I answered, fast and sharp. Conall jerked back, and it was my turn to clutch him to me. "I just woke. I don't—I can't—"

"I understand," he said. His parted lips pressed below the corner of my jaw, tongue swirling over the spot as I arched into him.

"And you're leaving," I reminded him in a ragged whisper.

"Not for hours," Conall breathed.

And if Asterion beats you to the exit? I wondered, but Conall's hands slid down, gently groping my ass before catching the backs of my thighs. He lifted me, my legs opening at the familiar interruption of his body between them.

"I try to remind myself that the others would be better for you in the long run," Conall said. He didn't take us back up the stairs, but to the right, into a cool, unfamiliar corridor.

"I wish you wouldn't speak of the future that way. I don't have it in me to consider much beyond a day or a week," I admitted.

I was too tired to cling to frustration or resentment, and Conall's hair smelled like the meadows we lay in together, and like the sweet, leathery tobacco leaves he pinched between his fingers and pressed into a pipe after dinner.

"I've lived too long to make plans when I know how well they can be destroyed in a moment, or how much can change in a matter of minutes, or how long a life might live beating against stagnancy," I said.

Conall turned into a small room, a parlor with a few chairs, one long couch under a broad window, and a bright fire burning behind a screen. His expression was illuminated once more, face lifted to study me.

I helped myself to brushing his hair back, strands gliding through my fingers.

"I can barely hold onto joy from one moment to the next, and pleasure is stolen as quickly as it comes. Deny me for your own sake, but not for mine," I said, adding privately, *I need you.*

It was selfish and base. At some time, Conall would've been exactly the kind of lover I sought out, spent years with, but I wasn't that woman any longer. I was as cavernous as Hywel's hoard, but without the treasure. The nightmares sapped me of the little strength I gained, and all I wanted was to feast endlessly on Conall's attention until he withered away in the wake of my demand.

Deny me, I thought to Conall, wanted to plead.

My hunger made me into something like Hywel's vast and toothy maw, his open gullet and waiting belly. I would devour the Red Wolf until he pried my jaws open and made his escape.

"I'm sorry now that I wasted days," Conall whispered, lifting his chin.

I bit at his lips, licked at his groan, tangled his hair in my fingers. "But you'll leave before morning."

"Return in days," Conall rasped.

I couldn't pick him clean to bones in just a few hours at least.

Conall turned us as we reached the couch, sank over me as he settled me on the cushions, but he didn't pull away. And I could never have pushed him back.

15.
THROUGH FEAST
AND FAMINE

"He shouldn't have left you."

I scowled down at the mass of sticky lump dough on the table, flour dusting over the surface and all down the tunic I wore. I was not going to have the same argument with Asterion that I'd barely finished with Conall.

"You may chase him if it pleases you," I said, my nails digging into the dough, grunting as I scooped the uncooperative mass up from the table and then slapped it down again.

Wooden stairs groaned and steps thunked against the stone tile floor. "What are you doing?"

"Trying to remember how to bake bread, but this is..." I raised a hand, stretching my fingers to show Asterion the mess that clung to my fingers. I turned to glance at him and then let out a yelp of surprise at the man at my back.

"Forgive me," Asterion gasped, stumbling backward, gloved hands raised at either side of the absurdly pretty human face.

My hand was over my heart and I looked down, frowning now at the imprint of wet dough. "What's possessed you to wear that ridiculous disguise *here*?" I snapped, going back to my work.

"I didn't want to frighten you."

"So you sneak up behind me looking like a stranger?" I let out a laugh, but it was a bitter sound, covered by another slap of dough. "I thought you knew by now that I prefer—"

"It's kind of you to say so, but—"

"Oh, Asterion, *shut up!*" I cried.

He did so immediately.

I sighed, falling forward and bracing myself against the table. My hair was tied back, but it had always been slippery and impossible, and strands were already falling loose from the effort of my botched baking.

A step retreated behind me.

"I like *your* face," I ground out, and the steps stopped again.

"I worry...I worry I will remind of your time at The Seven Veils."

"You are a minotaur. I am a demigoddess. Laszlo has talons. Conall, a tail," I recited, shrugging and standing straight again. "I'm not *human*, Asterion. I've—" *fallen in love with* "—admired many faces in my long life."

He fidgeted at my back, eyeing the door.

"I was never raped by a minotaur," I said plainly, and Asterion let out a gargle of anger and sorrow. "There were werewolves at The Seven Veils, but that doesn't mean I fear Conall."

It was a terrible simplification, but Asterion's mind was stubborn and I was exhausted. It was simplifications or smashing his thick head against the wall. But his horns would either stop the impact or get stuck in the plaster.

I tried to maneuver the dough once more, and it bubbled and slopped and stuck. I gathered it up in my hands and turned to toss it away.

"Don't do that," Asterion murmured, and out of the corner of my eye, he plucked his gloves from his fingers and returned to himself.

He'd given me so few opportunities to study him by daylight, and the kitchen seemed to be perpetually glowing with streams of sunlight, even on days when outside it was foggy and drizzling. His skin gleamed, burnished copper and dark brass, rich shades of brown and glimmers of red. The gold paint on his horns was slightly faded, and I wondered what ceremony he made of the decoration. Did he have a brush or use his fingers?

"You're very impatient," Asterion said, taking my hands in his and turning me back to the table. He pressed his own hands, palms and then the backs, into the bowl of flour I'd set aside, and then scooped a generous amount, dusting and spreading it over the table.

"I've already used so much," I said.

Asterion hummed. "So use a little more. If it were enough, your fingers wouldn't be glued together."

But he took the dough from me, rolling it in the flour, using the heels of his large hands and the backs of his knuckles to smooth and mix, rather than digging his fingers in as I had.

"What made you learn to make bread?" I asked him, slowly picking off the mess on my hands, watching the steady motion of his, the strength he used as the dough became elastic. His dark shirt cuffs were now coated in white, but he didn't seem to notice. I wished he would roll them back over his forearms, offer me a glimpse of the snarls of muscle I knew he must have.

"Hunger," Asterion said. "Same as you, I'd imagine."

"Years of feast, years of famine," I said, thinking of times long ago, times when whoring became too dangerous, or disease too widespread and food hard to find.

"Yes," Asterion agreed. "For the first half of my life, I was exactly the sort of creature Birsha believes monsters to be—a captive beast, and then a scavenger in hiding after I escaped the labyrinth."

"In the story, Theseus killed you."

"He nearly did," Asterion said, nodding. "But my half-sister, Ariadne, gave him false information about my body. It's easy to convince a man that the monster he faces in battle is wildly different than him. He missed my heart by a few inches, and he was far too eager to leave the labyrinth to wait until I finished bleeding out. He dropped his spool at my feet and followed the string out. Days later, when I was strong enough, I did too."

Asterion's motions were mesmerizing, a hypnotic rhythm in the rolling and stretching and shaping of the dough, the ragged edges smoothing to a silky finish. I entertained a whimsical fantasy of him transforming in the same way with those touches.

"I tried to give into the bull's blood for a long time, be the animal King Minos saw me as, the nightmare Zeus had fashioned as a joke, but...eventually, my mother's blood won out. I watched. I learned. I studied the hunters I hid from, and then the farmers whose land I circled. One night, I watched a pack of travelers turn into wolves. They sniffed me out immediately, but they had no qualms about my company, wild and untamed as I was. They taught me to cook, to speak, to survive with dignity. And they introduced me to the wider world of our kind, halflings and beasts and monsters."

He stopped, standing straight and rolling his broad shoulders. A rounded loaf of dough rested at the center of the table.

"There," he said.

"Hmph."

"Are Hywel's dreamers not cooking today? Laszlo and I can manage, you needn't—"

"I needed something to do with myself," I said, cutting Asterion off with a wave of my hand.

I'd needed to not fall back asleep. I almost had on the couch with Conall, drowsy and relaxed after his generous lovemaking, but then he'd kissed me goodbye, already dressed and heading for the door, and I'd roused myself, too afraid of what thoughts might claw their way up from my subconscious if I were left alone.

I pulled a clean square of linen out of the loop of my belt and draped it over the loaf to let it rest, debating over asking Asterion to let me follow him around the castle, asking him to tell me more stories or let me pore over maps with him. He was hovering too, neither of us speaking. We'd made hardly any conversation up until last night and just now, but I liked his mind, his low voice.

"I told him to stay," Asterion murmured.

"I don't care," I said, shaking my head. He hummed, as if to refuse my answer, and I snapped. My hands grabbed onto the broad collar of his coat, tugging him to face me. "Asterion, I am *using* Conall, the same way I used you in the carriage, the same way—That night, when you—"

Asterion's nostrils flared, and his eyes narrowed. "I remember that night perfectly, *théa*. You did not *use* me. I touched you while you slept. It was I who took advantage."

"I wish you would again," I spat out, a graceless invitation.

Asterion rumbled, his head turning to the door, and I huffed out a sigh, giving up on snaring this minotaur's attention. My hands loosened at the same moment that his grabbed my hips, clutching tightly and pulling me up to my toes. I gasped as Asterion bowed, my face already lifted to his, ready to accept the rough and slightly clumsy kiss. *Néktar* rushed over my tongue and down my throat, Asterion's delight in the kiss so incredibly potent, as strong as the fury with which his tongue took my mouth.

I moaned, an eager and languid form giving into his hands as one slid up my spine to hold the back of my neck. He groaned and the sound shook me down to my core, a pulse and throb of willing interest answering the sound.

And then, as quickly as he'd claimed me, I was released, set aside. I stumbled, unbalanced, and found Laszlo standing at the top of the short stairs that let into the kitchen.

"Excuse me," Asterion said, bowing to me and heading for the door.

Laszlo's eyebrows rose behind his glasses, but he stepped aside to let Asterion pass. I gaped at the broad back as it fled the room, leaned my hip against the table to hold myself up, and tried to catch my bearings once more. Laszlo's wings flexed absently as he approached me.

"I'm sorry for interrupting."

"It's fine. It certainly didn't take much for him to scurry off," I muttered. Laszlo neared, and I remained still as he bent, sniffing briefly at my hair.

"You smell fine to me," he said, adding after a pause, "A bit like wolf."

I snorted and shook my head. "Perhaps you appreciate Conall's scent more than Asterion does," I suggested, thinking of the obvious and antagonistic flirting Conall pressed upon Laszlo.

Laszlo hummed. "Perhaps. I came to see if you'd like to try and rouse Hywel."

I straightened at that. "You want to try and wake him? Do you think we could?"

"Nothing I've tried has worked thus far, but we might at least entertain ourselves." Laszlo stepped back, crooking one arm and opening the other toward the dark doorway that I'd found during my first search.

I linked my arm with his and followed down into the deep caverns under the castle.

"Were these passageways here, or did Hywel dream them as well?"

"They were here, or most of them, at least. The shortcuts are his creation. Everything but the cavern where he sleeps was here," Laszlo explained.

"How can he sleep in a cavern he dreamt of?" I asked, smiling.

"He doesn't. He sleeps in a hole he dug and burrowed into under the ground. It only looks so fine thanks to his imagination."

"And all the treasure," I pointed out.

Laszlo hummed in agreement. "He started napping in the pool centuries ago. I knew then he was getting ready to hibernate. He would paw and dig and slither deeper with every brief sleep. But he refused to bring his hoard down."

"Why?"

Laszlo was quiet as we turned down the steps leading to the hoard. "He didn't want to admit it was time."

"He didn't want to leave you."

Laszlo tipped his head in acknowledgement. "He hasn't."

"How long is he meant to sleep for?" I asked.

"No one knows. He slept once when he was much younger, but time wasn't as well tracked then."

We stopped at the foot of the stairs. The candlelight was flickering, wicks burned down low, and outside the hollow opening of the cavern, it was evening instead of morning, the sun already below the horizon and glowing red over Hywel's sea.

"What if...what if he doesn't wake up?" I asked.

"Do you mean today, or..."

"In time for whatever war Asterion wants to wage against Birsha?"

"Provided we are careful, none of us, not even Birsha, are going to run out of time. Asterion can plan with or without Hywel's help. It makes no difference to a dreaming dragon. Come," Laszlo said, leading me forward. "I was worried he might've rolled over, but he's in precisely the right position."

Hywel was on his side, facing us, limbs and neck stretched, belly exposed.

My steps slowed and Laszlo slipped his arm free, pausing at Hywel's back feet, beautiful long claws still gleaming from the polish I'd given them.

"What exactly do you have planned?" I asked.

Laszlo's hands went to the draping fabric at the front of his waist, untying the sash. The twin drapes of fabric slid aside, and at his back, folds and crosses of material swung loose, revealing smooth planes of golden skin and knots of muscle that grew thicker and more pronounced, trails of feathers falling down the lines of his shoulder blades where his wings sprouted from. I hadn't realized the many layers of his shirt were really one long, continuous garment that crossed and twisted around his wings, and my fingers now itched to touch, to assist, to unbind a body that was broader than I'd imagined, more structured than slim. Laszlo's long tails swatted through the air at his back, fanning the thin feathered threads open and then falling smooth and sinuous again.

His back and sides were covered in delicate golden-brown freckles that seemed to swoop and swirl in something like a pattern. He pulled his arms free of the shirt, and those too were carved and defined, covered in more freckles and a small burst of feathers on either elbow. He folded the shirt and I helped myself to staring at his chest, gleaming and dusted with glimmering curls, as he moved to set his shift safely out of Hywel's reach. His trousers were high-waisted, slitted at the back to provide room for his tails, and he made no gesture to remove them.

"You don't wear a disguise like Asterion, but this isn't your full gryphon form, is it?"

"No, I can change at will. I take myself flying over the sea sometimes, but I prefer this form," Laszlo said. "I like to read. And work with my hands," he added, smirking with the hint of a secret. He used one knuckle to slide his glasses up his nose and turned back to study Hywel with a tipped head.

"You don't have to join me, if you find you'd rather not," he said over his shoulder. "But you're welcome to touch."

I want to touch you, I thought, and wondered if that was included in the invitation.

He returned to Hywel, climbing over heaps of pillows, to stand at the base of Hywel's long stomach, directly in front of the thick seam I'd seen those weeping cocks peeking out of. Laszlo raised his hands, reaching out without hesitating, stroking firmly at the seam. It reminded me of a pair of lips, full and apparently tender, as Laszlo's hands pressed into the flesh, molding it under his grip.

A surprised laugh slipped out of me, and Laszlo glanced over his shoulder. "You plan on waking him...like this?"

Laszlo shrugged, and candlelight shimmered up and down his golden feathers. "Why not? However, as you can see," he said, twisting aside to reveal the first parting of the seam, the two dark red heads of Hywel's cocks appearing, "I will have my hands full on my own."

More like arms full, I thought, fighting off another laugh.

I lifted my tunic up over my head, still covered in flour, and then unlaced the simple gown I'd dressed in until I was wearing only a thin linen chemise, piling my own clothing with Laszlo's before joining him.

He was stroking and petting at the thick red cocks that were stiffening and sliding out of their sleeve, palms flat and swirling in a circle around the tops. He stepped back as I neared, one arm dropping to his side, making room for me to stand between him and Hywel. As soon as I did, his arm wrapped around me, nestling me between their heat. I wanted to lean back and press myself against his chest and hips, but I focused on the task before me. My hands joined Laszlo's, gasping at the sharper burn of Hywel's tender flesh, at how silky and vulnerable it felt under my touch, so unlike his firm scales.

"He's as eager as a puppy, really," Laszlo murmured, his lips close to my ear.

And certainly Hywel's arousal was growing quickly, thick tips butting into our palms. Even as I spread my fingers wide, I couldn't form a circle around him. But Laszlo was rubbing, petting, stroking, moving slowly and evenly around every inch provided. I worked with him, our hands and arms sharing one cock, then sliding to work separately.

I licked my lips, squeezing at the length, pulling toward the top, and watched as an opalescent droplet—although it was almost as big as my fist—beaded at the tip, dribbled down the slit. I scooped it up with the heel of my hand, spreading it back around the head and down the thick shaft.

Distantly, Hywel purred in his sleep. The cock I was petting jerked and butted forward, nudging into my chest and leaving a damp mark against my chemise. I laughed and bent my head, kissing the slippery flesh, finding a pleasantly sweet and salty flavor on my lips. Laszlo huffed as the cock he'd been attending bucked as well, as if asking for the same treatment.

"Greedy beast," he said fondly, and then he wrapped his arms around both lengths in a firm hug and pulled them gently.

Hywel's tail swung and beat, knocking down a pile of treasure, and both cocks dripped their pearly fluid into my waiting palms. Laszlo slipped his hands under mine, guiding them back to Hywel's cocks, his fingers linking over mine, sliding through arousal, over heated pulsing flesh. His chest pressed to my back, arms braced around me, and the whisper of the feathers on his jaw brushed against my cheek. His heavy breaths cascaded down my chest, cooling against the damp fabric sticking to my breasts.

"Have you...done this before for him?" I asked, trying to steady my voice.

One of Hywel's cocks was more fully extended than the other, and it nuzzled and thumped against my belly. I wanted to rise to my toes and press it between my legs, not that I had any expectation of mounting anything so obscenely large, only that I wished I could wrap my entire body around his lengths.

"Of course," Laszlo said, and this time the press of his feathers to my skin was more direct, his cheek rubbing against mine.

I obeyed the nudging, arching my head to the side, exposing my throat. Laszlo's spectacles glinted out of the corners of my eyes as his head bowed. Our hands stuttered over Hywel's flesh as Laszlo kissed a wet mark against the curve of my shoulder. His hips fit against my ass, arousal hinting as he leaned into me, crowded me closer to Hywel. Our arms slid around and over, petting Hywel's cocks, and then Laszlo was touching *me*, not Hywel, slippery hands sliding up my waist, around my ribs, to cup and lift my breasts. I moaned and arched, and Laszlo's wings fluttered at his back, shrouding us, the pulse and pound of flesh cradled against my body as he squeezed me tenderly.

That's very pleasant, but I'd rather you came up here where I can watch.

16.
THE ENTERTAINMENT
OF GUESTS

I gasped at the sudden boom and stroke of Hywel's voice in my head, but Laszlo didn't so much as flinch, his kisses trailing halfway up my throat and then back down to the slope of my shoulder.

It worked, I thought. Hywel had woken.

Laszlo was cupping and rolling my breasts in his hands, nipples caught between his knuckles, and Hywel was dripping arousal onto my nightdress. I squirmed between one enormous, wriggling cockhead and Laszlo's hips.

Laszlo, Hywel growled.

"You didn't share, why should I?" Laszlo rasped into my skin, but he sighed as Hywel snarled again, tail thumping and crashing into more gold. Laszlo lifted his head, nudging his temple against mine. "Would you like to let him watch, my dear?"

I nodded, mouth watering as I recalled the knots and lines of Laszlo's back, the freckles that dressed his skin and ran curving down below the waist of his pants.

He stepped back and I released Hywel's cocks, spinning and catching Laszlo's face in my hands, sticky and slick as they were. I jumped to the tips of my toes, pressing my breasts to his chest, and drew his mouth down to slant over mine. He tasted bright and sweet, like pears and cream, a hint of spice or alcohol as I slipped my tongue inside to taste more deeply.

Laszlo's arm banded around my back, lifting me off my toes and carrying us both out of the many pillows. His hand reached up, talons bracing carefully around my face, holding me as he pulled away, blinking down through the clear shine of his glasses. His talon stroked across my bottom lip, a sharp drag, and his pupils flared as he stared at the motion.

I wanted to touch him. I had before we'd fondled Hywel, and now that the dragon was demanding to watch...I knew what view we ought to give him.

I stepped back and caught Laszlo's hand in mine, guiding him along the length of Hywel's body, stepping carefully over the dragon's huge legs to where his head rested, catching the cool evening breeze rising up from the sea through the open cavern wall.

You wanted my attention, Hywel said.

"You need to wake soon, my love," Laszlo answered, glancing at the dragon over the rim of his spectacles.

Yes, Hywel agreed, but his eyelids still blinked slowly, a drowsy stare tracking our progress.

"Laszlo has taken good care of me since my arrival," I said, and the gryphon's fingers squeezed around mine.

He was always an excellent host.

"I should like to be an appreciative guest."

Hywel chuckled at that, and Laszlo's eyes were narrowed as I turned back to face him. I stepped forward, kissing his chin, reaching up to brush my fingertips over the feathers that wrapped around the sides of his face. Laszlo's mouth opened to speak, but Hywel rumbled in interruption.

Don't dissuade her, darling. I've missed the sight of you coming undone under another's touch. It's been years since you brought us guests to play with.

Laszlo blushed at the words, but he didn't argue, bending his head down to mine for another delicate kiss. It was brandy I was tasting, warm and sweet. My hands settled between our hips, studying the frame of brass buttons that ran down either side of the trousers he wore. When I pulled away to start my work of undressing him, Laszlo turned to stare at Hywel.

"Asterion says you haven't so much as winked at him," Laszlo said.

Asterion doesn't polish my scales...or my cocks.

"I'm sure he would if he thought it would ready you for battle," Laszlo answered drily.

My lips twitched as I plucked at the buttons in front of me. Laszlo's talons slipped into my hair, and my eyes shut of their own accord, a sigh escaping my lips at the delicate stroke of their sharp tips against my scalp.

"Look up at me, dear one," Laszlo murmured.

I hesitated, pulling down the corner of the placket, exposing downy golden fur and the defined cut of an Adonis belt. I leaned in, pressing a kiss to the line of muscle, and Laszlo's fingers tightened in my hair. My breath caught in my chest as he forced my gaze up to meet his.

His face was shadowed, but his eyes glowed behind his glasses, blazing with hunger and a longing so clear it made me want to shy away. I brushed my fingers into the soft, short fur around his hips and his eyelashes fluttered, an unsteady breath putting out of his parted lips.

"How does he like to be touched?" I asked, glancing briefly toward Hywel.

Slowly, gently. Kisses and licks, Hywel answered.

Laszlo's fingers relaxed in my hair, one soothing down the side of my cheek to cup my jaw. Part of me wanted to pull away, break the lock of our stare, his gaze too intense and tender. But Laszlo had been kind to me, and quiet. And he'd been lonely. I wanted to be perfect for him, to offer him exactly what he wished.

I finished unbuttoning his trousers, the fabric sagging and sliding down his thighs easily, the dense golden fur continuing down his legs. His length was just beginning to thicken, swelling and growing longer as I ran my fingernails down the tops of his thighs and broke the stare briefly to study him. His sac was heavy and thick, bigger than a man's, hanging low and softly covered like his legs. His cock was dark, a purplish red, and I bent my head to kiss its tip as it bobbed up toward my chin.

Laszlo let out a shuddering breath, and a thick pour of *néktar* slithered over my tongue and down my throat. He was as potent as Asterion, but a little less overwhelming. Such an impossible, careful, and gentle man. I flicked my gaze up, fighting my smile at his open-mouthed wonder, and alternated flicks of my tongue with sucking kisses up one side of his cock. My hands soothed circles over his thighs, his tails swinging around his side to bat and pet at me, one coiling loosely around my right arm.

He's rarely selfish, Hywel said.

"You mean," —Laszlo paused to grunt as I helped myself to an overflowing handful of his balls— "you're usually greedy."

He'd returned to combing back the strands of my hair, my braid loosening and blonde wisps floating about my head. I repeated my ministrations on the other side of his cock, resting at his base to suck a mark into the skin until he bucked forward. My hand circled him, his cock kicking in my grip, and I ran the tight circle of my fingers down his length, gathering the fluid at the tip and stroking it back.

Hywel purred in approval as Laszlo groaned and gasped.

"You mentioned guests," I said, catching Laszlo's eye, pleased with how thin the rings of yellow in his eyes now were.

His throat bobbed as he swallowed, and his tongue traced against his bottom lip, staring as I poised myself at the tip of him. When he didn't answer, I froze, arching an eyebrow and waiting as his chest heaved with ragged breaths.

"When others visit..." he started, moaning as my mouth parted and I leaned forward, suckling on his tip, swiping my tongue against the underside. "When others visit, sometimes we come down here together. I..." Laszlo's head fell back as I sucked him deeper into my mouth.

Laz fucks them until their cries wake me. I watch. I lick them clean, Hywel murmured.

I thought of Birsha's house, of all the monsters who came to possess creatures more vulnerable than them. I'd heard from Lillian that there were other houses too, ones that took more care with the humans who resided there. I'd never understood the fascination monsters seemed to have with the weakest race. If I could've traded my human blood for a monster's, I would gladly have. Perhaps then, I wouldn't have been caught by Birsha.

Laszlo's thumb caught under my chin, drawing my face up, sensing my distraction perhaps. I cleared my head and focused on his beauty once more.

I leaned back, kissing Laszlo's tip as he caught his breath and straightened. "Who was your favorite?" I asked.

"Hywel," Laszlo said, a weak note in his voice revealing the truth. The others provided touch, provided time with Hywel awake during his hibernation. But they weren't beloved.

He likes a werewolf's knot, Hywel added, a fangy grin shared with me as Laszlo blushed.

I pushed Laszlo's cock up toward his belly and kissed the underside down to his base, then nibbled my way back up, teasing him with the suction of my lips until he was rocking forward, talons in my hair tightening once more, trying to draw me back into position.

"Hywel likes to watch women's faces. And he liked the giantess who howled as she rode his dragon's cock," Laszlo rasped, retaliating.

Laszlo liked the sea beast who choked him with a tentacle as Laszlo took turns fucking all three of their holes.

I giggled around Laszlo's cock as he guided it onto my tongue and deep into my mouth. His chin dropped to his chest, and his fingers unraveled my braid, twining it around his fist.

"Hywel liked... Oh, Evanthia, I—" Laszlo started to use my mouth, his hands working my head as his hips thrust slowly and deeply. I stifled my brief flutter of panic and focused my gaze on his face, the urgent need and the flush of embarrassment. How long had it been since he'd been touched, treated as a lover?

I liked the nest of succubi who nearly starved Laszlo as they took turns fucking him. I liked seeing him covered in sweat and delirious with pleasure.

Laszlo was panting, grunting as he fucked my mouth, still slow, deep enough to touch the back of my throat. He wasn't aggressive, but he was demanding, holding me in place for him, moaning when I pulled my cheeks in as he dragged out. My own body answered, clenching on nothing. I'd loved this act once, long ago. Loved making my partner weak with need, at my mercy. It was a kind of restoration to claim that power again.

"I liked when Hywel nearly ate them when they wouldn't stop," Laszlo said, grinning briefly.

And then I tucked you into the hoard and licked their cum off you.

"I love you," Laszlo gasped, turning his head to Hywel.

Hywel's mouth opened and I thought he meant to answer, but instead his tongue flicked out, twining around Laszlo's throat and squeezing. I gasped, and then Laszlo was shouting, driving back between my lips.

"You are so beautiful, Evanthia," Laszlo said, starting a racing speech of praise that made me tremble on my knees. My hands tightened on his sac and around his length, pumping with his pace. "Your mouth is exceptional. So sweet. Hywel, she is —she is—"

The tongue around his throat tightened once more, and Laszlo's speech was shortened, only a strained and ecstatic note escaping.

You are divine, Hywel finished for his lover.

Laszlo's balls tightened in my hand and I braced myself, drawing in one breath and then sliding him to the back of my throat, holding him there as I sucked and he bellowed. *Néktar* was bright and heavy, flooding me as Laszlo jerked and spurted heat and a tart sweetness. It was a silkier texture than I'd expected, and I swallowed it down, let it glide over my tongue as I pulled and sucked and stroked against Laszlo's cock.

His talons dug briefly into the back of my head, and I soothed my hands around his hips, over his ass, and down his trembling thighs.

Laszlo released a brief, muffled whimper as Hywel's tongue unwound from his throat, and then his hands relaxed, sliding down to hold the back of my neck, keeping me in place. My nose was pressed to the fur over his groin, my jaw starting to ache, but I closed my eyes as Laszlo stroked the back of my neck, untangling my hair from around his fingers.

"Magnificent," he mumbled.

And then his cupped hands drew me back. My eyes opened to find his stare on my face, features smoothed into calm and only a remaining flush spread over his cheeks to prove the pleasure he'd just taken.

I can't shift yet, but I feel restless. Just a little longer, darling, Hywel said, the words slowing and slurring.

Laszlo nodded but didn't pull his gaze from my face. I was on my knees before him, my eyes watering from the strain of taking his cock, my breaths short. I stroked his length, and we both watched as he dribbled onto my chest, warm and glittering.

I was a little filthy from touching Hywel and then sucking off Laszlo, and his pants were down around his knees. There was no reason to feel the moment as sacred, except for the careful way Laszlo held my head, the gentle force of his stare.

He bent, pulling one hand from me to tug his legs out of his pants. I tried to lean back, but he held me in place. "Come. Let's wash together."

And then he was entirely naked at last, scooping me up into his arms and carrying me out of the hoard.

17.
TREASURES OF
THE HOARD

I hadn't forgotten about the giant underground pool, but I hadn't been brave enough before now to go there on my own. The water was warmer than I'd expected as Laszlo carried me down the steps. I was still in my nightgown, but he peeled the sullied fabric up out of the water as he set me on my feet, and it slapped roughly against the stone, landing behind us.

We paused, facing one another in the water, and I had the rare urge to cover myself. Not that Laszlo hadn't already had enough of a view of me or that I hadn't seen my fair share of him. He was just so *intimate*, his gaze so focused and determined. That was something I was very out of practice with.

His hands cupped my face and he lifted it up, bowing down and fitting our lips together. His back was warm as I circled my arms under his wings, feathers combing over my skin as my fingertips mapped his flesh. His glasses bumped against my face, his nose a little large, and his hands remained on my cheeks, tilting me just so and teaching me the kiss, pulling my lips apart to be open to him. Demanding. Careful. A fascinating contrast that turned me into an eager pupil. I let my hands roam, his wet tails swatting playfully at them as I gripped his ass, smiling into his mouth. His cock jerked against my belly—monsters were never done with fucking, as far as I'd learned—and I thought I might rise to my toes, invite him into me, when he stepped away.

"Wash," he said, and I was offended at how steady his voice was. "I have plans for you."

"Plans that can't start here?" I asked, no longer concerned with covering myself.

"They start here by us cleaning up," Laszlo answered, one sharp feather-tipped eyebrow lifting.

I snorted and then fell back into the water, letting it rush over me, soaking into my hair and then covering my face and nose as I sank for a moment. When I floated up again, Laszlo was swimming to the edge of the pool, the creak of old hinges echoing in the cavern.

"How did you get a sea beast here to the castle?" I asked, thinking of the delightful blush Laszlo had worn when Hywel mentioned the tryst.

"They came up from Hywel's dreaming sea," Laszlo said. "Once, there was even a strange ship from another time that found its way to the castle. It took weeks to convince Hywel to send it back again."

I smiled at the exasperation in the gryphon's voice.

"Swim this way, and I'll wash your hair."

"Does that happen often? Monsters finding their way in?" I asked.

"Only by accident. Like the nest of succubi that were looking for a new roost. I think they meant to finish me off and claim the castle for themselves." Laszlo paused as I reached him, standing up and letting water sluice off me. My breasts had started to grow heavy and full again in the weeks since Asterion had rescued me, and I recognized the interest in Laszlo's gaze as he studied them. Then he admitted, "Up until I realized they meant to kill me, the frenzy was a great deal of fun."

"I took an incubus lover for a time."

"Did your natures suit one another?" Laszlo asked, gesturing for me to turn.

I did and considered the question. "Our appetites did. Not much else."

Laszlo hummed in understanding.

"How did you meet Hywel?" I asked, biting my lip and letting my eyes fall shut as Laszlo dug his fingers into my hair, lathering the strands with whatever strange bottle he'd been holding.

I caught a sigh from his lips and tried to turn to find his expression, but he pushed my head to face forward once more.

"I suppose it's better if I tell you. He's insufferable when he tells the story. He...rescued me."

I grinned. "Rescued you from what?"

"Another dragon."

I waited, but Laszlo wasn't adding to the story. "I suppose I'll just have to wait for Hywel to wake up to get the details."

"Another dragon was trying to...acquire me. For her hoard. I had a good nest, with a great deal of treasure. I thought I'd kept myself fairly well secret, but dragons have a nose for gold."

I pressed my lips hard together to keep from giggling. Laszlo was exceptionally golden.

"I offered her a few choice objects, but she was going into a mating cycle. She wanted me included. Hywel is older, and he managed to chase her off. Sent her to a wealthy orc den north of me."

"And then he claimed you for himself?"

"Not...exactly," Laszlo said, starting slowly again. He was thorough in his work on my hair, and he guided me back into the water with a steady hand on my shoulder, rinsing me clean as I stared up at the ceiling. "He accepted a few treasures in gratitude, and then he just...continued to return and visit."

I closed my eyes and smiled. "He wooed you."

"He did. He brought me gifts from his own hoard. Very rare from a dragon. I suppose he knew in the end that he'd be getting them back, and all my own in the bargain," Laszlo muttered. "But I *do* like his castle. Our home."

"Do you know what happened to the female dragon?" I asked, standing again.

"I heard she feasted and fucked her way through the whole den for several months," Laszlo said lightly. "I believe she might even have stayed."

"Good for her. I would've been very put out if I'd been robbed of a pretty gold gryphon," I said.

Laszlo's arm snapped suddenly around my waist, drawing me crashing back into his chest with an whoosh of breath. His hips nestled into my ass, and his talons combed my soaked hair away from my left shoulder. He held me there, as we'd been pressed together while stroking Hywel's cocks, and our breaths stuttered in the wake of the sudden movement.

"Would you really?" he whispered into my ear.

I'd been flirting unconsciously, not even aware of myself, and now pressed by the question, I found myself awkward and uncertain again. But my head was nodding.

"I'm not sure I would've given up so easily," I said, speaking carefully to keep from stammering. I pressed my ass back, but Laszlo moved with me, not allowing me to grind into him. "Not for orcs, certainly."

It'd been a long time since I'd fucked an orc. I'd seen almost none at Birsha's establishment, as they tended to be fairly precise lovers when it came to their partner's enjoyment. They liked cries of lust, not of terror. I remembered some rowdy, aggressive sex with a small den and a lot of crawling around on my hands and knees. A good meal, but not my preferred flavor.

"I think it wouldn't have taken Hywel much convincing to make a bargain with you," Laszlo admitted, laughing softly. He stepped away slowly, and his back was to me before I could turn and catch his mouth with mine. "Would you do me a favor?"

"Of course."

"Tending my wings is tedious on my own. But I can give you instruction."

I gaped at the broad spread of his wings, stretched to keep themselves out of the water, the ends just barely submerged.

"I'd be...happy to." Honored was a better word. Feathers were a tricky business from the little I knew, and even my incubus hadn't allowed me the opportunity to groom his.

Laszlo reached the edge of the pool, hauling himself up and then sitting down on the stone, next to the open old trunk. He put the bottle he'd used for my hair away and then pulled out a fine comb with a sharp end, a small blade, and a bottle of oil.

"The edges will be the worst, and up at the joint usually needs tidying. Cut any ragged ends. Pull out ones that are turned at odd angles. Polish what's dull," Laszlo instructed.

"Will it hurt if I pull out your feathers?"

"I'm used to it. Just warn me," he said, glancing over his shoulders. He drew his knees up and rested his forearms on them, hunching forward so I could reach the undersides of his wings too, where there were more ruffled spots.

I paused, taking in his wings, noting the different areas of issues he'd mentioned, the places that needed trimming; the broad middle that wasn't shining quite as brightly, probably harder for Laszlo to reach. I planned my movements and then reached for the blade first.

"I've missed this the most," Laszlo murmured. "Even more than sex with him. I've missed having my mate awake."

I didn't ask if he'd had any guests do this for him. I knew the answer. I just didn't know why he offered *me* the privilege. I wasn't sure if I was ready to know, so I set to work silently.

TENDING LASZLO'S WINGS HAD SOOTHED ME INTO A RARE calm. He'd taken my hand when I was finished, dressed us both in robes, and led me through the castle.

We would go up to his roost, I thought. He would tuck me into his nest, and I would draw him down on top of me, fit him inside of me. It wouldn't be wild and spontaneous, like with Conall in the meadow. It wouldn't be secretive and sleepy, like with Asterion either. Laszlo would be intentional, demanding, intimate.

And I was calm.

Except we did not go up to his nest after all, but stepped into a large room filled with racks of weapons and dummies dressed in pieces of armor, swords and axes and rifles mounted onto the walls.

I paused, and Laszlo's hand slipped free of mine.

"If we are at war, you must learn to fight," Laszlo said.

My calm evaporated immediately. "No," I said, stumbling back from him, my throat squeezing tight.

"I'm not asking you to step onto the battlefield, dear one," he said, turning to face me, his arms crossed over his chest. "But you've been captured once. Mistreated. I will do everything in my power to avoid seeing such a fate befall you again, including arming you and teaching you to fight."

"It won't matter," I said, my head shaking, heart slamming wildly in my chest. "I'm not strong. Not strong enough. I have one gift, and it's—"

"You have many gifts," Laszlo said sharply, glaring at me over the edge of his glasses. "They are not up for critique. And you may not have more than human strength, but that doesn't mean you shouldn't train what you do have."

All the heady warmth of the past few hours cooled to ice. I wanted to return to Hywel's nest, tuck myself against his scales. But Laszlo and Asterion and the others were waiting for Hywel to wake, and I wouldn't be able to sleep and dream calmly next to him when he went to war.

"I don't want... I don't—"

Laszlo walked forward. Unlike Asterion, he knew better than to read my flinches and winces and draw away from them. His arms unfolded and his hands cupped my shoulders, steadying me. "You will not be abandoned. You will not be left alone to defend yourself."

But...but perhaps these men would fall. Would fail. If they did, I stood no chance.

I glanced over Laszlo's shoulder to the steel and iron that surrounded the room. Was there any weapon that might offer me safety? Any monster who could provide me with impenetrable shelter?

Maybe not.

But I wasn't handing myself over to Birsha like I had the first time.

"First, we fit you in armor," Laszlo said, reading my surrender. He stepped to my side, wrapping an arm around my shoulder. "It's perhaps trivial of me, but I've set aside some of the armor Hywel and I have collected from the great female warriors of history. Boudicea should be just your size, I think. Although perhaps Artemisia's might be more...optimistic," Laszlo mused, his brow furrowing as he slid away toward a large armoire.

"Were you a warrior?"

Laszlo threw open the doors of the cabinet, his wings shrugging. "On occasion, when it was necessary." He paused, head turning and eyes focused on a distant thought. "My father was a warrior. He trained me from when I was a hatchling. But that was a very long time ago." Laszlo dug through the armoire, pulling out a pair of kid leather leggings and a long dress, slitted for movement. "I prefer scholarly pursuits now, so training will likely be good for us both."

"Would you...would you fight Birsha if not for..." *Me*, I thought, but said instead, "Asterion pressing the case?"

"If not for *Asterion*," Laszlo said, eyes glancing over the edge of his glasses to me, "Hywel and I may not have heard of any concerns at all. The minotaur is quite a champion of goodness."

He struggles to find it in himself, I thought, but that was Asterion's business, so I kept it to myself.

Laszlo passed me the garments and then surveyed the room. "Now we must choose a weapon for you. A sword, I think. You'd look just like a valkyrie."

"No," I said, shaking my head. "No, not that, please. I don't want to be the woman who guides souls off a battlefield."

I don't want to be the reason you or anyone dies fighting Birsha.

Laszlo blinked through the shine of his glasses. "You're right. An Amazon's spear then. Hippolyta was about your height."

"You have Hippolyta's spear?" I asked. My mother had told me stories about the queen of the Amazons, daughter of the god Ares. She was a divinity too, like me.

She'd married Theseus, who stabbed Asterion. The many myths of the day were starting to tangle in my head. I'd spent so long in the dark, so long a possession and a physical tool for others, I'd forgotten the world I was born into, even if I'd arrived many years too late for the best stories.

Laszlo returned to my side, a spear in each hand. He passed me the older looking of the two, the thick length marked and nicked with the impact of battle.

Laszlo stepped back and raised the spear horizontally. "We'll start with stretches, how to hold and move the spear between defensive motions and offensive strikes. Do as I do."

I sighed. I would've preferred Laszlo had taken me up to his nest and bedded me, or at least let me nap as I soaked up all the good *néktar* from our hour in the hoard. This was decidedly not the sort of activity to feed me. But it would be good to regain some strength. And I would enjoy watching him move.

I raised the spear in my hands and nodded for him to begin.

18.
COURTING
RITUALS

"Y̲ou have to remember she is nearly human," Asterion snapped.

I whimpered as his hands dug into my shoulders, but he misunderstood the sound, starting to pull away. I reached back to grab at him, and my shoulders protested that motion too. I groaned and Laszlo huffed, watching us from his armchair.

"She is no such thing. She is out of shape," Laszlo said, and then added after a beat, watching me scowl through the ache of every little movement, "Tomorrow we will only stretch."

"She doesn't need to know how to fight."

"Of course she does. All of us must know how to defend ourselves. And because she is weaker and a daughter of Hedone, she will be coveted."

"She will be *protected*," Asterion growled.

Laszlo gifted the minotaur with one of his sharp, dry glances. "Says the man who runs out of the room at the first opportunity."

I choked on a laugh. *I used to laugh loudly and often*, I thought. I missed Conall. He could still make me surprise myself with the sound of my own laugh. It hadn't even been a full day, and I'd been so irritated with him, but I missed him already.

Asterion returned to working the knots out of my shoulders. There was no needless caressing, sadly, but he was skilled with muscle, and I was grateful that he'd joined us for dinner and noted my stiff movements. Laszlo had made me work with the spear for hours, lunging and balancing, thrusting and swinging and blocking his attacks, until my thighs trembled and my arms refused to raise over my head.

"I am concerned about her nightmares."

"Nightmares? What nightmares?" Asterion asked, sitting up. "She shouldn't have—"

"I'm right here," I murmured, too tired to put up more of a fuss.

"I agree. She should be safe here. I think they are Birsha's doing," Laszlo said. "She shouldn't sleep alone."

"A-Alone? She is meant to be *free* here," Asterion stammered through the words.

"I would recommend Hywel's hoard, but he might roll over and crush her," Laszlo said lightly.

I snorted, but Asterion's hands tightened on my shoulders, drawing a pained grunt from me. He snatched them away again, and I was too weary to argue.

"You can't force her into your bed so Hywel can have her later, Laszlo!"

Silence struck hard and I stiffened, turning to glare at Asterion, who flushed and looked away.

"I'd like to not sleep alone," I said.

"Good, it's settled," Laszlo answered as Asterion sputtered. Laszlo rose up from his chair and approached me in my huddle on the carpet. "You'll come up to the nest with me."

Asterion reared back as Laszlo lifted me from the floor, a brief whine of protest escaping my lips. I caught a glimpse of Asterion on the couch as Laszlo carried me away. His hands were braced on the cushion and arm, fingers digging into the plush stuffing, face turned away from us. He was tense, apparently struggling to hold himself in place. I sighed and rested my head on Laszlo's shoulder, and he adjusted his grip on me to open the door to the terrace.

The moon was bright and full, the sea air warm tonight, and Laszlo paused at the center of the tile.

"Do you mind that I stole you away?" Laszlo asked.

"I like that you don't make me coax you," I said, lifting my face.

His smile was brief, cast in the glow of moonlight, and then his head ducked down, offering that same simple slotting of our lips together, an easy fit. His nose nuzzled against my cheek as he pulled away, and I opened my mouth to ask him to continue when his wings beat at the air, gusting it around us both. With the next great swoop of feather and muscle, he jumped high, carrying us up off the terrace.

My breath hitched and my arms tightened around his neck, but his grip on me was steady. The terrace dropped and shrank beneath us, and the high tower of the castle glittered with candlelit windows as we rose. Laszlo's shoulders flexed as his wings worked, heavy strokes of effort that lifted us in smooth measures.

"You don't mind bringing me into your nest?" I asked as our ascent slowed and twisted.

Laszlo's nest had its own smaller balcony, not overlooking the terrace but down directly to the rocks and sea. His wing beats relaxed, and we dropped elegantly down to the stone.

"I would've liked to bring you here sooner," Laszlo said, and before I could ask why he hadn't, he opened the door and carried me inside.

Laszlo's nest was not like Hywel's, and though there were a great many curious items arranged on shelves and tables— revealed by gleaming brass candelabras generously decorating the room—it was all arranged with a meticulous attention to detail that suited the gryphon I'd come to know.

Books lined shelves in a tidy order, the tops of their spines matching neatly, and I knew at once they must be Laszlo's favorites. On another shelf was a careful display of small statues, objects of idolatry. There was no fireplace, but the walls were shrouded in a deep blue velvet and the floor was heavily layered in carpets, these in better condition than the others around the castle. A massive bed, larger than any I'd ever seen, was built out of the far corner of the room. Sheer curtains shrouded its high platform, the fabric stretching high up to the vaulted and beamed ceiling.

In the left side of the room, near an open cabinet filled with polished bottles and small decorative boxes, a large steaming tub waited, a water pump poised near its edge. Laszlo carried me in that direction, and I patted his shoulder for him to put me back on my feet, exhausted as they were.

"You've already washed me once today."

"That was because you were covered in...you know," Laszlo said primly. "Now it's because you are sore, and you were sweating a surprising amount while we trained—"

"It was not a *surprising* amount," I squawked.

"It was to a gryphon."

I huffed and Laszlo ignored me, carrying me to the edge of the tub before finally setting me down. His hands made immediate work of the battle tunic he'd leant me, lifting it up over my head. It was loose enough I didn't even have to raise my arms very high, but I sighed with relief as I dropped them again. My nose wrinkled as I caught a whiff of myself. I did smell like sweat.

Laszlo continued to undress me, placing my hand on his shoulder for balance as he undid the lacings of the leggings and worked the leather down for me to step out of.

"I take it gryphons are particular about their grooming," I said, sighing as my toes sank into the hot water of the tub.

"It is something done together in the nest. A group cere-mony. From parent to child. And a...practice between mates," Laszlo said, helping guide me to sit.

I melted into the hot water, sighing and sinking back into the high, curved shape of the long tub. Laszlo stared down at me for a moment and then moved to the cabinet.

"Does Hywel clean you when he is awake?" Did Hywel tend Laszlo's feathers as I had earlier in the bathing pool?

"He does," Laszlo said, nodding. He lifted a green bottle and held it up to the candlelight from a sconce on the nearby wall. "This will help with your aches."

He unstoppered the bottle and poured a generous amount into the water, reaching down between my bent knees and swirling his hand. His gesture made the bath churn and lick pleasantly against me.

"Don't sink further. Let me get a comb for your hair," Laszlo said.

I didn't care if my hair got wet again, but I bit off my smile and sat up straight as he hurried to the other end of the room, opening a shallow gilded box. Rubies glimmered, then a glitter of diamonds, and finally Laszlo pulled out a delicate hair piece with long, sharp tines.

"Ares fashioned this for Aphrodite. She asked him for a pretty trinket, something to complement her beauty. He made her a weapon," he said, brushing the longest dagger point of the comb against his thumb. The metal was delicate and smooth, with great blossoms of silver and gold and steel pressed together in a bouquet at the top of the comb, every dangerously sharp tine etched with twisting knots. "He sold it to Hywel during one of their spats. It was one of the pieces Hywel used to woo me."

I stilled in the bath as Laszlo returned to my side.

If Hywel had gifted it to Laszlo in courting, was it right for him to offer it to me, even briefly? Was it right for Laszlo to ask me to groom his wings, to take me up to his nest and wash me, if that was a custom between mates?

Or were these intentional offerings?

Laszlo lifted my short braid from my shoulders and wove the comb through my hair, pinning it up against the back of my head. His talons fell to my shoulder, their sharp tips delicate against my skin.

"Lean back now."

I should go back to my own room. Or find Asterion, who refuses to make a claim on me, who would probably run out the door at the suggestion.

I did neither, leaning back into the support of the tub, sliding down to submerge my shoulders. Laszlo stood and unwrapped his shirt, peeling away the long layers, revealing his chest again.

"Will you join me?" I asked.

He shook his head and strode back to the cabinet full of oils and serums and who knew what else.

"I have a soap rumored to be made by Morgana le Fay. She made bars of it for Arthur and his knights to wash their wounds and tired bodies after battle," Laszlo murmured. "An oil that comes from Vasilisa the Beautiful—or her mother, really. She claims she used it and it added to her good luck in facing Baba Yaga."

Laszlo continued, and I pressed my eyes shut. Every bottle came with a myth, some familiar and some new. Their contents were precious, both in value and in meaning to Laszlo. He hummed with thought, and I blinked away the tears that had fought to escape.

I didn't know what I could be to this gryphon, to his dragon mate, or what was right to accept from him. But I craved his tender attention, his stories. And when he returned to the tub with three little bottles chosen and told me to lean forward so he could wash me, I did so without argument.

"I have a good sponge too, let's see," he murmured. "Aha. Narcissus's very own."

It was plush and deliciously scratchy, circling smoothly over my back. "Laszlo, what happens after my bath?"

Laszlo was quiet for a few minutes, stroking the sponge up and down my back. He lifted my right arm, washing me from fingertip to the hollow of my armpit, down my side. The sponge tickled, but I was too tired to squirm.

"You know what happens, dear one. If you want it," Laszlo said at last.

I turned my head to rest my cheek on my knee. "I'm clean enough, then. Or I could be quickly."

Laszlo's smile was soft, his head shaking. "I am not like the others, Evanthia. I will not chase you or tease you or wrestle you into a frenzy. You had your way this morning. I will have mine tonight."

I bit my lip, warmth curling through me. "What will you do?"

"Wash you. Dry you. Anoint you in fine oils," Laszlo said, rising and circling to the other side of the tub. "I will lay you in my bed and join you there."

"I know that part."

"I believe you know the rest too," Laszlo said, arching a brow.

"Not with you, I don't," I said.

He nudged my shoulder back, and I followed the movement, hoping he would caress my chest and breasts next. Instead, he reached into the water and pulled out my foot, working on my legs next. My skin grew goosebumps from the change of temperature, and his thumb stroked over a small patch along my ankle.

"Be patient then, and you will learn," Laszlo said.

I sighed as he washed down into the water, my legs falling open in an invitation he ignored. For now.

19.

A CEREMONY
OF PLEASURE

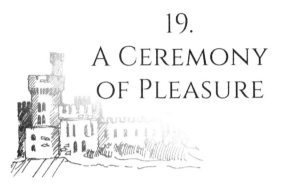

I ran my hands over my belly, studying the easy glide of my skin, the silky-smooth finish on almost every inch of me.

Laszlo's bare back faced me as he stoppered the cut crystal bottle of lightly fragranced oil he'd been pouring over me.

"We're done now, yes?" I asked, thighs squirming together.

Laszlo had spent far too much time preparing me for something I'd been eager for most of the day. I wasn't suffering as Laszlo touched nearly every inch of me, but it *was* maddening. He'd ignored a few choice areas, and I was looking forward to those attentions in particular, even more so with every passing second.

"You and Hywel share a similar impatience," Laszlo murmured, digging through a small trunk and pulling out yet another bottle. This one was gold and smaller than the first, but I sighed at the sight of it. I was tired. I wanted to be in bed. I wanted what Laszlo had promised in the bath—the pair of us together, joined and satisfied.

Or I wanted to be allowed to go to sleep, if all else failed.

"This oil is designed to heighten pleasure, sensitivity," Laszlo said. "Cleopatra had it created for her. It's very potent. May I apply it to you?"

"Laszlo, I think you underestimate your own potency," I teased.

He smiled but turned, holding the bottle, waiting for me to answer.

I sighed again and nodded. "Of course."

"Thank you. Spread your cheeks for me," Laszlo said softly.

My breath hitched at the gentle command, so direct after so much chaste skirting around. I reached back to obey, my gaze fixed to his. My breasts were thrust out in this position, and his stare remained there briefly, traveling down to my hips, before he finally moved to circle behind me. My lips pressed shut as warm oil dribbled down between my ass cheeks. I held back the whimper in my throat and remained still, standing on a towel placed over a carpet at the center of the room. I trembled as I waited for his touch, and all but jumped into the air as the back of his finger landed, smoothing and spreading the oil down the line of my ass.

A gasp escaped me as his knuckle circled over my hole. "Laszlo, please," I whispered, voice ragged.

"Hush, we are nearly finished."

My fingers had to dig into the flesh of my ass to keep my grip and I closed my eyes, imagining his body against mine, the way we would slide as we rocked into one another.

His knuckle ran down nearly to my core, before gliding back up again. "Turn."

I swayed as I moved, and a faint warmth started to bloom on my freshly anointed skin. Laszlo was wiping his hand and then pouring new oil out into his palm, dipping his talons into the little puddle. My lips parted, and my breasts were rising and falling at an embarrassing rate as he reached up to their peaks.

A shattered moan fell from my lips as his dripping talons traced circles around one nipple and then the next. A dribble of oil slithered over my puckered skin, beading on one tip, and my head fell back, another moan rising as the warmth against my ass built to a gentle throb.

Laszlo's head ducked, and it was his tongue rather than his knuckle that spread the oil on my breasts. My hands flew up to clutch in his hair, my chest bucking forward, my ass cheeks clenching as if to cling to the warmth and the pulsing sensation.

"Ohh, Laszlo, I *need* you."

He pulled from one breast to attend to the other, and my

toes curled into the towel, body bowing into his as he swirled and sucked and laved at my breast.

I whined as he pulled away, and he tutted when my fingers wouldn't untangle from his hair. My hands were shaking as I released him, and they hovered in front of my breasts.

"Go ahead," Laszlo said. "You won't rub it off. It soaks in quickly."

I groaned as I groped myself, squeezing and rolling my flesh in my needy grip, and the warmth bloomed quicker with my touch.

"How-how long does it last?" I asked through gasps.

"Until you sweat it out," Laszlo said. "Open your mouth."

My mouth was already opening on another moan, but the sound muffled as Laszlo stuck two fingers inside, his talons pressing down on my tongue. I sucked on the digits, surprised by the caramel-sweet flavor of the oil, almost like mead. But of course, lovers would want something that tasted so appealing. I leaned forward, locking my stare with Laszlo's, watching arousal turn the gold of his gaze into a darker amber as I licked and sucked on his digits until his talons tickled at the back of my throat.

The warmth built here too, making my tongue sensitive, aching. As Laszlo's fingers pulled free, I dove forward, abandoning one breast to grab the back of his head, drawing him in for a starving kiss, my tongue thrusting against his. His groan mingled with mine, but his hands were busy between us and he yanked himself away far too soon for my liking.

My cunt was already throbbing as if he'd dressed that spot too, even though he'd painstakingly avoided touching me there. I was dizzy and mindless, too much of me requiring attention all at once. Laszlo reached up between us, gripping my chin with one firm hand to keep my head from tossing as he traced my lips with more oil.

"Laszlo—I-I can't take—Please."

Slick fingers pulled on the lobes of my ears, his palms stroking down my throat, and then he pulled away, taking himself out of my reach.

"Lie back on the bed, dear one," he said.

I'd been about to fall forward, my knees quaking, but I liked his demand so I spun, drunk steps lurching me toward the bed. Everything was warm, hazy, the fragrances of the oils mingling, the candlelight dreamy. I was crawling up onto the bed when Laszlo grabbed one of my feet.

I fell onto my belly, rubbing my breasts against the sheets as he poured a thin line of oil down the arch of one foot, then soothed it over my sole, into my toes.

"Oh, fuck!" The words burst from my lips as I started to grind into the bed, my entire body an unsteady chorus of pulsing sensations. My hands clawed at the sheets, trying to drag myself up to the pillows and brace myself as I spread my legs and twisted my hips down for friction. Laszlo lathered my other foot, and I sobbed as an orgasm rose up to the brink and then shivered away.

"Onto your back, Evanthia," Laszlo murmured.

"This is insane," I rasped, and I could barely gather the strength to lift myself, to toss myself haphazardly to the side. I lifted my head just enough to catch Laszlo set the bottle aside. "Fuck me."

"Not yet."

I growled and he only smiled, picking up a strange tool and bringing it to his fingertips. "Two or three?"

I gaped, and then fell back, flattened with another teasing threat of an orgasm, only for it to be stolen away again. "What?!"

A strange crunching, clipping sound echoed with my gasping breaths, and I sat up again to see that Laszlo had cut away one of his talons.

"No!" I cried, sobering briefly. "You don't have—"

He clipped another away. "Two or three?" he asked, filing the dulled tips to round them.

It seemed a shame, but since he'd already started and I could easily guess his goal... "Three," I murmured.

He rewarded me with a smile and clipped the third, filing it to a tidy, smooth stub. For the first time, he pulled his glasses off his nose and set them aside, and I ignored the needy pound of

my body to study this new view of him. There were little inden-
tations on the bridge of his nose I wanted to kiss, and he
squinted at me briefly before his forehead smoothed, eyes
adjusting.

He dipped one finger into the oil, bracing his left knee on the
edge of the bed. Then another.

"Spread your legs."

They were already spread, but I raised my knees, shivering as
the soles of my feet throbbed with every brush against the bed.
It was as if I could feel every individual thread touching me. My
own lips pressing together was a heady kiss.

"I'm already wet," I whispered.

Laszlo dipped his third finger into the oil, and my hips lifted
from the bed, arching toward him. "That's nice," he said, smile
twitching.

He reached for me, and I rolled toward him. It wasn't the oil
that made me cry out with relief as he spread and stroked his
fingers over my folds, only the anticipation and joy of his touch
at last.

"More," I gasped.

"Yes," Laszlo agreed, and then he brought the bottle closer,
pouring it directly onto my skin.

I whined, reaching down to my core, my fingers tangling with
his. I spread my lips, pulled back my folds to expose my clit.
Laszlo huffed, ducking down, kissing the small nub and then
licking the oil around my skin. I was thrashing, fingers slipping
and sliding too easily, as he finally notched one finger inside
of me.

"Oh, please! Your cock—My ass—I need—Laszlo, *anything*!"

His chuckle rumbled against my sex and I shuddered, my
eyes rolling back and my too-sensitive toes digging into the bed
as I tried to ride my hips into his face. He pressed another finger
inside of me, and I had no idea if the heat and throb in my core
was the oil already at work, or simply arousal clawing up to a
crescendo.

Laszlo hushed me, purring slightly into my cunt as he kissed
and licked and nibbled on my flesh. The third finger burrowed

not into my cunt, but my ass, and I howled and arched, clutching his touch inside of me as I was suddenly dragged under the wave that had skirted away so many times before. The room vanished and my eyes squeezed shut, brilliant light flooding my thoughts.

But there was no settling, no slide down from the height. Only another flurry of throbs echoing from every sensitive, tender, begging part of my body.

"More!"

Laszlo nudged and worked his fingers in me, ignoring my shout for a few more seconds, but when he pulled away, sitting up on his knees between my spread legs, his cock was high and dark and eager.

I caught my breath, a brief moment of clarity granted by the stunning sight of him. "I want to touch you."

He lifted the bottle and held it out. "Dress my cock in oil."

The room spun as I sat up, snatching the bottle from his hands and pouring a too-generous amount into my trembling palm. Laszlo took the bottle back from me before I could empty it, and then I had him in my grip, my touch clumsy but ardent. His head fell back on a moan, his cock bobbing and pulsing as I slathered it in oil, and then down to his heavy balls. His hips jerked forward, and I was vengefully pleased to see his inner thighs quiver as I touched him, uneven and messy and probably a little too rough.

He grabbed at my hands, pulling them away and clasping our palms together. There was heat and pounding there too, but I only had a moment to note it before Laszlo was leaning forward, pushing me back down into the bed. The warmth of him over me was exactly as I'd hoped, his weight demanding a surrender I'd been ready to grant in the bath.

"Look at me, Evanthia."

My eyes met his, as golden as Hywel's hoard of treasure, and my breath was stolen as the head of his cock kissed my sex, sliding around my lips, nudging my clit, and then down to my opening.

"Your body honors mine," Laszlo whispered, his head lowering to mine, our lips brushing as I tried to chase for a deeper kiss. "And my body honors yours."

I stilled at the words, and then our voices mingled wordlessly as Laszlo pushed into me, full and heavy and hot. His chest settled against mine, my sensitive breasts recording every grazing hair, every ounce of pressure. He stretched me as he fit himself inside me, my channel starting to pulse and flutter as his thick length spread me open to hold him.

"Laszlo—I—"

What if I'm not a good mate? What if I can't love? What if I'm not—

He released my hands, his arms circling my back. My own wrapped around him, clinging, finding a grip to hold at the base of his wings. His eyes fluttered nearly shut at the touch so I stroked my palms around the tender, muscular flesh at his back, careful not to push feathers in the wrong direction.

I shuddered as he seated himself inside of me, our bodies fused to one another, my legs squeezing around his hips, heels planted on his ass as his tails flitted and teased at my toes. Laszlo's nose brushed against mine, beaky and handsome, drawing a smile to my lips. My body was pounding, begging for more, for a frenzy, but there was something sinking into me with this closeness, this moment of stillness together.

Laszlo's mouth grazed over mine as he started to move, not long strokes at all, but a simple rolling of his body, friction and pressure. My breath caught, and the pulses—at my ass and breasts and core and even in my toes—all finally caught the same rhythm.

"Like this," Laszlo said, his hands soothing up my shoulder blades to cup my shoulders, to brace me close to him. His face hung over mine, easy to reach, to nibble at his mouth, to receive his nipping bites in return.

I tried to hide my face against his shoulder and he shook his head, drawing away, forcing our gazes to join again.

"No hiding, dear one," he said. "Not when I am inside of you."

Our breaths were sweetened, tongues both candied with oil, twining together as we gasped for air, moved slowly and deeply. Laszlo's body demanded more room inside of me, somehow drawing me closer and tighter to his strong frame with every nudge and push.

This wasn't fucking or rutting. It wasn't the lurid licking of Hywel's tongue. This was...possession, and a sweeter, mutual version than any that had been claimed from me when—

I banished old memories and opened my eyes again, pressed my head back into the pillows, and found Laszlo's face torn with pleasure above mine, brow furrowed and lips parted on uneven breaths.

"Your body honors mine," I whispered, lifting my chin to kiss his cheek, over to his ear. "And mine honors yours."

Laszlo shuddered and he braced his hands into the bed, lifting his chest from mine, staring hard down between us as he rocked slowly, inching out and in again, fusing our hips together in a slow, circling pressure.

"Ev-Evanthia—I—"

"Yes," I gasped as he started to throb inside of me, forcing an echoing pound out of me. I slid my hands down to his ass and held us together as his rhythm faltered, as his wings beat and drummed me into the bed beneath him.

Laszlo glittered suddenly, every feather on him, every silky short fur and gleaming amber strand of hair catching the light as he came. The sight was stunning and shocking, and I struggled against my own sudden rise of ecstasy, savoring the view of him, the blaze of his stare, his brilliant voice arching with a cry.

His eyes fell shut and I surrendered, melting into the bed, shaking through the storm that rushed in my veins, arms and legs losing their strength. Laszlo settled into me, weighing down the thrum of the orgasm, pressing it into my bones. His mouth caught mine as I opened it to moan, and our lips fastened perfectly.

We stilled, wrapped around one another, his wings and tail feathers brushing my arms and legs. One of his hands stroked down my back and over my ass to cup the back of my thigh, a trail of warmth following. He breathed, and my breath hitched as our chests brushed together.

"It's—it's not over."

Laszlo's forehead rested against mine, his head shaking softly. "No. Not yet."

But neither of us moved, our resting bodies comfortingly sewn together while we let the slow pulses and little flares of gentle heat lift us. Laszlo kissed me as I whimpered, arched his throat for me to return the favor when he groaned. The oil did its slow work, leading us to fall together again in clutching stillness.

20.
AT ARM'S
LENGTH

Pages hissed as they were turned, and the slow and steady heartbeat of Hywel's dreaming sea called from an open window. There was light on the other side of my eyes, the sun shining.

Which meant it was morning.

I wasn't sure when Laszlo and I had finally succumbed to exhaustion. Even if we did sweat out the oil, we were too tightly pressed to one another to do anything but rub it back into each other's skin.

Another page whispered somewhere behind me.

Had I fallen asleep during the act? I couldn't remember what was real and what was some beautiful, decadent dream. Except I didn't have beautiful, decadent dreams, did I?

A feather stroked down the back of my leg, one of Laszlo's tails.

My heart squeezed roughly in my chest, and my eyes pinched tight. I'd had no nightmares. I wasn't sore. Even my eyelashes and toenails were thrumming with fresh *néktar*. Laszlo had held me like I was as precious as any of his or Hywel's treasures, a wounded gratitude and devotion in his stare.

I wanted to tell myself it was because he'd been so alone, drifting around this castle full of shadows, waiting for his mate to wake, but...

Another page turned. "Are you hungry, dear one?"

He asked it softly, and I thought he might not be certain I

was awake. I could ignore the question, not quite ready to face him. Or...

I rolled over in the bed, eyes still pressed shut, and Laszlo moved, ready for me. One arm lifted as I burrowed into his side, pressing my face into his chest, throwing my leg over his. His wings were tucked beneath his back, sitting him up slightly, but he didn't object to my added weight. He was still naked and I wasn't aroused, but I wanted to climb onto his lap, fuck him roughly. I didn't know if it was to thank him, or to try and establish a dynamic I *understood* between us. A relationship I was prepared for. Instead, I cuddled myself closer, tense and at the edge of weeping as he settled his arms easily around me once more, his book propped on my shoulder.

He didn't repeat the question, and I relaxed slowly as we remained silent. A page scratched softly over my skin.

Dear one.

"Are you sore?"

"No," I whispered.

"You're upset."

I am afraid to ask you why you call me "dear one." Why you want to wash me and dress me in oils. I am afraid that if I tell you I am afraid, you will stop doing those things.

"Last night was wonderful," I said.

A kiss was pressed to the top of my head. Another page turned.

"I am a little hungry," I added when Laszlo seemed to accept the compliment rather than press me for the truth.

His nose nudged into my hair as he nodded. "As am I."

The book was set down on the bed, but Laszlo's arms tightened around my back, and instead of sitting up and going in search of food, I was rolled back into the mattress. Laszlo hovered above me briefly, squinting in study. I leaned up to nip the tip of his nose.

"Hywel calls it my beak," Laszlo said drily.

"It's dignified," I said, kissing him.

"It's particularly useful in one regard," Laszo said.

"Smelling?" I guessed, a grin growing on my lips.

He shook his head. "Shall I show you?"

One of his legs wedged between mine and he started to shift back, sitting on his heels and lifting the sheet to expose my breasts to his ridiculous squinting, farsighted gaze.

I held back my laugh. "Please do."

And when Laszlo moved to spread my legs, tossing away the blankets and settling himself on his belly, face nuzzling into my sensitive sex, I sighed.

"Ah, yes. I always did appreciate dignified noses for this reason," I murmured as Laszlo helped himself to a generous serving of me.

❦

I WINCED AS THE SETTING SUN TURNED LASZLO'S FEATHERS into blazing blades of light.

"Are you tired, dear one?" Laszlo asked, turning away from the view over the terrace.

The sun was high by the time Laszlo and I left his nest, and I'd coaxed him out to the meadow for our stretches, the warmth and summer breeze soothing my stiff body. In turn, he'd wheedled me into more training before dinner. I would've like to protest, but in truth, our night together, uninterrupted by parasitic nightmares, had restored me almost completely.

"A little. But..." I didn't want to go to bed without him. And while I wouldn't have objected to a repeat of the bath and oil and sex, I mostly just wanted to savor another peaceful sleep.

"We'll go up together when you're ready," he assured me.

He was so beautiful, so bright, it almost hurt to look at him, golden, amber, and a bright fiery orange as the sun gave its last bleeding gasp on the horizon. But I would gladly go blind before I gave up the view of him.

Strands of music burst suddenly to life, weaving through the halls of the castle to reach us. Laszlo and I turned in unison.

"Another ball?" I asked. "Does that mean he's dreaming more or less?"

"Less, I think," Laszlo said, and he lifted his arm for me to take, his closest wing stretching to enclose me. "Shall we? Dinner's always grand when he brings a ball."

I linked my arm with his, told myself to breathe through the sudden urge to claw and clasp the gryphon to me, to bite his skin and claim him, even though I didn't know if I could bear to keep him.

"Conall should be here to dance with you," Laszlo said, brow furrowing.

"I enjoy dancing with you," I said, although I did still miss Conall and his bright eyes and blatant hunger.

"As do I, but his wildness suits you. The rest of us don't have it in quite the same way," Laszlo said as we stepped into his study.

The rest of us. I mused over the words and then paused at the sight of Asterion hovering in the opposite doorway. Asterion had never been especially casual around the castle, not like Conall or even Laszlo on occasion, but he was not dressed in one of his elegant dinner suits now.

Riding boots, coat, horrible gloves clenched in his grip.

"You're *leaving*?"

Asterion ducked his head. The gold was pulled from his horns, and he looked...strange somehow, sheepish. "There's work to be done in the city. Conall will return soon and—"

"No," I said, shaking my head. "This isn't about work."

"Do you want me to stay?" Laszlo murmured.

I shook my head. I knew what Asterion saw when he looked at the pair of us. I supposed I should've been grateful he waited to speak to me rather than simply vanishing in the night. If I was going to get anything meaningful out of him, it would be when we were alone.

Do you need *anything from him?*

I stopped at the thought. Laszlo raised my hand to his lips, kissing the back of it and then stepping away. Asterion seemed to waver for a moment, deciding between escaping out the door or stepping through to make room for the gryphon. He settled on the latter.

Why did it make me so angry that Asterion wanted to leave? That Conall insisted on doing so? Wasn't Asterion right, in a way? I liked Laszlo, his company. Hywel too. The pair of them could provide for and protect me for as long as I required them. Wanted them.

So why did I want to grab at Asterion's switching tail, take his horns in my fist, and drag him to my bed? He was beautiful, certainly. I had no doubt he'd be a powerful lover. He had rescued me at least once already.

Was that all it took for me to try and lay claim on him?

"I don't want you to leave," I said when we were alone.

Asterion stepped forward once and then stopped himself, head turning down again. "You're safe here. Conall and I were only ever an extraneous precaution. It's obvious Laszlo would never allow anything to happen to you. And you must realize he is...Hywel too... They are..."

"I don't want you to leave the castle. I don't want you to leave the room when I enter it. I—"

"They are mating you, Evanthia," Asterion said, looking up at last, endless dark eyes meeting mine.

The words hit me roughly, dried my tongue and tightened my throat. I would've looked away if I could have, but Asterion had always been too powerful, too potent, for me to hide from.

"They will keep you safe. I won't even call Hywel to the battlefield. He should remain here with you—"

"Stop, please," I gasped, my head shaking.

Asterion stilled, and his head tilted, a line creasing down the center of his brow. "Do you...not want them?"

My mouth opened and closed, my hands rising to fold and press over my rampaging heart as it stormed in my chest.

Asterion moved to me at last, huge and solid, every step making floor beneath my own feet more solid. "Have they hurt you?"

"*No*," I managed, head shaking. "It's not—I want —Asterion..."

Asterion's head ducked, and his hands hovered around my shoulders. If I swooned, he would catch me, but not before. "Tell me what you want, *théa*."

I have, I thought. But he hadn't listened.

"I don't *know!*" I moaned. "I don't know what I want. I don't know what I *am*. I don't know if I am a lover or if I am only someone who needs to devour you all. How can I be their mate when I am not myself?" I cried out. My eyes were filling with acid, but I blinked it away, and since Asterion would not touch me I had to grab him myself.

"Of course you can be—"

"No! Asterion, *listen*. There are parts of me that are *gone* now. They will not come back."

"Evanthia," he whispered, voice choked.

"I need *you*. And Laszlo. And Hywel. And Conall. But not... not the way any of you would like to be needed. I don't want you properly. I know that isn't fair to you, but I will stand here and beg you not to go," I admitted, crying openly now, ignoring the sound of my voice or the painful cut of the words on my tongue.

"You are whole, I promise you, *théa*."

"I am not a woman to be loved, Asterion. I am a pit to heap into and never be filled!"

"Stop," he said, his hands grabbing my arms at last, shaking me slightly with the force of his own refusal.

"I would take every bit of you and the others for myself. And if you must *run from me*, do so for your own sake, but not for mine!" I shouted, my voice cracking like glass with the truth.

"Stop, Evanthia!"

"*Enough!*"

Asterion's fingers clenched on my arms, and the room spun briefly as I sucked in a lungful of air—the first since I'd started to spout the bile inside of me.

Over Asterion's shoulder, a glimmer of gold winked in the doorway.

"Release her," Laszlo said, words stern but quiet.

For once, Asterion seemed to refuse the notion. He drew me closer, my body having to arch back to look up at him. His eyes were wide enough to glimpse white at the edges, nostrils flared.

"You are none of those things, *théa*," Asterion whispered. "You are—"

"Asterion, I will speak to you," Laszlo cut in. Asterion sighed, his head drooping toward mine. "*Now*."

Asterion's head lifted and he stepped back, hands gentling and then releasing me entirely. I stumbled around his side, lurching toward Laszlo at the door. How much had he heard? Did he know now? Know how unworthy I was for everything he'd gently offered the night before?

But Laszlo was as difficult to read as he had been when I arrived. His eyes were on Asterion, but his hand reached for mine, rubbing his fingers over my numb palm.

"Go up to the nest, dear one," he said softly. "There will be dinner there. I will join you shortly."

I opened my mouth, not sure what might fall out. An apology? Or more horrifying confessions?

Laszlo's gaze met mine, and it was too soft, too tender. He'd heard it all, and he would be gentle with me, whisper reassurances, promise me that time would change me, heal me.

I slipped away, letting the castle lay out the path to the nest ahead of me rather than trying to hunt and find my own way. It should've made my legs burn as I climbed the stairs up to the nest. It hadn't been a brief flight up from the terrace, but I arrived at the arched door far quicker than it had taken for Laszlo and me to come down this morning.

The room was dark, all shadows, barely lit by a low, smoldering fire in the fireplace. There was a table, the scent of food, but I ignored it in favor of the bed. The sheets smelled like the oils Laszlo had anointed me in, like sex and salt and sweat. There were a few stray feathers, their roots pinned into the mattress, and I pulled them free, pinching them in my fingers as I climbed into the blankets and pillows.

I'd been happy this afternoon. Yesterday too. There were fragile, jeweled moments in the past weeks that fooled my tired mind into brief seconds of peace, not of forgetting, but imagining that there was ruin behind me and new growth ahead.

If I'd let Asterion leave without a word, it would've been a bitter taste in my mouth, but not *this*—this horrible maelstrom of self-pity and disgust. But I hadn't let him leave. I couldn't release him, couldn't let him. I wanted to leash him at arm's distance.

I'd set aside a whisper of happiness in favor of throwing myself down a rough mountain, making rubble out of my body and emotions once more.

I needed to wait for Laszlo, have another slow and painful conversation that would leave me raw but not ragged. Apologize for taking what he offered last night when I wasn't prepared to reciprocate.

Weariness added weight to my eyelashes, made my eyelids sink and flutter. If I fell asleep, I would dream. I didn't fool myself. I knew what would come.

But I was craving punishment, so I gave in to sleep.

21.
WAKING,
CRASHING

On the fourth floor of *The Seven Veils*, the walls were painted green for envy. The staircase opened to a single hall with three doors on either side, and they were the first rooms filled for the night, never left empty when customers were in the house. There were no windows in the rooms, no view of the quiet woods surrounding the dark house. If the occupants of the rooms were quiet, which was rare in a house like that, they might've heard rustling from those empty walls. Might've noted the rooms were too narrow to add up to the building.

But of course, they already knew they were being watched. We were always being watched.

Two more hallways existed on the fourth floor, hidden staircases leading to the long corridors at opposite edges. Dark, enchanted windows looked through gilded mirrors onto beds and settees, where humans were used roughly and regularly. Staff passed through those quiet places, as well as curious newcomers and clients who liked to look but not touch.

In the early hours of the mornings, those rooms were emptied out at last, the hallways cleared. All except one room.

Someone had to answer to the appetites of the monsters who kept the house in working order.

For a time, that had been me.

The door clicked shut behind them once, twice, three times, and a final, snapping fourth. A guard for each floor of the house.

I moved as little as I could manage, studied a single elaborate cobweb that made beautiful scrollwork between two arms of the chandelier above me. My head was turned toward the false mirror, watching the door, *wondering if one of the doormen might appear, or the imp who watched the beasts in the basement, but the house was strangely still.*

All except for a soft, faint, rhythmic brushing from the other side of the wall.

A viewer.

I waited. I was alone, still, open to their gaze, but sullied and soiled too.

The sound continued. Not a brushing. No gasps. A scratching?

"I know you're there," I said.

I would not speak.

Not a scratching. Tapping. Tapping on the glass.

I frowned—

Show no emotion.

—and rolled toward the wall.

"Who is it?"

"Evanthia."

I sat up, not naked but wrapped in a silk robe, fine and soft and smelling of the sea air.

The mirror cleared, and I gasped at the sight of Conall's face smiling brightly at me. "Evanthia!"

No.

"Help!" I cried, drawing in on myself, turning my head to the closed, quiet door. "Conall, help me!"

"Evanthia, come here!"

"I—" I looked at the door again. There would be a man in the hall— he always came to me last, he liked me stretched—who would hear Conall's shouting.

"Théa," Asterion called, and I stared at the mirror once more, the minotaur there taking up the whole frame with his broad shoulders, his horns gleaming with gold. "Théa, come through."

I rose from the bed and lurched toward the mirror, an uncomfortable hollow in my core and all the embarrassing evidence of my use on my thighs.

"Come through, dear one," Laszlo coaxed, and the mirror was larger now, to my waist.

"I can't," I said, watching the door to my room through the reflection, as if Laszlo were only standing behind me.

But no, he was in the hall of the castle, his bedroom door open behind him.

"Come through, Evanthia. You'll be safe here."

I reached for the glass and sobbed as it was solid beneath my hand.

"Break it, Evie," Conall said, the meadow glowing behind him. "Break it and come through."

I searched around me and found a small, golden statue of a woman holding an apple, the snake wrapped around her arm. I had seen the statue before in Laszlo's—

No, in this room.

Or—

"Break the window and step through, théa," Asterion said, solemn and steady. A promise. "I'll keep you safe."

I struck the mirror, tall enough now for me to step through, just as I glimpsed the door behind me cracking open.

There was nothing but the black hall behind the shattered glass, but they called to me altogether, a trio of familiar, safe voices.

Wait, Evanthia!

But it was too late. I lurched into darkness, falling out of the dream and through the shattered window of Laszlo's nest.

For a moment, as cool sea air rushed over me, caught the tangled hem of my dress and licked around my legs, I was relieved. Relieved to be out of The Seven Veils once more. To be here, at the castle.

Except I was falling from the high tower, screaming, hurtling down toward brutal rocks that rose like fangs from the water. I heard the call of those voices that had lured me in the dream, but they were too far away and I was dropping too quickly.

I heard the roar of the world rushing past my ears, the sea and the rocks soaring up to meet me.

A louder roar than I'd ever known, one that shook the marrow in my bones. One that made me weep, even as the air stole the tears from the corners of my eyes.

And then there were no rocks beneath me, just a huge, dark shadow, a glimmer of opal and ruby. It swooped up to meet me, circled away to expose my demise once more, black wet stone jutting up from churning sea foam.

The world whipped and turned, unbalancing my fall, twisting

me in midair, and suddenly I was caught, talons clamping around my waist, all my breath stolen by the grip of the dragon hauling me up from death and back into the air.

"Hywel! Bring her—"

No. You nearly lost her, Hywel boomed in my head, and my hands slipped over the long, black claw circling me carefully, holding me in a tight grip.

Hywel was awake. Hywel was flying!

I'd been sleepwalking again. I'd thrown myself out of Laszlo's bedroom window and—

Hywel had woken.

He turned us back toward the castle, below it, the sea moving madly, splashing mist up to my toes. There was a dark hollow in the cliffside, the cavern opening, and Hywel flew there with me clutched in his grip.

You scared me, **blodyn bach.**

The cavern was warm as we dove inside, and Hywel dropped me immediately into a pile of pillows and bedding—his nest. He growled and grunted, hovering above me in the too-tight space, wings beating the stone overhead, an unsteady rain of rubble landing around us. The talons that released me reached down to the floor, wings knocking treasure in every direction, thrashing tail making chaos of the space.

And then suddenly, there was no dragon snarling above me, bringing the hoard down around us. Just a tall, pale man yards away.

My breath was ragged and loud as the hoard settled back into place. My hands were clutching the pillows around me, and the world was still rushing up, up, up to meet me roughly, even as I sat still and frozen, staring at the new face before me, his red wings a smaller version of Hywel's.

He was exceptionally lanky, with sharp cheekbones and a faint glimmer of opal-pink scales near his temples. His stride was long as he moved toward me, pausing once to frown and bend his knees, bouncing there for a moment.

"So strange," he murmured, and the voice was a simpler but perfect match for the incredible low and heavy tone of the dragon's.

I had never imagined Hywel as a man—Laszlo had never described him as one—but there was no other explanation. That he was standing before me now as one wasn't so complicated in the scheme of the world I lived in, except that I had just thrown myself out of a tower window to certain death before being snatched up by a dragon.

And now he was not a dragon but a *very* tall, very pale man, with spectacularly broad shoulders and an extremely narrow waist and—

"Hywel!" Laszlo shouted, footsteps thundering down the stairs to the hoard. "Quit making a maze of the castle!"

"No," Hywel bellowed back over his shoulder, his steps growing faster, feet tripping over pillows. A wing snagged on a bit of velvet and he growled, and then his wings were gone entirely. "Damn mess. Come here, *blodyn*—No, you can't, look at you."

I flinched back as he loomed over me, and he scowled but didn't stop from scooping me up from the floor.

Thin, but very strong. All muscle.

"Hywel." It was the first word I'd managed. I was surprised I wasn't still screaming.

Hywel was awake.

My hands were vibrating as they landed on his face and he blinked slowly, lips stretching and curving slightly. He purred at my touch, and I gasped at the familiar, smaller version of the sound. His cheekbones *were* sharp. My goodness, he was as spiky and beautiful as he had been when huge, except in an entirely new way, and—

"Why are you wearing clothes?" I asked. His shirt was untied at the collar, hanging open, and his breeches were a little loose, but still...

"Because I fell asleep in them, darling," he answered, smiling.

And then Laszlo and Asterion fell down the stairs and into the hoard. Hywel turned us to face them, his arms tightening around me, holding me under my legs and around my back.

"Is she "

"You. *Fools*." Hywel's voice carried, not shouting but not

leaving room for any other sound in the cavern. "She was *an instant* from the rocks."

"Hywel," Laszlo started primly.

"You were to keep her *in the nest* until I woke," Hywel answered, dark and stern.

"I was in the nest," I said.

"Not *alone*," Hywel continued, now rising in volume.

Asterion stepped forward. "Evanthia, are you—"

"She is in *my* care now, King of the Labyrinth."

"She is *free* to go where she pleases," Asterion snapped back, but his head bowed as Hywel glared at him.

"*Not* out the window," Hywel snarled.

"I was dreaming," I said, and the men all quieted. "A nightmare. I was—" I stopped myself, and Hywel looked away from the others to stare down at me.

"I told you," Laszlo said under his breath, and both Asterion and Hywel tensed, so I wasn't sure who the words were meant for.

Hywel growled and then choked on the sound when I shuddered.

"Put me down," I whispered.

"No," the dragon answered me, and I sank into him with a contrary relief. "I want the pair of you to leave. I will keep her here for the night, and we will speak in the morning."

"Evanthia—" Asterion started, but he must've expected Hywel to interrupt him because he stopped short at my name. His shoulders drooped, and then he sank forward into a bow.

Laszlo remained standing as Asterion turned and headed for the stairs. Would he leave the castle? I considered calling out to him, but only watched his back retreating. Laszlo was staring hard at Hywel. "We can't risk her again, Hywel. Are you sure you're...rested?"

"I won't so much as blink for years," Hywel answered. "I should... You could..."

Laszlo's expression softened and he walked forward, reaching out and resting one hand on my back, one on Hywel's shoulder. Hywel bent to hover his face over his lover's, and the anger melted away.

"I've waited centuries, my love. I can stand another night. Take care of her."

They kissed over me, a slow, savoring press of their mouths, a teasing drag of Hywel's teeth on Laszlo's lip. Laszlo drew away first, not hesitating before diving down and pressing a harder, more urgent kiss to my own lips. He pulled away, his eyes wide on mine.

"I'm sorry," I gasped out. They should be together tonight. I struggled against Hywel's hold, but he didn't so much as budge or seem to notice. "I'm sorry, I was—"

"Hush, dear one," Laszlo said, brushing his hand through my hair once, then drawing away. "Don't quiz her, Hywel."

"An instant from the rocks, Laszlo," Hywel answered tartly.

Laszlo stiffened and then gusted out a sigh. "*Morning.*"

"Morning. Late morning." Hywel shrugged.

The gryphon huffed and turned for the stairs.

"You should...you should be with him," I managed, trying and failing once more to put my own feet back on the floor.

Hywel spun away with me in his arms and I stilled, dizzy from the fall, from the sudden halt of the fall, from the dragon who was now a man who was also a dragon.

"He missed you," I said as Hywel headed for a shadowy corner of the cavern.

"I know," Hywel said, opal-gray gaze glowing down at me. "Why did you fall asleep? Did you feel drugged?"

I pressed my lips together, and the dark tapestry of red roses ahead of us slid to the side, revealing an even darker opening.

Hywel's eyes narrowed. "Did you *want* to have a nightmare, *blodyn bach?*"

"Not want," I said, flinching and freezing in Hywel's hold as we stepped into blackness.

He tutted, and three lanterns in three corners of the room flared to life. One was made of red glass, one of blue, and the third of green, all the colors painting over Hywel's pale skin and hair, catching in the open light of his eyes, dazzling and strange. The shadows changed his face, and now at last he was familiar. This was the dragon I'd touched and flirted with.

I gasped and pressed my face to his throat and jaw, breathing in the damp, earthy scent of him, wisps of smoke and lavender too.

"*Hywel.*"

His hand soothed over my hip. "There now, I have you. Down we go."

I hadn't taken note of the bed, but it was soft and dense beneath me, sinking under my weight, swallowing and cradling me. Hywel came next, stretching me by his weight on top of mine, lifting my hands above my head and pressing my legs under his.

"You didn't want a nightmare, but you went to sleep knowing you'd have one," Hywel murmured, more to himself. "You were upset. Did Asterion say something foolish?"

Hywel's long, lean frame on top of me was shocking and relaxing all at once. His hip bones dug into mine, and I squirmed beneath him to open up, but he braced his knees outside of mine, holding my legs closed.

"We'll assume he did, because Laszlo's far too wise."

"Kind," I whispered. "Laszlo is kind."

"Mm, that's true too." Hywel released my hands, patting them, and then pushed himself up. I could just make out his face, one half green, the other red. "Does *kindness* bother you?"

My eyes watered, and Hywel's head tilted. "I can't—I can't— He let me groom his feathers. He washed me. I can't be—"

"Mate," Hywel said.

I squeezed my eyes and lips shut and shook my head roughly, refusing tears and refusing that word too.

"Hm. I still think I'll blame Asterion."

My breath hiccuped with a watery laugh, and the humor in his voice cleared away the threat of weeping. "Blame me," I said.

"No," Hywel said, sitting up on his knees and staring down at me. "I'm going to undress you, *blodyn bach*. You were very small before. I'd like to look at you when you don't remind me of a meal. No, don't move. I will unveil my treasure myself."

"What woke you?" I asked.

"Your scream," Hywel said, scowling, shifting on his knees to pull the hem of my dress up to the tops of my thighs. "I warned Laszlo not to let you sleep alone."

"It's not his fault."

"Mm. Ahh, just as lovely as I recalled. But perhaps more accommodating," Hywel said, leaning back to admire my hips as he pushed the fabric up to my waist. He lifted one knee and then the other, nudging my legs aside to kneel between them. I moved to reach for the dress, to pull it over my head, and he tsked. "Don't move, pretty morsel."

I stilled and glanced around the room. The walls were rough stone, a glimmer of some metal vein in the rock sparkling in the green lantern out of the corner of my eye.

My breath hitched as long, elegant fingers reached to my sex, spreading my lips. Hywel was staring speculatively.

"Such a tiny little hole," he mused, glancing at me with a wicked smile. "And yet I know how much it can hold."

My heart had only just begun to steady after the fall, but its beat picked up again at the remark.

"Will you undress?" I asked.

"In a moment. You first. Sit up, darling."

I licked my lips. Hywel looked...hungry. And if I was aroused, it had more to do with a wave of panic looking for a better outlet than a natural response to the moment. Or even the sudden plummet of my energy after the nightmare's thieving.

Hywel *was* beautiful, elegant and haughty and eerie too. I'd let him lick me as a dragon. I'd touched his cocks when they were the size of his current torso.

"I can't be your mate," I whispered, unsure if that was even implied in the moment as it had seemed to be with Laszlo.

Hywel smiled, and his eyes narrowed a touch. "Sit *up*."

I obeyed and lifted my arms as he yanked my ties loose and drew the dress and my chemise up over my head.

"Lie back." Hywel sighed as I sank back into the bed. He stretched out on top of me again, and I let out a startled laugh as he rested his head on my chest, nose nuzzling at my right nipple. "I missed breasts," he said wistfully. "There's no pillow like them. Oh, except... Roll over."

He sat up, a little gleefully, and I found myself wearing a shaky smile, pulling my leg up to roll over on the large bed, furs and velvets and silks in a tangle beneath me. Hywel hummed and then moaned as he wiggled down the bed and rested his cheek on my ass. I laughed into the fur beneath my face.

"Lovely," he murmured, and then his hands slid under my waist and up, cupping around my breasts, squeezing them gently. We both moaned.

"Oh, I love lady flesh. Delicious," he said, nipping my ass and making me squeak. "And so soft. *Squishy*. Like fruit. And you smell like fruit too."

He was moving on top of me, turning his head from one side to the other, peppering kisses over the base of my back. His hands were working on my breasts, and he shimmied over the back of my legs, making me spread open once more. A fur throw tickled against my bare sex, and I gasped as he took another bite of my ass, the bottom of my left cheek. He breathed in deeply, and air rushed around tender flesh.

"If Laszlo were here, he would make me behave," Hywel growled. "Which is a shame, because he is so exquisite when he's misbehaving."

And then Hywel groaned and buried his face between the cheeks of my ass. I yelped and clutched at the velvet under my fists, panted into the fur. My ass clenched, and Hywel laughed and then licked me, lapping and nipping and tonguing hungrily.

"I never behave," Hywel rasped into my flesh, shifting lower, finding my tight hole, poking at it with his tongue.

Néktar floated around me, gliding over the bedding, rushing up my spine. I let out a warbling cry and then melted, forcing myself to relax, giving Hywel room, even focusing on opening myself for him.

He purred in approval and his hands left my breasts for my ass, spreading me open, feasting on me there, occasionally twisting down to lick my cunt too.

"You were not behaving when you went to sleep like that, were you, *blodyn bach?*" Hywel asked.

"No," I whined, shaking my head.

"No," Hywel agreed before thrusting his tongue past the tight muscle and into a small and tender place.

I groaned and softened again, limp under his searching tongue. He pulled it free, and I whimpered.

"Laszlo's sweetness makes you feel guilty, doesn't it?"

"Y-yes," I whispered.

"And so you wanted punishment."

I nodded, unable to speak the words but certain Hywel knew my answer.

One hand released my cheek and then came down with a sharp smack against the flesh of my ass. I cried out at the sudden crack and the burst of heat, jolting upwards.

"Lie down," Hywel growled.

I froze for a moment, a soft ache blooming where he'd spanked me. No one had hurt me since Asterion had pulled me off the streets and—

"Lie *down*, darling," Hywel repeated.

I stretched my arms in front of me and flattened myself on the bed, hiding my face in the fur blanket.

He was quiet, his hand returning gently to the spot he'd slapped, and he spread me open again. When his tongue returned, prodding and plunging, licking up and down the crease of my ass, I remained still and quiet. But not for long. He was fucking my ass with his wet tongue, and it was silky and hot and made me pulse with need. He stopped as I started to rock into the furs wadded up beneath me.

"Asterion would like to tell you that you are free. You are not free to put yourself in danger. You deserve to be completely free, perhaps, but I am very old and very strong and I refuse to allow it, and I will get my way. Do you still want to be punished?"

My eyes were open, my hands spread fully flat, and I was braced for another hard spank, but it didn't come.

"Not...not tonight," I said, turning my head so my voice was clear.

There was a soft rustle, a shimmer of white fabric tossed aside out of the corner of my eye. Warm skin grazed over the cheeks of my ass, and soft lips pressed to the center of my back.

"Very well. Did I hurt you?"

I shook my head. The spank had hurt, but it had felt good too, and the remaining burn was only pleasant. Mostly, it had shocked me. The others hadn't dared to touch me with any violence. If they had asked, I would've refused it, too afraid of my own reaction. Strangely, I was pleased—pleased I hadn't screamed and fallen into the past, hadn't shrunk away from Hywel. Pleased too, at what he offered for the future.

I whimpered as he pulled away again, but his hands returned to my sides, rolling me back over. His pants were loosened, one red cock rising up from the waistband, decorated with a trail of scales leading down his waist and even over a few inches of his shaft, another jutting into the fabric.

"I'm going to put you on my cocks, *blodyn bach*," Hywel said, staring down at me. "We can fuck. Or you can sleep, and I will watch over you."

"Why...why put your cocks in just to let me sleep?" I asked, brow furrowing.

"Because it will feel good," Hywel said, shrugging. "And I want to. You can refuse. I think you know that, but I'll say it just in case."

I did know. Not just that I *could* refuse, but that he would listen.

I opened my legs, but he held my gaze as he smiled. "Good little treasure."

His lower cock wasn't scaled and was paler and slightly less thick, although it was longer too and weeping profusely, as if preparing itself to ease the way. I licked my lips, staring and considering the pair.

"Do they both have to go in at the same time?"

It had been a while since I'd taken two cocks at once, and usually it was a kind of back and forth motion, not two thrusting in unison.

"Tonight they do," Hywel said, arching an eyebrow, daring me to argue. His hands were spreading his leaking arousal over both cocks, squeezing the lower cock to produce even more.

"All right," I murmured.

Suddenly, Hywel's authority broke, a soft huffing laugh escaping him, his broad shoulders softening. His head shook as he stared down at me.

"I *see*."

I opened my mouth to ask what he meant, but then he was sliding over me, his strong chest with smooth scales pressing to my breasts. His hand slipped between us, and he didn't protest as I reached up to his shoulders. I licked my lips as two hot, stiffly-pointed tips pressed to me, Hywel adjusting them until they were fitted to my openings. My entire body pulsed in anticipation.

"Push yourself onto me," Hywel said, a touch breathless.

I held my breath and arched my hips, and we both grunted as he notched inside my cunt, and then with a little encouragement from him and a reminder to myself to relax, into my ass.

The top felt wonderful, the bottom...more like a nerve-wracking challenge.

"Hywel—" I said, courage faltering.

"Lovely little morsel," Hywel sighed.

I forgot my own voice and moaned as he sank in. Silky wet warmth pooled in my ass, even as my body burned in protest. I gasped for air and Hywel continued, making room for himself with gentle thrusts, my body seeming to swell as he filled me all at once. He was too tall to kiss, so instead I opened my mouth and bit hard at his chest.

Hywel shouted and bucked, and I yelled with him as the first of the scales on his cock pushed inside of me, a notable and curious rub on my inner walls.

"Ohhhh, two holes. Just perfect," Hywel squeezed out in a tight voice.

I let out a garbled laugh, and he groaned. His hands grabbed my hips and then he was yanking me to his base, ridged scales pressed to my clit, hot and full sac tucked against my ass.

We sucked in a breath together, chests swelling to press skin close, sighs softening us around one another.

I waited for him to move, even though I wasn't *nearly* ready. Having him filling me twice over was outrageous. Painful and wonderful, so much pressure that I thought one breath would be all it would take for me to come or to suddenly explode into a thousand pieces.

Hywel's arms wrapped around me, and I whined at the adjustment, the slight grind of my body against his scales. Then he turned us to the side, dragging the fur over my back. The pressure eased slightly with the removal of his weight, and I could breathe again.

And it felt *spectacular*.

I moved, rocked my hips, and Hywel purred.

"No one could take me better, *blodyn bach*," Hywel said, his voice slurring slightly.

I lifted my head from his chest, blinking as his arms moved back, crossed behind his head. He sighed, and the tiny motion shifted and rolled him inside of me enough to make my eyes flutter shut.

"Fuck me or sleep on me," he said, settling into the bed.

I laughed, and that too threw me toward the edge, made Hywel groan. My entire body was throbbing, but he was wedged so deeply, so *tightly*, I couldn't do more than squirm on him. Not that I needed a great deal more than that.

"You-you can't sleep," I reminded him, rubbing myself against his scales, my voice cracking as his cocks nuzzled, as good as touching inside of me for how fully they filled me, each one stretching me, together threatening to split me.

"Wouldn't dream of it," he teased. "Who could sleep with their cocks strangled so sweetly?"

I whimpered, my head falling to his chest. I was terrified of coming, of what it would feel like plugged and speared like this, but there was an imperative to move, a compulsion. Just a little more, just a little deeper—

I yelped at the first clench of my body on his cocks, and Hywel laughed. My face was on fire, my nipples scratching against his chest.

"We nearly lost you, treasure," Hywel whispered, one hand moving to sweep damp strands back from my brow. Was it sweat or sea mist?

Hywel's scaled ridges were rough but perfect. I scratched at his ribs, trying to press myself closer, closer, please, just a little—

He lifted his hips, and my eyes flew open.

Explosion it was then. My body ignited with the slight buck beneath me, and I screamed as the lamps seemed to brighten the room, bathing the dragon beneath me in light. No, bathing me. Hywel's gaze locked with mine as I shattered, his stare vivid and consuming, watching my parted lips, my frozen breaths, the shudder that melted through me and then returned for another cruel helping when I was already bled dry.

My eyes rolled back, the pretty vision lost as I gave into the drowning sensation I'd narrowly avoided earlier.

Sneaky dragon. Wonderful, strange rescuer.

His hand slid up my cheek when I swayed unsteadily, at the edge of a second orgasm or about to finally fall from the first. His thumb brushed my temple.

Trickster bastard.

I dropped, not to his chest, but deep into sleep.

22.
WELL-RESTED
BLESSINGS

I woke still stuffed. Hywel was panting, barely moving on top of me, and the lanterns were dimmed, but I could've sworn the dragon was blushing as he glanced down at me when I opened my eyes.

"I may have..." —he groaned, throwing his head back as I squeezed on his lengths— "...slightly overestimated my ability to resist fucking you in your sleep."

"You *put* me to sleep."

"But in my defense, you've been riding me gently for twenty minutes."

I'd dreamt of nothing in particular but *pleasure* and *néktar* all night. Of swimming in the ocean and being fucked by waves. Of relaxing in a meadow and having flowers suckle my clit and breasts and throat. Of riding invisible cocks and mouths and fingers, of tongues that tasted like almond candies thrusting against my own.

"Only twenty?" I asked, swallowing a whine as I joined his motion. I didn't know how long I'd slept, but my body had happily adjusted to Hywel's body joined with mine in that time, still a stretch, but now one that only made me sensitive and shivery.

"You rested for a while," Hywel rasped. "After squirming and coming a handful of times more in your dreams."

"They were very good dreams," I said, wrapping my legs around Hywel, grinning as he shuddered and faltered in his rhythm. "*Thank you.*"

Hywel paused, blinking and clearing a fog of lust from his gaze. He smiled down at me, sliding one arm beneath my shoulders to arch me in his grasp. His head ducked down, broad mouth nearly in reach. Oh...we hadn't kissed.

"My sincere honor," he murmured.

His mouth glided over mine, our lips opening easily, tongues stroking before hunting each other for new flavors. Hywel surged gently into me, the plunge and retreat smooth and slow, the soft press of his scales into my sex painfully sweet, my body so tenderly used that the grind hovered at the edge of too much.

"Laszlo will be down soon," Hywel said on a gasp, thrusting deep inside of me and holding there, body arching up as he groaned. "I've kept you long past my promise."

"You should be with him now," I murmured into his chest, not sure I wanted the words to be heard, growing selfish for the feel of him inside of me.

Hywel only chuckled. "It has been hundreds of years of waiting since we touched this way, it's true," he said, voice too ragged to sound melancholy. "But, *blodyn bach*, it has been thousands of years that we've waited for you."

I twisted away but Hywel fisted long fingers in my hair, tugging and drawing me back to his mouth, his tongue plunging and hips growing urgent in their pace against mine. I clawed at the flesh of his back, and he purred into my mouth, his arms circling me to hold me tight against him as he bucked and thrust. His skin was silken and scorching, a sizzle of sweat between us evaporating as he started to growl and snarl.

I knew the moment Laszlo entered the room, a prickle of awareness tickling my toes and rising up my calves where they clutched around Hywel's hips. Shame washed over me first, quivery and warm, and then the arousal of being observed. This was his lover I was stealing for the moment, just as I'd stolen him when I could too.

"Sit up, let me look at you," Laszlo said softly.

Hywel gasped, but he released the clutch on my waist and hair, gripped my hips, and rose up onto his knees, pinning me on his cocks. Laszlo crawled onto the bed at my left, his piercing gaze behind glinting spectacles focused on where I was swollen and spread and fastened on Hywel's lengths.

Hywel turned his head, and I gaped at the soft pride and dark hunger that stole over his expression when he looked at Laszlo. When it turned back to me, remained fixed and glowing, running over me from head down to our union, I shivered.

"What do you think?" Laszlo asked Hywel.

"You've outdone yourself," Hywel answered.

"I thought so too, though I can't properly take credit," Laszlo murmured, and then he bent over me, smiling with barely disguised mischief. He hovered above my lips, and they parted in invitation, my back arching. "It was Asterion who brought her here, after all."

His hand brushed over my breasts as Hywel started to move in longer strokes. I shivered and soaked up every detail, the relaxing ease on my body of his retreat, the shocking pressure and possession of his thrusts in.

"Not for our sake," Hywel muttered.

"I'm not treasure," I said, but the words were thin and high as Laszlo plucked at my nipples, offering me a filthy, licking kiss that made Hywel moan as he watched us.

"Everything and everyone is treasure to a dragon," Laszlo whispered, nipping my lip, laving it with his tongue. His nose stroked against mine, and then he rose enough to smile down at me. "Mates included."

"Mates are the very best treasure," Hywel rasped in agreement. His head fell back on a groan and his cocks throbbed inside of me, thickening and dragging, rubbing higher and harder.

I squeezed my eyes shut, and Laszlo released my lips, scooting down to my breasts and adding rough kisses to his fondling. I ran my hands down the strong rib of his wing, catching a loose feather against my damp palm and cried out as one of Laszlo's talons circled my clit.

Hywel shouted with me, faltering in his long strokes, holding himself inside of me with short, rough kicks of his hips into mine.

"Shall I...save some for you, darling?" Hywel gasped.

Laszlo released one nipple to answer. "No, fill her completely."

I gasped and threw my hands back into the pillows, shocked by the words, by the throb of my body in answer, by Hywel's low laugh as I squirmed on his cock.

"You like that, *blodyn bach*," Hywel said.

"You said you wanted to devour us, dear one," Laszlo whispered, sitting up, curving an arm under my shoulder and smoothing my hair back from my face as Hywel shook me with his driving pace. "That you could not be filled."

"I-I—Please," I gasped, eyes growing wide, gaze flashing between the two men. I had said those words, hadn't meant for Laszlo to hear them, only wanted to shut Asterion out or draw him in—I didn't know really. But they were true, and I desperately wanted the cure, as if it could be found in this beautiful and base act, as if Hywel could—

Hywel stiffened, his cocks swelling once more inside of me, a sudden sharp pressure snapping through me, another great boom of release. He came and the sudden burst and flood in my core forced my own orgasm, a clawing, raging creature of ecstasy, one that stole my breath and turned my blood to fire and wiped my vision clean.

Laszlo held me and murmured soft, meaningless words, his talon still lightly circling on my clit as Hywel pumped inside of me, one dazzling rush after another. My lungs seized and burned until suddenly I was breathing again, gasping, Hywel's weight settling above me, the pair of us cradled in Laszlo's embrace. Mouths stroked over my throat and cheeks, lips pulling my own into heady kisses.

My vision cleared and my body thrummed, and I caught the dragon and gryphon kissing, heads resting against one another before they hunted for another press, a murmur of an old language on their lips. Hywel was still emptying himself inside of me with little jerks, a shocking pool of slippery warmth growing beneath us, and he pulled away from Laszlo only to return to me, kissing my temple, my earlobe, sagging on top of me. Laszlo joined him, brushing his fingers into my hair, pecking kisses at my shoulder.

It was the haze of *néktar*, so thick it ran like syrup down my throat with every breath. Or it was the depth and stretch and pressure of Hywel inside me, on top of me, Laszlo surrounding us with a blanket of wings. Or it was the brief and hazy peace that came with release.

But for a moment, I did not feel empty.

"I DIDN'T REALIZE THE SEVERITY OF THE NIGHTMARES," Asterion said, pacing in front of the fireplace.

"That's what comes of avoiding a young woman's delightful company," Hywel answered, stretched along the large couch, one of his legs bent over my lap, trapping me in the seat between him and Laszlo.

"I assumed they were a result of my recovery," I admitted, shrugging.

"You accepted them as such," Laszlo said, glancing at me out of the corner of his eyes. "You took them as—"

Hywel's foot nudged his lover's thigh, and Laszlo fell silent.

As punishment.

For what? I wondered. What was I to be punished for? My brow furrowed and I stared into the flames, occasionally interrupted by Asterion's passing stride.

"Then he is reaching her," Asterion said. "From such a distance? Is there a link we can destroy? *Théa*, did he ever give you anything? A...tonic, or—"

"I was fed and denied many things, Asterion," I said, eyebrows raising.

"There are no marks on her, no tokens," Hywel mused. "It's more likely that the connection exists because she fears and thinks of him. Little toad of a man that he is."

"He is more powerful now, Your Majesty," Asterion said, but there was an edge to the title that hinted at mockery.

"He is a parasite latched onto powerful monsters. But none more powerful than—"

Laszlo cleared his throat. "Less ego, if you please, and more solutions for Evanthia."

"She will sleep with me," Hywel said, waving a careless hand and shrugging. "Problem solved. And then we will kill him, and there won't be a problem at all."

Asterion stilled and glared at Hywel, eyes just bare sparks in the shadow, the orange glow of the fire surrounding him, mythical and huge in its halo. "She is free to *choose*—"

"I will sleep with Hywel. By choice," I said, not wanting another ridiculous argument about my ability to choose from the man who elected to *ignore* me when I chose him.

And then Asterion flinched.

I wanted to strangle him, but his neck was too big for my hands.

"But I would like... If there *is* some connection, some link that makes it possible for Birsha to enter my dreams, I want it broken," I said.

"I've started my research, but Hywel will be able to get a better sense of how your mind is being invaded," Laszlo answered.

"It will require leaving you vulnerable to start," Hywel said, reaching down and drawing my hand in his to his lap, somewhat conveniently poised above the mounds of his cocks. "I swear I will shut him out as soon as possible, even if I can't tell how he enters."

I considered the promise, aware of the three sets of stares watching me. "I've survived them thus far." I squeezed Hywel's hand in mine before he could point out how narrowly I'd escaped my most recent nightmare attack. "I'd rather you learned what you needed to know than draw me to safety before it's necessary."

Hywel nodded slowly. "No more naps alone. If you so much as feel drowsy and I'm not there, you scream," he said.

"I promise," I said with a nod. It was an easy bargain.

Asterion cleared his throat. "I should return to London. Now that you're awake—"

"You'll do no such thing." Hywel sat up abruptly, swinging his leg down from my lap but immediately draping his arm over my shoulder. "You promised us a guard for Evanthia."

Asterion scoffed and gestured between Laszlo and Hywel. "But you—You're obviously...*adequate*."

Hywel stiffened, and I thought the slight was intentional, that Asterion wanted to raise Hywel's ire in order to make his escape. A part of me didn't want to give up on the minotaur, on the early hints of emotion he'd aroused in me. But I had two powerful monsters who were staking a claim on my time and body and affection. Maybe Asterion was right to leave, and maybe it was time for me to stop fighting for him.

"We are," Hywel said tightly. "It doesn't alter your commitment. You vowed to protect her, not to pass her off to someone else, regardless of how capable we are. Laszlo and I will train her in weaponry, but you must prepare her for hand-to-hand combat, self-defense. At least until the wolf returns."

"Hand-to-hand *combat*?" Asterion snapped.

"Wrestling," Hywel replied cooly. He smirked and continued, "You're too large, of course. But you can teach her evasive maneuvers. You're good at those."

Asterion turned his back to us.

23.
EVASIVE
MANEUVERS

"You don't have to do this if you don't want to," I offered.

"Hywel will tear my horns out if I leave you alone," Asterion said, his eyes fixed to the golden feather that Laszlo had braided into a lock of my hair while we'd been catching our breath that morning.

He and Hywel had bullied Asterion into taking me to the training room after luncheon, and I might've objected to being managed, but I thought the pair deserved time for a reunion without me.

I shrugged and turned my back to the minotaur. He was still dressed formally, standing stiffly at the center of the large room, staring at me as I wandered, aimlessly inspecting the weapons on display. "Then stand sentry, if you must."

Asterion stirred briefly, as if he meant to prove me wrong by sudden action, but then fell still just as quickly.

"I understand why you want to leave," I said, and his eyes widened. "There's nothing to do here. We're cut off from your purpose, all your connections to help you challenge Birsha. There's no point in you being here."

"You are here," Asterion said abruptly, blinking. "You are worth protecting."

I lifted a large battle axe from the wall, laughing as I nearly dropped it. Asterion winced as he watched me. "You don't want to be in the same room as me."

"That's not true," he muttered. "I...wish it were. I know what they call me, but I promise you, *théa*, I'm not a coward."

"You act afraid of me."

"You underestimate your power if you think I shouldn't be," Asterion said.

I sighed and shook my head. I wanted to walk away from this conversation, give up on this man. I couldn't. It wasn't even that he had searched for me, found me, *saved* me. I *craved* touching Asterion. I wanted to claim that power he said I held and use it to bring him to his knees in front of me. "Asterion—"

"I've loved women before."

Before. I spun, still struggling to hold up the axe as I stared back at him.

The broad bridge of Asterion's nose crinkled. "I've...experienced passion. Affection. But I've never been the man a woman loved. *Preferred*. There are always...*others*. It didn't matter before now."

Before. There was that damn word again.

He was staring at the feather in my hair, stepping slowly toward me.

"I will devote my life to protecting you. I will be your knight, your shield. I will stand between any danger and you, make any sacrifice," he said slowly, low and heavy and solemn. "But I see the way Conall looks at you. The way the Kings of Clouds and Dreams dote on you. I won't be lesser, not with you, Evanthia."

I had not taken a breath during his speech and I did so suddenly now, a sharp inhale as I realized he stood within reach. Tempting and torturing all at once.

"I meant what I said last night," I whispered. "I feel only *greed* when I..." I fell silent, shaking my head as my throat tightened around the words. The lie.

It was a lie. Conall made me bright with humor and joy. Laszlo made me ache sweetly with need and affection. Hywel thrilled me, made me want to be wild and violent and brave again.

And Asterion... I wanted to step into the shelter of his body, the quiet depth he carried with every step and word, and I wanted to press my lips to his skin as if I could return the beauty

I found in him, convince him of it. I wanted to give as much back to these men as they gave to me. I didn't know if I could.

"It would be easier to resist kissing you if you didn't look at me like that," Asterion rumbled, looming over me.

"I don't want you to take a sword for me, Asterion," I answered. "And I would never ask you to be lesser."

"If I had fucked you when you first asked it of me, taken your body with mine, would you still want them?" he asked.

I opened my mouth to say no. To say yes. To say it was impossible to answer.

"I asked for sex. Not for possession. Not for claiming. And I don't ask for those things now, either," I said instead.

Asterion's gaze shuttered and he nodded. "But that's what I'll take, when you're ready. I've known that since the night I saw you in The Seven Veils." His body bent and I rose to my toes, arched back to shape myself to his body, nearly touching. "I leave a room you enter because every time I am near you, I'm at the mercy of your scent, your gaze, the potential of your touch. I have memorized your features, and I dream of them."

I was breathless, or I was gasping, drowning in his scent too, a smoother, cleaner fragrance than I'd expected, so soft and vaguely sweet.

"I know every piece of you as well as I know myself now. You *are* mine. Your scent tells me so. Your touch," Asterion murmured, barely audible, teasing me closer, higher, my chest brushing to his with every heaving breath.

His hand rose and cupped the back of my neck, and my entire body quaked. There was truth in his words, an understanding sinking into me that I'd either ignored or been ignorant of.

"But fate has always toyed with me," Asterion whispered, that line digging between his eyes, wrinkling his brow. His other hand raised, and a single thick fingertip lifted the braided feather up, the gold glinting out of the corner of my eyes. "And I am not alone."

He wants more than I can give, I tried to tell myself. But with him towering over me, touching me, speaking so privately and plainly, I wanted to throw myself into him. Perhaps possession would be a simpler course of action than fighting for my own identity. I could let Asterion pour his love into me, use it to fill all the empty caverns of my soul once more. I would not be my own, but I would be *someone's*.

But would I give up Laszlo, who had tended me and soothed me and lavished me with all the delicate presents and touches and the ceremony of lovemaking? Or Hywel, who had saved my life and kept my dreams safe, who'd sworn vengeance on my behalf? Or Conall, who teased and chased me and reminded me of the sound of my own laughter, of being wild and silly and care-less again?

I wouldn't. Perhaps I'd already lost the war I'd been waging against my own feelings.

I reached for Asterion and his head sank heavily into my palm, velvet fur and strong jaw vibrating with a restrained moan.

"Asterion, you *are* their equal," I said.

You can be their equal with me too, I wanted to add, but the door to the training room opened with a bang, cutting my words off as I gasped. I expected Asterion to jerk away in reflex, but instead he hauled me to his chest, twisting us so that his body was placed between myself and the door.

Playing the part of a shield, I thought bitterly.

"Come," Laszlo said, taloned hands bracing the doors open, face straight and solemn. "There are...ill tidings in the sea."

"Stay here," Asterion said to me.

Laszlo answered before I could. "No. She remains with us. Hywel is disturbed, and he wouldn't like her alone. Now, quickly."

Asterion kept his arm around me as we hurried to follow Laszlo out into the hall, the steady weight of his touch a relieving contrast to my rioting nerves. There were no dreamers in the shadows we rushed through, and I tried to recall if I'd seen any since Hywel had woken. We'd been served lavish dinners, but was there another magic to the castle than the shadow figures who roamed about?

A sudden, deafening roar startled me from my musing, and Asterion clutched me closer.

"Was that Hywel?" I asked. "Is he in his dragon form again?"

"He's stronger that way," Laszlo answered.

"Are you sure it's safe to bring her out—?"

"Yes, yes," Laszlo snapped, cutting Asterion off. He spun in place, features tight and eyes vivid, searching wildly for a moment before settling on me. His hand reached out, but he didn't grab at me. "She's safer *with* us than alone, haven't we established that?"

Asterion tensed at my side, the cut in Laszlo's words clear. But Laszlo's own fear was just as obvious, worry shaking his hand as it extended to me. Asterion had confessed to me just minutes ago his concerns about being lesser in my affections, but I couldn't turn away from Laszlo when he'd been the man caring so diligently for me recently, touching me so tenderly. Perhaps Asterion was right, even if I wanted to prove otherwise.

Hywel roared once more, making the brick and stone of the castle tremble with its force. I slipped free of Asterion's arm and accepted Laszlo's hand, reaching to hold his face.

"It will be all right," I said softly.

They were the words spoken to me so frequently of late, and I doubted them more than I trusted them, especially now when I had no idea what we were about to face. It didn't matter to Laszlo. His eyes fluttered shut and he sucked in a deep breath, jaw pressing into my cupped palm.

His arm snapped out, sudden and tight, banding me to his chest. He groaned softly, nudging his face into mine, and held me in place for a moment.

"Yes," he breathed, ruffling my hair with a sigh. He relaxed and then tucked me into his side, wings stretching. "Yes, it will. Come."

I resisted the urge to twist and search for Asterion behind us. His hooves were a steady beat, still following. Had I proved him right by taking Laszlo's hand?

It can't be one or the other. It has to be them all, I thought, then realized what the words meant and found myself blushing.

I'd just told these men I could be nothing to them, nothing real. I was accepting too much as it was—their protection, their attention, their bodies. But it irritated me that Asterion believed that he would be lesser. I should've been convincing him that he meant *nothing*, not *less*, but that would've been a lie, and instead I found myself wanting to prove to him that I *did* hold him as dearly as the others.

I wished Conall were here to enjoy the tangle I'd found myself in. He'd find humor in it and remind me to do the same.

We were nearly to Laszlo's study when piercing screeches cut through the roar of the sea's waves.

"A harpy?" I cried, freezing in my steps and clapping my hands over my ears as the sharp notes dug into my skull.

Laszlo shook his head, frowning, and shepherded me forward. Asterion crowded at my other side, the pair of them flanking me. We stepped into the study, and Hywel's swooping figure blazed from outside of the terrace windows, streaking across a violently clouded sky.

Hywel roared once more, so fierce and loud and endless that the clouds clogging the sky shuddered and crackled in answer. He spied us as Laszlo pulled me through the open door, and twisted through the air to dart in our direction. I hadn't seen much of his flight the other night when he pulled me up before the crash, too caught up between terror and relief. I'd thought of him as a massive, lazy house cat while snoozing in his hoard, but now, elongated and razor-sharp in the sky, I understood *why* Asterion had been so determined for him to wake once more.

He was terrifying and exquisite. Enormous and powerful. Had he shrunk himself to fit in the hoard, as huge and cavernous as it was? He seemed as large as the castle now, filling the sky with his huge wings, long bladed tail trailing down to the churning water, talons spread in warning.

My mouth gaped, body trembling. I wasn't frightened of *Hywel*, but nothing could convince my body and some deep instinctual part of me to not recognize him as the fiercest predator.

Birsha would shrivel at the sight of him, I thought, and I stood straighter, leaned in Hywel's direction, wanting to run to him. I would throw myself over the balcony edge, and he would snatch me up in those talons once more. The most dangerous grip in the world. The safest.

We crossed the terrace as Hywel shrank in the air, swooping

closer and then shivering into a drop, landing on two feet, long legs and narrow waist arrowing suddenly out into familiar broad shoulders. He was scowling, severe and dour in his long features, and he reached an arm out toward me in a clear command. Laszlo and Asterion both released me, and I only hesitated a moment before dashing to his side. My gaze was on his face, studying the snarling lip and the tense squint of his eyes, but I glanced over his shoulder as his arm snapped around my waist and saw the sea.

Red with blood, twisting like a whirlpool, flesh and chum and gore mixing with a pink froth of the turning sea. Something long and serpentine splashed out of the water, a tendril of muscle and flesh, slapping back down to the surface in expressive rage.

I gasped, stepping toward the edge. "What—?"

Hywel's arm tightened, pulling me back, twisting us so that his wide chest blocked my view. He caught my chin in a firm grip, tilting it up so our eyes met, and shook his head, a grave frown pinching the corners of his mouth.

Laszlo stopped at my side and Asterion passed us, running to the bannister, releasing one deep bellow of shock and mourning as he stared down into the water. He turned, the flesh of his lips and around his eyes pale and stark.

"The akkorokamui," he said.

"It's a dream," Hywel said, voice heavy and carrying. "It's... not *real*..."

There was an unspoken 'but' left on his lips.

"It's a warning," Laszlo said.

"Or a threat," Asterion continued, his gaze returning reluctantly to the sea, flinching and whipping away again. "We haven't heard from them in weeks. This may not be their true body, but it may be an answer to what's happened."

The red in the sea was spreading, shifting color to something sour and acidic.

"Can you make it go away?" I asked Hywel.

His lips flattened to a line, and he and Laszlo shared a brief frown. "Not without *dreaming* it away."

"It's too soon," Laszlo murmured.

Hywel might sleep and not wake quickly, they meant.

"Leave it, if it isn't real." Asterion gave the sea his back with a sturdy and intentional turn of his heel, marching toward us with firm steps. "Don't tear your attention away from her," he added, looking hard at me. "That's what he wants."

Hywel rolled his eyes a little, bristling at the orders. "Obviously." His lips moved, but he didn't give the word voice.

With Asterion standing behind Hywel and Laszlo, the last of my view of the water was firmly hidden.

"This *does* need investigating. The akkorokamui is our ally, and a powerful one. If this is a threat of what *might* come to pass, we need to do whatever it takes to prevent it from happening," Asterion said. He spoke softly, but the shelter of the three of them made his voice clear. "I need to find a way to contact Conall or do the work myself. Discovering the truth shouldn't take long."

The words were deliberate, an offering to me. He was leaving, but he wasn't *running*. And he meant me to know it, even as Laszlo and Hywel seemed to circle me between them in their arms.

"I understand," I said, nodding at him. *I don't know if I am worth returning for*, I thought.

Asterion was as still as a statue for a long moment, his stare locked with mine, a slow study of my features, and in the heavy pause I wondered if he might tell the others to move aside for him, or if he was waiting for me to pull away from them.

Just as it occurred to me to slip free of Hywel and Laszlo, Asterion nodded, and then he was marching once more, around our cluster and toward the door. I twisted to watch his back, a familiar and not unpleasant view, even though I was tempted to call out to him to stop. He ducked out of sight without a backward glance.

Hywel's eyes were narrowed on my face, watching too closely, but he smiled as I turned and reached his hand up to tuck back strands of my hair that had been coaxed loose by the breeze.

"Inside with you, *blodyn bach*," he purred gently. "We'll leave this nightmare to wash away as we dine and dance into the evening."

24.
THE FACELESS MAN

"I-I-I can't! Not—Oh!—Not again," I gasped, trying to squirm away from Hywel's persistent fingers.

The dragon chuckled, his breath gusting against my swollen sex. Behind me, with his body wrapped around my back, Laszlo grunted as I pressed my ass to his half-hard and well-used cock.

"You'll know when you can't," Hywel said.

"He means you'll pass out," Laszlo murmured in my ear.

I moaned, and Hywel's hands wrapped around my thighs tightly, tugging me back to his insatiable mouth. I yelped as his tongue returned to lave and lick and torment my clit, bucking into his caresses.

"Can't you just—Oh, Hywel!" I whimpered, swallowing and fighting for air as he spread me gently open, a tongue too long for his human disguise slithering inside of me to plunge as his lips and teeth sucked and grazed.

"She wants to know why you can't just put her to sleep," Laszlo guessed.

I nodded, more or less, and only partly because my entire body was rocking in a natural demand, thrusting myself onto Hywel's tongue, his mouth, his probing fingers.

Hywel grunted, and Laszlo took that as his cue. His hands stroked over my chest, through the uselessly thin fabric of the nightgown they'd put me in, talons plucking playfully at my nipples as I whined.

"If he uses his powers to put you to sleep, it'll be impossible for Birsha or whatever wretch he's using to reach you. It must be your own natural sleep," Laszlo explained, kissing my cheek and then suckling on my earlobe.

Hywel snarled as my body started to clutch on his tongue, and the sound shuddering into my body set me off once more, a painful and perfect snap and unraveling of pleasure. I cried out and clasped Laszlo's knees, bracing myself against the onslaught, sagging as it claimed me.

"Also, this method is delightful for all of us," Laszlo said lightly, cupping my breasts and nibbling on my throat.

I was drunk on *néktar*, coated in sensual oils from Laszlo's collection, in sweat and release too. Laszlo and Hywel had taken turns with my body, back and forth, until Hywel laughed and said he was impressed with my appetite and would have to get more creative.

In truth, I should've surrendered under the weight of the *néktar* hours ago.

I was frightened.

I didn't want to go back to The Seven Veils. Not even in a dream. Not even with Hywel and Laszlo carefully watching over me, protecting me from danger.

Hywel licked me clean, he and Laszlo stroking me from head to toe as I trembled and quaked through an orgasm that did not quite want to release me. Hywel's lips were swollen from kisses, mine and Laszlo's, and they trailed over my mound and belly as he slithered up my body.

"I don't want to sleep," I admitted, a weak slip of the tongue in the loose and languid aftermath.

"Mmm, I thought as much," Laszlo said, still kissing every inch of skin he could, throat and shoulder and cheek and temple, up one direction and then back down.

"It's not a hardship to continue, I assure you," Hywel said, resting his chin on my belly button and grinning up at me between my breasts.

I stroked clammy hands through his hair, my touch heavy and lazy. The room seemed darker now than it had minutes ago, although crawling up to the height of pleasure always did seem to make the world more vivid, sharper and louder and brighter.

"You needn't be afraid, though," he continued, turning his head to suck a kiss into my stomach. It was much softer, gently rounded, than it had been when Asterion first found me. My appetite sometimes struggled, faded away for days, but when it returned it did so with a vengeance, and Laszlo had always been a determined host, tables never empty until we were all truly full.

"It's a shame Asterion hasn't settled yet," Laszlo whispered, the words distant and I thought not for me. "Minotaurs, you know...quite exhausting."

"Are you calling me inadequate, darling?" Hywel growled, rising up and then nipping at my breasts, startling me into blinking my eyes open.

"Not at all. But adequacy isn't the goal. She needs to be *overtaken*," Laszlo said.

"Pulverized, more like," Hywel muttered. "She's too delicate."

"Is she? Was it very challenging for you to *stuff* her on a few minutes' acquaintance?"

I snorted, lips curling, and realized my eyes had shut again. I forced them wide open, drawing in a deep breath to speak. Hywel showed no sign of the murmured argument, smiling at me with a lazy grin, all promise and warning at once.

"Once more, I think," he said, glancing up at Laszlo.

Laszlo hummed and jostled me with a gentle shrug, and then they were rolling me between them, draping my body over Hywel's chest, Laszlo stretching over my back. Wings rustled and my brow furrowed, eyelids drooping against my orders.

Hywel's mouth caught mine, tangy and dark and delicious, and I moaned into his kiss, clawing at his chest as Laszlo slowly and gently slid his cock inside of me. Feathers brushed my side as Hywel's tongue paced with Laszlo's thorough and tender strokes.

I realized too late what Hywel meant by "once more," but it didn't matter. I didn't even make it to the end, falling into a decadent sleep before either Laszlo or I reached our finish.

MY CELL.

Strangely, I was relieved.

The room was cold and black and it stank, but I was alone. I couldn't bear to be stolen away from Hywel and Laszlo's embrace to be dropped into a memory of a client.

While trapped in The Seven Veils, the hours or days or weeks alone in the dark were often the worst, left to starve and go mad and forced to survive it all.

But I knew now I would wake again. I would be safe again. I would be tucked between a doting gryphon and an incorrigible dragon.

I held my breath, found my knees with my hands, and waited in the dark for Hywel to finish whatever it was he needed to do. There were no dragging steps, no claws slowly carving into my skin, no rutting weight or heavy growls in my ear. Just quiet. Just dark. And the unpleasant scent of my body left to wither and soil and decay.

I swallowed a gag and shook my head.

I was safe. I would be safe. In minutes.

Not long.

My chest burned and I sucked in a breath, swallowed the foul flavor of the air, squirmed and bit my lip against the pinch and poke of the horrible mattress, too familiar.

Some of the smell was from the last of Birsha's clients to visit me. A—

No. Don't remember.

Not long.

I would be safe. Not long.

I wanted to call for Hywel, but I was meant to be quiet. To wait. Better to not alert whoever made the nightmare that the dragon was watching too.

Just wait. Not long.

My body was sore, my belly hollow. Were they stealing all my strength again, all the néktar *I'd fallen asleep soaked in, gorged and healthy? If the dream took too long, would I wither once more, wake empty and ravenous?*

Not long. I chanted the two words over and over in my mind until they blurred together, slurring into meaningless gibberish, even in my thoughts.

It was too long already. Not minutes but hours. I was stiff and brittle.

I tried to move, and a chain rattled, a cold cuff I hadn't noticed before jostling on my ankle.

It's growing, I realized. The nightmare was growing. When I sat still, not moving, just holding onto waiting, holding onto Hywel and Laszlo, waiting for rescue, there was nothing to be afraid of.

And Birsha wanted me afraid.

But I'd had to breathe—hadn't I?—and now the air was stale and sour and foul. I'd moved my sore body, and the bed had pricked me, tried to stand and found myself cuffed.

I don't want to see him. Seeing him again would be the worst thing, the most terrifying, *I thought suddenly. It wasn't hard to conjure the thought, because it was true. The one real blessing of the nightmares was that I hadn't had to see Birsha again. He was a phantom to me, so rarely present in the centuries I'd lived under his rule and yet there in every brick of the house, every client's stare, every bowl of rotten food and ordered word from guards.*

He hadn't needed to threaten me face-to-face, to tower over me—he wasn't a very large man, anyway—to hurt me directly. Birsha and his actions, his control, had surrounded me every second of every minute of every hour of every day. There was no escaping that.

A match hissed in the dark, blue and then orange light flaring in a small pool, just barely illuminating the white gloves its fine stick was pinched between.

My fingers dug into the ragged mattress beneath me, a clammy squish and the slow blooming arrival of a figure in the room with me making me stiff with fear.

And deep down inside of me, a tiny flare of victory that was easily squashed.

"The difficulty with men and monsters who make pretty vows is how often and how quickly they are broken."

I couldn't swallow the bile rising in my throat, too strangled with terror, and the acid burned hotly on the back of my tongue.

Birsha leaned forward, the unremarkable profile of his face shifting in the flare of the match. He was unrecognizable, impossible to remember, indistinguishable from any male face. Not ugly, not handsome, not interesting. A phantom that refused to make an impression.

The match licked at a whisper of paper, larger flames growing and curling, a tendril of smoke before a true fire caught.

A hearth, modest but certainly not anything that had existed in my cell.

Birsha stood with his back to me. "I imagine they promised not to abandon you, to protect and shield you from my reach. Did you know they would prove false? You've lived too long to make fantasies of knights in shining armor. Not from monsters, certainly."

The firelight should've reached farther, but the room was opaque. All I could see was Birsha's undefinable figure standing at the edge of the hearth. The light didn't even reach my own hands and feet. I was lost in the dark, alone, with him.

He turned and proved that the shadows belonged to him too by staring directly into my eyes. His features stretched into the mask of a smile, eerie and discomfiting by how clearly it didn't reach his eyes, didn't even seem to sit properly on his plain mouth.

"They've done me a favor. I see now I was too strict with your upkeep. You were quite losing your shine, not worth what I paid for you."

He'd paid me a small stack of coins. To watch.

Birsha did not blink, did not so much as twitch. "You will make me a grand fortune once more. Perhaps I should release your leash every few decades or so. Let you run wild, and then bring you back to heel refreshed. It did not take long. A few months, and you've fucked your way back to health."

I tried to tear my stare away, tried to flinch, but I was frozen.

"Rabid little creature. All appetite. No grace. You repulse me," Birsha said, voice oddly bright, delighted. "You are exactly what they want, the rutting beasts. You match them perfectly. Just cunt and cock, claws and mouth, the lot of you grinding yourself down to useless stubs in pursuit of nothing. How easy you make it for your betters to take the reins."

"I've heard you've had a difficult time lately."

Silence echoed, burned, pounded through my ears. I could not move, but I had spoken, stared directly into the hollow nothing of Birsha's gaze and said my thought out loud.

"You had to run." A strange heat, pride and fear mingling, oozed through me.

Birsha's eyes tore away from mine and I gasped, gagged convulsively at the air of the cell, but then swallowed and found a strange new flavor on my tongue. Incense. Amber and myrrh. Sea salt too.

"Who's there?" Birsha barked. He strode forward, but there was no

progress in the movement. He didn't loom closer, didn't reach me, didn't even seem to cross space. His nothing eyes blazed in the dark, but he couldn't reach me. "Little spy," he hissed in something like approval. "They used *you. Child of a goddess no one remembers, and all you're good for is the use of others. Just a* tool," *he spat. "My tool."*

"You ran. You were frightened," I said, finding that Birsha was not the only one now wearing the garish impression of a smile on their face. Mine was fierce and painful, the horrid twist of muscle I'd practiced for hours in the mirror.

"Enough!" Birsha shouted, the word like a blade of ice. He clapped his hands together, and the fire went out with a snap, dropping me back into darkness.

But I thought I saw the muscles of his face convulse in a flinch before he vanished.

I screamed and lunged from the bed, suddenly freed from my trapped pose. I reached for him as if I had Hywel's talons. Or Laszlo's. As if I might sprout Conall's fangs in my open mouth, Asterion's horns from my temples. I howled and reached out into the darkness. I would draw Birsha back, tear him open myself, end the nightmare—the one I'd lived through for centuries—in a flash of blood and claw.

But the cuff around my ankle caught, cold and cruel, and my foot slipped on the moss and grime of the stone floor, toppling me forward. Down, down, I would crash into the—

25.
A TENDER TRAP

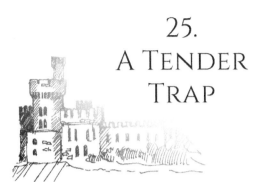

I gasped, upright and thrashing, gripped tight by my shoulders.

"Lovely girl, wonderful creature, *blodyn bach*," Hywel murmured, rising up from the bed in front of me, holding me tightly in his warm hands, gently cuffed.

Laszlo's nest was cool and dark, only a few candles tucked inside of glass lanterns at the edges of the room. The cloying memory of incense lingered in my nose but was quickly replaced by the fragrant oils and the soft, dry scent of feathers.

Kisses fluttered over my shoulders, crisp presses of tender lips. I shook, but Laszlo didn't retreat, his nose trailing over my skin.

"You did beautifully. So patient, my treasure," Hywel continued, one hand releasing me to pet at my cheeks. He smeared tears away and I gaped at him, lungs and body heaving for air. "My fearless goddess, you did so well. So brave."

I shivered as Laszlo traced careful fingertips up and down my spine, rewriting the sensation of my own skin in my mind. My head turned toward the window I'd crashed out of, but it was already repaned in glass and sealed tightly shut.

The sea air, I thought, not quite connected to my surroundings but ripped from the nightmare too.

"Never again, *blodyn bach*, I swear to you," Hywel said, still wiping my cheeks, pushing back sweaty strands of hair, drawing me into his warm chest.

I was burning up and frigidly cold all at once.

"Never again," Hywel repeated, kissing my temple.

Pretty vows.

I bit my lip, and Laszlo combed my hair back, tied it into a straight braid that brushed against the nape of my neck.

"Birsha has an—"

"Hywel, let her recover," Laszlo said, his arms sliding around my waist.

"Facts will ground her," Hywel answered, and continued, "He has an oneiros—a creature that feeds on dreams and forces nightmares—and an impressive witch working together. They steal your strength to keep from killing themselves with the work. But they're easy enough for me to shut out."

"He was there," I said, words barely audible.

Hywel was glowing in front of me, cool and handsome and fierce, and the longer I looked at him, the easier I found it to breathe. He nodded, thumbs still stroking my cheeks. "They have some of your blood, I think. The witch creates a channel. The oneiros opens your dreaming."

"Then it *was* him?"

"The cell you were in was part of the nightmare, but yes, that was Birsha," Hywel said, eyes flicking back and forth, watching me, my reactions.

I sucked in a deep breath and released it slowly, softening between them. "I could smell smoke, incense, like a church. And sea air." I glanced to the window once more to be certain, but it was still sealed shut, and there was no hint of brine and salt in the room.

Hywel blinked and looked over my shoulder at Laszlo. "She's right. I was focused on how they were manipulating her, but he skittered off like the rat he is for a reason—he didn't want us to see him, which means there was something to learn. Perhaps a hint of his location."

"Clever, brave, strong, wonderful," Laszlo whispered into my shoulder, his arms circling my waist, stroking my sides. I swallowed my whimper of protest and let my eyes slide shut.

"You must be exhausted," Hywel said, and warm lips pressed to my forehead.

I forced my eyes open and shook my head. "No, I-I don't

want to go back to sleep——" Hywel opened his mouth to reassure me, and I pressed my fingertips to his lips. "Please. I know you can keep me safe, but not yet."

His eyes narrowed, but he nipped sweetly at the pads of my fingers and nodded.

"Did they drain you very much?" Laszlo asked, petting my belly and down between my legs, along my inner thighs.

I tipped my head back to rest on his shoulder, taking a moment to breathe, to ground myself back in Laszlo's nest, between these two men. "I'm all right, but..." I was well stocked before falling asleep—*generously* so—and there was no hollow feeling in me now, even if I wasn't bursting at the seams with *néktar* any longer. But even if I wasn't starving, I wanted these men, I wanted their closeness, their skin and scents and sounds to erase the nightmare I'd escaped.

"Mm, well 'all right' certainly isn't good enough," Hywel said, grinning.

"Hywel, please——" I started, sighing his name out.

It was his turn to seal my lips shut, but he did it with a kiss, pushing me into the cradle of Laszlo's embrace. He pulled away but only just enough for his mouth to graze mine as he spoke. "You don't have to plead with us, *blodyn bach*. You never have to beg...although you sound so pretty when you do."

I blushed and turned my cheek to him, both wanting the lavish sweetness and affection they offered me, and feeling as though I ought to reject it for their own sakes.

But Hywel must've read something in my expression, because he continued. "I know what you think you deserve. Or, more accurately, what you think you *don't*. But I've seen proof to the contrary. Laz——"

Laszlo took his cue before I could argue, although the words to fight the pair of them didn't arrive readily to my lips, anyway. Laszlo's hands slid up, one to my chest to cup and cradle a breast, nipple teased between his knuckles, and the other to turn my face to the side. He twisted and caught my mouth in a deep kiss, our breaths quickly ragged and tongues teasing one another. Kissing Laszlo was always sweet, always thorough, and the taste of him reminded me of a rich white wine, oaky and golden.

Hywel took advantage of my turned head, nibbling and lapping at my throat. His hands completed the work Laszlo's could not, a rougher contrast on my neglected breast, an aimless circling path around my sex.

If he thought I'd meant to object to *this*, he was mistaken. Sexual distraction was exactly what I wanted, more sweat and scratches and straining for release. As much of myself I had left to recover after my captivity, this had returned easily. Whether arousal came to save myself from starvation or was a natural gift of my mother's blood, I was grateful.

I melted into Laszlo's chest, arching until my body pulled in complaint to take deeper draws of his kisses. Hywel's hand tugging and squeezing on my breast pushed me back, and Laszlo didn't hesitate, falling into the mattress with his wings spread out beneath him, drawing me down. Our mouths separated and I gasped for air before Hywel took his place, licking in, hungry and snarling, tongue hot and breath spiced. His fingers spread the lips of my sex open and I stretched, pressing one foot to the bed to cant my hips up, ready for him to slide his cock into me.

He only teased his fingers into my cunt, purring into the filthy kiss. He lifted his head, and Laszlo pressed warm, wet kisses to my cheek and shoulder.

"Do you know what I think?" Hywel asked.

I was catching my breath, squirming and finding Laszlo's cock between the cheeks of my ass, a little dew of precum kissing my skin.

"I think you could take the pair of us," Hywel continued, low voice rasping beautifully, the sound calling to me, peaking my nipples and making my core throb.

I sighed and found a coy, artful smile curling my lips, the kind of smile I'd used centuries ago to tease and tempt great men. It faltered briefly, rusty and unused, but only for a moment.

"I know I could," I said, now intentionally rocking, rubbing Laszlo's cock between my cheeks, arching my breasts up to catch Hywel's eye. It worked, and a rare shot of pride warmed me as he licked his lips and stared at their bounce.

"I think I could take you both too," Hywel said, smiling.

Laszlo's groan shuddered through us both. "Hywel, *yes*," he gasped.

My eyes widened as Hywel's face lowered to my chest, his glimmering gaze shining up at me, white eyelashes feathering and shrouding his stare as he looked down to my breasts again. His teeth looked sharper as his mouth opened.

"Would you like that, *blodyn bach*? The three of us all knotted together?"

"Yes," I said, nodding rapidly, then blinked. "How?"

Laszlo chuckled, his hands stroking my sides. "Yes, darling. How?"

Hywel gave us both a fangy grin, and I yelped and twitched on top of Laszlo as he nipped one breast and then the other with those sharp teeth.

"You first, *cariad*," Hywel said to Laszlo, and then his hand on my cunt slid down, taking Laszlo's cock and pressing it to the tight hole of my ass.

I moaned and shimmied my hips, and Laszlo's breath in my ear hitched.

Hywel had used my ass earlier in the night when they were still trying to exhaust me into slumber. I was tender and a little sore, but only enough for the press of the blunt tip to start a warm and needy awareness. Laszlo's hand replaced Hywel's, and the dragon pulled away momentarily, stiffening cocks bobbing between my legs. He returned with another bottle of oil, grinning and pouring the liquid generously over his cocks and into his hand.

"You really have the most exquisitely formed legs," Hywel murmured. "Lift them high for me, there's a good girl."

Laszlo and I both gasped as Hywel stroked his cock, my ass, even my pussy with the oil until every inch of us that touched was slippery and warm and sensitive. He pulled Laszlo back to my hole, and the oil, gravity, and a little buck of the gryphon's hips did the work. I released a wavering cry at the sharp stretch, but it softened quickly, my body so cheerfully familiar with these men.

Hywel pressed his thumb inside of my cunt, fingers stroking my sex aimlessly, and stared down at the pair of us. Laszlo was moving in a shallow mimic of a wave, rising gently into me. My legs trembled in the air, tired and weak and overwhelmed by the dense pressure of my ass being filled. Hywel caught one before it fell and smiled at me, bright and shining.

"Laszlo, you next," Hywel said, and then he pulled his hand free of my sex and grabbed Laszlo's softly furred calf, pushing it back, folding the gryphon slightly and changing the angle of his cock inside of me. This time we both cried out, barely covering the sound of Hywel's laughter. "Pretty holes. Pretty loves. My treasures. I've been desperate to do this since the pair of you fondled me in the hoard."

"I'm surprised it took you this long," Laszlo said, voice ragged, body still nudging sweetly into me. His hands guided my legs to rest over his, stretching me open wider, my breath catching on a whimper. Laszlo's head turned and his voice softened, pretending to whisper in my ear. "Hywel's not known for his patience—Oh!"

Laszlo yelped, his arms latching around me and hips bucking roughly up as Hywel grabbed us both around our thighs, hauling us to him. The tip of his cock nuzzled and rubbed and slid against me, but it was Laszlo who received the abrupt plunge, and it made the gryphon go taut and wild beneath me.

"Some things are worth waiting for," Hywel said, winking at me as Laszlo shuddered and settled. "Are you ready, *blodyn bach*?"

He was moving gently into Laszlo, his upper cock rubbing against me, and I joined him in the motion, riding Laszlo's cock, stealing the friction from Hywel, the pair of us tormenting our gryphon lover. Poor Laszlo was trapped beneath me, filled and clasped and surrounded. His breath was ragged in my ear, full of little sighs and grunts.

I was jealous.

"Fuck me, King of Dreams and King of Clouds," I said, just barely loud enough to be heard.

Laszlo groaned and nibbled on my lobe, but Hywel just beamed that sharp and feral smile down at me. He reached down, and the slick stroke of his cock became a thick and determined plunge that stole my breath from my lungs, left me still and tense, marveling at the sudden possession of my body.

So exquisitely full. Such incredible, dense pressure. My eyes squeezed shut, and my body arched and braced for more.

Sharp teeth pricked at my breasts, jolting me. I gasped for air, and Hywel rolled into me, Laszlo echoing the motion with a long moan. Their hands pet and soothed and groped at my skin and I writhed between them, a compulsive need to *move* and *feel.*

"You're perfect, Evanthia," Laszlo whispered in my ear, his hands stroking over my legs.

"Divinely delicious," Hywel hissed, fangs scraping delicately over my nipple.

I whined and squirmed, rocking between their cocks, one hand flying back to dive into Laszlo's hair, another reaching to grasp Hywel's ass and pull him closer.

"So beautiful, so *tight, my go*—" Laszlo's praise died off with a choked sound of pleasure.

Hywel's hand reached to my cheek, rubbing there until I opened my eyes again to firelight and the dragon hovering over me, body close and taut, so deep inside of me and barely moving. His gaze glowed as it held mine.

"You give your body so sweetly, *blodyn bach*," Hywel said.

I shook my head. I wanted fucking, not this...this assault of sweet lovers' words. "Hywel—stop, please—"

His hand on my cheek slid over to my lips, and I couldn't help but bite and suck on his digits. But with me muted, it gave him room to speak.

"Such a warm, loving treasure," Hywel said, his own voice growing rough. Laszlo's motions were urgent, fucking us both, forcing Hywel deeper into me, into *us*, a perfect tangle of our hips all fastened and circling for more friction, more contact. "Such a strong heart. Yes, you take us so well, don't you, my *blodyn bach*? You were made for this."

"Yes," I gasped, lost somewhere between their bodies and his speech.

"Yes, made to be loved," he said.

I snarled, trying to grab Hywel by his broad shoulders and pull his mouth to mine to shut him up, but he laughed. Laszlo caught my hands, drawing them back up over both our heads. Hywel gazed warmly down at us, and Laszlo's mouth sucked and laved at my throat until I could barely stand to keep my eyes open.

"You're ours to love now, dear one," Laszlo whispered.

I tried to open my mouth to object, but then Hywel touched me at my core, pinching my clit and making me yelp before treating it with gentle pressing circles.

"Our pretty, perfect mate," Hywel growled. He moved now, thrusting softly into us both, Laszlo panting into my throat.

"Please," I gasped, but I no longer knew what I was asking for. This wasn't sex for relief, wasn't wild abandon; it was *adulation* and devotion, and I couldn't tell them to stop, couldn't beg them for more, either.

"We're going to take your heart, Evanthia," Hywel whispered. "We lay claim to it and to all of you. And if you want to fight us with your pretty claws and sweet little teeth, we will take your scratches and bites too. *All* of you."

I was dizzy. The pair of them had taken me to some strange and impossible height, not ecstasy or panic, but some mix of the two. It was only Laszlo's hands that connected me to the real world, his touch and Hywel's eyes on mine as he thrust and snarled and groaned. Hywel's fingers stroked and swirled over my clit, thumb kissing and sliding in to join his cock, grasping onto my sex.

"Mate," Laszlo whispered into my throat, his voice breaking and body bucking wildly in contrast to Hywel's steady movement. "Love. Oh, Evanthia, I—"

Their words had found fissures in me, all the tiny places I threatened to break apart, and it was Laszlo's pleading and Hywel's fangs scratching sweetly on my breast that cast the final blow. I shouted wordlessly, body wracked and quaking, and then I was all in pieces, beautiful, glittering shards that should've torn through them both, cut the very fabric of the air and world apart. Except that Laszlo and Hywel were holding me so tightly, arms and legs wrapped around me.

Their bodies shifted, someone pulling inside of me, and I moaned in protest, shivering, rattling in all my little broken parts. They stilled, arms tightening around me, until I realized there must've been some whole pieces, because my bones ached at their grip. My face came back together as Hywel licked my cheeks, cleaning tears away.

"No," I breathed out, but I didn't want to move, didn't want them to release me to be wreckage on the lovely bed, all fractured in candlelight.

"Yes," Hywel said, kissing my mouth. That too was still in one piece, and my tongue tied easily with his. He pulled away too soon, and my lungs filled with air, no cracks to let it escape. My eyes opened, and Hywel was fuzzy, milky with tears, and too close for my gaze to know where to look. "Yes, *blodyn bach*. If your heart is not whole yet, you have use of ours."

Laszlo kissed the back of my neck, nose nuzzling the spot. "My wings are yours, dear one."

"And my fire," Hywel whispered, kissing me once more.

And as if to prove his point, our hearts did seem to match tempos, Laszlo and Hywel pressed so closely to me that I could feel them drumming together, easing and slowing as Hywel kept my objections silent with his steady kisses.

26.
WINNING
HAND

I didn't remember sleeping, but I woke with dawn curling tendrils of light through nests of clouds.

"You don't know me," I whispered, the argument ready on my tongue, as if I'd slept with the words just waiting to burst free.

Hywel was awake, of course. He was still careful not to sleep, sitting up in the bed with me leaning against his hip and Laszlo still tightly fastened to my back. Long, pale fingers stroked my hair back from my face, and then the dragon shimmied down into the bed until we were nose to nose.

"You think I don't know the woman who dreamed in my lap? Who washed my scales while I was sleeping? Who saw the loneliness in my mate and gave him hope and reminded him how to feel affection?" Hywel blinked at me and waited for a moment, but I'd only had the single sentence ready and I was still foggy from the restless night, warm and pleasantly sore, surrounded by their bodies. "What have you hidden from us, Evanthia? What lies have you told?"

I nibbled on my lips, swollen and tender from kisses, and Hywel waited patiently, touching me everywhere he could reach in an absentminded pattern.

"What if I can't love you back?" I asked at least.

I expected him to frown or growl or object or correct me in some way. Instead, he simply took a deep breath and continued touching me, looking at me. "That's not quite the same thing as you not wanting to be loved," he said. He shifted, turning onto his back, still pressed against me. I couldn't help myself. I leaned in and rested my cheek on his shoulder, traced the elegant muscle of his arm with my fingertips. "Let's say, hypothetically speaking of course, that years go by and you find yourself never really in love with us, not wanting to remain at our side..." He paused, and I held my breath. "We wouldn't *force* you to stay."

Asterion had demanded I be free to stay or leave as I chose, but I suspected if I told Hywel now that I was leaving the castle, he would *not* allow me to do so. It ought to have rankled me or made me tense with the sense of being trapped. Except I didn't *want* to leave. I didn't want to leave this bed, these men, this castle. I felt as though I should, but Hywel had more or less refused to let me turn away.

"What if I was in love with someone else?" I asked, less determined to prove to Hywel that he shouldn't care for me and now more curious about the terms of such a relationship.

He only shrugged. "It would depend on how detestable they were. *I* am in love with someone else, you know," he pointed out, nodding over my shoulder to Laszlo and taking a moment to smile at the sight of the sleeping gryphon.

"That's different. He's—He and I—I mean, we—"

Hywel's eyebrows rose, mouth twitching, and I licked my lips and tried to think of a way of making my point without making it sound as if I'd already settled myself as their mate.

"Are you in love with someone else, *blodyn bach*?" Hywel asked gently.

I opened my mouth to say no. To say that if I was going to fall in love at all, if I *was* capable, it would probably be with a whole mess of men at once, but I wasn't in love *now. I'm not, right?* I wondered, a little panicked. Any possible *theoretical* other gentlemen in question weren't at the castle. Not at the moment. But was that as good as admitting that I was already on the way to falling in love?

What had *happened* to me?

I'd been so...so frozen, a captive in my own body, and now I was basically squirming under Hywel's stare, thinking about horns and fur and feathers and scales.

"No," I forced out. The word felt odd on my tongue.

He smiled at me. "Well, then. Nothing to do about it but let things be as they are. How about breakfast? You ought to be hungry after last night."

I gaped at him as he slid from the bed, rifling his hand through his hair, pale strands fluffy and sticking up at odd angles. His body was fascinating, all sharp corners and elegant lines, shimmering scales beneath his skin. My mouth went dry as he bent, rifling through a pile of clothes, his lower cock peeking out between his long, lean thighs. He twisted, eyes sparkling with laughter as he caught me staring.

I tugged the sheet up to cover my blushing cheeks and nodded. "Food is good," I said stupidly.

⚭

"You're completely neglecting your left side," Laszlo said, frowning and backing away from me, his head shaking.

"I'm exhausted."

"Well, trouble never comes when you're well-rested and ready for a good fight, my dear," he answered primly, chin jutting up. "You have to be well-trained, regardless of the circum-stances. And right now, you are *failing to defend your left side*. Again."

I scowled at the gryphon and didn't move.

"Evanthia," he said, slightly sharp.

"I'm going to pluck out your feathers while you're sleeping!" I blinked and stiffened, gasping at the venom in my tone.

Laszlo arched an eyebrow. "You could *try*," he answered coolly. I could've sworn he was holding back laughter.

We stared at one another for a long moment. I was sore from sex before I'd even walked into the training room, but Laszlo had shown me no mercy.

Is this loving? I wanted to ask, but was too afraid to speak the words. I'd been afraid of Hywel and Laszlo treating me with tenderness, afraid of how I was supposed to respond to longing looks and heartfelt words.

Instead, I was being snapped at for poor posture while defending myself with a battle axe.

"Evanthia, I *know* you can do better," Laszlo said firmly. "Even exhausted. Now...*again*."

I sighed and ignored the burn and tremble of my arms as I raised the weapon once more, pausing to consider the angles we stood at, the patterns of movement Laszlo used when "attacking" me in practice. I'd been leading with my right side, the side I held the weapon on, keeping my left tucked behind me. But Laszlo had repeatedly managed to twist around and catch me there.

My right side held the weapon...my left needed defending...

Laszlo watched, patient, as I puzzled out the issue.

I switched my feet in the stance, turning my left side forward, twisting my body. Now my left side was guarded, but I could easily swing the axe back if Laszlo attacked me on the right.

"Much better," he said with a small smile, and then he leapt forward, wings beating and talons raised.

❦

I GLANCED UP FROM MY HAND AT ANOTHER ROUGH PUFF OF breath from Hywel's lips. His eyes were narrowed at his own hand, at the cards dropped to the table, and there was a frustrated wrinkle on the bridge of his nose.

"He's very bad at bluffing," Laszlo said to me in a false whisper, earning himself a quick glare from his mate. "But he also has a tendency to catastrophize his hands. He's tossed out entire winning hands before, assuming everyone at the table had better."

"Yes, thank you, *cariad*," Hywel snapped, discarding a knave of hearts to the table roughly.

The deck was old and stained, hand-painted with an ink that had turned from red to rust over the years. I'd seen similar decks before my captivity, and there was something about the castle, these men, and a game of cards by the fire that transported me back to centuries ago. I was going to end up the loser of this game—*two* aces in the hand and not a chance to rid myself of them yet—but my heart was strangely light, a smile almost constantly poised on my lips.

I slipped my right foot free of the heeled shoe I'd worn to dance in earlier and tucked it under my voluminous skirt, leaning back in the armchair that smelled of rose oil—some long-lost visitor's perfume, perhaps.

"Perhaps he should be worried this time," I murmured to Laszlo, smiling.

Hywel glared at me now, and his scowl deepened as he pulled a new card, but Laszlo gave me a canny glance from the corner of his eyes and his lips twitched. I had a feeling the gryphon already knew what we were all holding in our hands, what was left in the deck, and how the game would all shake out by the end.

"It will be better when the others return," Hywel muttered. "We'll have proper numbers. Three for Losing Lodam doesn't quite count out right."

Laszlo hummed out a noncommittal agreement and then deftly settled a king to the table, winning the trick. Hywel grumbled, and I tucked my grin against my shoulder.

Laszlo reached for the deck to determine our next trump suit when the loud thunder of knocking sounded through the castle.

I stiffened in my chair, and Laszlo's wings rustled, but Hywel threw his cards down with a grateful shout and jumped up.

"See?" Laszlo said to me, nodding to Hywel's discarded hand. All modest values in a good mix of suits. He probably would've won.

I forced a smile while I chewed on the inside of my lip, more concerned with who was at the door than our abandoned game. Laszlo reached for my hand, and I snatched at him gratefully.

"It's all right," he said softly.

"I smell wolf," Hywel called from the hall.

My breath caught and Laszlo smiled, rising from his seat and holding out his arm for me to take. I tucked my foot back into the shoe I'd abandoned and slipped my arm through Laszlo's, smoothing my skirt with my free hand. It wasn't until I'd calmed my nerves that I realized Laszlo was also fidgeting, smoothing back his hair and rolling his shoulders, stretching and folding his wings in and out.

"Are you nervous?" I murmured to him.

Laszlo stiffened, chin bucking up proudly, and then blinked and glanced at me, a light blush blooming on his cheeks. "They haven't met yet."

It took me a moment to realize who meant. Hywel. Hywel and Conall. Which meant the undercurrent of flirtation and sexual tension I'd noticed between Conall and Laszlo hadn't been my imagination.

"Did you and Conall ever..."

Laszlo glanced toward the open door. "A long time ago. But his heart wasn't in it, and I was lonely. It had possibility, but he didn't strike me as...sincere. Until you."

Laszlo's hand was covering mine on his arm, and I raised my own free hand to link our fingers together. I had no idea what Hywel and Conall would make of each other. And I wasn't sure how sincere Conall really was, at least romantically. I didn't want to offer Laszlo empty reassurance, so instead I leaned in, kissing firmly at the corner of his jaw, nuzzling the delicate feathers there. He gusted out a sigh that ruffled loose strands of my hair and then nodded.

We were just stepping into the hall to follow Hywel's path when we heard the dragon's growling words.

"What on earth is *that* doing here?"

"Hello, pigeon," a silken, masculine tone greeted.

"Oh dear," Laszlo murmured, pausing in his step and glancing at me, wincing. "The Wyrm."

I'd heard the name mentioned a few times now, a possible nearby ally, and curiosity to see them at last made my steps quick, but Laszlo tightened his arm around mine.

"Stay back. Hywel won't want you tangled up with the Wyrm," Laszlo whispered before we turned a corner.

"Are they enemies?" I asked, surprised Asterion and Conall would go to someone Hywel deemed as a threat.

"They were lovers, ages ago," Laszlo said, waving his hand. "They nearly killed each other before the end of it."

We turned the corner, and the three men stood at the door at the end of the hall, Hywel's spine rigid and proud as he blocked the other two from entering.

"Rolant."

Rolant, the Wyrm, was a few inches shorter than Hywel, about the same height as Conall, with lovely, refined bone structure and long, straight brown hair. He was quite attractive, except that when his gaze glanced around Hywel's shoulder and he found Laszlo and me at the back of the hall, there was something cold and almost lifeless about the pale eyes staring at me.

"I don't mind the pair of you hissing at one another here in the cold, but I'd like to go inside, if you don't mind," Conall said, stepping forward.

He looked tired and a little ragged, and I wondered where and how long it had been since he last slept. Hywel's arms were holding the doors open and blocking Conall's entrance, and for a moment I wondered if Hywel would shut the door on them both, his forearms taut with tension.

Conall looked up at the dragon who had claimed me and spoke a few words I couldn't hear, although I thought Laszlo must've caught them because he choked on stifled laughter.

"I will manage Hywel and Rolant," Laszlo murmured to me. "You...settle Conall in. But be sure to come up to the nest before you retire."

I nodded, still watching Hywel and Conall, and Laszlo pulled his hands from mine, kissing my temple. He stepped in front of me, wings blocking my view briefly, and then he was halfway down the hall and Conall was practically charging toward me.

Was it my imagination, or was there a sunken quality to his cheeks? Had he not eaten in the past few weeks? Not slept? He was marching toward me with shoulders hunched forward and a dark stare, almost angry, and I braced myself, placing one hand against the wall as a snarl erupted from his throat.

He didn't slow, even as he was only feet away, and I stumbled back for a brief moment until his arms snapped around my waist, hauling me roughly to his chest. His entire body was shaking, and I gasped at the viselike grip of him around me. Tangled red hair filled my vision as Conall pressed his nose and mouth to the side of my face, hot breath rushing over my throat, tongue swiping out to stroke along my jaw.

"Conall?" I breathed, startled by the force of him.

He smelled like the woods and he was still moving, pushing me around the corner, out of sight, which was a bit of a relief because the Wyrm was still *staring* at me, watching with narrowed eyes.

"*Mo chroí*," Conall growled, spinning me, pinning me to the wall and pressing himself firmly against me until I was forced to open my legs to make room for his.

My arms settled around his shoulders at last, stroking him through his coat, shocked by the quake of him, the way his entire body seemed to rattle with every breath, full gasps of air against my throat. Conall's arms only loosened enough for his hands to slide down my skirt to grab roughly at my ass, tugging our hips firmly together.

"Are you...are you *all right*?" I asked, a startled laugh rising from my lips. Bitter smoke clung to his hair and coat, but he was warm and familiar, and my nose was nuzzling into his hair.

"I *missed* you," Conall breathed, and the grip of his hands shifted to gather up fistfuls of my skirt, hauling it up around my waist.

I laughed properly now and reached back to still his hands, my head against the wall, nudging his back so I could find his gaze. Dark circles hung heavily under his green gaze, the color sharp in contrast to the little lines of sleepless red that surrounded his irises.

"I need you, Evie," Conall said, eyes wide, lips turned down. "Please, *mo chroí*. I *need* you."

It wasn't seduction but *desperation*, and it washed my humor away. I let go of his hands, but he didn't start to tear my skirt up my legs again, and when I took his face in my palms he moaned and leaned his cheek into my touch, sagging bodily into me.

"Please," he rasped, bucking weakly against me.

I brought his mouth to mine for a soft kiss and Conall shuddered and pressed closer, weak, entreating sounds falling from his lips as he hunted for another kiss, and then another, tongue flicking and teeth nibbling. Not rough, not *demanding*. Begging.

I pulled away and kissed above the scar on his right brow as he whimpered.

"A little privacy, and I'm yours," I whispered.

27.
HOWL AND
KNOT

Conall kicked the door open to reveal a dark room with the large and looming figure of a bed at its center. His arms were full of me, of my skirt, his face buried in the now torn collar of my dress, roughly shaven jaw scraping against the top of my breasts as he bit and laved at my skin.

I gasped as he yanked the torn collar open wider and rooted in to find my nipple, suckling on it roughly. He marched us inside the room, the door hanging open behind us. For a moment, I considered reminding him to close it, and then I was dropped onto a large, slightly dusty sheet that covered the bed.

A little privacy, I'd said, and that was what he'd done. I'd always appreciated his eagerness, and I couldn't help but be flattered by it now.

Conall clearly didn't intend to stop. Oh, he would if I asked, I knew that, but he was climbing onto the bed, snarling and trembling, vibrating with holding himself back.

"Do you like this dress?" he asked, pausing with one clawed hand wrapped around my collar, his knuckles grazing my nipple as he waited for my answer.

I arched an eyebrow up at him. It was dark, but I knew he would see the look clearly. "I did before you tore it."

He grunted and then yanked, tugging me up from my splayed position on the bed for a moment before the fabric gave way, silk shredding open down to my navel. "Sorry."

I barked out an awkward laugh at his meaningless apology, and Conall hovered above me, waiting for me to recover.

"God, I missed that sound," he whispered, bending his head and kissing my now exposed shoulder. He moaned and rubbed his bristly cheek against my skin. "I missed the scent of you." He stifled another growl and then he was rising up, pulling at the skirt of the dress, distracted by my hips, groping my ass and burying his face in my stomach. "You're getting stronger."

"Rounder," I allowed. I'd been gaining weight back under Laszlo's diligent care, and I was starting to feel familiar in my own body, soft and lush once more.

Conall managed to shimmy the waist of the dress over my ass, and he took a moment to study those restored curves appreciatively, hands stroking with something akin to reverence. He pressed hot, open-mouthed kisses over my stomach and then down to where my legs were trapped together, a soft tangle of pale curls covering my mound.

I hadn't bothered with undergarments—Hywel wasn't much more patient than Conall at the moment—but I felt strangely exposed, stretched out on the sheet in this bare and dark room, with Conall still fully dressed in all the layers for traveling.

"So soft," he murmured. "Want to sink into you. Claws, teeth, cock. All of me."

I'd wanted much the same when I first found my sexual appetite with these monsters, and it made me sit up and reach for him.

"Conall."

"Need to taste you," he muttered. "But fuck, I need to be *inside* of you."

"Conall," I repeated, a little sharper.

He stiffened, almost flinched, and looked up, eyes wild and glowing in the darkness.

"Conall, what happened?" I asked, scooting back and pulling my legs free of the skirt. He stared at my limbs as they appeared, licking his lips. "Are you all right?"

He blinked, shook himself, and then delivered me a crooked smile that didn't quite reach his eyes. "*Mo chroí*, you don't need to worry yourself for me."

I frowned and tucked my legs closer and he blinked at me, at the wadded-up dress he was lying on top of now, torn down to the waist. He sat up, drawing in a deep breath, shoving a hand into his hair to comb it back and wincing as his fingers caught in tangles. He shook his hand free and then stood at the foot of the bed, tearing off his coat and dropping it to the floor, claws tugging ruthlessly at the buttons of his waistcoat and then shirt until they both hung open over his chest.

"Come back to me, Evie," he said gently, kneeling on the bed and already crawling in my direction.

I stretched and he caught me, pulling me close so our bare chests pressed firmly together. He sighed and tucked his face into my shoulder, cradling me in his arms.

"I came at you like a beast, I'm sorry," he whispered.

I settled my hands in his hair, my own gentler, patient fingers working at the tangles for him. "I don't mind that. But you seem...on edge."

He leaned back, rolling to lie down on the bed with me clasped to his side. There was a little light from the woods outside the window and a faint glow from the staircase we'd entered the room from, just enough for me to make out his face as he gazed up at me.

"I meant what I said—I missed you," he said, one hand stroking slowly up the back of my thigh, over my ass, to cup and squeeze briefly before moving up and over to my shoulder. "I missed your mouth, your skin, your taste." He lifted his chin and I bent, offering him a slow, shallow kiss that teased. "The sounds you make. The way you smell. Asterion's not here, is he? Idiot. I should've stayed."

"Hush." I kissed him again, smoothing my fingers through his hair before sliding them down his chest to clasp his length through his trousers.

Conall groaned eagerly, bucking up into my grip, his cock jumping and jerking through the fabric. "Need you," he ground out through bared teeth.

"I know you do. Help me undress you."

Conall was as respectful of his own clothes as he had been of my borrowed dress, and a button of his trousers went popping off and rattling over the stone floor. I had to climb off him to avoid being elbowed as he tore his pants off and tried to tear his shirt away without managing the waistcoat first. He still had an arm tangled in one sleeve, cuff buttoned too tightly, when I leaned into him, laughing at his urgency, and his control snapped.

I was thrown to my back, Conall's arms tight around my thighs, holding them open and high, his face buried against my cunt. I howled as he feasted, and my fingers made new tangles in their grip. Conall's mouth was deadly on a woman's sex, I thought. He worshiped me with his mouth, kissing my body like a lover he'd lost for years, starving sounds echoing into my tender skin. When I moved, shamelessly grinding myself into his face, he only encouraged more, rocking my body in his hands, painting my arousal over his chin and cheeks and nose, lapping his tongue inside of me to draw out more.

Hywel would laugh and goad him on. They'd make a sport of eating me in this way, a lewd meal of my pleasure, I thought, and then Conall nipped and sucked on my clit, kissed it sweetly before claiming it roughly with his lips. Ecstasy flashed, whip-quick and just as fierce. I let out a sharp cry, tipped at the edge and falling, when Conall pulled away.

I moaned at the deprivation, tumbling weakly over the edge but without his touch to heighten the sensation.

He scrambled over me, and I was just about to pout, to scold him for abandoning his efforts, when he plunged mercilessly inside of me.

The knife's edge returned as if dragging me backward through the release. I shouted, my body enfolding him in my grip, legs and arms and cunt clasping him to me. His mouth found mine in that same hungry possession he'd lavished on my sex, and I licked my own tangy flavor from his tongue, our bodies rolling into one another. He was speaking into me, groaning and growling, but I couldn't tear myself away to make out the words. One clawed hand clasped around the back of my neck, the other digging into my ass as we rutted clumsily, desperately, all appetite to make up for the lack of seduction, the failure of finesse.

"Yes, those sounds, those wet sounds your body makes as I fuck you," Conall hissed in my ear. "I missed those."

I shook my head, face hot, now trying to *ignore* those sounds.

"You get so slick when I talk to you," Conall said, and this time his grin was wild and broad and real, sparkling in the dark as he raised himself enough to meet my eyes. "I tell you that when I snap my hips like this, push my knot at your opening" — I moaned and my heels pressed into his ass to make him do it again— "you splash against me, and you turn pink all over and just *gush* a little, even before you come."

I turned my face away and Conall's hand on my neck tightened, forcing my stare back to his.

"You smell like dragon cum. And gryphon too. You have them all over you, you practically *shine* with it. But when I'm in you, you smell like a bitch in *heat*."

I growled at him and darted up, snapping my teeth into the flesh on his shoulder. Conall yelped, and his whole body tensed and stretched, and then his weight flattened me on the bed and his hips pressed hard, and that heavy stone of pressure that pounded against my opening *pushed* and *burrowed*. I howled, and Conall snarled and stopped, making to draw away.

I smacked his back without thinking. "Don't. I want it," I gasped out, my hips trying to rise to chase his knot. "You said— you said, in a bed—"

Conall whimpered. "Fuck. Fuck, *mo chroí*, you don't know what you're doing to me."

The fragile tear in the words made me pause and I tried to twist, to find his face, to ask him to explain, but then he was pushing again, nudging and digging at my body, the dense hard heat of his knot threatening to tear me open. Conall groaned, head thrown back, throat flexing, and then he wiggled, just a little shake of his hips, the same way he'd shimmied the dress off my hips, but this was *in*, forcing and shoving and—

I clamped around him, thighs and arms squeezing, as his knot lodged itself inside of me like a *boulder* that had made me its home. The pressure seemed to compound and expand and grow and grow, in my core, my heart, my throat, behind my eyes, until there was nowhere left for it to travel.

Conall bellowed and his hips churned forward in a beautiful swooping motion, and the pressure burst. I sobbed as I came, an earthquake that ran through me, stole my breath, wiped my vision clean and bright. Conall kept moving, slow and deep, and his mouth was at my ear, my jaw, my cheek, brief kisses and licks. He was gasping, molten heat flooding me. His hands scooped under my ass, tilted me just an inch, and we fastened together like a perfect single piece, as if we'd always meant to fit this way. The painful pleasure sweetened, turned syrupy and soft, left me limp and drunk and grinning. It rode me in the waves of Conall's movement, his brow furrowed as he stared down at me and rocked inside of me, tender flutterings echoing out of every motion, running a decadent path through my muscles.

"Oh, Evie," he whispered, and I could barely hear the plea of my name under the roar of my own blood rushing through my veins, his gasps ragged and loud in my ears.

"Kiss," I begged, and his mouth sealed to mine.

A perfect circuit, I thought, our bodies now twice fastened. Our tongues licked and twined, our breaths wove through one another. I wasn't empty at all. I wasn't broken. I just hadn't tried putting the right pieces together before now. I'd been missing *this*.

"I can't fall asleep," I murmured, fighting to keep my eyes open under the assault of Conall's gentle, thorough massage.

"Not if you keep forcing yourself to stay awake," Conall agreed lightly, thumbs stroking firmly down my spine, pleasant little pops echoing and tingling after his touch.

"No, I mean..." I groaned as he dug into my lower back and then shook my head. "I mean that Birsha has been getting into my head while I sleep. Using nightmares to drain me, torment me."

Conall stiffened as I started to speak, and by the end he had me rolled onto my back.

Sometime after the endless rocking storm of sensation of his knot inside of me, Conall had calmed and slipped free. I'd watched, curled on my side, as he'd built us a small fire in the hearth, his lean lines glowing in the light, tail swinging absently against the back of his bare thighs, brushing through the curling red hair on his legs. He returned to the bed, wrapping himself around me and kissing me until I couldn't breathe.

I looked up at him now and studied his face. Was it the glow of the fire, or were the circles under his eyes now softened?

"Evie, he's been *what?*"

I opened my mouth to tell Conall about the nightmare that had thrown me out of a tower window and then shut it once more. He was more relaxed than when he'd arrived at the castle, and I thought that might ruin his mood. Instead, I explained what Hywel had learned and how.

"Hywel keeps them from returning," I said, letting my hands wander over the firm, broad planes of Conall's chest.

Conall stared down at me, holding his breath for a beat before releasing it slowly. "Well, I suppose the sleepy beast is good for something."

"Generous of you."

I startled, but Conall must've known Hywel was there, hovering in the dark hall outside of the bedroom, because he only winked at me and rolled to his side to face the still open door.

"I did wonder why the Wyrm was so eager to visit in person. Did you toss him out the back again?" Conall asked Hywel.

Hywel leaned in the doorway, ankles crossed, a sweetly scented smoke rising from a rolled cigarette held between his fingers. Not tobacco, according to Laszlo, but dried flowers—a treat Hywel liked to indulge in. The dragon's gaze flicked between us, but he didn't seem tense or irritated to find me with Conall, just curious. "I considered dropping him into the dreaming sea, but I'd feel sorry for wherever he washed up. I would've warned you not to involve him. He can't be trusted."

They both looked to me, and Conall's wily smile faded.

"Do you think he'd help Birsha?" Conall asked.

Hywel snorted and shook his head, rolling the cigarette in his fingers but never bringing it to his lips. "No dragon would. But he'll steal whatever he thinks is most valuable here. And you and

I both know what that is," Hywel said. And this time neither one of them looked at me, simply held each other's gazes. Conall nodded once, first, and then Hywel dipped his head in answer. He straightened and smiled at me. "It's time to come back to the nest. Unless we're all sleeping here in this dusty little guest room."

"Conall tore my dress," I said, sitting up in the bed, stealing the sheet to wrap around me.

"Wicked puppy," Hywel purred.

Conall remained stretched on the bed, exposed as I slid to the edge and took the sheet with me, long and languid, all muscle and scar and lovely coppery red fur. Hywel examined the smoke curling around his fingers with a focus that pretended to be lazy but was really quite intentional.

"You can come along too, wolf. Laszlo certainly won't mind, nor our lovely treasure, I'm sure."

I ducked my head to hide my smile at the carefully casual invitation. Either Laszlo had said something, or Hywel missed nothing. Perhaps both.

When Conall didn't immediately answer, I turned to look back on the bed. Conall was staring at me, some cross between the desperation he'd been full of earlier and a cool reserve. He was sprawled on the bed, bare to our gazes, but I thought he seemed braced as if ready to fight or run.

"No nightmares," I murmured, reaching a hand out to him. "Just sleep."

Conall looked at my hand as if it were an asp that might lash out and bite him, as if it were a life rope he could latch onto. Slowly, his head shook, arms and legs stretching a little wider over the bed.

"I'll do just fine here, *mo chroí*. You go on and get your rest. We'll run the meadow in the morning."

I wanted to dig into his thoughts, make him answer all my questions. Why was he falling to pieces to touch me when he'd arrived and now so terrified to come to bed with me and the others? Was he like Asterion? Did he want to claim me for himself and no one else? But he didn't seem *jealous*.

Hywel's smoke drifted into the room, lavender and rose, and

I sighed. I'd had enough of questions and confusion. Hywel and Laszlo made their feelings clear, their intentions known. It frightened me, yes, but it was a comfort too.

I turned, and my extended hand slid into Hywel's free one as he led me back to the nest.

28.
THE WYRM

"Why...why *is* Rolant here?" I asked through gasping breaths, hands clasped around my ribs to keep them from splitting open, which they clearly wanted to do.

I'd thought Conall's morning meadow run was just an excuse to have me alone again, but instead he seemed to take up his training in earnest.

"He's as old as Hywel, and he doesn't go about sleeping for centuries," Conall said, his own voice a little rough as he fell back into the grass, splayed out under the rising sun, tall shadows of grass streaking lines across his white linen shirt. "He doesn't help out of the goodness of his heart—everything is a transaction—but he's been cooperating, getting us in contact with some of the...less conversational monsters. A lot of the older monsters take issue with Birsha, not because of his actions, but because to them, he's an upstart human not minding his place."

I puffed and fell to my knees in the grass just a couple feet away from Conall. His head turned, and the green of his eyes matched the stalks that obscured his face.

"Come here," he said.

"I want more information," I answered.

"Then you'll have it...over here."

I crawled to his side and Conall pulled me to straddle his lap, pressing my hips down to sit firmly.

"You're going to distract me."

He shook his head. "I just like the way you feel right here. I like holding you this way," he added, and his hands squeezed my ass but he didn't move us into a grind. I was tempted, but I braced my hands on his chest and stared down at him.

"Well?" I prompted.

"I didn't know the history between Hywel and the Wyrm. He's never been *that* willing to speak to me. I'm next to human in his eyes, even if I do have...a reputation. But when I mentioned Hywel was starting to wake, he was all charm suddenly. He gave up the locations of three ancient beasts we've been searching for in exchange for me allowing him to join me on my return."

I frowned and twisted to look back at the castle. "That seems suspicious."

"I thought so too, but Asterion said he could be trusted if we needed his help protecting you, and on our journey, Rolant seemed to know the way here. Are you worried for them?" Conall asked. I blinked, and he added, "Hywel and Laszlo? Or for yourself?"

My lips parted and I paused, staring down at Conall. "Not for myself—I know none of you would let anything happen to me. For Hywel, I think. Laszlo said they nearly killed each other before they left one another. What if Rolant wanted to come and finish the fight?"

"Then he'll end up dead, I expect," Conall said. "Hywel's a mated dragon now, nicely refreshed from centuries of rest and power accumulation. In a real fight between the pair of them, Rolant wouldn't stand a chance."

"Being mated makes a difference?" I asked.

Hywel called me his mate too. Did it matter if I was or wasn't when he was already mated to Laszlo?

Conall's stare drifted away and he shrugged in the grass. "It does for almost all monsters. There's a doctor who...makes a study of us with our consent. He says it changes something in the blood. Amongst werewolves, having a mate is having someone to fight *for*, a reason to survive a battle. It's an honor from the gods to find that in life," he said with a strangely bitter note to his voice.

"You sound like you don't believe that," I said.

Conall stiffened and then relaxed once more, meeting my gaze again, his eyes narrowed slightly as if he were looking up at the sun, even though it was ahead of me, safely out of his view.

"I do," he said slowly. "I think it is also... To have something so precious, so perfect, so much a part of yourself...it changes you. It makes everything else in the world...*less*. And I think that's dangerous. If not to you or to your mate, but to the rest of the world."

I opened my mouth to ask if Conall had been mated, but he sat up before I could speak, wrapping his arms around me and rolling us in the grass so that he stretched out on top of me.

"Hywel thinks he'll try and steal something, and I suspect he's right," Conall said, arms and hands cradling my shoulders, the back of my head. He bent, holding my gaze, a smile crinkling the corners of his eyes.

I could guess his meaning, and I rolled my eyes. "I'm not a *thing*."

"Oh no, *mo chroí*, you are infinitely more valuable than any *thing* in this world," Conall murmured.

I growled in annoyance but when his mouth met mine, sweet and playful and so very welcome, irritation melted away under the morning sun.

MY FIRST REAL INTERACTION WITH ROLANT DIDN'T COME until the evening, after Conall had run me ragged in the meadow and Laszlo had trained me in sword fighting until my arms refused to hold the weapon up.

The dreamers of the castle were growing scarce now that Hywel was awake, only enough left to manage the upkeep and offer the occasional whisper of a melody from one of the instruments.

"You ought to bring in a village to keep the castle for you, dazzle them a little. They'll only live a few decades anyway, and they'd liven these old stones up a bit "

Rolant's voice was careless, an old French accent galloping

through the words and down the hall to reach my ears as I walked between Conall and Laszlo to the dining hall.

"If the accommodations of my home are not to your liking, Rolant, you may always retreat to your own little house. Or is it a cottage? Such a dainty little place, as I recall."

"An abbey," Rolant bit out.

"But not a castle," Laszlo whispered in my ear, just a hint of wicked humor flashing behind his spectacles.

"The monks must be rolling over in their graves," Hywel murmured. "Ah! There you are, my loves. Rolant is feeling quite *dull* without entertainment this evening. We will have to do our best to amuse him."

"Conall knows some very good poems," I said, mostly under my breath, making the werewolf with his arm around my waist snicker in stifled laughter.

But Rolant must've heard me, because he turned as we entered, cold eyes immediately fastening to my face, making my brief attempt at humor feel awkward and dangerous.

"Ah, the divinity," he said, studying me. He bowed shallowly, not removing his stare, and the gesture mocked gallantry. "I have heard such mixed reports of you, madam, I had no idea what to expect. There was an old acquaintance of mine, a very respectable ancient vampire named Yvain, who many years ago waxed poetic about your elegant sexual manner. So much so, I almost considered seeking you out in your little slum in London," Rolant said. He turned to share a brief smirk with a glowering Hywel. "Although you know I never pay."

I remembered Yvain, a lovely vampire from a nomad tribe who'd been turned while he was out alone, during a ceremony meant to declare him an adult male. He'd always made love with the enthusiasm of a virgin, never quite able to hold off his release as long as he wished, and had been excessively sweet, always with a beautiful gift at the ready for each visit.

Rolant continued, turning back to me. "Of course, recent reports have been...less complimentary."

Hywel huffed, and a little smoke expelled from his nostrils. Conall tensed and started to vibrate with a growl at my side, and Laszlo's wings stretched behind us.

"How is Yvain?" I asked, not rising to the bait.

"Oh, quite dead," Rolant said with a cruel laugh. "But *you*, my dear, have clearly recovered. Yes, I see why he was such a devotee of yours. Beautiful, naturally, but there is something altogether *profane* about you too, isn't there? Those eyes. Sorrowful, starving, seductive. You look ready to suck a man dry."

I glanced at Hywel and raised my eyebrows. Why on earth had he ever entangled himself with such a horrible, petty person?

"Rolant, you will cease or you will leave," Hywell said, the words firm. "Actually, you had better just—"

"I'll be good. I'll be tame," Rolant cooed, hands raised at his sides. He grinned at me, and the expression was almost grotesque in his vicious glee. "I'm only playing, darling girl. I am quite jealous of you. Such a collection of handsome beasts you have acquired for yourself to play with."

Somehow, that stung more than the reference to my captivity. I was still struggling with my relationships with these men, my willingness to let Laszlo and Hywel pour affection into me. I turned my cheek away, letting the dragon have his win.

Hywel had enough. His body swelled and his voice deepened, a sudden gust of red leathery wings taking up every available inch of space at his back. "I won't put my hands on you, Rolant. I swore off that vile habit millenia ago," he snarled. "But I can still find ways to rip that venomous tongue of yours from your mouth."

Heat shimmered in the air between them, a warning of a potential blaze. Conall and Laszlo pressed in close on either side of me, no doubt prepared to sweep me from the room if the pair decided to transform into their true shapes. Rolant was ice to Hywel's fire, cool and almost magnificent against the blaze of my dragon's anger, but he tensed, bracing himself for attack—not foolish enough to make the first move.

"My venomous tongue has information you would rather not miss out on."

"If you know anything of use, then so does the person who told you," Hywel said, shrugging, but his wings folded back into nothingness and the air in the room settled.

"True, but Birsha has her now," Rolant answered, sliding past Hywel and helping himself to a seat at the table.

Hywel scowled at the other dragon—Hywel had courtly manners, and Rolant sitting first was rude, especially to me—but held out his hand to us. Conall pulled my arm free of his first and stepped aside for Hywel.

You're just one woman; you can't have them all holding you at once, I reminded myself. And it was natural for Conall to defer to Hywel, both as a guest in his home and as a werewolf to a dragon.

"Has who?" Hywel asked, pulling out a chair for me.

"Nimue."

I fell into the chair at the pronouncement, and Laszlo released an audible gasp as Hywel rumbled with a low snarl.

"Birsha has our Lady of the Lake? You *let*—"

Rolant scoffed. "Don't be absurd, Hywel. I had no idea she was under any kind of threat. You may know the worst of me, but you can't imagine I would stoop so low as to risk *her*."

I'd heard plenty of legends about the Lady of the Lake, the enchantress who'd presented Arthur with his sword Excalibur, who'd been tangled in so many myths told when I was a child. But even the basilisk Marius had said Arthur hadn't existed.

"And the sword?" Hywel growled.

"Excalibur is real too?!" I blurted out, dizzy at the turning conversation.

Hywel and Rolant paused, glancing at me as if they'd forgotten my presence. Hywel studied me with an absent frown, and I suddenly realized how *old* he was, how old both dragons were— more ancient than I could properly understand, I supposed.

"The sword was broken hundreds of years ago in battle," Laszlo said slowly, sinking into a chair at my side, the feast laid out before us neglected by the conversation.

Rolant rolled his eyes and nodded. "It *was*. And then people went and made a *story* out of it. And her. And all the silly little human warriors she fussed over. You know what *legends* do."

Hywel let out a heavy sigh, and at last he and Conall sat too. "The Sword of Victors healed?"

Rolant grunted. "And became *Excalibur.* Silly to name a sword like that."

"A sword...*healed?*" I repeated.

Hywel hummed and reached for my hand under the table, squeezing it briefly and running his thumb over my wrist. "The sword was always an object of power. Nimue is high fae, next to a goddess in strength. She imbued the blade with magic, gifted it to those human men she found *worthy.* Those legends about Arthur aren't based on one warrior, but rather many—knights and kings and lords. She made them a sword that would guarantee their victory in battle, as long as they remained worthy of the gift. But one after another, they all fell. Sometimes within years, sometimes decades. Infallibility tends to corrupt the noble natures of men."

"If the sword requires a noble nature, surely it's not in any danger from Birsha," Conall mentioned.

"One would hope," Laszlo murmured.

"Better never to underestimate your enemies, dear boy," Rolant said blithely to Conall.

Rolant looked hardly a day older than Conall, but the werewolf took the patronizing tone in stride, only briefly sharing a dry look with me. We were the children at this table, even me with my centuries of life.

"Birsha will make his play for the sword," Rolant said gravely. "Or he will try and force Nimue to make him something new. Something to suit his nature, or whatever champion he chooses for battle. However, if I were him, I'd do my best to take Excalibur out of the equation before your lot found someone to carry it to war."

Hywel leaned forward, elbows on the table, stare glowing. "He doesn't have it yet then?"

"Nimue has only been missing a week, by my reckoning. She won't give in so easily."

"How do we plan on finding a hidden, legendary sword?" Conall asked, eyebrows raising.

Rolant shrugged. "She told me where it is, of course."

Hywel snorted. "Outrageous."

Rolant glared at him and then muttered, low and quick, "Well, she didn't expect me to be able to carry it, did she?"

There was a polite pause of quiet, the faint clink of silver-ware being lifted at last, and then a sudden, startling burst of a giggle.

From me.

Rolant's eyes narrowed to a glare, and Conall's lips twitched.

Another giggle burst free, and I stifled the sound with the back of my hand, trying to wrestle my growing grin flat again. Hywel turned his head slowly toward me, eyes heavy-lidded and an indulgent smile curling over his lips.

"Yes, *blodyn bach*?" he purred.

I shook my head, and his eyebrows waggled slightly, coaxing out another gurgle of laughter that I choked on.

"S'just...clever," I squeezed out, pressing my lips hard and taking my knife and fork in my grip with more focus than cutlery had ever deserved.

Telling a dragon where one of the greatest legends of western myth was hidden. Knowing he wouldn't be able to retrieve it himself. Knowing he would never let another treasure hunter get their hands on it, out of jealousy.

"I don't know what you see in her," Rolant hissed.

29.
THE QUEST TO
THE MOUNTAIN

With Rolant in the castle, there was nowhere safe to speak privately but in bed. As a group, we'd made a polite effort to entertain the Wyrm in the study, but he'd grown antagonistic again, picking at Conall, Laszlo, and me in turn until it was safer for him and Hywel both that we all retire. I dragged Conall, my hand fastened tightly around his wrist, with the others up to Laszlo's nest.

I told myself it was because we all obviously needed to discuss Rolant's news together in private, but I knew the truth. As soon as my thoughts had started to entertain the idea of Conall being part of my nightly routine of lavish attention and murmured conversation, I craved knowing if it was possible.

Conall resisted crossing the threshold, but once inside he relaxed and grew nosy, wandering over the layered carpets and picking up each object to study it in turn as we talked.

"The difficulty with Rolant is there are so many possible directions he could be plotting, it's hard to anticipate," Hywel said, sitting in an armchair by the fire and pulling off his boots.

"He's as slippery as an eel, that one," Conall agreed, pretending not to watch out of the corner of his eye as Laszlo unlaced the back of my gown.

"Then we will methodically consider each path and how to best respond, together," Laszlo said. "We have the sword to consider, of course. And Nimue. But, Hywel..."

"Evanthia's safety is my priority, *cariad*, I swear it," Hywel said solemnly.

My eyebrows rose, and I stared at Hywel in the reflection of the mirror I stood in front of. "*My* safety?"

"Rolant won't act for Birsha, but if the right person approached him—" Conall started.

"With the right price," Hywel muttered.

"—then it's not impossible Rolant may move against *you*," Conall finished, setting aside a small statue and crossing his arms over his chest, leaning against the high back of the other chair. He was trying to look at ease, but I had a feeling he was still wanting to run from the room. The space was intimate, yes, but not so crowded with the four of us. I couldn't help but think that there was still room for another, if that person had been in the castle and so inclined to join us. Which was unlikely.

I batted Asterion from my thoughts and chewed over Conall's words.

"Birsha wouldn't be the only party interested in you, *blodyn bach*. Were you never pursued before him?" Hywel asked.

I hummed and nodded. "I suppose so." By men and kings and monsters. Usually that hunt came with gifts and seduction. A few times with attempts of force, but I'd always had protectors of some form and the ability to choose, even if it was from a short list of options rather than a long one.

It wasn't so different now, but somehow those choices seemed more expansive here with these men. I could turn them all from my bed, or leave Laszlo's in this case, and they would still keep me safe. If I was unsatisfied with what was available to me, they would take me elsewhere, or cart in what I wanted.

Oh. I was starting to get *spoiled*.

"But what would Excalibur have to do with me?" I asked, hiding the smile that appeared on my lips.

"A wild-goose chase for us to follow," Conall said.

Laszlo nodded, pushing the shoulders of my gown down, helping me step out of the pool of fabric. I was wearing my chemise but the candlelight, combined with the sheer, gauzy fabric, turned it into a hazy halo around my body, hiding nothing. Not that there was anything left to hide from any of them. Still, I watched with a sense of feminine triumph as they all paused to admire me, Hywel's gaze warm and openly approving, Conall swallowing hard and forcing his stare away, Laszlo sharing a secret smile with me in the reflection of the mirror.

"Rolant could lead us out of the castle, leave you vulnerable here alone. Or, if you come with us, we could be walking into a trap," Hywel mused.

"We could be walking into a trap regardless. I know you think Rolant won't side with Birsha, but we have no proof of that," Laszlo said gently, glancing over his spectacles to his mate.

Hywel didn't argue, just nodded in understanding.

"If we split up, we leave each other at risk either way," Conall said, frowning. "I'm not too proud to admit that I wouldn't feel like adequate protection for Evie if the pair of you left to retrieve the sword. And I can't say I feel worthy of taking it from hiding."

"Then you overestimate Nimue's taste in warriors," Laszlo said, flashing a sly smile to the werewolf.

Hywel huffed a laugh. "She liked them brawny, handsome, and a touch gallant. You'd do fine, pup."

"They were her lovers, weren't they?" I asked.

Laszlo nodded. "Of course. The ones she liked best."

I wondered then what "noble nature" had really failed. Had the men moved on to new lovers and lost the protection of the sword?

"We should wait for Asterion," I said, taking the robe Laszlo had brought over and sliding my arms into the heavy sleeves. I wrapped it around myself, kissing Laszlo's cheek in thanks, and then moved to sit in the chair Conall was propped up against.

"There may not be time to waste," Hywel said.

"She's right. If anyone is pulling Excalibur from whatever hidey-hole Nimue has hinted to Rolant, it's Asterion," Conall said. His hand shifted from the back of my seat and I thought he meant to pull away, but instead his fingers slid into my hair, stroking the back of my neck in secret.

"We could send Conall and Asterion with Rolant," Laszlo suggested, taking his own perch on the arm of Hywel's chair. Hywel fidgeted, wrapping one arm around Laszlo but looking away. Laszlo smiled knowingly and winked at me.

"You want to be there," I said, laughing at the dragon.

"It's one of the great *legends*," Hywel muttered.

"A legend you know the truth of," I pointed out.

He shrugged. "Legends change the nature of a thing. And I don't trust that Rolant won't try to wheedle the sword into his hoard one way or another. I can think of at least four methods he might try off the top of my head."

"Ahh, but you're much cleverer than he is," Laszlo teased, running his talons through Hywel's pale hair.

"And you'd much rather the sword came to rest in *your* hoard," I pointed out.

Hywel hummed and feigned innocence, eyes widening. "I mean, if it needs a resting place after Asterion is done with it, *naturally* I'd be happy to accommodate."

"Naturally," Conall and I said together, and I twisted to share a grin with him.

The flames of the fireplace added embers to Conall's glowing green gaze, and the heat there caught low in my belly. I wanted to rise to my knees and bring his face down to mine, kiss him in full view of Hywel and Laszlo, and let the consequences unravel through the night.

Conall leaned over the back of the chair, a tug in my chest calling me to him or vice versa. And then the fire popped, Conall blinked, and his face lifted, glancing at Laszlo and Hywel, then back at me. He stepped back from my chair and cleared his throat.

"Stay," Hywel said, a low and calm invitation. "You're welcome with us. And I promise you the sweetest of dreams."

Conall's gaze darkened on the dragon, turned hungrily first to Laszlo and then finally to me. He *was* tempted. He wanted to slide into the tangle of us, and I wasn't sure what shape we would take, what dynamic it might change, but I wanted it too.

I reached for him, to grasp his callous hand and draw it to my mouth, my kiss of approval for Hywel's offer.

Conall's head twitched, a small shake. "Not tonight," he said, a touch roughly. "I told Asterion I'd keep an eye on Rolant. You guard your treasure here, dragon. I'll watch the castle."

"If you wish," Hywel said.

Conall's calm smile faltered slightly, and he huffed out a

laugh. He did not wish. But he turned and left the room, the door shutting softly behind him.

Hywel groaned. "Oh, don't pout, the pair of you."

WAKE, PRETTY MORSEL.

I shivered and rolled in the bed, hunting for the heat of my companions but finding cool sheets instead. Low voices murmured around me, and I frowned. My head felt heavy and I blinked one eye open to find the room quite dark, just the fire down to coals and two candles lit, blocked from view by the large figures crowded together.

One of them turned, large horns glinting, and my breath hitched as Asterion's warm eyes found me on the bed. Hywel, Laszlo, and I had stayed up late talking more, planning, debating, and while they'd stripped me bare and pressed me between them in the bed, their actions had been chaste. I'd fallen asleep quickly. I glanced toward the window and found the sky outside nearly black, a wash of silvery-gray clouds lit up from behind by moonlight.

Asterion was still staring at me when I turned back to the cluster of men by the fire, his gaze hungry.

He'd returned, and Conall was back in Laszlo's nest. They were discussing Rolant's secret, and Hywel had called to me in sleep to rouse me, which meant they'd probably come to some decision.

Still, I held Asterion's eyes, twisting under the sheets, stretching languidly, letting the fabric slide along my figure and over my bent leg, dragging back to reveal my breast. The corner of his mouth curled and his stare made a slow study of me, lingering on my skin, even in the shadow of the sheet where it draped like a tent from my knee. He didn't alert the others, just enjoyed the view.

But Hywel didn't have to turn to know I was awake. "Dress, Evanthia," he called, a hint of laughter in the words.

Asterion started to turn and I moved, sitting up, sliding out of the bed. He froze once more, gaze avid and quick, sliding down my body, holding at my hips, grazing down to my toes as they curled in the carpet. His soft ears twitched, and his hands fisted at his side.

Conall huffed, breaking the spell, and I found him grinning at me.

I remained nude, unashamed, as they all turned to look. "What am I dressing for?" I asked, not making a move to cover myself. If Asterion wanted to turn away, he could. He was the only one who hadn't really seen me, even in that dark moment when he'd first brought me to the castle.

"Trouble," Hywel said, smiling at me.

"We leave to seek the sword as soon as possible," Laszlo said. He broke away from the group, passing me to open the closet. "You'll want something practical."

"Unless you don't want to go," Asterion rumbled.

"We discussed—" Hywel started.

"We can find an alternative," Asterion answered with a glare.

Laszlo twisted, holding out a pair of trousers from the depth of the wardrobe, and I took them, hurrying to dress.

"I'm coming with you all."

"Birsha's forces are stretched thin, and while I don't believe there are any nearby that might attack, I can't guarantee that. It isn't as safe outside of the shelter of the castle," Asterion said, striding toward me. He was keeping his gaze fixed above my chin, his hands clasped behind his back, as if it took all his effort not to reach for me.

Laszlo passed me a shirt, and I took mercy on the minotaur, shrugging it on quickly.

"I understand that. But I can't stay here forever," I murmured, lifting my hair out of the collar of the shirt.

"You certainly can," Hywel snapped.

Laszlo continued to toss men's clothing onto the bed—a wool vest with a high collar, a dark long-tailed coat—and I layered each one over the other.

"Not like this," I said to Hywel with a rueful smile. "Not hiding. Anyway, I am safest when I am with all of you, yes?"

"Yes," Conall, Laszlo, and Hywel all said at once.

Asterion stepped forward, his hands catching mine in a light grip. "You are, yes."

I nodded. "I trust you, the four of you, as I trust no one else. I'm coming with you."

"There will be some kind of trap. By Rolant or Birsha or Nimue herself," Asterion warned, his brow furrowing.

"Then we will find our way out of it," I said with a confidence I almost possessed.

He stared at me with that lovely, warm, penetrating gaze, and at last released a sigh. "Very well."

"We'd better go before he changes his mind again," Conall quipped, already heading for the door.

৩৵৩

"I should've let the wolf hold you," Hywel murmured in my ear.

I'd been gazing up at the sky. The day was cloudy but without the threat of rain, the sky hazy but gentle. If anyone had looked closely, they would've realized there were two sources of light tucked behind those milky white curtains. One distant and massive, traveling across the sky in a slow arch. The other was a smaller, swaying beam, almost a star directly above us as Laszlo watched from overhead. I'd seen glimpses of him, brief and shining, through cracks in the clouds, or when he ducked down to check that we were still safely alone, but he remained hidden the rest of the time.

I roused myself, stretching in the circle of Hywel's arms. We'd been riding since before dawn, and it was nearing evening now, but Rolant said we were close. I turned and caught a glimpse of Conall's dark scowl, although it washed away when he noticed me looking. What remained was a tense, false smile.

"We're all jealous of one another at the moment," Hywel continued. "But I think his instincts wear on him the most."

There'd been a strange moment when I'd left the castle and found everyone but Laszlo and Rolant facing off while holding their horses. Asterion had grunted, lifting himself to his saddle and riding for the gates with Rolant at his side, but Conall and

Hywel had watched one another warily until finally Conall snarled and also jumped into his saddle.

"Instincts?" I asked, resisting the urge to look back at Conall.

Hywel only hummed in answer. "Perhaps I'll be generous and share you on the trip back."

"A horse of my own is too much to ask, I take it?" I teased. It'd been a long time since I'd ridden, and I didn't mind being held against Hywel's warm chest.

"It would be fair but certainly out of the question," Hywel purred, unrepentant as he kissed my throat.

"We'll reach the cave around this bend," Rolant called back to us.

I twisted and whispered to Hywel, "Do *you* think he's set us a trap?"

Hywel was quiet for a few minutes, his arm around my waist delivering a reassuring squeeze. "I change my mind every few minutes," he admitted. "The most likely scenario in my mind is that he waits until we have the sword and then escapes with it. The level of danger that presents varies in my mind."

"How did you...end up in a relationship with him?" I asked, watching the back of the other dragon rocking gently as we climbed steadily up the barely present path of the mountain.

"We were both quite young. We had hoards to protect, and... appetites. It's not uncommon for dragons to end up in that kind of arrangement together. I can't say I was ever more than half in love with him, but I was attracted to the idea of having a dragon as a mate. And he made it clear often enough that he was more interested in the treasure we were amassing. Every item in the collection had to be clearly possessed—his or mine," Hywel said. "Eventually, temptation was too great. Rolant challenged me for the hoard."

I turned my face up to that second, smaller glow, and as if Laszlo knew I was looking for him, a little sparkle of gold appeared through the clouds. "It's different between you and Laszlo."

Hywel nodded, curling around me and tucking his chin on my shoulder. "Laszlo is part of me. All I am is his, including my treasure. He is the same. And luckily for me, my mate has *exceptional* taste."

That ever present itch of *why me?* crawled up to my tongue. Laszlo and Hywel brought one another leagues of treasure. What could I offer them?

But instead of the question, one that would've left a bitter taste in both mine and Hywel's mouth, a sudden shriek of an eagle's cry swung above us. Without a word, our horses were halted and Rolant returned to us. The path was narrow, and crowded together the horses stomped, a rattle of stone sliding down the side of the mountain. I kept my eyes turned to the sky, staring as the brilliantly golden, feline and feathered form of Laszlo swooped down from the clouds.

He was blazing bright, lion's legs and eagle's talons tucked into his huge body, wings spread and three feathered tails twined to one, an elegant arrow streaking toward us. I thought he would crash into us or continue down the mountain, when his body curled forward and his flight slowed almost to a halt. Above us, around the bend Rolant had promised would bring us to our destination, a chorus of haunting howls rang out, drawing a shiver down my spine.

"Werewolves," Conall snapped, leaping down from his saddle the moment Laszlo's paws touched the ground.

The gryphon straightened back into the familiar and elegant form of the man, gleaming glasses still perched on his nose. "A dozen," he announced.

"Easy," Rolant scoffed.

Laszlo didn't spare him a glance. "They're not alone. I counted at least five trolls clinging to the mountainside, and there could be more."

Asterion's hooves hit the ground, his white gloves torn from his fingers to expose him from the disguise he'd traveled in. "Birsha must've gotten the location from Nimue."

"Send the horses back down the mountain to safety," Hywel said, hauling me from my seat and passing me into the ready arms of Asterion.

I twisted in the minotaur's grip before he could carry me away. "I need a weapon."

"No!" Conall and Asterion both said.

"Of course she does," Laszlo argued. "Something with range. The crossbow. Evanthia, come here."

"We agreed she'd be with—" Asterion started, holding tightly to my waist as I rummaged in the saddle bags for the crossbow and bolts.

"There's nothing in the air," Laszlo said, reaching for me. "She will ride me, well out of reach."

Asterion didn't release me, even as I swung the arrow quiver over my shoulder, checking my reach and loading a bolt. I looked up and found Hywel smiling down at me.

"Look at her, Asterion. Laszlo will keep her safe, and her aim is the great success of her training so far," Hywel said, surprisingly gentle.

Conall tugged off his coat, revealing a holster ready with knives. He wheeled his horse around in the tight space of the path and then swatted it swiftly on the rear, sending it eagerly back down the way we'd come. All the horses were growing restless, aware of the tension or startled by the howls now calling once more.

"I'm going ahead to speak to the werewolves," Conall snarled, rolling his shoulders. His hair seemed to be thicker, eyes wilder and more vivid, almost yellow. "Give me one chance to convince them to stand down before you attack."

"Surely if they're here, they're aligned with Birsha," I murmured, frowning at Conall. "Wouldn't it be better if you didn't give them the chance to attack *you* first?"

His smile was crooked and fierce, and his claws were out as he reached to grip my jaw in his hand, pulling me close with a rough tug and slanting his mouth over mine. His fangs dragged against my bottom lip, and I was torn between irritation at him wasting time when we had enemies around the corner, and the urge to wrap myself around him and keep him fastened to me.

"I am King of Clans, *mo chroí*," Conall said, voice gritty and growling, his body halfway shifted already, cheekbones sharper and chest broader. "When I speak, they are bound to listen, even if they do not heed me."

He stepped away, jogging up the mountain, back hunching

and tail growing thick and full. Laszlo had shifted back to his gryphon form, and he was moving restlessly.

"No more earnest partings, I beg of you all," Rolant said dryly as Hywel ushered me toward Laszlo. "They may already have someone in the cave to retrieve the sword."

Laszlo was huge like this, his back as high as my chest. He had to kneel for Hywel to lift me to my seat, tucked between Laszlo's enormous wings with my legs folded around their roots.

"It's been a long time since he accepted a passenger," Hywel told me, winking. "Try not to pull his feathers."

Laszlo let out a piercing screech of objection, and I tightened the grip of my thighs and found a safe ruff of dense fur to hold onto instead of the long feathers at the back of his head. His wings began to beat, his entire body flexing and shifting beneath me, and my breath caught in my chest, eyes growing wide.

"Don't do any silly flying tricks, Laz. If you drop her, we'll all be very cross," Hywel teased.

I leaned down as Laszlo screamed once more at Hywel and then leapt up from the ground. My body slid against his thick coat, but my arms wrapped around his shoulders, my thighs squeezing desperately, and I held my seat on Laszlo's back as he soared almost vertically up into the air.

As if flying on a dragon is any easier than me, Laszlo thought to me, his voice heavier in my head but very welcome in the moment. *Let's keep an eye on our Red Wolf, yes?*

"Please," I gasped out, tucking my face into Laszlo's feathers as we continued to careen through the air, higher and higher, turning with the mountain.

Snarls and barks and growls grew louder as we rose.

How well can you see, dear one?

I sucked in a deep lungful of Laszlo's sweet, clean scent before braving a glance down. We were very high. I stifled the yelp in my throat, and Laszlo chuckled in my head as I tried to fasten myself even more closely to his back. His body steadied, circling and bobbing slightly above the mountain. I bit my lip and leaned to the right, staring down over his shoulder. The sun was sinking fast, but there was a slight glow on a large plateau of the mountain, where a flicker of figures could be made out. At the edge of the path, facing all of them, was a huge and blazing red form.

"I see Conall! They are...they're holding still. Listening. He's..."

Magnificent, Laszlo finished for me, and I nodded in agreement. The other werewolves were circling, stirring in slow patterns, but none lunged for Conall yet.

He's reminding them that he's challenged every pack leader within three thousand miles and is always the victor, Laszlo told me.

My eyes widened. "Is that true?"

He's boastful but not a liar.

I licked my lips. I'd known Conall was strong, powerful, and by the accounts of those I'd asked, a significant figure in the werewolf population. But this meant he was, by rights, the head of all those packs he'd challenged, and yet he traveled alone or with Asterion.

Oh dear, Laszlo murmured.

More figures were crawling out of the soft glow of the cave, one dozen now becoming two.

They're all new, recently bitten. They know their fate by fighting Conall, but they're taking the chance on—

"Him being outnumbered," I finished. "Laszlo, fly down. I want to be ready."

Later I would thank Laszlo for listening to me, for swooping closer to the growing crowd of werewolves, for not insisting on keeping me as far from the danger as possible. But for now, I turned the quiver of arrows to my front and took aim.

30.
THE CENTICORE
AND THE SWORD

ywel and the others will join him, Laszlo assured me as we neared the plateau. *See, the Wyrm is slithering up the mountain now.*

"And if he turns on Conall?" I murmured.

Laszlo turned restlessly in the air. *Aim at him for now. We will watch.*

Rolant wasn't the only one ascending the mountain. Asterion was climbing, the faintest flicker of his gold-tipped horns catching my eye for a moment.

"Where's Hywel?" I hissed, frowning.

Respecting Conall's right to the challenge, Laszlo answered. *See that breeze there, stirring the weed that clings to the wall around the cliff?* I hummed in assent when I saw it. *That's a troll. They'll attack at the worst possible moment. Hywel is watching them.*

I sighed, slipping my sweaty fingers through Laszlo's fur, soothing myself and taking a grip on the body of the crossbow once more.

Don't worry, dear one. There are unknowns still, but our odds are easy.

It was at that moment that a cluster of the werewolves, smaller beasts than Conall's broad body, streaked with white down their brown backs, all lunged together. I swallowed my cry, trying to watch Rolant and Conall at the same time, wanting to fire the bolt at the attacking werewolves.

Make them count, Laszlo warned, as if sensing my eagerness.

I nodded, stare bouncing between the tangle of snarling bodies and the slow glide of the dragon crawling closer.

The Red Wolf's strength was quickly obvious. Conall swiped his claws in one motion, and yelps of pain went up. He dove, catching one werewolf by the scruff of his neck in huge red jaws, tossing the creature effortlessly aside. With four against him, he still easily outmatched them all.

It was a test.

A sharp cry rose from my throat as the swarm of were-wolves all charged at Conall in unison. They leapt onto him from all sides until I couldn't see the brilliant fire of his fur under the mass of the attackers. Laszlo twisted us in the air, agitated.

"Take me lower!" I called.

Look! Laszlo answered.

Rolant was moving like a whip into the fray, and I held my breath, crossbow raised but knowing any shot I took would risk hitting Conall. And then Rolant's silver jaws snapped around one of the enemy werewolves, fastening to his back leg and tearing him off the churning mound. The werewolf was tossed over the side of the mountain with a broken yelp, and I winced but released a sigh.

The last red slice of sunset snagged on a crescent of steel crawling over the craggy edge. Asterion leapt onto the plateau and stood for a moment, assessing the scene. He'd peeled away his gentlemen's layers and stood bare chested, twin axes strapped to his back. Rolant was tearing werewolves away from Conall, who was starting to emerge bloody and fighting from the pack. Asterion reached back, bronze muscles rippling, and drew out the axes, hefting them in his grip.

"I feel useless!" I said, frowning down at the scene.

Better useless than sending Asterion into a panic, Laszlo warned me.

It was true. If I were on the ground, all of the men except Rolant would be fixated on not letting me get so much as a scratch or a bruise. With me safely in the air, they could focus and I could—

I gasped as a werewolf abandoned its savage grip on Conall,

leaping over Rolant's back while he was busy with another and sneaking up behind Asterion.

"*Lower!*" I cried to Laszlo, bracing and holding myself on his back with the squeeze of my thighs as he dove. I lifted the crossbow to take aim, and Laszlo's flight was a steady shot toward the ground. When the dark streak of the werewolf was safely out of range of Rolant and before he could reach Asterion, I fired.

Laszlo's wings beat, and I pressed myself to his back as we jerked suddenly upward.

"Did I—" I twisted, almost falling off my gryphon in my effort to see.

You got him, Laszlo told me. *You did well, dear one*.

We settled in the air, and I stared down at the collapsed figure of the werewolf, a white line of fur splayed over the ground behind Asterion as he engaged himself with two who had turned from Conall.

"Find me another," I said, my voice grim.

We have bigger prey now, Laszlo answered, turning us toward the rising heap of jagged rocks that rose up around the cave entrance. And as he spoke, the rocks shifted, weeds swayed, and the large, stony figures of mountain trolls shook themselves free of their hiding places.

"Will a bolt even hurt them?" I asked, gasping at the sight of the massive creatures.

I'd met river trolls and forest trolls in the past, as tall as mature trees, but these were practically giants, with flat, craggy faces and a tangle of grasses in their hair.

Aim for eyes, throat, genitals, Laszlo instructed.

I didn't wait. One stomp from these mountain trolls would seriously injure any of the men on the ground. I lifted the crossbow back into position, holding onto Laszlo as he shot forward.

Here comes Hywel, Laszlo told me, and a streak of heavy red was gliding around the corner, approaching from behind.

One of the trolls was turning toward Rolant, who was busy snapping and clawing at a cluster of werewolves that took turns diving and scratching at him. I took aim as Laszlo flew nearer and shot for the throat. I reached for another bolt immediately, twisting and staring as the troll screamed like thunder and scrabbled its four-fingered hands at the wound in its throat.

"Turn back!"

Laszlo spun us and I fired once more, this time at the troll's eye, a whoop bursting from my lips as the bolt struck true.

A little valkyrie, Rolant's voice boomed from below. His tail slashed, cutting down the troll's legs from behind, the mountain quaking as the heavy body hit the earth.

Hywel swooped from overhead, a scorching blaze striking three mountain trolls. **My *valkyrie*, *Rolant*.**

I grinned and Laszlo soared us up into the air, narrowly missing the swiping reach of another troll.

Conall, Laszlo snapped.

I was already putting the next bolt in place, strangely bloodthirsty and eager for my next target. Laszlo flew us toward the path where Conall was cornered against a rock by five of the remaining werewolves. I shot one from the air, only managing to catch it on the thigh as he leapt onto Conall's shoulder.

I need to go low, Laszlo warned me.

The ground below was beginning to thin out, Asterion clearing away the last of the werewolves as Rolant and Hywel turned on the trolls. I tightened my body on Laszlo's back, tucking my heels up and lying low as he dove for the weres attacking Conall.

Laszlo's talons reached out, snagging one werewolf before he lunged at Conall.

"Get her away from here!" Conall snarled at us.

Laszlo flew high with a sudden flex and beat of his wings, swooping us to the edge of the mountain and dropping his prey. I sat up, loading another bolt and firing it into the crotch of an approaching troll, cursing as the creature twisted aside and the shot was wasted.

We dive again, Laszlo said, and I made myself small on his back.

It was organized chaos—blood and screams, talons and claws, blades and fangs. It was ugly work, but my mind cleared, crystalline, shoving aside fear in order to better watch, plan, move.

Every shot that missed made me more careful the next time, and every one that hit my target left me stronger, surer.

Laszlo tossed the last of Conall's opponents over the mountainside, and I patted his back.

"Put me on the ground."

I don't think—

"The others need your help, and I need to see how badly wounded Conall is."

Laszlo spiraled. There were five trolls left, and they were sturdier foes than the werewolves. Rolant had twisted his long body around one, slowly crushing its stony body, but that left Hywel and Asterion to tackle the majority of enemies left.

Conall was limping toward them, and Laszlo hissed in my thoughts. *Get both of you safely out of the way*, he said.

"I promise."

He slowed, and I swung my leg over his back, dropping down before he'd even put so much as a claw on the ground. Conall froze, shuddering in his beastly form, huge green eyes staring as Laszlo turned and flew toward the others.

"What are you *doing*?!" Conall snapped.

"Stopping you from getting yourself killed," I answered back, just as abruptly.

Up close he looked even worse, deep scratches over both shoulders and across his chest. He reached out with shaking hands, his fingers and claws longer, and dragged me away from the fighting. He limped with every step, and his tail hung crookedly over the back of his torn trousers.

"Stay here—"

I slid my hands through his, grasping tightly to his thick forearms. Conall was all twisted in this form, shaggy red hair crawling in at his temples and over his elongated face.

"I stay here, with you," I said. There was an open wound underneath one of my hands, bleeding slowly, and Conall shuddered and glared down at me.

He shrank before my eyes, staggering in place, his shape shifting towards human once more. "*Mo chroí*," he rasped.

Without all the fur, it was easier to see the wounds, and I was relieved to find that most of the blood smeared and splattered over him probably wasn't his own. The ground shook beneath our feet and I spun, lifting the crossbow, staring up at the lurching face of the troll that had escaped the others and was making its way toward us, and then fired the shot.

The bolt plunged into the troll's throat, green-gray blood burbling from the wound, and a moment later Hywel had the troll's head in his jaws, dragging him backwards and down to the ground.

Conall gasped, hands clasping onto my waist, and he let out a huffing breath, sagging into me. "Fine, protect me."

"I knew you'd see sense," I said, feigning lightness even as surprise trembled through me. "There's alcohol and clean bandages in the bag on my hip."

"It looks worse than it is. I'll heal in an hour or so," Conall said, even as he started rummaging through the sack hanging over my shoulder.

"That's all well and good, darling, but we still don't know what's *inside* the cave," I muttered, loading another bolt into my weapon.

I eyed the fighting ahead of us with what might've been a pout. I needed to train harder with blades. The men might prefer I stick with ranged fighting, but even now I noted opportunities where I might weave through the ankles of the trolls to do damage from the ground, like Asterion hacking at the backs of their legs.

"Mmm, darling, is it? Fighting's put you in a good mood," Conall mused, then hissed as he rinsed his chest with the flask of alcohol.

It had, actually. I'd never imagined myself as a fighter, as having any interest in violence at all. I wasn't sure if it was the relief of defending myself after so many years of feeling utterly helpless, or if...

I took a deep breath, and my eyes widened. It wasn't strong, not like sex with my monsters, but there was a sweet lick of *néktar* on the air, tanged with the metallic edge of blood. I flushed at the realization.

Conall stepped up to my side, slippery pink rivulets still dripping down his chest and legs, but much cleaner than minutes ago. Already, his wounds were starting to knit back together.

"It's all right to enjoy this," he murmured gently, his hand settling on the base of my back, drawing me into his side as we watched Asterion help Rolant finish off one troll, Hywel and Laszlo another. "Survival *is* a strange thrill."

⚜

IN THE WAKE OF THE BATTLE, THE EERIE QUIET THAT ECHOED out of the cave's entrance was more chilling than the violence had been.

Hywel had dragged the troll's bodies away from us, and I'd busied myself with Conall's and Asterion's injuries as the two dragons made a hearty meal of the rest of the dead. At least they weren't wasteful.

"Do you think there's something else waiting in there?" I whispered, staring into the warm glow of two torches burning on either wall just inside, making the blackness that continued ahead of them appear limitless.

"Undoubtedly," Rolant said.

He stood left of me, wrapping a bandage around his waist to cover a wound on his side. Asterion and Conall were both cleaned up, buttoning their shirts over their still-bleeding chests. Hywel, Laszlo, and I remained spotless, although Asterion had insisted on looking me over twice once the last of the trolls was dispatched.

"I want a sword," I said to Laszlo.

"No," Asterion answered first. "If we come upon another enemy, Conall and Laszlo will take you directly out of the cave."

"Don't be ridiculous. Birsha could just as easily send more men to be waiting outside," Hywel said. "She stays with all of us at all times, like we agreed was *wisest*."

Asterion huffed, and Rolant's eyes rolled.

"Gentlemen, I believe if there is a trap waiting ahead of us, it was laid by Our Lady herself," Rolant said.

There was a thoughtful pause, and then Laszlo spoke. "That's actually...more concerning."

Rolant and Hywel hummed their agreement, and Asterion and Conall stepped closer on either side of me. As if hearing the conversation, a slow scratch and snarl called slowly up from the darkness, bouncing and rolling over the stone.

Rolant sighed and withdrew a sword from its sheath, stepping forward. "I can't grab the sword, but I'll do my best to keep all your limbs attached. Especially hers. Only to return the favor, you see."

"Thank you," I said, nodding at him.

Hywel scowled and marched after the other dragon, their footsteps blending with the scuttling sounds from the dark. Laszlo gestured for Asterion and Conall to lead me forward, but it wasn't long into the cavern before the path became too narrow for three, and then even forced Asterion to slide behind me, broad shoulders brushing either wall.

Conall's arm wrapped around me, holding me close to his side, and I shivered in the darkness. Rolant's torch bobbed at the front of our line, making the walls and shadows dance and bounce around us. It grew cool and humid the deeper we traveled, this slight path tipping us down, turning left and then right until I had no clear sense of what direction we were traveling in.

"She's enchanted the path," Laszlo spoke from the back.

"Canny old witch," Rolant agreed from ahead.

I wondered if it was similar to the magic of the castle and closed my eyes, imagining that the narrow hall would suddenly open once more. A moment later, the grunting, puffing growl of a monster grew louder, and I debated whether I really wanted to find the end of the passage after all.

"There's light ahead," Hywel murmured.

And the sound of water splashing.

Progress halted suddenly, and Asterion's hands reached for my waist, holding me still as Hywel and Rolant shifted, revealing a steep set of stairs leading down.

Rolant sniffed the air. "Fur, blood, magic."

"Water, stone, et cetera," Hywel muttered with a wave of his hand. "It's not as though we didn't *know* there was something waiting down there for us."

"Oh, very well, Your Majesty. Yes, let's just stomp down the stairs into who knows what kind of danger," Rolant snapped back.

"That's the spirit," Conall said, releasing me and clapping them both on the back, sending them stumbling down a few steps.

The splashing and growling grew louder, anticipating our arrival, but neither Hywel nor Rolant wanted to balk in front of the other, so instead they forged ahead.

"There's nothing coming from behind," Laszlo murmured.

Asterion nodded and squeezed his large body past mine, leaving me with the gryphon as the rest hurried down the stairs.

"Are you all right?" Laszlo asked me, taking my hand as we made to follow them.

"I'm..." I licked my lips and paused before admitting the truth. "I'm enjoying myself, actually."

Laszlo just smiled at me and nodded. "You've been cooped up too long. A little adventure and treasure seeking is good for the mind and body."

A great booming roar and the shout of familiar voices broke the moment. I ran down the stairs with Laszlo just behind me, my boots slipping over dew-slicked stone. He caught me, and we came crashing into the tight cavern together.

Ahead of us was a beast unlike any I had ever seen, stomping and jolting in a pool of glowing water. It was enormous, and resembled a goat, if a goat resembled a boar which also resembled a cow and they were all the size of a house.

"Centicore!" Laszlo cried, almost in triumph, eyes huge and bright behind his spectacles. "I haven't seen a centicore in a millenia!"

In answer, the centicore's horns, which had been twisted back with their points turned down, spiraled on his head, now curling forward and prepared to gouge flesh as it lunged toward us. A sharp scratching sounded, and the centicore howled, slitted eyes rolling back as a gleaming silver chain pulled its throat taut and it skidded back in the water. Its fur was spotted brown and golden, with a streak of white down its throat, the gentle colors only interrupted in one place where brilliant scarlet spouted from its ribs.

I clapped my hands over my mouth at the sight of a ruby encrusted sword hilt sticking out from the beast's side.

"The Lady of the Lake put the sword *in* the beast?!" Conall cried.

The chain around the centicore's thick neck only gave us a few safe feet along a slippery stone ledge, and we all remained pressed to the walls, watching the animal scream and stomp and thrash in the water.

"Very clever," Hywel said, frowning.

"It's awful!" I said, glaring at that glittering steel hilt, more red blood oozing from the beast's side. "How long has it been left like this?"

"She's *fae*, what do you expect?" Rolant scoffed. "Hywel, can you shift?"

"Not without bringing the mountain down on top of us," Hywel answered.

"Neither can I. Perhaps your little pet bird—"

"*Rolant.*"

"I'll go," Asterion said, pulling out the axes from the holsters strapped over his back.

"Wait," I gasped, but he had already jumped down into the water, crouching low as the centicore shrieked, a shockingly human cry that made pebbles and dust shake loose from the ceiling of the cavern.

He raised the axes up like a shield and they clashed into the hard, golden bone of the centicore's horns, sparks flashing from the metal. The centicore screamed again and Asterion roared back, pulling one axe free and swinging it low, aiming for the centicore's throat.

My stomach jumped, my hands planting themselves over the spot, and I shook my head, staring at the hilt embedded in the centicore's side.

This was wrong.

"Asterion, stop!" I cried, but he was defending himself now as much as he was fighting the creature.

I lunged toward the water, and all around me, men shouted and hands reached out for me. I dove down, and my breath was ripped from my lungs at the icy shock of the water. It must've been coming from deep within the ground, and for a moment it made my body freeze, the plan in my head shaken loose. Fingers swiped at my ankle and sense returned.

I kicked myself loose and swam, body adjusting to the brutally cold temperature. I tore myself free of the heavy coat I'd been wearing and circled the churning where the centicore stomped its hooves. I resurfaced at its back, and the sounds of my men shouting and Asterion bellowing and the centicore's haunting cries all made me want to retreat back under the water.

Instead, I grabbed onto the soaked fur, braced my leg on the centicore's knee, and climbed onto its bucking back.

"Evanthia!" Asterion shouted, stunned and staring up as the creature screeched and tried to toss me off.

"Hush," I said, my eyes wide and staring back at the five gazes gaping at me. "Hush, it's all right."

I stroked my hands down the neck of the centicore, grunting as it leapt straight up, knocking both our backs against the ceiling of the cavern.

"Get back, Asterion," Laslzo hissed.

The breath was knocked out of me, the room spinning, but I stroked the fur under my hands and squeezed my thighs tight like when I'd been flying on Laszlo.

"Shhhh, shhhhh, settle down now," I murmured.

"Everyone, quiet," Rolant said as Conall and Hywell dragged Asterion up from the water back onto the ledge, their horrified stares settling once more as I caught my breath.

The centicore screamed in protest, leaping up once more, but I was petting the sides of its neck, and it didn't knock me into the stone again.

"Evanthia," Conall breathed.

"Shhhhh," I said to him and to the centicore. "It's all right. You poor thing, hmm."

It kicked its hind legs up, and the chain rattled as it tried to dive forward. I held on and waited, petting it gently, speaking softly.

"Wicked woman to put a sword in you," I whispered, and the large, palm-sized ears in front of me twitched. "That was cruel, yes."

Rolant snorted and then stiffened as the centicore stirred and yelped restlessly.

"Don't mind them. It's all right. I won't hurt you. It's all right now." I sat up slightly, and the centicore stomped but didn't toss me about. Our audience sighed.

Laszlo spoke, his voice low and soothing to match mine. "It's going to put up a fuss when you retrieve the sword."

I nodded, keeping my tone light as I dug my hands into the thick fur, scratching and petting. "I know."

"We can all try and grab it at once, keep it from hurting you, but—"

"I'm going to break the chain," I said, eyeing the heavy rings of metal that dug into the centicore's throat.

"Evanthia, no," Asterion said, careful but firm.

I licked my lips. It was an outrageous plan, and probably not what Nimue had intended with her horrible puzzle, but it would serve her right.

"I think you should all step safely away from that staircase," I said, talking as though I was proposing we all go on a picnic together, while I leaned over to examine the distance between the sword hilt and me. Well out of reach. I would have to leap for it and hope the centicore didn't crush me in its panic.

"Evanthia," Conall hissed, jerking forward.

The centicore's calm broke at his sudden movement, and it lurched up onto its hind legs. I released my grip and slid back, all the men shouting together at once.

"Hold it!"

"Conall, grab her!"

"Evanthia!"

I twisted, falling from the side of the centicore's body, toward the water, and reached for the hilt that stuck out from the bloodied fur. My fingers slipped around the hilt, and icy water soaked into my trousers once more, but I kicked my feet against the floor of the pool, surging up and grabbing onto the jewel encrusted hilt with both hands. The centicore screeched and the water surged and tore around me, pulling my legs out from under me as I yanked on the sword with all my strength, trying to keep it straight and true to avoid doing any more damage.

"*Evanthia!*" Conall's voice roared behind me.

The blade was scarlet with the centicore's blood, dragging slowly out of the beast's flank, and a strange, violent shout crawled up from my chest, an echo of the creature's scream, born from equal parts sympathy and determination.

All at once, the blade came free in a long, streaking arch of red. Iron bands of strength caught me as I fell backwards, and I leaned into Conall, still shouting as I swung the blade toward the metal chain. The others were surrounding the centicore, fistfuls of fur in their grip, Asterion's arms holding one leg down in the water.

"Get back!" I shouted, and he released the leg, surging away as the centicore bucked, leaving the chain exposed beneath its chest, buried down in the water.

What good can a sword do against a chain? a part of me wondered.

But this was Excalibur, Sword of Victors. A strike of glee and pride hit me as the blade struck the metal, shattering the chain links as if they were made of glass.

"Back!" Asterion bellowed, the word echoing over every cranny and crack of the cavern.

The route we'd followed down from the cave should've been too narrow, but as the chain broke, the hollow opening of the stairs gasped as if it were a lung expanding to fresh air. There were no stairs, no endless dark path, but a great maw of an exit that led directly to the freshly bloodied plateau we'd entered from.

The centicore bolted, waves from the pool around us surging up as it dragged its heavy, wounded body up and out, into the night.

Conall collapsed, the pair of us sinking into the water briefly, his arms still fastened around me, my open mouth gulping down water. I choked and he dragged us up once more, back toward the ledge, which had expanded like the enchantment on the cave.

"How dare you," he rasped. "You risky, foolhardy, careless—"

I yelped as he spun and hauled me up out of the water, sword clanging down onto the stone at my side, my cold, wet body slapping down in front of him. His stare was blazing, face hard and furious.

"Conall—" Asterion warned, standing in the slowly settling pool.

"You could've been *killed*," Conall growled at me, his jaw ticking.

He was right, of course, and I had no defense except that I'd been revolted at the use of a living creature all for some *challenge* set to protect a sword, regardless of its power. Conall's teeth were grinding, and I was shivering, the now open wall of the cave letting in a breeze. I lifted my hands to smooth back his slick and tangled hair, and he snarled.

His own hands snatched my face in their grip, and he pulled my mouth to his, kissing me roughly, biting and laving over the spot. He was trembling as he had been when he arrived at the castle, and I tried to wrap him up in my arms and legs, but a throat cleared farther off in the room.

"Gently, wolf. She could be injured," Hywel snapped.

Conall groaned, our mouths open and his tongue stroking mine, and he held me in place as he pulled away, glaring at me out of the corner of his eye.

"I'm fine," I gasped.

Which was not true. I was already feeling quite sore and bruised, and being soaking wet in a chilly cave didn't help.

Hywel was already out of the water, his clothes steaming dry as he held a hand out to Laszlo and helped him back onto the stone landing. Asterion stood at the center of the cave opening, staring out into the darkness, his shoulders bouncing.

"Stand up, *blodyn bach*, let us get a look at you," Hywel muttered.

Conall crawled up onto the stone at my side as Hywel pulled me to stand, tucking me between himself and Laszlo. Laszlo's glasses were sitting crookedly on his nose, golden wings dripping.

"Oh! Your feathers are ruffled," I said, smoothing a hand over some of the bent and broken feathers at the edge of Laszlo's wing.

"I'll be fine. Turn and let us see your back," the gryphon fussed.

"I'm tempted to send you flying *straight* home with Laszlo—" Hywel fumed.

I rose to my toes as Asterion's horns ducked out of sight. Rolant had also pulled himself out of the water, his temple bleeding and an annoyed scowl plastered over his face as he watched my lovers hovering around me. And Asterion was bent over, body shaking and breath puffing, his hands planted on his knees. I tried to squeeze between Hywel and Laszlo, but there were too many hands on me.

"Asterion? Asterion, what's wrong?" I called, heart hammering in my chest. Had he been kicked as the centicore charged out of the cave? Was he fighting for air?

Laszlo and Hywel paused in asking me questions and turned to check on the minotaur, who let out a sudden sharp bark of sound. Another followed a moment later, Asterion's back heaving, and then a great many in succession. I sighed and rolled back on my heels, bumping into Conall crowding close behind me.

Asterion was laughing. Bursting, bellowing laughter, his body shaking with the sound and the effort of holding it in.

"You just loosed—" he wheezed out, trying to straighten and then leaning forward again, arms wrapped around his stomach as he guffawed. He shook his head and turned, standing and meeting my gaze, a lovely crooked smile stretched over his lips. "You just loosed one of the most ancient and feared beasts into the countryside, *théa.*"

Rolant huffed and sagged against the wall of the cave, shaking his head. "It will hide itself. It didn't live this long without adapting like the rest of us."

"Oh, we can certainly hope not," Asterion answered, still grinning. "Our Lady of the Lake won't be pleased."

I huffed. "I'm not especially pleased with her at the moment. That was a horrible trick."

"Well, I doubt you're quite the hero she expected to retrieve the sword," Rolant muttered.

"But you *are* worthy of it," Hywel declared. "Pick up your sword, Evanthia."

I blinked. "It's not mine," I said, even as my eyes fell naturally down to the blade at my feet. The pool had washed the metal clean of the centicore's blood, and the long shaft of the sword was as brilliant and bright as starlight.

"Nimue always meant the sword to be wielded by humans and halflings," Laszlo said, eyeing me over his crooked glasses. "You were the natural choice of our party. And you *did* pull it free."

I opened my mouth to object and Conall growled, his hands on my hips tightening. "Pick it up, *mo chroí*. You're riding back with *me*."

There was an edge to the words and an almost biting possession of his grip on my hips. I turned to look at Conall and found him still tightly-wound and glaring. I glanced at the others, unsure if Hywel would protest, but he and Laszlo didn't seem surprised, only petted their hands over me and then stepped away. At the entrance of the cave, Asterion's gaze glinted on me, his huge grin now a slight smirk, a secret understanding in the look, a reminder of the competition for my affection that he was refusing to partake in.

"Evie," Conall whispered, desperate.

I bent and picked up the sword, startled by how light it was in my grip, how perfectly it fit in my hand.

Rolant was eyeing my hand on the sword with something between anger and envy. Hywel's shoulder knocked against his as he passed.

"My mates always find the *best* treasure for our hoard, don't you think?" Hywel taunted.

31.
THE RISE OF THE RED WOLF

"**A**re you still angry with me?" I asked upon waking on horseback, warm and cozy against Conall's chest, his legs around mine and the horse we rode moving gently along its path.

"Yes," he said, but the word was soft, and he bent his head to nuzzle against my throat.

"Even if you'd all been able to kill that poor creature—"

"That poor creature the size of three carriages put together, with horns designed by the devil himself—"

"Nonsense," I said. Conall huffed, and we were quiet for a moment.

Asterion's large human disguised form swayed with the movement of his huge horse in front of us, the shadows of trees passing over us. I thought we were close to the castle now, these woods almost welcoming us home.

Conall's lips grazed against the shell of my ear, the teasing touch curling heat through my veins. And then he breathed out a handful of words so gently they almost vanished under the steady beat of horse hooves below and rustling leaves above.

"I'll go mad if I lose you."

I stiffened, and Conall nudged my tangled hair back, pressing a chaste kiss to my jumping pulse. I pulled away, twisting to look at him, but there was nothing to his expression but a barren and serene honesty.

"Sorry," he said, a little brighter and clearer, the corner of his mouth quirking up. "It's dramatic, I know."

"Are you joking?"

"No," he said, shaking his head. "It's what happens, *mo chroí*."

"What happens," I repeated.

Conall's stare shuttered for a moment, eyes dodging away. I was patient.

"If a werewolf loses their mate," he sighed out.

Oh. I recalled the brittle tension he'd arrived at the castle with, the immediate need to devour me, touch me, possess me, the starving man falling upon the feast.

I didn't know what was more surprising—the fact that a part of me had already started to understand what was happening, or the fact that Conall's confirmation didn't make me want to launch from the horse and ramble out protests. I leaned back, resting my head against his shoulder, and he laid his cheek on top of my hair.

"You made the right choice," Conall murmured. "That was a rotten fae trick, but they're a ruthless race. And for all we know, Nimue meant this to happen exactly as it did. You're a nobler hero for freeing that beast than we would've been for killing it."

I knew as much, but I reached under the blanket that covered me and found Conall's hand on my waist, tangling our fingers together.

Conall's voice lowered and tightened. "But you ever do anything so reckless again and I'll..."

I smiled as he floundered for words. "You'll be right there by my side. After all, *who* was it who insisted we let him take on two dozen werewolves on his own?"

Conall snorted. "I've faced worse odds."

The shadow of the castle was starting to take shape in the mist through the trees, and I wasn't sure what would happen when we arrived. I hadn't forgotten the way Conall had spoken about being mated just days ago. He wasn't at peace about the fact that he saw me as his mate, and the reluctance in his confession wasn't shyness. He might understand the instinct that made him desperate for me, but he wasn't excited or determined like Laszlo and Hywel.

Was it the competition of the others, like Asterion's reservations, or something else?

"Why don't you have a pack?" I asked, thinking of what Laszlo had recounted to me while we were in the air above the fighting.

Conall was quiet for so long in the wake of my question that I thought he might not answer. His arms remained wrapped warmly around me, our hands linked, his cheek against my head, but it was as if I'd never spoken. I rolled my lips between my teeth and tried to think of something else to say, to let him know I didn't mind moving on.

His voice sounded, low and steady in my ear, before I had the chance to offer him an out.

"I come from a long line of pack leaders. A clan, we call them, when packs join together."

King of Clans.

"A clan is stronger, has a wider territory, more ability to protect each other. They require a hierarchy too. My father was the leader, but there were those beneath him, werewolves he trusted from each pack family line to follow his rule. His father before him had brought in a new pack before he died, when my father was a young man. My mother was that pack leader's daughter. She and my father were mates. It was a happy accident, a good way to secure the pack's cooperation in what is usually a... volatile transition."

"They were mates?" I asked.

"Mmm. *Enthusiastically* so. They were almost obsessed with one another. I don't remember a lot, but... No, we'll get to that later. Suffice it to say, however reluctant the rest of the conquered pack might've been, my mother was very satisfied to be mated to my father, and even more so when my father stepped forward to challenge my grandfather and won. It was a bit of a ceremony to pass it down like that, but a leader must always be the victor of a challenge.

"Our family line was old, and my parents' mate bond settled the nerves of the most recently added pack of the clan, so there was no argument to my father taking the position as leader. My mother was pregnant with me already, and an heir was just another promise of my family carrying on protecting the clan."

Conall's fingers fiddled with mine under the blanket. "I

don't...I don't know which of my parents it was who was more ambitious, or if that was just another aspect of their personalities that was so perfectly entwined. When my grandfather died within a year, my father was already looking for another pack to conquer and absorb into the clan. That's very quick. Usually when a new pack is challenged and brought in, a clan gives things time to settle, for werewolves to find mates and start families, settling the new blood in with the old."

"Your father didn't wait."

"No. No, he found a growing pack who'd settled into open territory south of us and set the challenge immediately." I twisted, and Conall arched an eyebrow down at me, answering my question before I had to ask. "Oh, he won. He won that challenge, took that pack. And the next one, a year later. And another, just a couple years after that."

"Oh."

"Mm. Yes. Oh. By the time I was old enough to remember pieces of this, we were the largest clan in Ireland. My father called himself the King of the Red Wolves. He planned to take the entire country. My mother called me the little red prince. It was a *terrible*, idiotic idea. But they encouraged each other. When someone warned my father of the risks of growing too quickly, my mother insisted that they didn't have enough faith in her mate. They were blind to each other's flaws, obsessed with each other's victories. And...and in truth, there was no pack or clan in Ireland that would've been strong enough to win my father's challenge."

Conall's gaze went distant, and I licked my lips. "None but his own," I said softly.

Conall's lips twitched. "Ahh, clever girl," he whispered, grazing a kiss over my forehead. "Yes. It was quite a mutiny. My father did have supporters, of course, other wolves that wanted the power and prestige of being an entire nation united. But that's not a natural state for werewolves. There are too many of us who *know* we could lead, if not under another's thumb. And a challenge amongst werewolves is not a simple act of one fight. It's *war*.

"The only thing the werewolves of Ireland were united in was battle. We lost...an enormous number of our kind. Hundreds of wolves slaughtered against one another. Packs dissolved into chaos, families split apart. All to defy my father."

It was as if I could see the carnage firsthand, watching Conall's expression shift, his brow furrow, the reflection of screams in his eyes.

"Your parents were killed."

Conall swallowed. "My mother first. Obviously. What better way to destroy my father than tear apart his life and soul and the sun he orbited around?" His face was blank, eyes blinking, just the vaguest hint of tears in the open horror of his gaze. He smiled, and it was haunted. "She was ferocious in her own right —she would've become the leader after her father, if not for my grandfather. I bet it was the same number of wolves I faced today that she faced on her own."

He'd been there—that slack faced recollection of his worst memories said as much.

"My father lasted...two weeks, maybe less, after she was gone," Conall said numbly.

"Did they... Conall, did they come for you?"

He blinked and stirred, drawing in a sudden deep breath and glancing down at me. "Not like you might think. There was fighting for a number of weeks after my father's death, but it was small battles, the cleanup and rearranging of the survivors. I was kept at first by a pack of loyalists to my father...and then kidnapped by the opposition. They weren't cruel to me—I was still a child—but I think they feared me being raised to follow in my father's footsteps. In the end, I was given a choice. I could join one of the packs that killed my parents, where they could keep an eye on me, keep me leashed..."

"Or," I prompted.

"Or I could choose exile," Conall said flatly. "For the sake of the peace negotiation, no pack could offer me shelter. I would be utterly alone and left to survive on my wits."

It would've been considered a death sentence for a child. Even a werewolf.

"You chose exile," I said.

Conall smiled at me and nodded. "I did."

"Conall, you were just a *child*."

"I was. And quite a feral little beast I became too. Kept to my werewolf form more than human. It was easier to hunt that way, and predators didn't like my scent. Oh, don't fret for me now, *mo chroí*. I survived," Conall said, and then tightened the hand I held beneath the blanket. He winced and glared ahead of us before adding, "Some might even say I thrived."

"The packs that exiled you, you mean."

He hummed and nodded. "I didn't seek them out. When I was first exiled, I kept myself well out of any pack's way. But eventually I was more beast than man, and the lines of the territories didn't mean anything to me. It was winter and I was hunting, following the migration of a collection of deer, and I ran into one of the packs that had belonged to my father's clan and turned against him. I recognized two of the werewolves, who were there when my mother..."

My breath hitched and Conall stirred, rousing himself from the old memories.

"I'm sure they saw me and...and thought I'd come for vengeance, but really I was just frightened. I didn't mean to challenge them, exactly, but I needed the food and I wanted them to retreat."

"You won," I said.

Conall blinked and sighed. "I suppose so, yes. So the story goes. I'm not really sure how, if I'm honest. I wasn't thinking clearly. But the leader of the pack was with the hunt that day and I...I broke his arms. They assumed I was there to challenge them, and so they declared me the winner."

"You would've been the new leader," I said.

He huffed. "And if I'd accepted, I would've been dead within a week, I'm sure. Poisoned or slaughtered when I finally succumbed to sleep. But the words did clear my head, just a little. I remembered who they were, and who I was, and why I'd been so frightened of them. I rejected their pack, told them I wanted nothing of traitors. I took the hunt I needed to survive and I left, determined to keep away from other werewolves once more."

I chewed on my lip. The castle was close now, but I wanted

the rest of the story. I stirred against Conall and he laughed softly at me, sensing my impatience.

"What happened next?" I pressed gently.

"This part I learned later. With their leader defeated, the pack had to go find another. There were still lines of allies after the disaster with my father, and so they went and told another pack who'd fought against my father about their run-in with me. They didn't trust that I wasn't after the same goal as my father, and I don't know if I can blame them. I did want a kind of revenge on them all."

"They hunted you," I guessed.

Conall nodded. "They did." He sighed and sagged against me, weary in remembering. "They did. That went on for...a long time. Years. Sometimes I hid, and sometimes I faced them eagerly. Evanthia, I have no idea how I won some of those challenges."

"You were angry, and you wanted to survive. Wanting to survive is the hardest part," I said.

He growled and kissed my cheek, my jaw, licking up to my lips. "I did. I wanted to defy them. I wasn't thinking about what it meant to these packs for me to defeat their leaders, leave their authority broken and the pack in humiliation. No, that's a lie. Eventually I realized, and I relished their shame."

"They should be ashamed," I muttered.

"Should they?" Conall asked lightly. "What my father was doing was pure, selfish ambition. And werewolves live by blood and claw and fang. Our sense of diplomacy is...rickety, at best."

"I can't say what I think of what happened to your parents, only that I wish you hadn't been involved," I said.

We passed under the gates that opened to the castle, and Conall held me in quiet.

"I'm not a tragic hero, Evanthia," he whispered. "I did realize what was happening. One of my father's sympathizing packs finally discovered the rumor and sought me out. They wanted me to take up my father's crown again."

"You didn't."

"Perhaps," he murmured. "Oh, I challenged them, and I won them, and I rejected them. Over and over again. It was... I was searching for a newly-formed clan, enemies of my father, when I found the castle," he said, nodding ahead of us.

"The castle?! Oh, do you mean—?"

"I met Laszlo when I was quite young, maybe twenty, twenty-two? The years are muddled," Conall admitted with a grin.

I looked up in the sky, searching for the glint of gold, catching it as it cut through the clouds and flew into the mist surrounding the castle.

"He all but dragged me in by my tail," Conall said, chuckling. "Restored some of my sanity. Put me through so many baths, I turned into a prune. Bullied me into oils and civilized meals and just...kindness." His voice broke on the word, and I wanted to turn in the saddle and wrap myself around him. "He gave me back to myself."

"He has a tendency to do that," I rasped, and Conall nodded. I wondered if Conall knew that what Laszlo had done was courtship, or if he thought it was only charity.

"It was very tempting to stay. He never really said I could, but he never asked when I would leave, either. When I realized... when I realized how *badly* I wanted to stay and forget everything else, just live in that strange dream world Hywel fueled, I made my goodbye."

"Were you lovers?" I asked, unable to resist the question.

"We came together a few times. I was all appetite back then, no charm at all, and no real...appreciation for what he offered," Conall said, and I was surprised to see him blush. "After I left Laszlo, I decided I could be the hunted enemy or I could be the coming conqueror, and the latter suited my pride. I'm not sure when it shifted. I was on a mad mission to prove to all the were-wolves of the world that I was the most powerful—"

"No," I spat, and Conall froze. I swallowed and shook my head, turning to meet that brilliantly green gaze. "No, Conall. You were on a mission to prove to them, and to yourself, that they couldn't *hurt* you. You might've been angry, and you might've enjoyed victory. I don't blame you. But you were a young man, a boy, who'd been shaped by violence and fear and a determination to survive. You didn't want to be hurt, hunted, killed."

Conall slid his hand from mine, pulling it free from the blanket, and studied my face as he brushed my hair back, smoothing it and soothing us both.

"When did it change?" I asked, my brow furrowing. "They're not still hunting you, are they?"

He grunted and smirked. "Not so often, no. I'm not sure when it was exactly. I left Ireland, traveled south through Europe first, and somewhere in Spain I realized that word of me was traveling faster than I was. The packs weren't just ready to defend themselves from me, they were welcoming. Eager. Trotting out all their unmated members to me, accepting the challenge as if my victory was a foregone conclusion. It...it went to my head more than I'd like to admit."

"They *wanted* you to defeat their leaders?" I asked.

Conall laughed. "I was as baffled as you, believe me. They gave me *gifts*. Sat me at their tables. It was so strange, but I was so *starved* for kindness. Finally, I came across a clan with a very old and very noble leader. Everyone knew I would give the challenge, but they made a sort of event of it, held feasts first, revelry, meetings with all the greatest members of the clan. I liked the leader—he was canny and kind and he cared about his people. I didn't *want* to challenge him, and I told him so."

"Was he relieved?"

"He laughed at me and said that if I stopped with him, I would just put a target on the clan's back. I'd been so single-minded for so many years. He sat me down, the pair of us alone, and made me really think about what I'd been doing. It was shameful for a pack leader to be defeated and the pack to be rejected, yes. *Unless*..." Conall said, waggling his eyebrows at me.

I thought, and it dawned on me slowly. "Unless it was happening to all of them," I said, and he nodded.

"It's one thing to be defeated by some wild, exiled youth of a werewolf who then spat on your pride and turned away, and quite another to be defeated by the *Red Wolf*, who is proving his strength to not one pack or clan but *all* of them."

"You'd made a legend of yourself. Oh, Conall, they were all spoiling you to get you to *stay*," I cried out.

He laughed and nodded. "Exactly. Thankfully, Andrés

explained that to my thick skull too. He was very patient with me. I don't know how much he knew of my story, of my father, or if he only had the sense to see me for what I was. I was even less inclined to challenge him after we spoke, but he was right—if I favored any pack over another, it would be as if I was stepping into my father's shoes, threatening to rule over them all. We had to make a bit of a performance out of the fight. And then I had to move on."

My heart ached for the young man he'd been, bound to be alone, to continue his own exile. I closed my eyes and Conall kissed my temple.

"After that, I was more...circumspect in my challenges. I watched packs from afar, waited to see how they were ruled, if it was worth proving myself once more. Occasionally, I'd hear a rumor that a certain region thought I hadn't come because I was frightened of their strength." He shrugged and grinned at me. "So of course, I went to set them straight. I started seeking out other monsters for company, rather than other werewolves, and discovered an entirely different world, a different hierarchy where I was an impressive curiosity rather than a legend."

"It feels quite absurd the way we talk about you now, so young, when really you are—"

Conall laughed and shook his head. "No, I like it. I *am* young by comparison. I'm sure Hywel has tales that could make my hair curl. It's an honest perspective, and I appreciate the respect I am afforded. I am glad I never took a pack. I wouldn't have a friend like Asterion, and I wouldn't have..."

Our horse stopped and I blinked, startled to find us suddenly in the orchard in front of the castle. Laszlo touched down from the air, straightening to two legs and murmuring to Hywel as he dismounted.

"I wouldn't have met you, *mo chroí*," Conall whispered in my ear. "Now you know all there is to know."

He jumped down from his horse and then turned, reaching his hand up to help me down. Cold air struck my back, the void of heat he'd stolen away. I reached a hand down, combing it into his tangled red locks, and shook my head.

"No, Conall. There is always more to know. That's the beauty of learning another person," I said.

The fixed charm he wore so easily faltered on his face, revealing an open and vulnerable terror, and my decision was set in stone. I would love this man. I would love him as no one else had tried to love him in his life. I'd thought love would come back to me, the sudden swoon and storm of feelings that had seemed to possess me of their own accord when I was younger.

I was making love a choice now, a course I would follow every day, actions I would relearn and practice and memorize. I knew where I wanted to start.

"Would you be offended if I admit I'm nervous?" Conall whispered.

I placed my hands on his shoulders, and he pulled me down to stand in front of him. I shook my head and offered him a smile. "No, I understand perfectly. But I'm going to tell you what you'll do next."

He grinned. "Oh, you will, will you?"

I nodded. "You're going to take my hand and follow me inside. And you're not going to let go until I tell you."

Conall sucked in a deep breath and stepped back, holding out his hand. "Very well, *mo chroí*. Lead the way."

32.
IN THE
NEST

A s we entered the castle, all of us weary and cold from our unexpected bath in the cavern, I gave Excalibur to Hywel for safekeeping. He kissed my forehead and tipped his head to Asterion, the pair of them heading toward the armory. Ronalt left for his guest suite, and finally it was only the pair of us, Conall and me. I already knew exactly where to find Laszlo.

I led Conall up to the tower nest. He balked as I approached the stairs, but I squeezed his hand and held his gaze until he swallowed and matched my steps once more.

Laszlo was inside the large room as if he'd expected us. No, he *had* expected us, his gaze glittering as it met mine, a pleased smile curving his lips.

"I started you both a bath."

I looked at the pair of them, Conall with fresh scars and bloodied clothes, Laszlo and his crooked feathers and ragged, windswept hair.

"Will it fit two?" I asked.

"Of course," Laszlo said.

I nodded. "Good. Then it's the pair of *you* going in. I'll play maid."

There was a fair amount of bluster in response.

"No, dear one, your bruises need to be dressed in oil."

"You're chilled to the bone, *mo chroí!*"

But Conall didn't drag his feet as I led him to the large tub

Laszlo had waiting for us by the fire, and when I tugged on our joined hands, he refused to release me for a moment.

"I'll join you. Once I'm done with you," I said, shrugging. "Now be good for me, undress, and get in the bath."

I held Conall's stare but the words were meant for Laszlo behind us too, and I glanced over my shoulder to share a bright smile with my gryphon as he approached, already untying the waist of his shirt.

"Last time I bathed with Conall, he made such a mess," Laszlo murmured, eyes on his hands as he undressed.

Conall's gaze darkened. "Of *you*, you mean."

Laszlo's smile was shy. "I do, yes."

Conall's cheeks flushed and he glanced at me, eyebrows lifting slightly.

"I'll undress too, if it will make you behave," I teased.

Conall barked out a laugh and released my hand, head shaking. "That's the last thing it'll do. All right. You'll have your way now, but I'll give you hell for it later."

In spite of Conall's claim and my determination to tend them both, I did actually want to get out of the clothes I was wearing, so I left them to undressing and stepped behind a screen to do the same. There was a warm robe—Hywel's, I thought—hanging from a hook, and I wrapped it tightly around my body before stepping out again.

Conall was already in the bath, leaning against the sloped back, gazing appreciatively up at Laszlo with a seductive smirk. I paused, hanging back, a shameless observer of their interaction now that I understood the history. Laszlo had offered Conall sanctuary when the werewolf was at his most vulnerable. There were feelings between the pair of them, but I suspected some explanations were also due. The tension and flirtation between them created intriguing possibilities and complications in relationships that had barely started to form.

"I did miss the view," Laszlo murmured, standing bold and beautiful and majestic, all gilded by firelight.

Conall's eyes widened, and he wet his lips. "I...always meant to return. To visit."

Laszlo hummed, sighing as he stepped into the water,

groaning as he crouched down and let it soak into his sore body. His head turned and he smiled, catching me spying. "You had somewhere else to be. And look, the fates brought you back after all."

Conall followed his gaze, and I crossed the room slowly. "So they did."

I grabbed a pillow from the bed and set it down next to the tub. Conall's hand was damp, reaching out from the water to skim over my hip as I knelt on the cushion, trailing around my waist and up to tweak my nipple through the robe. I huffed and batted him away, flicking water up to splash at his nose, which twitched in what struck me as an adorably canine manner.

"Help me with Laszlo's feathers," I instructed, nodding to the gryphon to turn his back to us.

Conall watched me trim and pluck, massage and oil, quickly picking up the skill. With Laszlo's back to us, I nudged Conall's elbow, showing him the downy spots around Laszlo's wing roots, digging my knuckles into sore muscles. Laszlo moaned and arched into the touch, and Conall grinned, fangs glinting, copying the movement.

"Where's Hywel?" Conall asked, his eyes glancing warily at the door.

Laszlo turned, his gaze catching mine over the joint of one wing. "He'll be fussing over the sword for a while before he's ready to join us."

"I should go," Conall whispered.

"No, you shouldn't. And you won't," I said.

"Are you scared of dragons?" Laszlo asked, intentionally goading.

Conall growled under his breath, but he combed his clawed fingers gently through the ruffled down under Laszlo's wing, making the gryphon shiver and blush.

"This is my nest, Conall," Laszlo murmured. "I issue the invitations."

Hierarchy, I thought with a roll of my eyes. Monsters were all bluster about their power and superiority, but the second the species intermingled, it became the most convoluted organization of who was bowing to whom—reluctantly or otherwise. Add sexual and emotional ties into the mix, and it was a wonder the entire monster community hadn't already come to blows before now.

I combed oil through the primary feathers at the tip of Laszlo's wing as the two hedged delicately around the topic until I realized Conall was genuinely trying to talk his way out of the bath, hands bracing on the ledge.

"Conall, *sit*."

Water sloshed as Conall thumped down in the tub. I didn't look at him.

"If Hywel and Laszlo don't mind my intrusion into their bed, they won't mind yours either. Quit trying to talk your way out of somewhere you want to be," I said.

I ignored their twin stares on me, examining a crease in a feather, deciding if it was broken or only bent. Laszlo's wing stretched, pulling itself free of my grip, and he twisted, hanging his wings over the back of the tub. He brushed my hair back from the sides of my face.

"Are you going to take your own advice, dear one?" he asked.

"I'm working on it," I admitted with a nod.

"Get in the bath, *mo chroí*," Conall murmured.

I shook my head. "Let me finish my work first." I shuffled on my pillow to sit behind his head, smiling over his shoulder at Laszlo.

There was a small pitcher on a table near the fire, and I dipped it into the water as Conall sat up. Laszlo turned, rising onto his knees and pulled sponges and soaps from a shelf.

"I know you lot think I'm savage, but I can manage my own bath," Conall said.

I took his thick red hair in my fist, tugging his head back, and Conall's breath caught, lips parted. "Just hush and enjoy yourself," I said, and then I guarded his face from the pitcher of water as I poured it into his hair.

Surprisingly, he obeyed, his eyes sliding shut so a thick fan of flame bright lashes landed on his cheeks, scarred and freckled. Laszlo passed me a bar of hair soap, fragrant with clove and making thick suds in my palms. Conall groaned as I dug my fingers into his hair, scratching his scalp as I washed him. His shoulders softened as I worked. Slowly, while Conall was distracted, Laszlo inched forward between the werewolf's spread legs, wetting his lips and eyeing Conall's bare chest with a focus that bordered on predatory. I caught Conall by the roots of his hair on the nape of his neck, and his eyes flashed open as Laszlo dove forward, stroking soapy hands and soft talons over Conall's chest.

"Cornered, am I?" Conall rasped, arching into Laszlo's palms, eyes heavy-lidded and dazed as he stared up at the ceiling.

"It's for your own good," Laszlo murmured, and then he leaned in, lapping his tongue over one of Conall's nipples.

Conall's knuckles whitened on the ledge of the tub, and I tugged on his hair, tipping his head to one side and offering myself his pointed ear tips for nibbling kisses. Water started to swirl and splash the edges of the tub as together Laszlo and I tortured our werewolf, cleaning him and teasing him and spoiling him with tenderness. Conall sagged in my grip on his hair, thrusting his chest up to Laszlo's mouth, hips rising slowly until the pointed and angry red tip of his cock peeked up out of the water.

Laszlo paused, one kiss pressed over the hair that ran a russet red line down Conall's belly, and then tipped his gaze up to mine. His cheeks were slightly flushed with arousal, and I couldn't see where his hands were, but I thought he was holding Conall's hips. There was an unspoken question hovering between us all, and it took me a moment to realize that Laszlo was waiting for permission. From me.

"Please, one of you...or both, I don't care. Just touch me before I burst," Conall breathed.

I nodded to Laszlo, and he struck, sudden and starving. Conall's hips darted up to meet Laszlo's open, tonguing mouth, the pair of them so perfectly in unison that with one swallow and thrust, Conall was howling. Not from relief, but the startling pleasure-pain of being sucked along Laszlo's tongue. I watched Laszlo groan and lick, head bobbing over Conall's crotch, hands now appearing between the werewolf's legs, looking intriguingly busy.

I caught my breath and reveled in their shared *néktar*. What a gift their passion was.

"*Mo chroí*, kiss me," Conall pleaded. "Tell me this is all—"

I rose up high, Conall's head resting against my chest as I leaned over him, peppering his face and mouth in kisses. His hands flew back, diving into my hair, clutching my shoulders as he growled and bucked into Laszlo's mouth.

"I should've asked the pair of you to let me watch weeks ago," I mumbled, dragging my mouth over Conall's jaw.

Laszlo was reverent and worshipful when he touched me, but he had a lusty hunger for Conall that was making the air heavy and lush, my head spinning and skin thrumming cheerfully at their offering.

"I would've been a distraction," Laszlo said, kissing the tip of Conall's cock and catching his breath.

I frowned at the words, but Conall only smiled. "A very welcome and delightful one," he said. His hair was trailing in the water, rinsing the ends clean, and he blinked up at me, studying my expression from upside down.

"You need her," Laszlo said to him, stroking his thighs.

Conall nodded, gazing at me. "I do. Come into the water, Evie, love. Your monsters need to touch their mate."

"The water will spill," I tried, but Conall huffed and Laszlo sat up, the pair of them reaching for me.

They wrestled me into the water, Conall barking out a laugh as I squawked and flailed. Laszlo had my legs caught in his arms, and he nipped at my ankle as Conall squashed me against his wet chest, play-growling and nuzzling into my hair. He huffed and blew blonde strands out of his face.

"You smell like centicore. Laszlo—"

I screeched as Laszlo tugged my legs up, sliding my ass out from under me and dunking me into the soapy water. I spluttered as I resurfaced, too many arms and legs tangled together in the bath, and the infuriating, snickering laughter of my lovers echoing above me as I wiped the water from my eyes.

"All of my thoughtful—" I started, but Laszlo leaned forward, wrapping my legs around his waist as he covered my mouth with his, a deep and languid kiss stealing my voice.

"You just like to have your way," Conall teased me, but his hands were slick with soap as they stroked down my back gently. "God, these bruises tempt me to go hunt that beast down."

Laszlo hummed into the kiss and pulled away, frowning. "Show me."

"They don't hurt so much," I said, but neither man was paying attention, just hoisting me up and twisting me around in the tiny amount of space afforded in the tub.

Conall's cock had softened slightly, but it cozied cheerfully against my sex, and he purred as my breasts rubbed his chest. He combed my wet hair back with his fingers, strands tangling on calluses, the bite of the tug drawing a sigh out from me. Laszlo's knuckles grazed over my back.

"I can treat this, but we'll have to be gentle with her tonight," Laszlo said.

"Not *that* gentle," I said, and Conall grinned.

"No massage, no scratching," Laszlo listed.

"*She's* the scratcher, not me," Conall objected.

I dumped a pitcher of water over his head, laughing and leaning back into Laszlo's chest as Conall choked and huffed. He glared at me from one brilliant green eye, the other shrouded in soaked hair, and then shook his head vigorously. I squealed and Laszlo drew me back, using me as a shield against the spray. The fire hissed and spit, steam rising, and I let out a bright laugh as Conall slapped his hair back from his face, grinning at me.

"*Children*, behave," Laszlo teased.

"Oh, you never spend any time around humans," Conall said, waving his hand. "You forget how to pretend that life is short and precious."

I sighed and softened between them, Conall's hands mapping my legs and thighs aimlessly. Laszlo circled my waist with one arm, scooping up handfuls of water in his free hand and running them into my hair.

"I am not around humans, but life does seem especially precious at the moment," Laszlo said softly.

Conall's gaze darkened, bouncing between us, and he bit down on his bottom lip briefly. He knelt, hands crawling slowly forward on either side of the tub until he was leaning over me, the soft hair of his stomach tickling my skin under the water.

"You like to watch, *mo chroí*?" he rasped.

I nodded slowly, squirming against Laszlo, whose cock stirred between my ass cheeks in response.

Conall lifted one hand, fingers delicately tucking my hair behind my ear, and then his hand flashed behind me. I pressed myself to one side, sighing as Conall and Laszlo sandwiched me firmly between their bodies, arching together over my shoulder. Conall's tongue slid obscenely over Laszlo's lips, teasing and retreating, returning to plunder. It took a little maneuvering, but I was able to spread my legs, and Conall's hips fit firmly between my thighs, cock nestled between my lower lips. I gasped when Laszlo gasped, moaned with Conall as Laszlo clasped his face and took command of their kiss. Conall's hand fell to the water, clasping Laszlo and me both, grinding himself against my sex.

I writhed between them, gulping down *néktar*, teased by the soft brush of feather and fur under water, using the press of Conall's cock to stimulate myself until the room was a rush of sound and hazy light.

Conall pulled away with a sudden gasp, water washing over the sides of the tub and over my starved flesh.

"Eager little cheat," he said, plucking one of my nipples.

Laszlo laughed and kissed my throat. "One night, she watched Hywel and me feast on one another. She came more times than we did."

I blushed but grinned at the memory.

Conall stood from the water, cock partly erect, eyes bright and smile easy. "We should take her to the Company of Fiends. She'd go happily mad in the frenzy."

"Someday," I said, considering the offer and all that might come with it. Too many people, I thought. Too many strangers and their appetites. I lifted a hand, and Conall helped pull me to standing. "For tonight, I just want you, Conall of no clan or pack. My red wolf. And I want to share you with Laszlo." I turned to the gryphon to smile at him, adding, "If that's all right with the pair of you."

Conall stared at me for a moment, breath hitching, and

then I was caught in his arms. The pair of us dripped over the carpet and stone floor as he rushed to the bed. Before he could toss me down and plunge himself inside of me as I was sure he meant to, I wriggled free, skirting just out of reach of his hands.

"Lie down, love," I said, nudging at his chest.

Talons clicked against the floor, feathers swishing, and Conall looked back to Laszlo.

"Across the bed," Laszlo said. "Hang your head over the edge."

Conall's face and chest flushed at the suggestion, and I fought my own eager grin.

"Go on," I urged, pushing him gently.

He sighed, shivering, and climbed onto the bed, lying on his back and crawling backwards with his cock bobbing in the air.

"Can I have the oil?" I whispered to Laszlo.

His eyebrows bounced, but then he pulled it from behind his back, hand already clasped around the thin gold bottle. "You read my mind."

My body thrummed, cunt clasping on nothing as Laszlo gifted me the bottle. This would be a treat for Conall, yes, but also for me.

"The pair of you are making me nervous," Conall quipped.

I eyed his stiffening cock and arched an eyebrow. "Are you sure that's the correct word?"

He huffed, and I unstoppered the bottle, pouring a small pool of oil into my palm and dipping one finger into it to trace around my lips. My mouth warmed gently as I leaned against the side of the bed, bending over Conall's lap and rubbing my mouth to the inner muscle of his thigh.

"Tease," Conall hissed.

I grinned and nipped his flesh before sitting up. My finger dipped into the oil again, and this time I drew directly over the inner crease of his thigh and hip. Conall's brow was furrowing, and I paused to admire his prone stretch. His wounds had knit back together, fresh pink lines cast over warm, pale skin. His chest rose and fell, the muscles of his stomach tensing as his breath hitched.

Laszlo stole back the bottle of oil, and Conall shuddered as the gryphon dribbled a line of the liquid down his chest.

"I should've shared this with you when you visited last," Laszlo said, staring down at Conall from the other side of the bed. He was nude, his own length darkening with arousal as he stared at the werewolf spread before us.

"You and your toys and tonics. I don't mind a good, plain fuck," Conall said, but his voice was growing rough and his cock was twitching as I spiraled a line of oil up his length with my fingertip.

"A *plain* fuck?" I asked a little tartly.

Conall lifted his head to glare at me. "Nothing with you is plain, *mo chroí.*"

Laszlo huffed and I laughed, shaking my head.

"He's usually so good with words. We must be making him nervous. Perhaps you'd better give him something more productive to do with his mouth?" I said to Laszlo.

Conall groaned and arched his hips into the air, arousal now stiff and dark and pulsing.

"A very worthy suggestion," Laszlo agreed, smiling at me, his hands reaching down to hold Conall's head. He stepped closer to the bed and Conall was ready, growling and tipping his head back, reaching to take Laszlo's cock onto his tongue.

"I've always noted that werewolves have very hungry mouths," Laszlo rasped, sighing and letting his eyes fall shut as Conall lapped eagerly at his length.

I laughed, and for the first time since my escape, I recalled the monsters I'd met before Birsha. Those ugly memories tried to rise too, but they weren't as quick, and I distracted myself with the view of Conall bucking and squirming on the bed, inching his way to Laszlo to swallow more of the gryphon's cock.

Conall's knot was starting to darken and swell, the tip of his length weeping arousal. I wanted time to torment him a little, so I used my warm, pulsing hands, stroking and tugging his sac until he was gasping on Laszlo, who moaned in answer. I climbed up onto the bed, tracing my fingers in the line of oil Laszlo had poured over Conall's chest and drawing patterns over his skin and around his nipples.

"Fuck," Conall gasped. "*Mo chroí*, please. I'm going to spill, and you know how much I like the pretty squeeze of you when I come."

I flushed, debating whether or not he ought to be punished for begging or rewarded. I decided a combination of both would do, and I settled my knees on either side of his hips. Laszlo watched, eyes wide and fixed to my sex as I spread myself open and took Conall in hand, guiding him to my entrance. I fit him just barely inside of me and Conall growled, pulling away from his feast to lift his head and glare at me.

"Evie, darling," he snarled.

But before he could thrust up and fill me, Laszlo leaned forward, planting his hands on Conall's stomach and holding him still.

"Damnit. I'll have revenge on each of you," Conall panted, head falling back and hands fisting in the sheets.

"You mean you'll express your gratitude," I said, just riding the head of his cock for a moment, drawing it out and stroking the slick tip around my clit until my breath caught and the magic of the oil started to make me throb.

Laszlo had distracted Conall by taking his face back in hand, fucking that snarling mouth with his own gasps and groans, wings flexing with the rhythm. My hands on Conall's chest brushed with Laszlo's, and I grasped his wrist as I sank down, filling myself with Conall's length. Laszlo tipped forward, his brow furrowed and cheeks flushed, and I caught his mouth with mine as I started to ride Conall. I licked into Laszlo's mouth, crying out in the kiss as Conall bucked and thrust beneath me.

There was a warm thrum that carried from my mouth to my cunt, a current of closed energy, and I wondered if they felt it too, if we were all tied together in the moment. Was that mating, or the oil Laszlo had shared? Or had I only forgotten what intimacy felt like, the way it seemed to let you share parts of yourself without a word or a look?

Conall let out a garbled speech that made Laszlo yelp and stumble back, freeing the werewolf's lips.

"Knot, please ma—*mo chroí*," Conall stammered. His face was lovely and red, sweat glittering around his temples. "Please. I want to be so tight inside of you, keep you on my cock all night, locked to me. Please, I need—"

I sagged forward, sinking down and pressing against his knot, swallowing his pleas with a kiss that tasted of him and Laszlo both.

Conall's hands grasped my hips and when I surged up, gasping for air, he pulled me roughly down onto his swollen knot. We'd only shared this once—the day before? Two days? Time was foggy in and out of the castle, and I was dizzy, the heat and pulse of pleasure already ringing through me. But I knew now I was addicted to this moment—the bite of the stretch, the pinch of pain as he seated himself inside of me, and then the rich, pounding throb that followed.

I sighed as we settled together, resting for a moment and savoring the sight of Conall straining beneath me, the lovely completion of being so full and closely connected. My werewolf, however, was not so patient.

Conall groaned and reached to my core, stroking and swirling his fingertips over my clit until I squirmed and ground into the touch.

"Jealous?" I asked Laszlo, who watched us with a studying stare, his hands still stroking Conall's hair and face.

"A bit. Of both of you."

Conall panted, fucking me with those tied nudging thrusts, working my clit under his thumb.

"You can have his knot next if I can watch," I offered.

Laszlo smiled, but he looked down at Conall. "Is it different for you now that you've found her?"

Conall paused and blinked, licking his lips as he caught sight of Laszlo's waiting cock once more. "Dunno. Still want you fucking the back of my throat. Don't see why I wouldn't want to knot your ass and watch your wings beat with my thrusts."

My laugh and moan tangled together, and my eyes fluttered shut as I pictured the pair of them, my hips rocking on Conall's lap.

Laszlo fed Conall his arousal once more, teasing his tip on Conall's tongue until we shook and rocked and Conall had swallowed him down. Conall reached his other hand back, clasping

Laszlo's ass, and we pitched and plunged and groaned. Laszlo caught my mouth in a kiss, the pair of us bowed over Conall's body as it braced between us, fucked from both sides.

Laszlo was the first to fall, shouting against my lips, wings stretching back, hips thrusting ruthlessly as Conall choked and thrashed beneath us. Laszlo stumbled back quickly, still dripping his release over Conall's cheek, and the werewolf gasped for air as if he'd been about to cheerfully suffocate.

I caught one exquisite view of Conall's face, cheeks red and victoriously painted, lips pulled back in an eager snarl, and then we were flipping over on the bed, Conall's patience shredded as he snapped and kicked between my thighs, his mouth and hands everywhere at once, pulling at my hair and breasts, sucking on my throat and nipping my shoulder.

He was in a frenzy, and he'd started to wrap his arms around me, gripping my bruised back, when Laszlo caught his hands.

"She's bruised. Take mine."

Conall growled, but he eased his movements and the sound softened into purr. His hips churned, not gentle, but rhythmic and deep, and my voice broke into whimpers as I started to quake.

"That's it," Laszlo said, voice soft and soothing for us both. He let Conall brace against him, the pair of them kissing my cheeks and lips and temple in turn. "She's yours. She's safe. We're all here together."

Conall moaned and his eyes went black, gazing down at me, canines flashing in the candlelight as he panted and surged inside of me.

"My mate," he rumbled.

"Ours," Laszlo corrected, but softly.

"Yours," I agreed in barely a whisper, but the word was nervous on my tongue, and Conall's smile hitched and he slowed his motion, tugging my relief away right before it surged up.

"It's all right, *mo chroí*. It will come," Conall murmured, and I didn't know if he meant my orgasm or my acceptance of belonging to these men.

Laszlo licked the shell of my ear and then nuzzled my hair. "Don't brace, dear one. Let it rise."

Conall let his weight settle, a perfect, grounding pressure that stole my breath. Their hands stroked me until I was loose and liquid on the bed, almost drowsy if not for the urge to chase the heat and shimmering pound of ecstasy that hovered at my edges. Conall groaned and shivered.

"Fuck, I can't hold on," he gasped.

"Don't," I pleaded, wrapping my arms around him, trying to pull him into my own flesh. "Don't hold, I love when you spill inside of me."

Those words were all it took for Conall to shudder and burst, heat flooding me and swelling the pressure of his knot in my greedy core.

I had no time to brace, and Laszlo was right—letting my release rise on its own was delicious, like drowning and flying at the same time, a slow and sugary whirling through my blood. Conall and Laszlo shared my mouth as I babbled wordlessly, quaking on the bed, clinging to them both to keep from being caught up and swept away in the tide.

A soft sigh carried across the room from the open door, and Conall stiffened on top of me.

"And here I was thinking I was too tired to possibly do anything other than fall asleep before I hit my pillow," Hywel murmured, crossing to us and pulling his bloodied shirt up over his head. He eyed the limp and quivering pile of us with a smile. "I hope you aren't done. I'm feeling very...inspired."

I squeezed around Conall's knot, and he groaned and bucked inside of me.

"I'm sure we could manage a good effort for you," I said. Hywel winked at me and reached for his belt.

"Good girl, *blodyn bach*."

<hr>

I STIRRED IN MY SLEEP, FUR AND FEATHERS CARESSING ME AS I rolled. A pair of low, hissing whispers caught my ear, and slowly, in piecemeal measures, the conversation woke me just enough to listen.

"You didn't bite her."

"No...she's not ready. I'm not sure I am either."

It wasn't Laszlo and Hywel, as I was used to sometimes waking up to their murmurs. It wasn't even Conall and Laszlo, as might've made sense after a long-awaited physical reunion.

"Hmm, but it leaves you tense not to turn the scent bond into a mate bond," Hywel murmured.

"It does," Conall admitted. My head was pressed over his heart, and his whispers floated above me. "But it's better already, now that I've told her."

Hywel hummed, and his claws reached over Laszlo's shoulder to stroke gently through my hair. "We won't give her up."

"I'm not asking you to. I'm not asking her to give you up," Conall answered. There was a pause, and then he added, "But I won't let you make me an afterthought, either."

I tensed and Conall's hand around my breast twitched as he realized I was listening. Hywel must've known. He knew when I was asleep or not. I could sit up now and make my own position on the topic very clear. But I waited to see what the dragon would say.

The bed shifted. Conall's breath caught. Warm, silken skin brushed over my shoulder, Hywel moving. I risked opening my eye just a sliver and realized he was arching over me and Conall.

"Werewolves may only have one mate," Hywel hissed, "but dragons and gryphons take as many as we please, pup."

There was a snag of breath and a familiar damp sound, and then Conall groaned, trying to arch up. They were kissing, and I was desperate to twist and stare and watch them. But it must've been their first kiss, and I was already enough of a voyeur.

Hywel moved away after a moment, settling back on the other side of Laszlo. "It's about time you let me give you some peace while you sleep."

"The nightmares are a part of me. They're a reminder," Conall whispered.

"They're penance," Hywel muttered, slightly bitter. "And you can set them aside for a night. Now go to sleep. *Both* of you."

I fought my grin, pressing it to Conall's chest as he heaved a sigh. And then we were all quiet, all at peace, and sleep swam back over me with a welcoming embrace.

33.
TRAINING
TECHNIQUES

"Easy, Hywel!"

"Guard your left!"

"You're wasting energy."

"No, she needs to attack!"

My teeth grit and I let out a rough growl, charging toward Hywel, taking out the aggression of being yelled at from four directions and trying to channel it toward our sparring. Hywel, who remained cool and languid even mid-lunge, didn't so much as blink an eye at the running commentary of our spectators. He met my thrust easily, sweeping it in a circle and then returning with a slash. I was slow and awkward compared to him, even with the advantage of Excalibur in my hand, and I narrowly dodged the motion, catching my heel on the mat and stumbling backwards until I landed hard on my ass.

"Hywel!" Conall roared, leaping forward from where he'd been pacing the perimeter of the room.

"I'm fine," I said, but I was too breathless to really give the words any voice, and the others were chiming in quickly with their thoughts.

"We have to improve her stamina," Asterion muttered.

"It's her absurd lack of balance that's giving her issues," Rolant said.

Conall and Hywel were both headed in my direction, and Conall snarled at the dragon, cutting in front of him.

"Cool your temper, pup, she's in no real danger," Hywel said, arching an eyebrow.

"You push too hard."

I sighed, folding my legs under me and preparing to stand, when I really wanted to spread out on the floor and cool down for a moment. "Conall—"

"Should I leave her under-prepared and unable to defend herself should the worst happen?"

"You should do something other than ruthlessly attack her until she drops!"

"Conall!" I cried out.

He spun, eyes wide and wild, rushing towards me. "Are you—?"

"Conall, calm down," I said, firm and gentle.

He blinked, steps pausing, mouth still hanging open and face pale with worry. He stared at me for a moment, the color slowly returning to his cheeks, until he was properly blushing.

"I'm *fine*," I said, rising and crossing to meet him. The others watched us, not bothering to hide their curiosity. Hywel reached past Conall, and I passed him Excalibur, and then Conall was drawing me to his chest. I coaxed my sweaty, tired hands into his hair, soothing it back and stroking down over his shoulders.

"I'm training, remember?" I teased.

Conall shuddered. "I know...I just—"

"Hywel is a very good dueler, which means he's going to make me look like a clumsy fool most of the time, but he won't let anything happen to me. Will you, Hywel?" I asked.

"Never, *blodyn bach*," Hywel said, offering me a soft smile.

I leaned back in the close circle of Conall's arms and cupped his face in my hands. "Can you stand to leave and *not* watch?"

Conall scowled for a moment, jaw ticking in my hands before letting out a sigh. "It...might be best."

I rose to my toes, nudging my nose to his, but Conall was greedy and tense, seaming our mouths in a smooth and deep kiss, his fingers digging into my lower back. Which was lovely, actually. I smiled against his lips and considered who I might best bribe for a massage later. Conall pulled away, glaring at me as if he knew my mind had wandered, but he smacked another quick press to the corner of my mouth and stepped away.

"Find me when you're done," he muttered.

"Laszlo, keep him busy," Hywel said, winking at his mate.

"I'll see what I can manage," Laszlo said drily.

Considering I'd woken to the sounds of their puffing breaths and slick touches, while Hywel kissed me under the covers, I was sure Laszlo could distract Conall from whatever mating related stress he was dealing with.

"Come along, Rolant," Asterion said, turning for the door before I could catch his eye. "We ought to let Hywel lead his own instruction."

"Thank you, Asterion," Hywel said, offering a shallow bow to the minotaur.

Rolant sighed and slithered after Asterion. "I suppose we can always correct the damage later."

Hywel rolled his shoulders and turned me away from the group, scooping my chin up in his fingers and lifting my gaze to his. "You're all right?"

I nodded, warmed under that opal stare, wanting to slide against Hywel's chest. "I know a battle will be distracting too, but—"

Hywel scoffed and shook his head. "In a battle, you'll be fighting for your life. Having a gallery of opinionated lovers barking contrary orders at you will be the least of your worries, and much easier to block out. Unfortunately...Rolant is right about your balance. Come, let's do some stretches."

I grinned, shuffling my steps after my dragon.

৩৵৩

"Laszlo, I'm—"

"Shhh," the gryphon whispered in my ear. "They're returning."

I shivered and bit my lip, turning my face into his chest and biting down on a button of his shirt.

Male voices from the balcony grew louder, turning away from the view of the sea and marching back to the study, where we all gathered after dinner. And all the while, Laszlo's fingers swirled softly over my clit, buried in the heavy flounces and folds of my satin skirt. I tensed as the approaching footsteps softened from stone to carpet, entering the room, and the hazy, hot height of pleasure that'd been rising up with Laszlo's touch suddenly burst.

I shuddered on his lap, quaking with my release, biting off my cry, as Hywel rounded the back of the chair and stood in front of the fire.

"Oh dear, *blodyn bach*, you look quite flushed."

Laszlo's fingers pulled away from my core while it still throbbed, leaving the frustrating promise that I might've enjoyed *more* if only we hadn't been interrupted.

"I'm f-fine," I answered, stuttering as Asterion crossed to sit in the armchair opposite Laszlo and me.

"You do, though," Conall said, smirking down at me and then throwing himself into the corner of the couch. "Come over here, you'll be farther from the fire."

Hywel was reaching for me at the same moment Laszlo was lifting me from his lap.

Rolant paused behind the couch, sniffed the air, and wrinkled his nose. "I'm going to bed. You lot smell like questionable decisions."

I blushed as Laszlo set me down, my back settling against Conall's chest, my legs draped over Hywel's lap as he joined us.

"He knows better than to think I'd share you with him," Hywel whispered to me.

While that was surely true, I also thought Rolant and I had settled on mild mutual respect and disinterest. I appreciated the help he'd offered in retrieving Excalibur, and I knew Asterion and the others valued his information, but I couldn't shake the sense that he was a bit more venomous than Hywel, if not as powerful.

Speaking of Hywel, he wasted no time in sliding his arm under the flouncing cover of my skirt, hand stroking and grasping my inner thigh.

I jolted, trying to slide my legs to the floor but finding them tight in Hywel's grasp. "I'm exhausted from training, perhaps I should also—"

Conall draped his arm over my chest, and I glanced down to realize that Laszlo had loosened my collar too, leaving it to gape open and reveal a good stretch of my chest and the flesh of my breasts. "Just stay and rest here, *mo chroí*," he said, his fingertips grazing absently along the line of that wide collar. "We'll go up together later."

This is a trap, I thought.

And then I looked up and found Asterion's eyes on us. He was settled deep in the armchair, a cut crystal glass of liquor cupped in one large hand, leg folded and hoof resting over a knee. His gaze was warm, and I couldn't tell if it was the shadow making him smile or if that was really his expression. But he was still here, waiting to see if I would stay. He must've smelled my arousal, my release, like Rolant had, but instead of fleeing the room he'd sat down to...watch.

I sighed and shivered as Hywel's fingertips spread, and his hand turned, one digit at a time rubbing between my folds. I relaxed back into Conall's chest, and my surrender had him sliding his hand inside of my gown, just barely skimming the outside of my nipple. Under the full spread of my skirt, Laszlo tucked his hand against Hywel's cock, and I bit my lip as his rubbing knuckles grazed my thigh too.

And then Conall picked the conversation up, asking about a sphinx.

Asterion answered and Conall's hand burrowed deeper, making no secret of the way he pinched the hardening tip of a nipple between his fingers. My eyes fell shut and my lips parted on a single, strangled whimper. Hywel's hand stroked up, two fingers hunting for an opening, his thumb skimming against my swollen clit, and I squirmed in place.

Around me, the conversation carried lightly, with obvious pauses—Hywel's breath catching as Laszlo's hand burrowed into his trousers, and Conall humming as he flicked playfully back and forth over my nipple. Was I meant to pretend they weren't tormenting me? I opened my eyes and panted as Asterion's thick tongue circled the rim of his glass before he took another sip. My dress slipped off one shoulder, just a scant inch away from exposing my ignored breast as I breathed too heavily, teased and touched and needing *more*. But he didn't acknowledge what was happening, not with words, and he didn't leave.

I wanted him to watch.

I gasped as Hywel pinched my clit, arched, and the shoulder of my gown slid down. Conall murmured, amused, and then cupped the revealed flesh, gripping my nipple between his knuckles, pulling on it until it was sharp and swollen. I tried to stay quiet, but small cries fought in my chest, murmurs of protest as Hywel and Conall pulled their touches away for scant seconds. And the more sounds I made, the more I jerked and trembled, the less Asterion spoke. Laszlo and Conall parried back and forth, nonsense conversations about acquaintances I didn't know, nothing about what was happening here in this room, this strangely beautiful and stilted moment.

Asterion moved suddenly, body bowing forward, eyes intent. "Lift up her skirt."

There was a pause of movement, a crackle of the fire, and I raised my own shaking hands before Hywel pulled his touch away and he and Conall bundled my outrageous skirt up to my waist.

"Asterion—" I gasped out, reaching for him.

"Go on," he said, glancing at Hywel. "Touch her."

Hywel needed no further encouragement, and I moaned, the spell of attempted silence broken by this blatant acknowledgement. My right leg fell down from Hywel's lap, my heel hitting the carpet, and I was left exposed to Asterion's stare as Hywel plunged his fingers inside of me. Conall turned, and then my dress was just a ring of inconvenient fabric wadded around my waist. Hywel's top cock was out, fisted and pumped in Laszlo's steady grip, and both the dragon and I were vocal and wordless, Hywel's touch unsteady.

"Stop before she comes," Asterion said.

"Don't be cruel, Asterion," Conall purred, but the minotaur didn't acknowledge him, just watched Hywel fucking my already swollen and satisfied flesh with his fingers, watched Conall pulling and twisting my nipples, apologizing with warm grips of his hands.

"Ast-Asterion is never cruel," I panted out, catching his eyes. Lovely glimmering amber swirled in his gaze, and he let out a long sigh and shook his head.

"Never to you, *théa*," he vowed.

Hywel curled his fingers inside of me and I moaned, head falling back, eyes growing wide as those long, elegant digits beckoned my satisfaction closer.

"Not yet," Hywel warned Asterion. "She remains quite close to the edge for a while. It's her favorite spot."

I blushed at the shared knowledge, at the way Conall's head nodded above mine. He ducked, kissing my forehead, plucking my nipples in both hands. I grappled, reaching for the arm of the couch, twisting my left foot under Laszlo's, bracing for the breaking moment.

A soft, slow cry rose in my throat, and for a moment, I thought Hywel might betray Asterion. And then, at the very brink, when I started to squeeze on his fingers, to lose my sense of who and where and what I was, Hywel spoke.

"Now."

A dark shape lunged forward, my thighs grasped in huge, warm hands, my body tugged to the edge of the couch and turned to face a kneeling minotaur, his mouth open and—

"Ahh! Asterion! Yesss!"

A scorching, thick, slick tongue delved inside of me, curling as Hywel's fingers had done, and Asterion tugged me down until his upper lip pressed to my clit, my arousal glossed over his lips and his breath caressed my needy flesh. I came with a grateful shout, body bucking onto that long, dark tongue as it fucked and swirled inside of me, my own release wet and shocking as it splashed from my core. Conall bent his head, suckling on my breast, but I tugged him away with a grip on his hair.

I needed to see the minotaur, needed to hold that liquid gaze as he feasted on my pleasure and answered it with his own. Had I ever met another being who offered so much *néktar* only at the pure joy of seeing another's release?

"Asterion, please," I squeezed out, trembling in his hands, not sure what I was begging for. It was more than sex. What I wanted most in that moment was his surrender, for him to draw me to his chest, and in spite of my uncertainty, to claim me as his without allowing me argument or excuse.

He groaned and his eyes fell shut, breaking the moment as his tongue stroked and licked every inch and depth of me before drawing slowly and thoroughly out. He cleaned his lips, his broad nose, and gusted a sigh out on my gaping sex.

"Thank you," he said softly. And then he rose, arousal obvious and straining in his tight trousers. "I'll retire now."

A strange, garbled bark of laughter escaped me at the bland words, and I gaped up at him. And then he grinned, as if the words were meant to be a joke after all and he knew how absurd it was to...to do *that* and then walk away.

But he did, turning so I could see the bold jut and arch of his hungry cock leaving us in front of the fire. My uneven breaths matched his short steps out of the room and down the hall, until there was only me, panting and baffled, cradled between Hywel and Conall.

"He's nearly there now," Conall said, hands groping my breasts to soothe the sting of his pinches.

"The suspense is killing me," Hywel said drily, rolling his head to lean toward Laszlo for a kiss. "Don't stop, *cariad*. We've only just begun."

Conall hissed a false whisper in my ear, "Insatiable old folks."

34.
MATING FOR
BEGINNERS

"If you're hiding in here, I can leave the way I came and not let the others know."

I froze for a moment, up in the hayloft of the quiet stables, dust glittering in the air as it passed through cracks of sunlight. Then I sighed and leaned forward, bracing on my hands to look over the ledge and down to where Laszlo was standing in the doorway.

"They're looking for me?" I asked.

"Hywel's trying to be subtle about it, recalling things he left lying about in every room of the castle. Conall's on a proper hunt, though."

"I didn't mean to be hiding," I said.

Laszlo's head tipped and he turned to the side, revealing more of his face as he checked behind him. "We've been... hounding you a bit."

"No," I said, shaking my head. "It's not like that. I just... needed some time to think."

Laszlo stared up at me, and in spite of my sudden craving for a little time alone, just looking at him made me want to climb down the ladder and tuck myself against his chest until his wings closed around me.

"May I come up?"

I let out a rough sigh and nodded quickly. "Yes, please."

He didn't need the ladder. He was in the air with a few beats of his wings, grabbing the railing of the loft and stepping into piles of hay. He had to crouch and tuck his wings in close at his back, but we met in a large heap of hay that smelled dry and also a little mildewy, a scent that was relieved by Laszlo's lovely tea and cream fragrance. He gathered me into his arms and then spread his left wing, giving me a downy bed to rest on.

"I think we're all making each other a bit urgent," Laszlo said, his arm cradling me close to his side.

I tipped my head back to study his sharp profile, wanting to trace the lovely hook and line of his nose with my fingertip. "How do you mean?"

"Mmm... A werewolf's mating instincts are more demanding than most. Conall's giving you time—or himself, I'm not sure—but it does create an atmosphere of *need*. And Hywel won't want to be outdone. Are you still...?"

I chewed on the inside of my lip and considered the unvoiced question. "I don't..." Laszlo's arm tensed around my back, just barely. He was bracing, and it broke my heart. I turned, leaning over his chest, and forced myself to meet his gaze. "I don't doubt my ability to love you."

Laszlo's face lit up, and the worry that chewed at my thoughts and the tight ache in my chest unraveled.

"I *do* love you, Laszlo," I whispered.

He surged up, joy glowing in his eyes as he dove for my mouth, a sharp cry pressed into the kiss, his free hand holding my face to his. We curled together, twining legs and arms around one another, tongues twisting and ragged breaths laughing.

"How could I not?" I gasped, kissing over his cheeks. "How could I not love you, my sweetest, gentlest, most patient man?"

"Not as patient as you might think," Laszlo rasped, sealing his mouth to mine once more, our faces pressed clumsily together, hands clutching at fabric and flesh.

The kiss was tinged with relief and reverence, deep and drugging strokes of tongue and drags of teeth, but it didn't escalate. We only wanted to enjoy one another, share the gratitude between us. Laszlo's thumb and soft talon brushed over the arch of my cheekbone as his kisses grew long and languid, and then trailed up to the cupid's bow above my lip, over my cheeks, and across the bridge of my nose.

He stared down at me with that liquid gold gaze of his, just a tinge of green in the mix, and offered me a rare and stunning smile. "You don't know how much you honor me."

I flushed and wanted to hide, but this moment and Laszlo were too precious to shrink away. "Is it enough?" I asked.

"Enough?" he laughed.

"Is it...enough to love you? I don't know what else mating needs."

His smile grew brighter, more tender. "Oh, dear one." He pressed a kiss to my forehead. "Yes, it is enough. You are..." He blinked, eyes glittering briefly before he drew in a deep breath. "You offer me more than enough. As for mating, it's different for every species." He shuffled us, drawing my legs over his lap and scooting back to sit up in the hay.

"I can't deny how I feel about you all, even when I am not sure how I can manage to feel anything at all—or in moments like this morning, when I need to retreat," I admitted, wincing. "But I don't know how to be a mate, to reciprocate everything you offer."

Laszlo caught my hand, and the pad of his thumb stroked a spiral from my wrist into my palm and around again. "You honor me with your trust and your surrender. You took care of my mate, and you took care of me when we couldn't take care of one another, when you needed and deserved so much yourself. You've reciprocated plenty, Evanthia. Would it help if we...looked at mating less in generals and more in specifics? Courting, ceremony, expectations, and the like?"

I softened against Laszlo's chest and nodded. Lists, rules, something more concrete and easier to swallow than the promise of endless devotion. I couldn't say I was still so broken, not when these men had done so much, offered so much, until I was all but overflowing with their affection and strength.

"I know dragons fairly well," Laszlo said lightly, and I smiled, resting my head on his shoulder and nodding. "I told you that it starts with an exchange of gifts, which is true. But Hywel will likely consider your actions while he slept as part of courting, because he's been mated to me so long. Also, Excalibur is rightly yours but you've brought the sword into his hoard, and there are very few items he could've coveted more.

So that, not to mention the spectacular sex, is courting managed."

I blushed, but Laszlo only continued.

"As for claiming, he's done so. You recall," he added with a wicked smile, which sobered quickly. "He will want to bite you. That's part of what has him restless at the moment. It will heal quickly, but it will change your scent to other dragons. Having Rolant here while Hywel hasn't bitten you is a bit tricky, but Rolant is behaving in spite of his temperament."

I frowned and leaned back. "I didn't realize. Hywel never said!"

"None of us are going to pressure you to commit to a claiming before you are ready. Before you're as *determined* as we are, really. We might be monsters with impulses and instincts, but we are also men falling in love with you, dear one. Your wants and wishes are the most imperative of all."

Laszlo kissed my forehead before I could hide my face against his throat and then returned to the topic.

"Now, onto our lovely werewolf. *He* absolutely will need to bite you to settle the bond. It's very permanent, and it usually isn't common practice to share a mate with others. But I think if it were going to be an issue, he would've expressed it by now. There's no courting, that I know of, aside from the use of the knot so..."

"When we're ready..." I started.

Laszlo nodded. "When you and Conall are ready, he will bite and mate you. Both Hywel and Conall will have some extra internal sense of you when that happens. It's a way of ensuring they can protect their mate, provide for them."

"Hywel can sense you?" I asked.

Laszlo nodded. "In generals. Emotions, physical pains, and pleasures. You can imagine how much Hywel takes advantage of the latter," he added with a chuckle. "Exquisite torture when he wants to keep me on the edge."

"As if he doesn't excel at that already," I said with a sigh.

"Quite," Laszlo agreed drily. There was a pause, and I watched his fingers toying with mine, returned the little touches and caresses. Below us, horses puffed breaths and whipped their tails at curious flies, the stable calm and quiet, an earthy and humble atmosphere for a conversation I'd been so afraid of just weeks ago.

"And gryphons?" I prompted, rubbing my cheek over his shoulder.

"I've told you some," he said, suddenly delicate with his words.

"You have. But how do you claim your mates?" I asked.

There was a long pause, and Laszlo's embrace tightened into a clutch. I wiggled in his arms, sliding up his side, and found his cheeks stained with a warm blush.

"Laszlo?"

He blinked at me, and I could've sworn my gryphon looked guilty. "We...groom one another," he said stiffly. He lifted a hand and combed it through my loose hair, finding the feather he'd braided in. "And we exchange feathers after passion."

Ahhh, he was expecting me to be upset. I might've expected that too, except that all I really felt at the moment was a sweet, delicate pleasure, both at Laszlo's claiming and his bashful reluctance to admit it.

"Sneaky gryphon," I murmured, bowing my head, teasing him by hovering my lips over his, pulling out of reach as he tried to arch up for the kiss.

"You're not angry," he said, gaze scanning over my face.

"No, I'm not," I answered before placing my mouth to his. He moaned as I licked outside of his lips, but the kiss was light. Laszlo and I breathed one another in, surrounded by gentle sips of *néktar* in the air that I let float away.

"What if I don't have feathers to give you?" I whispered.

He cleared his throat, and his blush deepened. "Ah. I have another confession."

I lifted myself up as Laszlo reached into his wrapped vest. He withdrew a simple silver locket from a pocket over his heart and passed it into my hand. The latch was fine and thin, a precise leaf that clipped over a small round bud. It opened with a soft click, and I blinked away tears at what I found inside—one small and glimmering red dragon's scale on the right side, one coil of warm honey blonde hair on the left.

"I'm sorry. I couldn't help myself," Laszlo said.

I lifted the locket to my lips, my eyes falling shut as I pressed a kiss to the scale and to the lock of my hair. My hands shook slightly as I closed the locket once more and returned it to Laszlo, who tucked it safely away in folds of soft silk.

"We only have to be as we have been," Laszlo said to me. "If you want to leave someday...I will still have a part of you with me."

A strange, broken cry tried to rise in my throat at the thought of leaving. I'd be fighting myself every step. I swallowed the sound down and wrapped my arm around Laszlo's shoulder, cupped his jaw in my left hand, and reunited our lips in another, deeper kiss. We slid together, Laszlo drawing one of my legs over his hips, arm twining around my back to hold my ass and fasten me close. The hand on my thigh rose up to my hair, clasping my cheek and jaw and throat, as if Laszlo were reassuring himself that I was really here in his arms.

"I don't want to leave," I breathed out. The words were a release, a weight off my chest.

Laszlo's smile stretched, his nose nudging mine. "Oh, good. I didn't want to lie to you, but Hywel and I might find ourselves following you."

I laughed, and Laszlo pecked sharp kisses across both of my cheeks before relaxing back into the hay. I softened and stretched out, content in the hazy nest we'd made, studying my gryphon as he did the same to me, his gaze warm and gentle.

"Would you like to know about minotaurs?" Laszlo asked carefully after a long stretch of pleasantly shared silence.

I hadn't seen Asterion yet today, although it was early still, and I wondered if it was him I'd come out to the stable to avoid. He made my head spin, so cool and removed for days, only for a scorching passion to snap and explode out of him suddenly.

'*Thank you,*' he'd said. Bastard.

"Please," I whispered.

Laszlo cleared his throat. "Minotaurs are comparatively simple to the rest of us. They scent their mate almost immediately, the bond entirely instinctive. Unfortunately, they have quite a reputation for aggressive behavior in that regard. Generally, they're a very...impatient race."

I huffed, and Laszlo stifled his laugh.

"Yes, Asterion seems to be an exception. There's not much in the way of courting for a minotaur. They usually discover their mate and claim them immediately."

"Do they bite like werewolves and dragons?" I asked.

Laszlo shook his head, and I was momentarily distracted by the bits of straw and hay that were starting to collect in his hair. It was rare to see him disheveled, and it made me want to climb on top of him and make him even more so.

"They...they coat their mates in their scent," Laszlo said, and I blinked at the slight stiffness of his speech. "They release onto their mate, let it soak in."

I stiffened.

The hot spill over my belly, soaking through my thin slip, slick over my stomach and breasts and down to my thighs.

"I shouldn't have said anything."

I shook myself and focused on Laszlo once more, trying to clear the dark and hot fog of the memory of Asterion gushing over me. Marking me. *Claiming* me.

Bastard!

"Did you know?" I asked, leaning in to kiss Laszlo's chin to soften the tense bite of my voice.

He huffed. "It was obvious, and it was meant to be. A less than subtle request for me to...keep my distance."

I gasped and sat up. "You mean—Ohhhh!" I growled, and Laszlo smiled.

"It was a challenge for me, I assure you. And then Conall decided to stir the pot."

I gaped down at Laszlo. "He knew too. He knew that Asterion had claimed me, and then he..."

"I'm not sure if he thought he was teaching Asterion a lesson, or if he'd already started feeling the mating urges toward you, or...if he simply knew what you needed, and wasn't afraid of challenging Asterion in order to offer it to you."

"These absurd " I made a choked sound of struggle as I fought for the word. "Machinations! Marking me, leaving me,

dancing around one another and not simply *telling* me what—what
—Argh!"

My fists were clenched, but my heart was pounding. Below
me in the cozy nest of hay, Laszlo folded his arms behind his
head, a slightly smug smile on his face in spite of my temper. I
glared at him for a moment, but my anger ought to be directed
elsewhere, and it softened quickly.

"Thank you. You and Hywel have always been honest with
me, and I appreciate that, even if I wasn't always ready."

"Well, in Conall's case, we have an advantage of experience
and wisdom. As for Asterion..." Laszlo shrugged. "Bullheaded."

I snorted at that and sighed. "He did tell me, I think, but not
in a way where he was actually trying to make me *understand*.
And that night...he left."

"Perhaps he thought you would need time," Laszlo suggested.

I opened my mouth to object and then shut it with a snap. I
wasn't ready. Over and over again, I'd told Asterion I wasn't
ready. I would not be loved, I couldn't return the feelings, I
didn't want to be claimed. He'd said it before he left again, he'd
told me I was his...

And I'd told him I wanted to be fucked.

And in the days that passed, Conall had all but mated me,
Laszlo and I exchanged feathers, and Hywel courted me about as
his queen.

"Damn," I whispered, settling back into Laszlo.

He kissed the top of my head. "Don't be hard on yourself,
dear one. You had more than enough to occupy your mind. Asterion will wait for you until the end of time."

I huffed. "That's the problem, I think. He says he's not sure
he can stand to share me."

"Does he intend to wait us out?" Laszlo asked, a bite of
offense in his tone.

"I have no idea what he intends. He barely speaks to me
lately."

Laszlo hummed and twisted his fingers into my hair, letting
his talons trail along the back of my neck, drawing a shiver
through my body. "Asterion will either have to accept the situa-

tion or leave you both endlessly disappointed. I think the other night was a good sign."

"If only I'd seen so much as horn or tail of him since," I muttered, cuddling closer to Laszlo.

It was such a relief to feel settled with one of my men—such a surprise too. I found myself smiling once more, kissing Laszlo's throat, stroking his chest with my hand. When had my protests started to melt away? I wanted this. I wanted to belong to Laszlo. I wanted to possess him too.

And not just him.

Asterion had told me I held a terrible power over him, and now I wanted to wield that strength, over him and all the others.

"You're getting an idea," Laszlo said.

I grinned. "How can you tell?"

"You're squirming, and you have a very pretty blush on your cheeks. Have I mentioned how much I like your ideas?"

I laughed and twisted, resting my chin on Laszlo's chest. "I'm not sure if this one is...maybe a little cruel. And unfair to you and Hywel and Conall."

"Will I enjoy the part I have to play in this plan?"

"Mmm, undoubtedly," I purred, sliding my leg over Laszlo's hips, pushing up to straddle his lap and press my palms to his chest. I stared down at him, and his eyes lit up.

"Ahh. I see," he said, voice growing thick as he bucked his hips to tease me. "Then I'm happy to help, dear *mate*. However you need me."

"I always need you," I said, shrugging away thoughts of anyone else. Perhaps I did have a wicked plan, but Laszlo and I deserved this moment just for ourselves too.

Laszlo smiled up at me, hands stroking up under my skirt, hiking it up my hips. "I am always yours, Evanthia."

Mine.

My fingers tightened on Laszlo's shirt, and I dove down to claim my lovely gryphon mate's mouth.

35.
TAMING THE MINOTAUR

Asterion knew the moment I stepped into the training room. His back was to me, and his bare shoulders tensed and flexed, muscles tightening with every step closer as I approached. He was glistening with sweat, heavy weights fisted in both his hands. My own sweat had just barely dried on my skin as I'd walked downstairs, and the cum dripping out of me was still slick—a messy mixture of all my lovers. I'd had to wrestle Conall to keep him from licking it out of me after we'd settled.

"I've come to train," I called.

Asterion's long tail switched at his back, slapping against his calves—an agitated twitch of warning.

"Not today," he growled.

"Yes, today. Now."

"Evanthia—" he started, turning, and then his voice stuttered and died as he faced me.

The robe I wore—in case I ran into Rolant in the castle—was untied, the folds of fabric gaping open, revealing my marked skin. Red kisses sucked into my flesh, the grip of desperate hands, my sex swollen and still tender.

Hywel had wholeheartedly approved of my scheme and emptied himself inside of me three times before letting me run off to find Conall.

I was filthy, claimed. I was so thoroughly gorged on *néktar* that my hair was curling, skin glowing, eyes bright and almost crystal blue. I was a daughter of Hedone, and right now anyone on earth would recognize that truth. I shrugged the shoulders off, letting the silk drip over my breasts and then down to the floor to pool around my feet. I tried not to smile as Asterion groaned, body hunching forward.

"You wrestle bare-skinned, yes?" I asked, arching an eyebrow.

"You're *cruel*," he snarled, but his eyes were roving greedily over me.

I ignored his meaning, crossing the space slowly, every movement sending a fresh drip to run down my thighs, the glossy sheen catching Asterion's glare, his brow furrowing.

"You swore to protect me. Teach me to defend myself," I said.

"Why? So you won't *need* me?" he burst out, and he backed away when I was almost within reach of him. His cock was jutting, fighting against the tight constraint of his pants.

I stopped and tipped my head, giving up my cool facade. "Asterion, I will *always* need you," I said, voice breaking. "Just as you will always need me. Can you bear to run far away enough from me that it will cease this craving?"

"There is no such distance," he said, fists clenched.

"Then can you stand to remain close enough to touch without giving into what we both want?" I asked, eyes wide.

His chest heaved, every inch of his body straining away from me, while his cock did the exact opposite.

"You smell like them," he rasped.

"I will always smell like them," I said firmly. I meant to have my way, to make Asterion surrender, but it would only work if he could accept the others.

"You—It's so strong, I can't—You don't—"

He couldn't smell the mark he'd left on me. Weeks ago. I'd been his from the start.

"So fix it," I said, shrugging.

Asterion stared at me, shoulders shuddering, mouth open on his panting breaths, like he was trying to avoid breathing through his broad nose. His eyes flicked over my shoulder, and I frowned. He was considering running for the door.

"*Don't*," I snapped.

His gaze flashed back to me.

"It's time, Asterion," I said, more gently.

He groaned and lurched forward. I reached for his shoulders as his arms wrapped around my waist. My mouth parted, and Asterion's head tipped, tongue stroking in. We couldn't kiss, not in the usual way. I could only surrender to him, allow that thick dark tongue to invade my mouth, to fuck and lick and taste me. His hands roamed, squeezing and stroking, hunting for new flesh. When he reached between my legs to thrust a blunt finger inside of me and tried to scoop out the thick fluid that filled me, I grunted and wrestled my body away.

Asterion moaned and chased me for a moment before pausing. I pressed my lips between his nostrils and shook my head, nuzzling and refusing him at the same time.

"No, Asterion. You take me like *this*. Fuck me, and fill me with your scent *and* theirs. You will be equals. You claimed me, and not one of them will change that. But you won't erase their claims either."

"This is torture," he hissed.

I wanted to roll my eyes. I slid my hands over his terrifyingly strong shoulders and up his thick neck to hold his heavy jaw. "I am so wet, Asterion," I murmured, and I rocked my hips into the hand that cupped me, leaking into his palm. "They made me so ready for you. Hywel stuffed me, and Conall's knot stretched me. I will take *all* of you so well. Give me your cock," I pleaded, sweetening my tone as I trailed my lips over to his soft ear.

Asterion's breath puffed roughly over my shoulder, and his tongue stroked out to caress over a mark from Conall, the line of his teeth, hard enough to bruise but not to break the skin, a bite he'd barely held himself back from taking.

"I want you to put your entire heavy, brutal, perfect cock inside of me, Asterion," I whimpered into his ear. "I was made for you."

His forfeit was a tremble in my hands; it was the way he bowed over me, his own knees faltering as he scooped me up off my feet.

"Yesss," Asterion moaned, holding the backs of my thighs and lifting me to wrap around his hips as he fell to the dense mat.

I gasped as he fastened me close. He was so *broad*—just holding him between my legs like this made my body burn. His mouth hung open, hands cupping my waist as he bent forward. I gripped his shoulders, nibbling my way back to his rich lips, feasting over them as Asterion lowered me down to the leather surface, suede and soft against my bare back.

He sat up slowly, leaving me in a stretched arch, his thighs tucked under my back, my body splayed and spread, exposing my swollen sex.

"Beautiful," he murmured, reaching his hands to my inner thighs, his thumbs spreading me open, stretching my hole to his gaze.

It was my turn to be breathless, startled, and squirming.

"Are you sore?" he asked, voice lovely and dark, velvet and sturdy.

"Almost never," I admitted.

"We'll see about that," he said, quiet and private, bowing over me once more and licking his tongue up the length of my stomach to my breast.

I cried a soft sound of praise as he circled my breast, swiping that long and lovely muscle wide, around my side, up over my collarbone. His hands stroked my thighs, and cum dripped down to my ass.

"I may not fit," he said. "Not all of me. Minotaurs have killed mates with too much haste."

"You will fit," I said, stroking my hands into his soft mop of curls and then over to hold his horns in my grip. "I am *yours*."

He groaned and reached between us, knuckles brushing over my tender flesh and catching on my clit, but not with intention. He nudged and lifted his hips, fabric tugged down so the soft, short hairs of his hide rubbed the inside of my thighs, and then a sudden, heavy staff of scorching flesh slapped down against my clit.

I arched and cried out, and Asterion's cock dribbled eagerly onto my belly.

"Ohhh." I gaped at the shocking length of him. I'd felt him in the dark, but we'd been exhausted and it had been too dreamlike.

Now daylight was streaming in through tall windows, and

every vein and inch of him was stark. The color of his cock shifted from the russet brown of his skin down to a charcoal black before warming to a purply red at the very tip.

"You're magnificent," I whispered, barely able to catch my breath. He was *huge*. I swallowed hard. *Would* he fit? Inside, yes, but all of him? I wasn't sure. I'd never been presented with such a challenge that I was so eager to conquer.

He spilled more arousal onto me, and it collected in my belly button, another trail running over my side. Asterion hummed, hands sliding up my ribs, claiming my breasts in his grip. He rolled his hips back until only the first few inches rested against me.

At last. *Finally*.

And yet—

"No more avoiding me, Asterion," I said, covering his hands with mine, words urgent and nervous. His gaze met mine, and I caught my breath. "Please. Please, say it "

He bowed and lowered his snout to my chest between my breasts, between our hands. "I am yours, *théa*. You are my mate."

"Asterion—"

"I will share your bed, alone or with others," Asterion said, looking up at me. I sighed and nodded, urging him to continue. "I will claim your body, alone or with others. I will protect you, alone or with others. And I will love you, no matter what."

I sighed and released him, and Asterion moved the head of his cock to my entrance. It was a fat, thick tip, and it pressed to my opening bluntly as he hovered his face over mine.

"Thank you," I whispered, stroking my fingertips over his cheeks. I lifted my face as he lowered his, our mismatched mouths fitting gently together.

His cock nestled inside of me with a slow, dense pressure, and I breathed hard against Asterion's lips, his chest rumbling into a heavy purr.

"I need—" He gasped, inching away. "I need to see."

I wanted to watch too, but the sight took my breath away as Asterion sat up. His hands clasped my hips, holding me steady, and sunlight reached over the leather mat to cross along my hips. I was stretched wide, my already tender flesh red and glistening.

"More," I gasped immediately, trying to buck and draw him into me.

Asterion made a throaty sound of assent and pulled me onto his length rather than pushing inside. I whined at the strain—a good match for Conall's knot, but one that continued much deeper than he'd ever fit.

"Ohh, what a greedy, sweet cunt," Asterion whispered, eyes bright and steady on where my body was swallowing his shaft. He tugged out, and I shuddered. He slid in, deeper than before, and we both moaned as he pushed some of the cum still inside of me back out, gathering it on his yet to be devoured flesh and over my own.

"You feel perfect, please don't stop," I sighed out.

But he did stop, stopped and stared, studying me from the crown of my head to where we were joined, even glancing over his shoulder to gaze down at my toes curling into the mat.

"If I didn't know better, I would say you were the goddess, not her daughter," Asterion said. "You were designed by divinity."

I blushed and squirmed. "Designed for what?"

Asterion blinked, and then he slid out just an inch before gliding deeply in. "This."

"Show me," I gasped.

He groaned and repeated the motion, claiming new territory in my body that made me cry out.

"Who was I designed for, Asterion?" I asked, but my voice was begging.

He growled and trembled. "Me. Me, my little *théa*."

"Prove it," I gritted out, trying to rise to meet him.

He was so deep, my body so full I thought my belly seemed to swell, or I was just tensing, trying to force him in.

"Prove it. Give me all of you."

Asterion let out a garbled shout, and his right hand struck the floor by my head, shoving his cock hard inside of me as his weight sank down. I shouted, squeezing on his length, and a rich heat started to swirl in my core, higher, up even into my chest. Asterion snarled and bucked, and still there was more of him to take.

"All, Asterion. *All* of you," I snapped.

His arm folded, elbow to my shoulder, and together we howled as he struck hard in the heart of me, the downy sheath that tucked his length away brushing against my clit.

"Oh, Evanthia," he moaned, his body sagging over mine, his hand on my hip sliding back and down to hold my ass. "My mate."

"Yours," I breathed out, kissing his jaw, claiming his horns in my fists.

He groaned and started to move. "I can't—I can't be gentle. You will be *fucked*, my lovely goddess."

"Fill me, fuck me," I pleaded, wrapping my weak legs as much around him as I could, even when his weight and breadth pressed them wide.

Asterion bellowed and surged, body drumming a rough rhythm inside of me, every clap of flesh stealing my breath and making stars burst behind my eyes, colors swarming. His tongue swiped over my throat and against my ear, occasionally claiming my open, shouting mouth. I braced myself by his horns, yelping into his ravenous kiss, the pound of his cock inside of me brutal and beautiful at once. I *would* be sore, and I would walk bowlegged, and I'd do so with pride.

"Mine," Asterion growled. "*Théa, mine.*"

He chanted the words, hissed filthy praise for my body in my ear, and still made room for his length in my willing body. The sheath that rubbed into me tightened and swelled, a perfect friction and pressure against the stretched lips of my sex, lovely bites of ecstasy snapping at my edges.

"Mine," I said, but there was no breath to make the word, and all my strangled sounds were reflexive, tiny cries and shouts with every rough thrust, so wholly possessed.

I settled instead for claiming Asterion's flesh with my teeth, biting on his throat, as the storming orgasm ripped through me. I screamed into him, and Asterion howled. His cock went off like a cannon inside of me, a sudden bolt of hot, rushing pleasure. I released his throat and Asterion braced his hands on either side of my head, pinning me to the floor and rutting me madly as he bellowed, one flood of his release splashing out of me, and then another mixing with my own bursting response.

My hands clamored over his chest, a sudden panic rising in me that I might drown in this moment, suffocate under the sweep of *néktar*, and I didn't *ever* want this to end, not even in such overwhelming pleasure.

"Asterion," I whimpered.

He must've heard my panic and understood it instinctively, because his arms snapped around me once more, cradling me to his chest, and he rolled on the floor, planting his back down on the leather mat, a slippery mess sliding beneath us. Being on top lodged his length inside of me, my legs too weak to lift myself, and we both moaned, my eyes squeezing shut as I seemed to choke around him.

"Forgive me," Asterion rasped, and I wanted to snap at him for saying such a thing, but then he continued. "Forgive me, *théa*, but I must have you again."

He was still gushing inside of me, but he grabbed me by the waist and bounced me on his length, using my fluttering sheath to fuck himself, to fuck us both. I had been used this way at The Seven Veils, but I couldn't recall a single one of their faces, not now, not with Asterion's beautiful chest glittering with sweat, warm eyes fastened on my breasts as they shook with his thrusts. I reached down to rub over my sodden clit, and Asterion moaned and quickened the pace, ass slapping against the floor as he thrust in and out of me.

"If they want to smell themselves on you, they'll have to have another turn when I'm done," Asterion rumbled. "Oh, you will never wash me off now, *théa*."

I laughed at the claim, grinning with him at his triumph, and my head fell back as he huffed and gasped and groaned. "Lick my breasts, mate," I teased.

He growled and hunched, and I grabbed a horn, yanking him into place. Asterion suckled with tender attention, laving and stroking his tongue with a sloppy reverence. His thumb joined my hand, a better judge of what I needed than even I was.

I came once more riding my minotaur, hands fisted on horns to steer his mouth, thighs burning, cunt biting down cruelly on his throbbing staff. Asterion followed me, holding me tightly, a broken shout buried in my breast, another obscene flood nearly tossing me up off his length, if not for his grip on my waist.

He collapsed as he finished, chest stuttering as he fought for air, eyes wide, cock unflagging and starting to make me ache. I leaned down and crawled up his chest to ease the burn, sighing and sagging against him when the stretch went from painful to reassuring. We rested like that, and I had a feeling—a stiff, thick, long one—that Asterion would need me again before we left this room. For now, we enjoyed our peace together.

"I liked watching them touch you," he murmured.

I sighed. "Good. I like... I'll want you all quite often. I *am* very greedy."

He stirred and then grunted and seemed to realize he was still exhausted. "I won't always want to be last."

I kissed his jaw. "It won't be like that, Asterion. I promise. They'll like to watch you touch me too. As long as that's okay with you."

He hummed, thinking it over. "I won't mind. I thought I would, but...as long as I have you, *théa*, I will be very happy." He lifted me up a little more, and I whimpered at the tug of him in my swollen sex. We twisted so we were eye to eye, and I couldn't resist kissing his upper lip once more. "You make me very happy, Evanthia. I intend to do the same for you."

I smiled at him and gave him another kiss as his eyes crossed to watch. "You will. You can start now," I said, and I waggled my eyebrows before adding, "With your tongue."

36.
ADIEUS AND
INTRODUCTIONS

The first morning I woke with all four of my men in bed with me ought to have been a very slow, languid, and most likely profane treat. Instead, it started by opening my eyes to find Rolant at the foot of the bed, staring at us all.

I screeched, bolting upright, before diving back under the covers. Asterion, whose cock had been nestled between my thighs, leapt from the edge of the bed, erect length swinging like a weapon. From the other end of the bed, Hywel jumped out too, less obviously aroused and significantly less surprised than the rest of us.

"Get out," he said with a sigh.

"I came to say goodbye. You all took entirely too long to rise," Rolant said, eyeing Asterion with a bored quality I found both relieving and a little offensive. There was *nothing* unremarkable about Asterion's...anything.

"It's barely morning. It might've waited," Conall grumbled, rolling toward me as Laszlo slid from the bed. He gathered me close in his arms, not bothering to lift his head from the pillow.

"I want to reach home before nightfall," Rolant said, shrugging.

"And you wanted to take one last chance to annoy Hywel," I said.

Rolant blinked at me, his stare cool and superior as ever, but I thought he might've been laughing with me in private. Asterion sat back down on the edge of the bed, an arm crossing over my hip and blocking Rolant's stare.

"We'll escort you down," Laszlo said, rifling through piles of discarded fabric to retrieve robes for himself and Hywel.

"To make sure you don't accidentally place any of my hoard in your bags on your way out," Hywel said drily.

I squirmed out of the circle of Conall's arms, clutching the sheet around my breasts as I sat up. "Goodbye, Rolant. It was... not unpleasant to meet you," I teased.

He broke out in a laugh, striding toward the door. "You weren't an utter disappointment yourself, divinity."

Laszlo and Hywel followed close on his heels, shooing the other dragon from the room. Hywel paused in the doorway, glancing back at us. "Stay in bed. We'll bring up breakfast."

I nodded and fell back into Conall's embrace, and he and Asterion sighed as the door shut.

"Move over," Asterion said.

Conall huffed, tightened his arms around me, and rolled once more, taking me with him as I yelped in surprise.

"Conall," Asterion growled.

I laughed as Conall pressed me down in the bed, burrowing his face into my throat. The bedsheet waggled with the thump of his tail, and he squirmed on top of me, making room for himself between my legs.

"You had her to yourself all night," Conall said as Asterion scooted closer on the bed, tugging at the twisted sheets.

"She was between us! So did you!"

"Your hands were on her best spots!"

"My *what*?" I squawked, wrestling against Conall and only managing to rouse his cock where it pressed to my belly.

Asterion chuckled. "You've had plenty of time with her best spots," he said. "I deserve to catch up."

I had a vague recollection of Asterion's huge hands cupping my slick and messy sex, as well as groping absently at my breast through the night.

"Just give me a few minutes like this, and I'll share her again," Conall rasped, rutting playfully on top of me, nuzzling and nipping at my throat, licking his tongue over my pulse as he groaned.

"This is very rude," I muttered, but I was meeting Conall's

thrusts, rubbing my sex to the base of his cock for the dull friction.

"Don't you dare knot her," Asterion warned. "I'll have *your* ass."

Conall lifted his head and winced at me, pausing his motion. "I'm a coward. I don't know how you manage the size of that thing."

I snorted and sagged on the bed, arms tossed up over my head. "I'm told I'm gifted."

Asterion shouldered Conall out of the way, leaning on his side, snout brushing against my forehead. "Gifted. Fated to take me. Whatever you like to call it. Are you sore?"

Conall sighed and slid to my side, the pair of them compromising my body between theirs, the werewolf nestling against my ass, one hand sliding around to cup a breast, as Asterion's free hand slid down between my thighs once more, lightly plugging my core with two fingers.

Just his small touch forced my body to recall how...ambitious I'd been the day before, claiming my—my lovers a number of times each.

"A little," I admitted, blushing.

There was no disguise for the glow of pride in Asterion's stare. He ducked his head, offering me his mouth, and I stretched up to gift his lips with kisses as Conall toyed and twisted a nipple absently.

"Rolant left abruptly," Conall mused. "You think he's up to something?"

Asterion pulled away from me, nudging his chin against the top of my head once before relaxing onto his back. He drew his fingers that had been inside of me up to his lips and sucked on them before answering.

"I think spending a week in a castle of mating beasts was enough for him," Asterion said.

His cock was still half-hard, which was an impressive view on its own, and while I was a little relieved he and Conall were content to cuddle and relax, I couldn't help myself from reaching out and petting at the long staff of flesh. His skin seemed more dense than Conall's or Laszlo's, but he was just as responsive to a light touch, bucking into my palm. Conall scooted closer to my back, replacing Asterion's fingers inside of me with his own, watching me circle Asterion's cock with both hands and stroke.

"It's...it's good that he left," Asterion said, watching my face.

I smirked. "Did you want more privacy?"

"I invited guests. They should arrive soon." Asterion groaned, horns piercing back into the pillows as he arched into my suddenly tight grip.

"Guests?!"

Conall kissed my shoulder to soothe me, and for a moment Asterion could only fuck himself through the ring of my hands, a thick syrup of arousal pooling at his tip and then spilling over. It was silken, sliding into my grip, making his motion beautifully smooth, and it smelled vaguely sweet. My mouth watered with the influence of *néktar* in the air.

"Friends." Asterion's breath hitched as he stumbled over the answer. "You'll-you'll like them, *théa*. Good people."

"How many?" I asked.

"I—Fuck—Evanthia, I-I can't count right now," Asterion gusted out with a shaky laugh. His hands were fisting in the sheets, and more precum was spurting and dribbling over my knuckles. His dark, soft sac grew swollen between his parted thighs.

I glanced over my shoulder at Conall and he grinned, releasing me and letting me rise to kneel between Asterion's thick legs. Asterion moaned at the sight of me, naked, bowing over his long cock.

"Do it," he rasped.

I ducked, brushing my lips over the flat, round head of his cock, glossing my lips and licking them clean. Sweet and salty, like dark sugar.

"Am I watching or joining?" Conall asked us.

"Joining," Asterion and I said in unison.

"If she's sweet, reward her," Asterion said, voice low and dark. "But if she's tormenting me, *punish* her."

I gasped and Asterion smirked at Conall, who laughed and crawled behind me, stroking his hands down my back and lifting my hips.

"Your choice, *théa*," Asterion said, giving wicked meaning to the words. His smile stretched broadly over his face, such a rare sight it stole my breath.

"I'll be good," I murmured, lapping him clean, stroking my hands up and down, Asterion's tension unwinding and hips flexing to butt his tip against my cheek. Behind me, Conall kissed down my spine, fingers trailing down to dip between my legs and swirl my own slick interest over my sex.

I nipped the side of Asterion's length and he shouted, jolting in my grip. "For now," I added with a grin.

⚜

I STIFFENED AT THE FIRST RATTLE OF WHEELS ON GRAVEL, churning closer from deep in the woods. On either side of me, Hywel and Asterion claimed one of my fidgeting hands, offering me a grounding grip to occupy my nerves.

"I promise you, *théa*, you'll enjoy their company," Asterion said, twisting to kiss the top of my head.

"And if you don't, I'll eat them," Hywell offered lightly.

Asterion snorted, but Hywel's promise drew a smile out of me, so he said nothing.

"Are Marius and Lillian coming?" I asked. Asterion had been especially tight-lipped about the visitors, and even Conall swore he didn't know, though I suspected he had guesses.

"Marius is keeping an eye on London," Asterion said. And Lillian would remain with her basilisk. "But we can arrange another visit with them, when we're able."

I nodded. I missed the quiet woman, missed riding with her and drinking chocolate. It'd been a long time since I had a friend, and while I certainly didn't lack companionship lately, it wasn't the same. I wanted to spend time with Lillian now that I felt...alive again, wanted to be as kind to her as she was to me.

A bright giggle rang in the woods as two carriages turned around a bend, clearing a line of trees and appearing on the horizon. Well, I certainly wouldn't lack company now. The second of the two carriages was driverless and loaded with luggage, following along after the first, which shook slightly on its wheels.

Another cry, *less* like laughter, sounded from the occupied carriage, and I glanced up at Asterion with arched eyebrows.

He winked at me. "That will be Miss Reed and her gentlemen."

The carriage rolled closer, carrying a soft cloud of *néktar* with it and murmurs of affectionate laughter. I rolled back my shoulders and took a deep breath, letting the power of sensual pleasure chase away some of my stress.

Conall stepped up to my back from behind Asterion, whispering in my ear. "I met them briefly. Flirtatious little human and a pack of monsters that dote madly on her. She stabbed Birsha once."

My eyes widened as the carriage halted, and before I could ask more about *that*, the flirtatious little human in question threw open the door and jumped down, darting out of reach of a warm brown hand that tried to catch her.

"Asterion!" the woman cried. She was pretty, with rich brown waves of hair that looked tangled from lovers' hands. The collar of her dress was unbuttoned and open, and her skirt was wrinkled, but she didn't seem the least bit self-conscious, gaze glittering with mischief as she scanned over us.

Asterion squeezed my hand, releasing to step forward and take hers, bowing over her knuckles. "Miss Reed."

"Oh, Esther, please!" she said, patting over his head and beaming up at him. "We are old friends now, surely. It's good to see you again."

From either side of the carriage, more men poured out. Either the carriage had a charm to increase the size inside, or the group had been *very* cozy on the ride. Possibly both.

Hurrying to join Esther Reed was a tall, handsome man with bronze skin, feline features, and a pair of large wings in shades of black and brown and bronze.

"Amon," Asterion greeted, shaking this man's hand and bowing to him too.

With a glance I could tell that whoever this monster was, he was *significant*. His gaze took in the castle, Asterion, and the men who surrounded me with a cool, studying quality, but those warm cat-like eyes paused on Hywel and Laszlo.

"Dragon," he blurted out, eyes widening.

"Sphinx," Hywel answered, smirking slightly and nodding his head.

If I'd been asked if I knew whether a dragon outranked a sphinx, I would've answered I neither knew nor particularly cared. But apparently, in this case, Hywel did rank higher. And Amon, whose wings rustled and who bowed stiffly from the waist, did seem to care. Behind him, the rest of his party eyed one another, exchanging surprised glances.

"I thought you invited us to one of your own homes," Amon said to Asterion.

"Ah, did I give that impression?" Asterion asked in a too-innocent tone that led me to believe he'd known exactly what impression he was giving. "Amon, allow me to introduce Hywel, the Welsh Dragon, King of Dreams, and his mate, Laszlo Bladewing, King of the Western Clouds."

Amon's jaw grit a little tighter at that, and he and Laszlo bowed to one another with equal respect.

"You know Conall, of course," Asterion said, waving at the werewolf before turning to me. "And this is Evanthia, daughter of Hedone." He wet his lips with his tongue and tilted his head, asking me for some permission. I nodded, and he added, "Our mate."

Our

Behind Amon, the others had gathered. A man flickered in and out of view, his arm slung over pretty Esther Reed's shoulder. Two others looked fairly human, although one was quite pale, hiding from the sunshine under a dark umbrella and sporting a pair of flat black sunglasses. The fourth was an enchanted statue. It was a curious group, I thought, but they all looked quite friendly.

"An honor," Amon said to me, and he bowed low—gallant, even.

I couldn't remember how to curtsey, and my tongue was tied at the presence of so many strangers, but the sphinx spoke once more before my silence became awkward.

"We met the Wyrm on the road. I am surprised you trust him with such a significant mission," Amon mused.

A stunned silence met the announcement, the five of us Rolant had left glancing at once another.

Hywel gathered himself first, voice low and dangerous. "Mission?"

Amon seemed to buoy at our obvious confusion. "Sending him to collect the last of the cauldron of Murias."

"The cauldron?!" Laszlo asked with a gasp, turning to stare at Hywel, whose pale expression took on a remarkable shadow, a fluff of dark smoke expelling from his flared nostrils.

Amon looked like he wanted to step back, but to his credit, he stretched his wings to shield the pretty Esther.

"He told us quite cheerfully you got word of its location and sent him—" The Irish brogue announced the redheaded, rascal-looking fellow before he appeared in earnest.

"No wonder he took his leave so eagerly," Conall said, barely restraining a laugh, which seemed to put our guests at ease. He turned to me and whispered, "The cauldron is one of the four gifts from the first fae to arrive in our realm. It serves food endlessly and was meant to keep the Irish people out of famine. But of course, it was stolen."

Hywel sucked in a dramatic breath and released it slowly. "It is no matter," he said in a tone that implied this news *very* much mattered.

"Are you sure?" I asked, stroking his stiff arm.

Hywel relaxed slightly, blinking and turning to offer me a genuine smile. "The cauldron is nothing to the treasure I already possess. Especially our more recent acquisition. I merely like to keep abreast of these sorts of discoveries."

Laszlo nodded, shrugging slightly, and I suspected that *more* treasure was always welcome, regardless of what was already possessed.

"Our debt to Rolant will be cleared, at least," Laszlo said.

"Ah yes, that is a relief," Hywel admitted.

The conversation returned to greetings, and Hywel and Laszlo did their best not to glare at the horizon *too* much.

"I've never been in an English castle before! I'll be very disappointed if there aren't a great many secret passages," Esther said brightly, grinning.

"Oh, there are dozens," Hywel promised, and the young woman clapped and bumped her hip into the currently invisible man at her side.

"Here come the others," Asterion said, nodding toward the road, where another carriage turned into view.

"More?" I murmured, but thankfully the chatter of Esther and her men covered my voice.

Conall wrapped an arm around my waist, and Hywel's hand squeezed mine.

"Be brave, *mo chroí*. We got through an entire round of fussy introductions and no blood's been spilled yet. That's not bad when you mix species," Conall whispered in my ear.

37.
DANCING AND
GOSSIPING

"**I** thought you might've been downstairs already."

Hywel's reflection appeared in the mirror behind me, his pale, cool coloring warmed by candlelight.

"Everyone seems lovely," I said.

His head tipped. "But?"

I sighed and fidgeted with a bottle of perfume on the vanity in front of me. "But there's an awful lot of them. And it's been... just us for so long. And Rolant," I added.

Another young woman had arrived after Esther Reed, a Miss Hazel Nix, and with her another small collection of monsters. The two groups had greeted each other eagerly, apparently arriving from different directions, and the quiet castle had become quite full and noisy in no time at all.

"We can send them all away," Hywel said easily, shrugging.

I huffed and shook my head. "Asterion must want them here for a reason, and...they do seem nice."

"Is it the demon? The Gemini?" Hywel asked.

I'd thought I hid my reaction when the demon stepped out of the second carriage, skin shimmering bronze and violet, eyes skirting up to me nervously, but Hywel must've felt my flinch.

"No. No, I... We didn't do more than cross paths, and he was as much a captive as I was," I said, frowning.

"Not one of the other men ever visited The Seven Veils."

I shook my head. "It's not that. Although that is a relief to know. But they...they know that I was there." The lovely redheaded Hazel Nix certainly looked at me as though she knew, although there was something gentle in her stare, and in her voice too. She reminded me a little of how Laszlo had treated me when we first met.

Hywel sank down to his knees at my side, and I twisted on the chair to face him, wrapping my arms around his shoulders.

"They do. They know what you survived, what you've risen from. If we didn't know better, I would say you have phoenix blood in you too."

I blushed and glanced away, but Hywel wouldn't let me escape, catching my chin in his long fingers and drawing my gaze back to his.

"I am king of this castle, *blodyn bach*. If I tell them to leave, they will leave. If I say you and I will hide away here, or in my hoard, then they will manage fine without us," Hywel said, stroking my hair up off my neck. He picked up a hair pin from the vanity and slid it into my hair, twisting the strands into a chignon and fastening it in place one pin at a time. "If I tell that sphinx to put on an apron and fix you dinner, he will."

"Hywel!"

"I wouldn't—that would be outrageously disrespectful. And I *do* respect him. Anyway, from what I've learned, it's that strange day-walking vampire who is the cook of the group. Do you know, I caught the one with the vanishing act trying to *steal* from the hoard! Nearly bit his hand off, but Laszlo dragged him off to set him straight." I laughed, and Hywel sighed. "It is strange to have the castle so full once more. But I think it's good too. We can't hide from time passing forever, can we, my love?"

I licked my lips and slid my hands around to rest on his chest. "I suppose not."

Hywel nodded. "There will be a feast tonight. And a ball. I want to dance with you, and I want to see you dance with the others. Will you do that for me?"

A little ache of grateful tears rose to my eyes, but I blinked them away, nodding. "Yes, I'll dance."

He picked up a jeweled pin and slid it into my hair. "Beautiful. But you need a necklace. Stand up."

"Hywel," I said in protest, but he stood first and drew me up with a tug on my elbows.

"I've brought you a present, something I've had for quite a long time and known it never really belonged to me. I was waiting for you, you see," he said, that heavy stone voice of his feigning ease.

And from the back pocket of his trousers, Hywel withdrew what looked at first like a handful of dripping wet stones, shining pebbles and sparkling crystals, drips of fresh dew preserved by diamonds. I stared until he grasped the jewels from either end and it dropped and cascaded down into a stunning necklace, each stone barely held together by threads of silver.

"I know she's not your favorite, but this was made by Our Lady of the Lake," Hywel said.

"Hmph," I grunted, but my fingers itched to touch the necklace. It looked as though the fae woman had scooped big pools of water and jewels up in her hands, then spread them into a stunning creation, natural and perfect all at once.

Hywel raised the necklace, and I couldn't help but lean in and allow him to wrap it around my throat, the kiss of stone and silver soothing on my skin. "She disguised herself as an old woman, waited for a knight who was gallant enough to come to her aid, and then gave him this necklace that would grant its wearer the gift of being unfathomably loved." The clasp clicked shut, and Hywel's hands stroked up my neck to hold my face, his smile subtle but glowing in his opal eyes. "Which you are, *blodyn bach*."

My breath hitched, and Hywel's hands stroked down my back, pulling me close against him, his head turning and bowing to my throat. I arched for the kiss, gasping as sharp teeth scratched over the left side of my neck instead.

"I will bite here," Hywel whispered.

"N-now?" I squeaked out, surprised by how willing I was, not just for the bite, but what it would mean.

"Mmm, no," he said slowly, scraping his fangs once more before pressing a chaste kiss to my pulse. "No, tonight we have guests and dinner. And you will dance with me, and I'll watch you dance with others. And tonight, I will share your body in this bed with the rest of your mates, *blodyn bach*. Because we've all waited too long for you to be selfish, as much as we might like. But soon, yes?"

He leaned back, catching my gaze, waiting for my answer.

Yes?

A cool stone slid over my chest, down to kiss between my breasts, as if Hywel had directed it there. I shivered and panted slightly, and still he waited for my answer.

It came, breathless but clear. "Yes."

Hywel beamed at me, and it was his arms around my waist that kept me upright.

"I don't...I don't have any treasure to give you, but Excalibur—"

Hywel turned me and slanted his mouth over mine, swallowing the offer. His tongue traced around my mouth, and he shook his head, nose nuzzling against mine. "Excalibur chooses its owners. No, you've given me *plenty*, mate. Besides, we have many years ahead of us to collect and exchange gifts," he said, kissing my cheek.

I circled my arms around his shoulders, holding him to me, closing my eyes and breathing in that soot and lavender scent of him. Hywel purred, hands stroking my back.

"Courage, my pretty morsel," he whispered.

I nodded against his chest, my arms sliding down over his shoulders, hands trailing to his own, our fingers tangling as we stepped apart. Hywel's scales glimmered under his pale skin, and for a moment I wanted to ask him to transform back into his dragon form, to escort me down to dinner, huge and terrifying. I would be afraid of nothing with a dragon at my side.

He grinned, sharp teeth glinting and pointing out the obvious. I *did* have a dragon at my side. For as long as I wanted one.

"Ready," I said, nodding my head and linking my arm through his.

⬥

"OH, NIREAS, PLEASE," HAZEL NIX LAUGHED, TUGGING HER giant lover by two of six arms away from the collection of instruments on the balcony. "They're managing fine, and we never get to dance together."

"That's because I'm a terrible dancer," the giant murmured, but the young woman only laughed and drew him toward the stairs as the shadow musicians continued to play merry tunes for our large party.

The vampire and the handsome young man who looked bookish and human danced past Asterion and me, whispering in one another's ears. Laszlo and Hywel were dancing too, using the steps of old-fashioned courtiers, ones I'd seen centuries ago. Esther spun by, the quiet enchanted stone man chasing her skirts, and what I suspected was an invisible partner crowding closer to her front.

Amon the sphinx, Hunter the orc, and my own werewolf Conall stood together, heads bowed.

"They don't look as though they're plotting war, do they?" I asked my own partner, Asterion, nodding toward the small cluster.

Asterion huffed. "More likely gossiping."

I laughed and craned my neck to watch the men as we turned away from them. "Gossiping? That seems awfully frivolous."

"We monsters are not much better than the gentlemen we seek to emulate," Asterion said, shrugging.

"Hmm, I'll reserve my judgment on that," I murmured. I did not mind human men, or what I remembered of their company, but they didn't measure up to the society I kept these days.

"Should you like to know what they're speaking of?" Asterion asked, nodding to the others.

I raised my brow. "Are you trying to get out of dancing with me, Asterion?"

He rumbled, a pleasant vibration sinking into my chest and gentling at the nerves that came and went this evening. "Never," he said, arm tightening around my waist. "I won't retreat from you now, *théa*. I hope you knew as much when you drew me into your body."

I flushed at the words, flattered and aroused, my hand on his chest gripping at his collar, tempted to drag him down for a kiss, even with so many others around us. And then it occurred to me that was exactly what I should do. I rose to my toes, unclenching my fist to slide my hand up his vast chest, around the wide neck and to the soft fur at the back of his head. Asterion's eyes widened as I drew his mouth to mine, our dance faltering while we gave focus to this new pursuit. Asterion's lips were only briefly frozen against mine. He groaned and I sighed, opening to him, knees turning soft as his tongue swept in, overwhelmingly thick and deftly teasing at my own.

"Ah, I see you are a favorite at last, Asterion," a sweet voice called.

Asterion lifted his head, gazing down at me in a way that sapped all remaining strength from my muscles, before glancing up and nodding at Esther, who must've been the one to speak.

"My dear mate has no favorites," Asterion said.

"On the contrary," I said, meaning the words for his ears only but aware that the room's conversation had paused to watch us instead. "I have *four*."

Asterion's lips twitched.

I frowned. "You don't believe me?"

"I do," he said, brushing his nose and mouth over my forehead. "I am learning to."

"I am very happy for you, my friend," Esther said, patting Asterion's shoulder. She beamed at me. "Your gentleman did me a good turn a year ago, and I will not forget it."

"It was a small favor," Asterion muttered, and I could've sworn the soft skin over his face was coloring slightly. "And if I recall correctly, you sought to repay me by disappearing and giving us all quite a scare."

"She's a pretty little ball of trouble, this one," a roguish and cheerful voice announced from Esther's side.

Esther waved her hand airily. "My vampire needed me. All worked out in the end."

"For everyone but Birsha," the disembodied Ezra noted.

Esther's pretty features twisted in a scowl. "I should've thrust the knife even deeper."

My eyes widened, and Esther twitched as if someone had nudged her. She glanced at me, paling briefly, and then spoke in such a scramble I could barely make the words out.

"Asterion, have you heard the latest goings on of your house? It is a great and delightful scandal, after all the trouble she has given you!"

"My house?" Asterion asked, blinking at the young woman.

But I knew her meaning almost right away. "You mean Isabel?"

Esther rushed out a breath and nodded, dark curls bouncing. "Yes! After all her squawking, to bring a monster in—"

"A monster?" Asterion prompted, head tilting.

Esther flapped her hands. "Well, I mean, it's only Byron, but—"

"*Byron?*" Asterion pressed, even more surprised now.

"Who is Byron?" I whispered.

A voice appeared so suddenly and unexpectedly—given the man was still staying invisible—it made me jump. "The guardian of the house camping in the woods, another werewolf."

"Isabel installed Byron *inside* the house?" Asterion asked.

"Oh, you haven't heard," Esther said, eyes widening. "Oh, dear. Perhaps..."

"Miss Reed," Asterion rumbled in warning.

"Amon, come explain the London latest to Asterion!" Esther called.

Strangely, I found myself withholding laughter. The music had paused, and the room was gathering together at Esther's call, Asterion looking flustered and annoyed and too polite to say so directly.

"Someone please come tell me about Grace House," he said tersely.

"It was attacked, Asterion. Last week, shortly after you left." It was not Amon who spoke, but the most well-dressed and composed orc I had ever met.

"*Attacked?*" Asterion gasped. "Why did no one say anything before now?"

"It was over before it properly began, my friend," Amon said. "Byron did his job admirably and killed the villains. No one made it farther than the woods, didn't set so much as a toe to the front steps."

"Byron was, however, grievously injured," Hunter explained,

raising a hand before Asterion had to ask. "Marius is installed now, with his bride."

"Bride?" I asked, but the conversation was moving on. Lillian and Marius were married, though? That was very sweet.

"It appears Isabel does have *some* sense of decency. She tracked Byron down in the woods and dragged him back to the house. She's playing his nursemaid now, poor fellow." Conall let out a rough laugh and added, "Wonder if he wouldn't have rather taken his chances in the woods."

Asterion was silent and stiff at my side, and I braced myself for the announcement. He would decide he needed to leave, I supposed. To go back to London and set things to rights.

Then he let out a long sigh. "What a relief for us that Marius found Lillian."

I blinked at that and glanced as several of the other monsters murmured their agreement.

"He all but *ate* the Grendel," Hunter laughed. "No one will move against Grace House while he guards it."

"The *Grendel*?!" I cried out.

"It's quite a story," Asterion said, nodding and smiling at me.

"Well, for goodness' sake, let's settle ourselves somewhere more comfortable so you can tell it," Hywel said. "I find myself quite curious to hear what went on while I was sleeping."

❦

THE NIGHT WAS SILENT, THE DEEP HOURS JUST BEFORE BIRDS rose once more to call on morning. My lovers dozed around me, barely fallen asleep after the party had finally broken up. It was not one story I'd heard tonight, but *many*.

"Did it hurt you, *mo chroí*, to hear so much of his name tonight?" Conall rasped in my ear, still trying to snuggle closer to me when he was all but fused to my back. Asterion lolled on his other side, sprawled carelessly, and I suspected Laszlo might be listening in front of me, Hywel curled around his back as Conall was to mine.

Birsha. So many stories about Birsha. About these new

acquaintances' triumphs against him, the torments he put them through too.

"No," I said, blinking at the realization. "No, it didn't pain me. It was...nice, actually."

Conall stirred, propping his head up to glance down at me, and I tilted back to lean against him. We'd let the fire burn out while we were downstairs and hadn't bothered lighting any candles before falling together into bed, so my view of him was soft and hazy above me.

"It makes me feel...as if I had not been so alone as I thought," I whispered, my eyes stinging.

Conall's breath hitched, his head lowering to rest his brow against mine.

"You had no notion of me, and I certainly wasn't imagining that there was anyone *fighting* him, but it's almost like...now that I know..." I laughed and shook my head. "I don't know. Hope can't be passed back in time, I suppose."

Conall's kiss was gentle, his breath rough, clearly holding himself back. "I wish we'd fought sooner," he whispered, and the tension of his expression wrinkled over mine.

I reached up, smoothing his features. We would always wish that. I knew as much. But it wouldn't serve to dwell on the unchangeable years of our past.

"We are here now. Hold onto me," I whispered, lifting my chin for Conall's kiss.

"Always, *mo chroí*," he gasped, diving down to seal our lips gently together.

At my side, Laszlo's fingers tangled into my grasp, clutching tight.

38.
THE COMPANY OF FRIENDS

I took slow steps through the castle halls, bright murmurs of voices rising up from one of the larger rooms we rarely used. Laszlo had brought me breakfast in bed, rubbing my tired feet and kissing me senseless before joining the others for a meeting, retrieving a promise I would not fall back to sleep. I was still strictly unallowed to do so without Hywel to watch over me.

I passed my hand over the stone wall of a staircase, pausing as my fingers trailed through *néktar* still lingering in the air. My lips twitched. Who of the many lovers now occupying the castle had a tryst in the staircase? Or one of the windowsills, for that matter? There were little traces of stolen pleasure all over the place. And in just one day!

I was beginning to understand why Asterion had invited his friends to come and stay.

I startled as a pale figure appeared in an archway across from me.

"Sorry!" Hazel cried out, hands raised, a sheepish smile on her lips. "I didn't mean to sneak up on you. Your dragon said you'd be down soon. They're all plotting in the study, aside from maybe Esther, who is—"

There was a bright giggle followed by a low moan twining out of one the hallways that branched off.

Hazel's lips quirked and she stepped forward, lowering her voice. "She is the lustiest person I've ever met, and *I* am part nymph."

I nibbled on my lip, recalling what I'd heard last night. "You are...you are my liberator," I said, staring at her.

Hazel gasped and looked away. She was lovely, tall and willowy with dark russet red hair. She'd told absurd and charming stories last night about working in the theater I'd heard of, performing entertaining sexual acts with monsters for an audience. It had been her lovers who'd told the story about the night they'd attacked The Seven Veils, and she'd fallen quiet, tucked between the imp and the demon, slightly shy of the story.

"I know you didn't do it for me," I said, wondering if it made her uncomfortable.

She spun to look at me once more, eyes wide. "I would have. If I'd...known I could've. That was a recent development. And I..."

"You went to save your demon," I said, nodding, recalling that part of the story.

She blushed and nodded, smiling softly. "I'm glad Asterion found you."

I huffed. "So am I. I was starving to death." And looking forward to it, at the time. How long ago that now seemed, as if my life was speeding up, soaking up beauty to blot out the tragedies of the past.

Hazel's eyes narrowed. "So it's true that you...umm— I can't believe I'm bashful about asking anything anymore, but—"

"I need sexual pleasure to survive," I said, offering her stumbling questions a reprieve. I thought of Asterion's finery and poetry treatment for me when I'd first come into his care. "Or pleasure of some kind, anyway. As a nymph...do you—?"

She smiled and laughed. "Not so literally, no. Has the doctor asked for some of your blood yet? He's studying us all, you know, and he's been very curious about Jude and me, since we're half-human." She stepped forward and lowered her voice. "I think he's not quite convinced Esther is all human, given how well she keeps up with them."

I laughed at that, and from whatever room the young woman and her partner were in, another great sighing cry of pleasure sounded.

"Men often underestimate women's appetites," I mused.

Hazel snorted. "True."

My hands twisted in front of me as I stared at her. I'd told Conall last night that I couldn't pass hope back to myself, but it wasn't quite true. Learning so much about the past year, about these women and their monsters and all they'd been through, all they'd done, had colored my captivity in the faintest shades. I would never forget the cracking stone of my cell, the certainty the house would come down on top of me, only to see a sudden circling twine of roots tearing my door from its hinges. I would never forget the sudden rush of air that flooded the room and my lungs, the scream of metal tearing that called to me to *run*.

I would never forget the moment my toes touched the earth for the first time in over a century. I would never forget the night of huddling beneath a pile of broken crates in the alleyway behind a public house and knowing I was, if only temporarily, *free*.

"Thank you," I gasped out, unable to keep the words inside of me any longer.

Hazel Nix was a watery blur in front of me, but she swayed and grew larger, and I did not flinch when her arms wrapped around me. I fastened my own tightly around her back too, a sob of relief escaping my lips.

"My pleasure," she answered.

I BARED MY TEETH AND SWUNG, A VIOLENT ROAR BARELY constrained in my throat, my arm vibrating up into my shoulder as metal crashed together. Hywel shouted and dodged away, his chest glistening with sweat between the open flaps of his loose white shirt.

"Ah! Get him, Evanthia!" Esther screamed from the sidelines.

Hywel laughed and shook his head, dancing back as I raised my sword once more. "I yield, *blodyn bach*. I yield!"

My arm dropped like a stone, Excalibur tilted just enough to avoid clanging against the floor. "Ughh," I said, knees wobbling.

"Oh, that was wonderful!" Esther laughed, hands clapping as she slid from Amon's embrace to come running in my direction.

Hywel reached me first, taking Excalibur from my stubbornly locked fingers, wrapping an arm around my waist as I threatened to droop. He was dewy with exertion, while I was *drenched*.

"You *were* wonderful," he murmured in my ear. "I'm very proud of you."

"How ferocious you are," Esther praised me, smiling brightly. She spun to face her crowd of men. "Why have none of you ever taken pains to teach me to fight?"

"Too afraid of the havoc that you would no doubt cause, *mon coeur*," Auguste answered.

Strangely, that was the answer that seemed to please Esther best. Amon was scowling at the very suggestion, but Ezra, who'd managed to currently hold his visible form, nudged the sphinx's side and whispered in his ear.

"Will you go to battle?" Hunter asked me, his arms crossed over his bare, green-toned chest. He'd been circling my training with Hywel, watching us with a similar study as Laszlo did.

I opened my mouth to answer what I thought was obvious and found something entirely different falling from my lips. "I don't know."

My men bristled, Asterion and Conall looking stormy and full of objections, Hywel and Laszlo only exchanging a glance.

"That's not something that needs a decision presently," Laszlo cut in quickly. "We only seek to arm Evanthia to our best ability. She has our swords, but she deserves her own."

Hunter glanced speculatively over his shoulder to where his own little family was gathered. "It is of great relief to me to know Hazel has her own defenses," he said gravely, nodding. Then his head tipped, and he grinned at the woman. "Little one, would you like to learn to fight?"

"I wouldn't mind trying," Hazel said gamely.

The six-armed giant followed her up, scowling, but led her to the wall to choose a weapon.

"Oh, come now, Amon, what harm can it do?" Esther coaxed, her arms around the sphinx's shoulders.

"Oh, swinging about blades for fun, yes, of course, no one was ever injured by the edge of a sword," Amon muttered, but Esther was pecking her lips along his jaw and his own mouth was twitching with a smile. If he was objecting now, it was only to keep her drawing him out.

I turned to Laszlo and smiled. "Now see what you've done."

Laszlo peered over the rims of his glasses at me in a stare that made my toes curl in my boots. "Instruct them, dear one. I want to see what you remember."

"Aren't you clever, *cariad*," Hywel purred to our gryphon before leading the rest of the men away.

⚜

"DOES IT HURT MUCH?" I ASKED ESTHER, LEANING TO HER EAR and glancing down at the small bandage wrapped around her upper arm.

She was dressed in a grand confection of a gown, jewels and lace dripping over her bound form, full skirts puffing softly at her waist. She had, in fact, been injured during training, a small cut on her upper arm that had sent the whole room into a flurry of action, her men rushing toward her and everyone else sweeping quickly toward the exit. I'd heard the vampire snarl and Esther squeal, and then the doors had been discretely snapped shut on the scene.

"Not at all," Esther said, shrugging and smiling. "Auguste can heal that sort of thing."

I glanced across the table at the vampire who was speaking with the half-fae, Jude Piper, and thought he looked rather pink in the cheeks tonight.

"If I didn't know better, I'd guess you got that cut on purpose," I murmured to her.

Esther laughed and choked on a sip of her wine, her own cheeks flushing. "Who's to say you *do* know better?"

What a wonderfully wicked girl, I thought, grinning and turning away before she and I both started cackling over our desserts. I caught the eye of the shimmering demon at Hazel Nix's side and paused, holding my breath. We hadn't spoken yet, and he was one of the more taciturn members of the party, but I wondered if that had anything to do with our shared history. Slowly, deliberately, Constantine nodded to me. I answered the gesture and his shoulders eased, Hazel leaning unconsciously into him as if sensing his nerves.

"Our paths never crossed," Constantine said, low enough it barely reached my ear. His head tipped, a bird-like movement, and he blinked. "I was worried we might have."

My heart thumped unsteadily in my chest, and under the cover of the table Conall's hand clasped tightly around mine, his eyes turned warily toward the demon.

"He knew better," I said, and that seemed to catch the attention of others, Hazel glancing between Constantine and me.

"Knew better?" she asked, frowning. Her shoulders straightened, and it was clear she was ready to defend the man.

"Is it...is it true one of your aspects gives extreme pleasure?" I asked carefully.

Constantine dipped his head. "Not the one he preferred. He used Antin solely as a brief balance to the pain, a method to remind the victim of their suffering."

I resisted my shudder, held my spine straight, and ignored the stares we received from around the table. "The pain wouldn't have done me any harm, though. And I suspect one...one *taste* of the pleasure would've cut through my starvation quite smoothly," I said, an awkward laugh crawling up from my chest.

"You mean if Antin had touched you—" Hazel asked, frowning.

"Anyone," I said, my hands now holding onto Conall's so tightly, I wondered that he didn't beg me to release him. "He could've touched anyone, if I was near enough."

"It's not just your *own* pleasure that sates you?" Dr. Underwood asked, eyes bright and eager with curiosity, leaning forward to crane around Esther to look at me.

I flushed and shook my head. "It's like... It's somewhat like... humidity? When the air is heavy before rain. Only more tangible, I suppose. I can taste it. It's like drinking pleasure when I breathe."

"Oh," Esther mused, blushing. Her lips wobbled, and then she burst out with a laugh. "Oh, dear. Not so sneaky now, are we?" she asked her lovers, blushing cheerfully.

"And there's a..." Dr. Underwood hesitated, hand fluttering in the air as he thought. "A sense of measurement?"

I nodded and shrugged. "Monsters are much stronger than humans, of course. And within monsters, there's...all sorts of levels," I said, hoping that was tactful enough. Monsters seemed to be eager to point out the hierarchy as long as it was in their favor, but I imagined they'd be less pleased to know I could *taste* it too.

"And the *kind* of pleasure?" the doctor pressed.

"Jonathon, darling," Auguste murmured, glancing at me apologetically.

But I didn't mind the questions, actually.

"There is variation, yes," I said, voice slightly rough as I considered the corrosive feedings I'd received by some of the clients at The Seven Veils, ones who only took pleasure in another's suffering.

Dr. Underwood pursed his lips like he wanted to ask but knew better than to press there, at least. Across from me, the imp Ronan rolled his eyes and nudged Hazel's side.

"Our good doctor wants a demonstration, if you aren't too shy, nut."

Dr. Underwood blushed and retreated at this, sputtering out a faint objection, but Hazel just laughed.

"When have I ever been too shy for a demonstration? Do you mind, love?" she asked Constantine, whose eyes shimmered like the surface of a brightly polished coin.

"Not at all," Constantine said, and then he wavered and stretched strangely, and I had to squint to sort out the confusion of my stare as he had two faces in opposing shades of red and blue turning away from one another. Their bodies were not entirely separate, but the red demon, with full lips and a flat plane of skin where his eyes should have been, reached for Hazel's cheek.

Her eyes fluttered up, lips pressed shut to withhold the cry of ecstasy, and she crumpled into the touch. I flushed as *néktar* burst into the air, a sudden wave and boom that was almost stifling. Conall caught me around the waist before I could swoon, and I tried to hide my response, tucking my face slightly into his shoulder.

Constantine—or Antin, as this aspect was named—drew Hazel's mouth to his for a kiss, and there was no disguise for her moan or the shudder of her body against his and the way she melted into the spiraling relief he offered.

I laughed into Conall's neck and closed my eyes, taking shallow breaths and letting the *néktar* soak into the room as Antin released his lover and fused back into the gleaming bronze demon. Hazel gasped roughly and sagged in his embrace, catching her breath and laughing with me.

"Far too powerful," I said, my own voice not quite even. *Néktar* was pleasant fuel more often than not, but the sheer amount Antin was able to produce from those he touched was aphrodisiacal to me. Perhaps not just to me. Everyone around the table was looking inspired in that moment, Conall's fingers digging into my hips like he was resisting the urge to tug me onto his lap.

"That—" Dr. Underwood cleared a rough, low rasp from his voice and started again. "That display would've restored you?"

I licked my lips and tried to straighten, but Conall wouldn't release me. "Not...restored," I said, thinking of the incredible hollow that had formed in me in my centuries of captivity. "But certainly strengthened."

Constantine seemed almost to preen at this, and I wondered if he didn't often receive praise regarding his abilities.

Hywel cleared his throat at the head of the table, able to catch everyone's attention with a single note. I glanced up to find his gaze hot on me, eyes smiling with wicked intent. "We have just finished our final course, but I wonder, *blodyn bach*, if you might still be hungry?"

39.
AN EVENING
INTERLUDE

"Did you—" I squirmed against thick fingers, trying to catch one at my opening, whining when it skirted away. "Did you know this would happen?"

Asterion chuckled in my ear, tracing another slow, uneven circle over my glossy lower lips, his heavy jaw tucked over my shoulder as we watched the others. Everywhere in the room, tableaus of entwining flesh glittered by candlelight. The air wavered in my vision, as hazy and heavy as a summer day before a storm, the room so thick with *néktar*, it seemed to pool in little droplets on my mouth, licked away with each breath.

Two hearty cries broke out from the chorus of gasps and moans, and my eyes darted to the left, where Auguste and the enormous Mr. Tanner—what a fascinating surprise he had been —had Esther fastened between them, their tangled shapes boldly illuminated by the firelight.

"Perhaps not so...explicitly," Asterion said, chuckling as my breath hitched and my hips chased his fingers. "But I did think these friends might suit your nature."

I hummed my agreement and turned my head, gaping at the cluster of my other lovers. Conall was trapped between Hywel and Laszlo, their attention lavished over his chest in licks and bites, Hywel's hand deep in Conall's barely opened trousers.

"Not just me," I said. Hywel looked up, catching my eye and offering me a wink. Laszlo lifted his head and Conall caught his mouth, the pair of them greedy for one another's kisses, as Hywel soothed a hand through Laszlo's feathery hair.

"Mmm, yes, it's good to see Laszlo and Hywel remember they are alive again," Asterion whispered in my ear. "Laszlo did seem to often treat this castle like a temporary tomb while Hywel slept."

I wasn't sure if that was quite true, based on some of the raunchier stories they'd told me about Hywel's hibernation, but I knew their guests were few and far between. Laszlo and Dr. Underwood were eager conversationalists with one another, and Hywel had played the part of jovial host to everyone with a keen enthusiasm.

Now though, we were keeping to our own parties in one way, at least.

The rest of Esther's gentlemen watched her progress between the giant and vampire eagerly, murmured words exchanged. They were plotting, I suspected, but the young woman seemed up to the task, if her eager cries for more were any indication.

Sudden movement caught my eye from the other side of the room, two pairs of wings stretching as Jude and Ronan groaned together, pale and red hands tangled around their lengths as they thrust into their shared grip. Surrounding them, the figures of Con and Antin traded grazing touches. Ronan's wings trembled and then folded in close, and he sagged back, shouting as Antin dove and sucked his dripping cock between full red lips. Con circled around to Ronan's wide mouth, filling it with his own vividly blue length, making the poor imp thrash and buck between them.

Jude crawled away from the trio, over to where Hazel lounged between Hunter and Nireas, their own hands as busy as Asterion's. The fae settled his head against Hazel's thigh, nuzzling there for a moment, until Hunter and Nireas picked up her legs and spread her open for his mouth.

I looked up to the woman's face and found her smiling back at me, her eyelids heavy with pleasure, lips parted on a sigh. She didn't mind being watched, didn't even mind me witnessing the union between her lovers.

I wasn't sure I was so generous.

I twisted on Asterion's lap, drawing a grunt from his chest as

I nudged against his thickening length. His arms twined around me, head leaning back to watch me slink up his chest to face him.

"Would you be disappointed if I wanted to go up to the nest?" I whispered. I glanced back at the room, at the busy, twisting, moaning forms that surrounded us, and raised my eyebrows. "Is that...rude?"

Asterion's chest shook in a restrained laugh, head dipping to nuzzle against my cheek. "I'm sure no one would mind." I met his gaze, and he tipped his head. "Is the *néktar* not...good for you?"

It was my turn to laugh. I cupped Asterion's face in my hands, pressing kisses all over his jaw and lips and snout. "Did you arrange a feast for me?"

"I want you to feel strong, *théa*. Not for fighting," he added quickly, brow tangling between his dark eyes. "But because..."

Because I had told him I was hollow. I leaned in, wrapping my arms around his shoulders and resting my head over his steady heartbeat.

"I do feel strong," I admitted. "The nightmares drained me, and I wasn't...ready at first, as you know. But you've taken good care of me, Asterion."

"I was hardly here——" he began, gruffly modest.

"You found me, you sheltered me, you brought me to where I would be safest," I recited.

It was strange to have such a gentle, intimate conversation in this setting, with the eager moans of lovers surrounding us, but there was something natural in it too, I realized. I was no longer constantly starving, imagining myself an empty void, but Asterion was right that the waves of power and pleasure in the room did still shore me up. Prior to my captivity with Birsha, I had never been surrounded by so many monsters this way, and the energy of The Seven Veils had been a slow poison to all of me, body, heart, and mind. The pleasure in this room was purely shared and received, enjoyed by all, even appreciated at one another's benefit.

In a matter of weeks, I'd gone from wondering if I might ever feel sated again, to wondering if I could drown and be consumed by an excess of what I thrived on.

"You are my mate, Evanthia," Asterion rasped. "I will always find you, shelter you, protect you...love you."

I swallowed the whimper in my throat and sat up, stretching my thighs open over Asterion's lap. He had opened his trousers earlier to offer his swelling length some relief in the midst of our fondling, and I sighed as my slick folds immediately kissed at the butting head of him.

Asterion swallowed hard, his throat flexing against my knuckles as I undid the many buttons that confined his body from my view. "You said you wanted—"

"I changed my mind," I admitted, smiling and glancing at the room.

Esther had her head in Booker's lap, the cheeks of her ass bouncing with invisible thrusts, her other lovers avidly watching the open place where she was being filled. I recalled her words to Asterion, that he had finally found a woman who made a favorite of him.

I stared down at his half-bared chest, pushing fabric aside to offer my gaze the smooth planes and valleys of his strong body.

"Feed my body, Asterion," I murmured, gliding over his thickening staff. "I want to celebrate you here."

You deserve to be seen, appreciated, I thought privately.

He reached for me, tugging slightly on the ribbons that held my robe-like dress shut, but he only parted the curtains of fabric wide enough for his own stare, groaning at the sight of my slick folds straddled over his pulsing flesh.

"Lovely *théa*," he whispered.

"Beautiful mate," I answered, triumphant as my fearsome, gentle, beautiful minotaur shuddered at the praise.

On the floor at our side, Hywel and Conall used Laszlo as a bridge between them, Conall filling Laszlo's ass with a dark growl, knot pressing insistently. I spared Laszlo a studying glance, admiring the way he kept his hands and mouth impressively busy on Hywel's two cocks.

"Hmm, I hadn't considered how divided your attention would be," Asterion said, chuckling when I tore my stare away from the others and turned it back to him. "Perhaps we should—"

His words died abruptly with a grunt as I lifted up on my knees and pressed the tip of him to my entrance. His thick tongue swiped out against his lips, chest bucking with a rough breath as I paused staring, into his hooded gaze.

"I imagine you can keep me occupied, Asterion," I murmured. "If you put your mind to it."

Conall laughed at that, glancing over his shoulder at me to smirk, and then Asterion's huge hands grasped my waist, pulling me down one ruthless inch at a time.

"Asterion!"

"That's it, *théa*." Asterion's thumb stroked slowly over the curving inner line of my hips, where my skin was tender and delicate. "How well your pretty cunt takes me. So lovely, red, and *wet*."

I panted, my thighs going weak at his words, sinking me down to his base. "Are you seeking to scandalize me or inflame me?" I asked, grinning and stroking my hands over his chest, scratching briefly at his flat brown nipples.

"Both," Asterion said, and only the ragged edge of the light word revealed that he was as affected as I was by our union. "Is it working?"

I pressed my lips together to hold in my giggle, my cheeks warm at the explicit flirtation. "I'm not sure. Perhaps you should keep up the effort."

Asterion huffed and sat up, one arm snapping around my back to press our bare chests together. He twisted on the seat, turning my back to the room, the wide-open expanse of my dress hiding the view of us. He braced his other hand on the seat of the couch, hips arching into me slowly, my breath hitching.

"Your body gloves me so well, my *théa*." Asterion's arm tightened on my waist, holding me above him as he sank back to the seat. He released me, and I crashed down onto his lap with a shout, his cock pounding in my core. "Tight but generous. Your body cannot refuse mine."

"No," I gasped, clasping his face in my hands, my head shaking. "No, I could never. Asterion, please."

He lifted us together once more and I moaned, head falling back at the heavy pressure that built with the movement.

"I thought at first you would not fit all of me. I was going to train your sweet little pussy to take me," Asterion said, licking my throat as I whined. He sat, holding my body in place to let his flesh drag along my inner walls. "Feed your body another inch every time I fucked you."

"I wouldn't stand for it." I forced my head to lift and my eyes to meet his. "I wouldn't let you refuse me any part of you."

Asterion's smile softened, and then his hand slid up my back to my shoulder, tugging me down to sit fully on him once more, our moans rising together shortly before our mouths met in a starving kiss.

"What a gift you are, Evanthia," he whispered against my lips. Then he drew back, loosening his hold of me. "Conall, take her."

"What?" I squeaked as new hands reached for me. "No! Asterion!"

I was pulled from Asterion's lap with a cry and a thrash of protest, for all that I was gathered to a familiar and welcome chest.

"On her belly," Asterion ordered. "Keep her mouth busy."

I squawked, but Conall laughed and turned me to face him. Asterion's hands grabbed at my dress, peeling it down my arms, leaving me bare as I wrestled against my wolf, my words muffled by his plunging tongue. I'd lost track of the activities of others. Lazslo was fucking a beaming Hywel, and our guests were tangled in two separate but messy unions. And then Conall's hands wrapped around my face, holding me in place for kissing as we fell together to the floor, his back spread over the carpet and my body draped limply on top of his.

Long, stroking hands ran over my back, down to my hips, and I shivered. Asterion hadn't left us. I sighed, giving into Conall at last, smiling at his grunt as Asterion pushed our legs open to make room for himself.

"I knew he wouldn't hand you over so easily," Conall teased against my cheek.

I opened my mouth to answer back, something sharp and

chastising to them both, but my words were snatched from my lips as Asterion spread my sex open with his thumbs and then plunged himself inside.

"I'm going to fuck you next," Conall whispered as Asterion set a punishing pace inside of me. "Plug you up with my knot, fill you till you think you might burst." His tone was sweet, but the words made my eyes grow wide. Asterion shook me on top of Conall, rubbing my clit into Conall's half-hard cock. The fine weave of the carpet bounced in my vision, Conall's bright hair threaded through.

"And when you and I can't stand being tied together a moment longer, I will give you over to Hywel, I think," Conall continued as Asterion grunted, planting his hands on either side of our heads. His hooves thumped against the floor, and I let out a long, broken sound at the steady surge and press of his rhythm inside of me, his body braced perfectly to consume me, destroy me, leave me limp and sodden and ready for Conall.

"I heard the nymph tell the demon that they would be at it well past the rest of us retire for the night," Conall said, nipping my jaw as I started spouting out nonsense words, pleas and praises. "But I think we will surprise them after all. You know how Laszlo gets when you're all wrung out, *mo chroí*. He can't help himself but to be so delicate with you it makes you mad with wanting. By the time he's finished, Asterion will be jealous we've all had so much time with you. He'll need to fuck you again."

"Yes," Asterion growled, moving one hand to my back, arching me against Conall, who grew breathless and stiff under me.

"If he doesn't finish soon, I'll have to join him," Conall snarled, bucking his hips into mine, a clear, sticky pool gathering between us.

I wailed at the threat, my body snapping tight as a vise on Asterion's length.

"Bastard," Asterion growled out. He held my hips in place and then snapped his own, rough and uneven, bellowing out his pleasure as he painted his release inside of me until it flooded out in a thick stream.

Conall just laughed, finding my mouth once more to occupy us both until Asterion was ready to ease out and offer him his turn.

When I woke the next morning, sullied and sated and cradled off the hard floor by the bodies of my lovers, I couldn't recall who of our party had surrendered first, but I was fairly certain it hadn't been us.

40.
PUCKS AND
TRAPS

"Y ou'd really never done any combat before?" Esther asked me, blowing a loose strand of curling dark hair away from her face, her gaze narrowed on the target ahead of her.

"No. It wasn't something expected from women—" I said.

"It still isn't," Hazel murmured, her focus on her own target.

"—and I was content with my role in the world at the time."

Esther hummed and then loosed her arrow, scowling as it landed toward the edge of the target.

"Better," I said, nodding. "And consider, most monsters are much larger than that board."

"But not stationary," Esther noted, although her frown had softened.

Hazel loosed her own arrow, and the shot was far too wide, until at the last second, sudden green roots sprouted from the earth, dragging the target to the left. The arrow hit center.

"Cheater!" Esther cried, laughing.

Hazel shrugged, turning her smug smile away.

"It's not really cheating if it's something she can do when it matters," I reasoned. "We'll follow no rules of chivalrous battle against Birsha's numbers."

Esther huffed and flapped her arms at her side. "True, and he deserves everything we can throw at him and then some. But I'm very jealous."

I nodded and admitted, "So am I."

Hazel flushed and set her bow on the table, where Laszlo had left us a tea tray of refreshments, as if we were only a group of young women taking a turn about the gardens together. Drinking tea and eating scones in our light cotton dresses. Shooting arrows at targets.

"Do you...do you want to be in battle?" Hazel asked carefully, glancing at us.

"I thought after we left Rooksgrave in ashes that I wanted only to be safe and happy with my gentlemen," Esther mused, setting her own weapon aside. She lifted her chin high and continued. "Now, I want to face him again. I want him to know it was a little, insignificant human woman who helped destroy him."

My heart pounded in my chest, and I ached for the certainty, the confidence she felt as she spoke the words.

Hazel nodded. "He hurt my friends. I'd like to grow a tree where his heart should've been, turn him into mulch."

My hands fisted in my skirt as they both glanced at me and then looked away just as quickly, realizing what it was they were asking of me. Could I bear to face Birsha? The man who'd stolen centuries of my life? Broken the woman I'd been to pieces? Did I *need* to look into those cold eyes once more?

"I don't know," I whispered.

There was a pause of silence, and then a slim, warm hand pulled mine from my skirt before I could tear a hole through the fabric.

"You don't have to. I'd put another knife in his belly *for* you," Esther said.

"Gladly," Hazel agreed, nodding and lifting up my other hand, enfolded in both of hers.

I fought for air, fought to answer them. *Yes, I want to kill him myself. No, I want to forget that time in my life and never speak his name again.*

No single answer came, not before a rush of urgent footsteps skidding over stone and the call of voices from the castle.

"Evanthia, ladies, inside!" Conall bellowed.

"Sanctuary! Sanctuary! Hywel, Laz, *please!*"

Esther and Hazel released my hands, and we spun as a trio. Hazel's hands flung out in the direction of the small, charging figure that raced up the drive toward the entrance of the castle, and Esther bit off a cry of surprise as the intruder was halted with a sudden shout, arms and upper body flailing with their sudden stop.

There was an entrance to the kitchens from this side of the castle, and no doubt that was where Conall expected us to retreat to. Instead, we took off running through the meadow together, charging for the gravel drive where our men were barreling out of the castle in uneven numbers. As we neared, I saw what had put a sudden stop to the small person's running. Thickening roots burst up from the ground and twined eagerly around the mismatched trouser legs, squeezing tightly enough to hold him in place.

The man Hazel had caught was as small as a child but with a twiggy, uneven beard and the small horns of a young fawn.

"I told you to go inside," Conall hissed, catching sight of us and cutting away from the others. I threw myself into his embrace easily, suddenly realizing he was right, that I had darted for the possible danger rather than toward safety.

"*Puck*," Hywel greeted through gritted teeth. "What do you think you're doing, showing your face here? Did you *know* your little missive about the cauldron went *directly* into—"

"Wasn't me," the puck gasped out, shaking his head. He relaxed in the trap around his legs and leaned forward, planting his hands on thick thighs as his back heaved with gasps of air. "Wasn't me that sent that letter."

"Not this damn treasure hunting nonsense again," Conall snapped, sagging slightly against me, but Hywel raised a hand to hush us.

My dragon seemed to grow as he walked steadily toward the puck fellow, tall and broad and dangerously elegant. "If it was not *you*, Robin, why did the author know of my interest in the piece?" Hywel said, teeth biting around the words.

Robin the puck cringed and ducked his head. "I *was* looking for information for you, I swear it. Only mayhaps I was a...little loose with my tongue?"

"Hywel, do you realize—" Asterion cut in.

Hywel glared back at Asterion, settling into his usual size

once more, and sniffed with offense. "That the letter might've been bait for a trap? Of course I do. Serves Rolant right, I suppose. It *does* not, however, address your indiscretion."

"Robin, *who* did you give the information to?" I asked, sliding from Conall's arms to step forward. Hywel shifted in my direction, guarding me from moving too closely.

The puck lifted his face once more, and the shade of his skin was too pale, green and queasy. His eyes darted around the crowd that had gathered here to judge him, and he did not hide the trembles that quaked his small form.

"I didn't *know*, dragon. I had no notion—"

"Who, Robin?" Hywel bit out.

Robin's beard twitched as he swallowed hard. "It was Birsha who stole my secrets, my lord."

Hywel staggered back a step, and I caught his waist in my hands, less surprised by this revelation than I suspected Hywel was. Behind me, Conall cursed.

"Rolant will save his own skin," Asterion said with a sigh. "Birsha will have a dragon on his side too."

I startled at the declaration and shook my head, trying to control my expression before Asterion saw too much of my reproach.

"You don't know that," I said.

Hywel sighed and shook his head, wrapping an arm around my shoulder and twisting to face me. "I fear he's likely right, *blodyn bach*. But it won't make a terrible difference. I outmatch Rolant—"

"No!" I cried, stepping out of his reach, planting my hands on my hips and glaring at my mates, who looked troubled but *not* for the right reason, in my opinion. "No! We are not giving *Rolant* up to- to Birsha! He stood by you all against the werewolves and the trolls. He led us to Excalibur!" And when that did not make them look properly moved, a new notion struck me. I glared up at Hywel. "Do you really think Rolant is *stupid* enough to stand against you *and* the Sword of Victors?"

Hywel blinked at that, head tipping to the side slightly, expression shifting by the smallest amount. Around his shoulder,

Laszlo ducked his head and hid his smile by cleaning his glasses on the tail of his shirt.

"You may have a point," Hywel said. "More likely, Rolant might play the game. Go along with Birsha enough to survive. He could be a tool for either of us."

Dr. Underwood cleared his throat, gathering our attention, his frown somber. "I'm afraid if Birsha seeks to make a tool of a dragon, it won't be by their wits."

A grave chill soaked into my bones as I considered what I had learned from Asterion and the others about how Birsha had been surviving for so long. I stepped back and found Conall eagerly waiting to enfold me back against his chest.

Hywel let out a low, rattling growl and marched toward Robin, who'd remained watchful and silent as we'd argued. "Release him. We'd better get inside and decide what's to be done."

The roots relaxed around the puck's legs, retreating back into the ground, and Hywel grabbed him by the beard, tugging the yelping man along toward the open doors.

Conall held me in place as the others turned to follow, squeezing me close and pressing a long kiss to my temple. "Wise *and* lovely, *mo chroí*."

I huffed and rolled my eyes, but I leaned into the press of his lips, savoring the moment, knowing what came next would unsettle the peace I'd been soaking up for so many weeks.

❧

"WE HAVE YET TO SO CALLOUSLY DISMISS ONE OF OUR ALLIES to Birsha's mercies," Hunter growled, leaning forward with his elbows resting on his knees.

Feathers rustled from the corner where Amon surveyed us all. "The Wyrm was never, strictly speaking, one of our allies. He certainly never claimed as much."

Asterion sighed, scrubbing a hand over his forehead. "He took no action against us. Offered us invaluable information. Led us to—"

"Yes, yes, the sword," Amon huffed, waving a clawed hand.

Hywel bristled at the dismissal of Excalibur but remained lounging at my side, his arm thrown over my shoulder. He might've been the most prestigious monster of our gathering, but when it came to the tactical elements of this war against Birsha, the generals of our group were clear.

Auguste cleared his throat from the shadowed end of the room, where I'd thought he was sleeping. He must've been resting and listening to us all for the past hour. "You have to admit, Amon, that the Sword of Victors in our hands is a coup. We might've gone the war without it entirely, but the devastation if it had ended up in Birsha's keep would've been considerable."

Amon bristled, eyes glowing. "A rescue mission at this time, when we *know* Birsha has gathered the very worst he can still find—"

"Would be ludicrous, yes," Asterion said, catching the sphinx's attention.

A tense, sharp energy that had been gathering like a storm cloud in the room settled slightly, and both Asterion and I sighed, even at opposite ends of the small crowd.

Hywel had dismissed the puck after a thorough interrogation, and it had been Laszlo himself who went to the kitchens and returned with a collection of simple foods for us to eat. Not a single shadow figure had passed through any door or wall, only our three collections. It was curious that at the heart of each group there was a woman, I thought, each of us with some human blood. I was sure that if Birsha had ever expected an enemy to rise up against him, it would not have been in the figure of a girl like Esther Reed.

He was afraid of her, they said. She and her monsters were why he had run from The Seven Veils the night of my escape.

I wanted him to be afraid of me too.

Hywel twisted a curl of my hair around his finger, and Conall's hand squeezed around mine where he held it in my lap.

"I will not deny that of all of us, I owe Rolant most," Asterion said to Amon. "I can undertake an effort to find out what happened to him myself."

"Asterion!" I gasped, but my soft cry slid beneath Hunter's answer.

"I will join you, my friend," the orc answered easily, nodding to Asterion at the minotaur's glance.

Ronan murmured in Hazel's ear as she frowned, and there was a pause before she nodded, her cheeks pale but her expression firm. "I'll come along," Ronan said to Hunter. "Can't hurt to have eyes in the sky."

Hunter hesitated, staring at his nymph love before nodding. "The rest of you should remain here," he said slowly, probably afraid Hazel herself would jump into the fray.

A throat cleared, and Ezra flickered into view where he stood behind Esther, her hands twisting in her lap. "I'd be happy to help. Better to remove me from the temptation of Hywel's treasure hoard anyway," he joked. "I make as useful a spy as I do a thief."

Esther's breath was ragged, her gaze shuttered, but she reached behind her, squeezing Ezra's hand until her knuckles were white.

Conall cleared his throat and stirred uneasily at my side. "I should—"

Asterion wheeled around and shook his head. "No, stay here. You know how I feel about this, and anyway...I'm not sure I could stand you half-crazed and eager to return," Asterion said lowly.

Conall's cheeks flushed, and his eyes remained steadfastly away from my own.

"Amon," Esther urged softly, turning to face her sphinx in the corner.

Amon sighed and nodded, looking more amused than resigned. "Yes, my star. Asterion, I'll join your party. Someone has to keep MacKenna in line, after all."

"Very well, but I think we'd better stop there," Asterion laughed. "Any more of us, and Birsha will hear the stampede from across the continent. We'll seek out information about Rolant and where he might be, and then we'll make a decision together on how to act."

I frowned at my minotaur until he caught the look. He

387

answered it with a small smile, and my heart stuttered in my chest as he tipped his head to the door.

"Go on," Hywel murmured, although Conall relinquished my hand with a little more coaxing.

The room was thick with conversation, lovers making safe promises to one another and monsters planning. Asterion caught me around the waist, lifting me easily off my toes and striding out the door of the study.

"Asterion, you're not—"

"I'm not running, *théa*," he said before I could finish my question. We hurried into the next room, a small sitting area with a lit fire, and he settled us on the settee together, my legs spread over his lap. He squeezed my hips briefly before cupping my shoulders, bowing his head to rest our brows together. My own greedy grip reached up and caught him by the horns, holding him tightly in place.

"Birsha was likely seeking to trap Hywel and Laszlo, if not all of us."

I shivered, and Asterion rubbed his hands up and down my arms as if to warm me. "That means he is seeking *you* too, Asterion. I don't want—"

"It will be all right, *théa*," Asterion whispered, tugging his head back just long enough to nuzzle against my face.

"Maybe Conall should—" I started in a small voice, hating the words.

Asterion snorted. "I meant what I said. Until Conall settles his mark on you, he won't be able to stand being out of your sight. Same goes for Hywel, and the dragon certainly won't let his mate leave the nest without him."

"Oh, and I should?" I muttered, trying to turn my pout into a respectable glower.

Asterion was silent for a moment, one hand sliding up my shoulder to catch my chin and lift it high. His eyes blazed down on me, soft and hot all at once. "Am I your *mate*, *théa*?"

I twisted nervously on his lap for a moment. "Asterion, you're the one who said..." He glanced away, a low sound of assent in his throat, and suddenly the answer was on my tongue. "Yes. You are."

Asterion's breath froze in his chest, eyes snapping back to stare at me. I don't know which of us moved first, but in a moment I was pressed tightly against Asterion's chest, our arms so fiercely fastened around one another, I could scarcely breathe.

I would rob us of the truth no longer.

"You are my mate, Asterion. I never feel as safe as I do when I'm with you. You've possessed me from the first moment you touched me, and I—"

"Evanthia," Asterion groaned, burying his face against my slender neck.

"I love you," I whispered directly into his sweetly furred ear, trailing a fingertip up the back of it and smiling as it twitched. "For sheltering me. Waiting for me. Feeding me and watching me and knowing me better than I know myself."

Asterion's breath was heavy and fast, rushing over my skin and down under the collar of my dress, making my breasts ache as I arched into his embrace. "I thought...I thought it would be enough to know," he said, rough and aching. "To know what you were to me. I could never imagine how full my soul would be when touching you, fucking you, *loving* you, *théa*. My little goddess. My *mate*."

I dragged his face up, pressing my lips to his. For all that our features were a mismatch, there was a perfect rightness to kissing him, one that brought tears to my eyes.

"Show me, Asterion. Before you go. Show me again what it is to be yours."

Asterion groaned but relented, lifting me from the couch in the cradle of his arms, carrying us both up to the nest.

"Amon will have his way with plans while I'm not in the room," Asterion muttered, but his hands tightened eagerly on me, and I knew any concern over plots and plans would wait until we were satisfied with one another. If that was even possible.

41.
SETTLE THE
MATTER

O ur company was in accord the next morning at dawn, all of us together outside of the castle, tearful kisses and whispered goodbyes exchanged, hands shaken and backs clapped between friends.

"I love you, mate," I whispered once more into Asterion's ear, my legs dangling over the ground as he held me in a firm hug.

"I love you, *théa*. I'll be back soon."

I pinched the back of his neck. "You'd better. No more tarrying in London or—"

Asterion groaned and laughed, setting me on my toes but finding himself still caught in my arms. "Conall exaggerated. I *was* busy then, I swear. As if I could've really avoided being near you."

I sighed at that, not consoled but appeased at least. My arms slid slowly from around the broadest shoulders of my acquaintance, and I fought the urge to turn away and go running, sobbing, back into the castle.

"Settle Conall's bond," Asterion whispered to me, waggling his brow. "He'll be intolerable until you do."

Conall and Hywel *had* been keeping me close at hand to an almost obsessive degree. With Asterion gone for a few days—I refused to accept it would be longer—and Laszlo a patient saint, it would be a good time to come to terms with my two other mates.

Come to terms with myself, I admitted. Hywel had already said he was ready. Conall...was less clear. He had his own concerns over matehood, considering his parents. I wasn't sure now if that was still the source of reluctance, or if he was waiting on me.

"Be as sweet to yourself as I would," Asterion added, standing straight.

I sniffed. "We'll see. That's your job now."

He laughed and I caught my breath at the warm sound, a cheerful flush on my cheeks. Asterion and I were usually so serious with one another. It was a giddy surprise to flirt with him, to make him laugh. I didn't want to stop. He caught my hands before they could tighten on his collar. Esther and Hazel were being gathered into the arms of their lovers, who would remain here at the castle. It was time for my minotaur to leave.

"Be safe," I choked out.

"I promise," Asterion said solemnly, dragging his gaze away from mine with a furrow on his brow. He looked over my shoulder, nodding behind me, and gentle hands reached out to pry me away from him.

I shuddered, swallowing hard on the sob that tried to rise in my throat, and let Laszlo's soothing scent and careful embrace surround me.

One by one, the familiar figures of the monsters in front of us shifted. Ronan shrugged on a coat, losing his brilliantly red skin, horns, and wings. Amon shrugged his shoulders, his own wings and tail vanishing, slightly furred brow smoothing into gleaming brown skin. Hunter winked at Hazel, donning a hat and transforming into a handsome, human version of himself. Ezra remained invisible, however, a secret addition to their party.

Asterion's white gloves were in his hand, our gazes held.

"Go inside, *théa*," he said softly.

I nodded, knowing this was the last true look I'd see of him before he left, and turned away, allowing the others to shepherd me into the cool stone walls of the castle.

"Isn't that enough?" Conall snapped, glaring jealously at the little jar of blood Dr. Underwood was collecting from me.

Underwood gaped slightly, glancing at me. I shook my head, offering him a shallow smile. "I'm fine, really."

"Auguste will bring her and Laszlo a platter of treats in a moment," Esther assured Conall, watching from the edge of the room.

Hywel stood like a gargoyle at my back, no doubt measuring every drop that left me.

"I appreciate your cooperation," Underwood said to me, nodding his head to Laszlo to include him in the gratitude. He did not look up at Hywel, who had flatly refused to share any of his blood for "dubious experiments."

"I suspect divinity blood may have an entire category of its own, although this will be my first chance at finding any evidence," Underwood continued.

"Happy to help," I said, shrugging the shoulder not in use. I didn't understand exactly what the doctor's goal was, or if he was only naturally curious, but it didn't matter to me what a trusted source might find.

"Evanthia," Conall rasped, eyeing the nearly full bottle desperately.

"All done," Underwood said, looking a tad harassed as he pressed a swab of clean cotton to the small nick he'd cut in my arm.

Conall and Hywel both groaned in relief, and a giggle escaped my lips at their antics before Hywel arched over me, snatching my face in his hands and pulling my mouth roughly to his. I squeaked into the kiss, but Hywel knew me too well, and with a nip and teasing lick I was melting under his touch. I moaned and shivered as his tongue slid between my lips, coiling eagerly around my own with a length that was closer to his dragon form than his human one. *Néktar* lapped sweetly between us, and I stretched to chase his mouth, my hands fluttering in front of me before catching his shoulders in my grip. He pulled away as Esther murmured "Oh my" from her own seat and then smiled smugly down at me.

"What was that for?" I asked, breathless and blinking.

Hywel stroked his hand down my arm and then flicked away the cotton Dr. Underwood had pressed to my wound.

Underwood cried out, looking at my spotless inner elbow. "Oh! But how—"

Hywel cut him off, speaking through gritted teeth. "Not. Now."

"Very well," Underwood sighed out, stoppering the bottle of my blood and wisely tucking it away in his satchel before Hywel or Conall tried to steal it back.

"Come, my love, let's go find where Auguste is and see if we can't help him," Esther coaxed, winking at me as she guided the doctor from the room.

"It really didn't hurt," I murmured, relaxing into the back of the couch.

"Mm, I know, which is why the good doctor left the room unscathed," Hywel muttered, rolling his shoulders.

"We simply aren't inclined to share *any* part of you, *mo chroí*," Conall said, swinging himself around on the couch to rest his head in my lap.

Hywel grunted his agreement and launched over the back of the couch to squish himself in at my side. "In fact, as much as I've enjoyed the company of our guests, I wouldn't mind an evening apart, just the four of us."

He reached over my lap, resting his hand on Conall's chest. Conall's eyebrows bounced in surprise, but I put my own hand over Hywel's and Conall stacked his on top, linking us all together.

I rested my head on Hywel's shoulder. "It would be nice, although I'd hate to offend the others."

"I doubt anyone will mind. We've been elbow to elbow with each other for three weeks now. Not sure I really have it in me to sit through another night of *charades*," Conall muttered.

It'd been three days since the others had left, and Conall had finally broken the news to me last night that it'd likely be closer to a week or two before we saw them again. We had been trying to keep up a cheerful facade amongst the group, but it was starting to falter. Even staid and peaceful Booker had broken into a morose frown the night before when no one had been able to guess what he was meant to be acting out while simply standing still and frozen.

"Ezra would've guessed it," the stone gentleman said with a heavy sigh. "Blarney Stone."

Conall had laughed, but he'd cut the sound off abruptly as Esther fell into sniffling tears.

The door of the small, sunny room we occupied opened, and it was Laszlo rather than Auguste who carried in a tray of pastries. He paused at the sight of us, a smile lighting up his face and making the sunshine seem a bit more earnest.

"Ah, is it just us?" he asked, not hiding his pleasure.

"We'll have private dinners tonight," Hywel declared, kissing my head. "I'll have the dreamers take care of everything."

Laszlo waved a hand, stopping Conall from rising to make room for him, and sat on the floor instead, beautifully informal and cozy as he leaned into my legs. Conall's free hand rose to pet and stroke at Laszlo's wings, while the gryphon took turns feeding each of us. I sucked on his thumb, meeting the bright gleam in his gaze and letting it warm me.

THE SNARL CALLED ACROSS THE MEADOW, AND I BRACED myself, Laszlo and I both rolling our eyes heavenward.

"Conall—" Laszlo snapped, his infinite patience finding a breaking point at last.

It was too late. Tightly banding arms snatched me off my feet, yanking me away from the false threat of Laszlo and the fighting staff. I dropped the staff I'd been holding as well, before the temptation to knock Conall over the head with it grew too persuasive.

"I *can't*," Conall answered Laszlo with a desperate growl.

"We're only training," I murmured, feigning a sympathy that my werewolf had worn away in the past hour.

"I know," he moaned, pressing his scowling face into my breastbone. I sighed and stroked my fingers through his loose hair, frowning as I found the back of his neck. He was almost feverish, sweating when the day was actually quite nice and cool, shivering under my touch.

"You either must leave the field—" Laszlo started once more, marching toward us.

"No!" Conall barked, whipping around to bare brilliant fangs at the gryphon.

Laszlo stopped short, eyes wide and lips downturned.

"Conall!"

Conall shook but refused to release me, his eyelids sinking closed. "I'm sorry, Laz. I-I—"

We had moved my training outdoors when we realized that Conall was too agitated by the monsters who weren't part of our little unit, but he'd *never* snapped at Laszlo this way. I didn't blame Laszlo for the injured wince of his expression.

"You need to settle this," Laszlo said, sharp and cool, gaze glancing through his spectacles before turning away from us.

"Laszlo, wait, I—"

But Conall didn't chase after Laszlo or loosen his grip on me as the gryphon turned away and headed for the castle. He groaned and sagged, wobbling us both before sinking wearily down into the familiar meadow. I stroked my hands around his shoulder to his collar, flicking at buttons.

"Evie, no, what are you about?" Conall muttered, trying to catch my hands and pull them from their work.

"You're burning up. Are you sick?"

"It's just—No, I'm fine, darling, I just—"

It was the mating impulse. The one he was refusing. It had been a week and a half since Asterion left, and while I'd attempted to tiptoe into the topic of a mating bite with Conall, he'd deftly skipped around my efforts, turning me away with sweet flirtation and seduction so I could never really be offended by the change of topic.

I stepped back, a sudden thought nearly knocking me back to the ground. "Do you not *want* me as a mate?"

Conall's choking splutter of outrage was reassuring, but for every second he stammered, an oily thread of unease slithered through me. I pulled my shoulders back and inched away, and his eyes widened.

"No—I mean, damnit, Evie—I—Wait!" He gasped as I

started to turn, diving for me and catching me by my wrists. "*Don't* walk away. Not after asking me that."

"Conall—"

His hands tightened, not enough to hurt me, but refusing me any escape. "*Yes*, Evanthia, *mo chroí*, I want you as a mate. You are my mate, and you have no idea how glad of it I am. Grateful. Fucking *ecstatic*," he added in a rush, a grin wavering into place. "A touch terrified too, but Hywel promises he won't let me fuck it up. If I haven't already."

I sighed at the sight of this familiar figure in front of me, intense and playful in equal measure. "But?" I prompted.

"No 'but,'" he said quickly.

I rolled my eyes, and Conall tugged on my wrists, pulling me into his chest. "It will hurt, Evanthia," he said softly. I blinked and stared up at him. His gaze was soaking me up, hungry and anxious and loving—because I was starting to understand the meaning of that. "The bite will hurt, and I can't bear to. As much as I'm desperate to mark you as mine, and yes, I know it's driving me and everyone else mad that I haven't. It will hurt you. And I've never wanted to hurt anyone less in my life."

A fissure of sweetness cracked through my chest, and I sank into Conall's strength, tucking my face in his shoulder and kissing the skin of his fevered throat.

"Will it make me a werewolf?" I asked.

"No. Or it would, but only under the right circumstances. I would need to be fully shifted, a full moon, and that would be much, much worse for you, so don't even ask—"

"I'm not," I said, pulling my hands free of his and sliding them up under his shirt to stroke the bare skin of his back. "You know I'll heal quickly, Conall."

"You've been through enough," he whispered so softly I thought he probably hadn't meant me to hear the words.

I smiled into his throat, shifting closer, widening my stance so my feet trapped his between them. "It's just a little bite."

"*Little?*"

I laughed at his offense and leaned back to find his cheeks twitching as he fought a smile.

"A nip."

His eyes narrowed. "Evanthia, it will take more than a *nip* to—"

"Conall, I doubt I'll even notice—"

"Not notice?!"

I shrugged, and he scoffed. "I mean...if you think it's such a very impressive bite..." I stepped back, releasing him from my arms.

Conall stiffened, glaring at me. "Evie, what are you up to?"

"Nothing," I answered quickly.

"You can't *trick* me into biting you."

I grinned. "I wouldn't dream of it."

He scowled. "Where are you going?"

I jogged backwards out of his reach as he swiped out an arm to catch me. "Nowhere," I said, laughing.

He huffed and shook his head, but behind him, a bright red tail wagged eagerly. It gave him away so easily. "Evanthia," he said in a hard, commanding tone.

"Conall," I answered, mocking his voice.

He stomped toward me, and I darted immediately away, giggling at the open shock on his face.

"What are you doing?" he cried.

"What are *you* doing?"

Another brief chase ensued before he halted once more, arms wide at his side. "Evanthia!"

"Conall!" I teased.

"Quit running away from me," he said, just barely concealing the whine in his words.

I paused, locking my hands behind my back and tipping my head to study him. "No," I said, and he gaped at me. "Catch me."

I ran before he could refuse, laughing at the dark rumble that echoed at my back. I ran as fast as I could, a straight arrow through the meadow, only seeking distance. Conall was faster than me, and it wouldn't be long before he caught me. It wouldn't be long before I *let* him. I just needed enough time to...

I glanced over my shoulder and smiled as I realized he wasn't running full tilt yet, just trying to keep me in sight. I would give him something to look at, then. I turned to face him, catching my breath with great gasps, and he stopped, his hands on his hips and an unconvincing snarl twisting his expression.

It melted away as I reached for the long tunic of Laszlo's I'd dressed in this morning. Conall's curled lip slackened as I peeled the fabric up from over my head, baring my upper body and the tight fit of the leggings I wore. He mouthed something—my name, I thought—and tensed.

I turned and ran once more, my laughter loud and sharp, a screech of excitement escaping as he answered with a growl that curled and called to me through the high grasses.

"I know what you're doing," he called.

"So do I," I answered, flashing him a smile over my shoulder.

He'd gained on me, but he was still keeping a gentler pace. His tail was kicking seeds off the tops of weeds as it waved eagerly, and he slowed when I did. Claw-tipped fingers pulled white linen off his shoulders and over his head, bare chest gleaming under hazy sunlight. I reached down, tugging off the boots that were loosely laced on my feet. I tossed the first one toward him, and it dropped short. Conall arched a brow at me. I threw the next one farther and he yelped, dodging before it hit him, giving me the distraction I needed to take off into the orchard.

"Evie!" Conall barked.

I grinned and spared my breath for sprinting.

The orchard was in deep bloom, pale pink and white petals floating down from gnarled apple trees. Thick leaves would shelter the view of us from the castle, and the ground was dense and soft with white wild violets.

"Ouch!" I hissed, bouncing on one foot as I glared down at the ground.

Wild violets and dropped twigs, I amended mentally.

Conall laughed, and I startled at how close the sound was. I searched around me, eyes moving too quickly to pick him out in the shadows, and then I caught a brief glimpse of rust-red fur batting out from behind a tree.

I turned and reached for the low branch of the apple tree at my back, hauling myself into its canopy.

"Wouldn't you rather go inside to a nice, comfortable bed?"

Conall asked, appearing from his hiding place, watching me climb with an amused quirk on his lips.

"So you can spread me out in goose down and treat me like a chivalrous lover?" I asked, grunting as I climbed up once more. I found a V of branches to rest in and leaned back against the larger of the two.

Conall approached slowly, face flickering through budded blossoms and fat green leaves. "Is that so wrong of me?"

"It's lovely of you, and you know it," I said, reaching for the laces of the leggings. Conall stopped still and stared at my hands with avid interest. I pulled the leather through the eyelets slowly, teasing him with my progress before I continued speaking. "But I should hate for us to forget how we came together in the first place. I'm not fragile, Conall."

"You're the strongest person I know," he purred, his own hands moving to his waistband.

"And I'm not a *lady*. I've been many things in my life, but never that," I said. I dangled the leather cord and then let it fall, catching over a branch. The open placket of the leggings parted, exposing my hips and the top pale curls of my mound.

"Come down to me, *mo chroí*," Conall called, low and pleading.

I hooked my thumbs into the waist of the leggings and pushed them down, pressing my back into the support of the tree to keep my balance as I pulled my feet free one at a time. Conall caught the fabric as I kicked it off, his smile wide and his red hair shaking.

"We can't *rut* in a tree, Evie," he laughed. "I'm not a bird."

I settled one foot forward, parting my thighs, and reached between my legs to tease myself. I wasn't very ready yet, but my clit throbbed at my first touch. "Oh, Conall!"

Conall cursed below me, but my head fell back against the apple tree, my eyes up on the glittering sun through the leaves as I stroked and petted myself gently, drawing a little wetness from my core and smoothing it over my aching lips. Fabric rustled below, and leaves whispered and gossiped as branches shook, and I giggled and moaned as I dipped my fingers into my own slick heat.

I glanced down just in time to watch Conall's arms flex, hands braced on two branches, as he thrust himself up to meet me. I braced one hand behind me, expecting him to stand, to match my pose, to bury himself into my needy body. Instead, he caught the foot I'd planted for balance, throwing it over his shoulder as he sat in front of me. I yelped, but his hands were quick, grasping my hips in a nearly bruising possession, but one that kept me steady.

"Damnit, Evie, you'd destroy the resolve of a saint," Conall growled.

"What on earth would I do with a—Oh, yes!" I cried out, digging my fingers into Conall's hair as he thrust his face between my legs, licking and sucking with an aggressive hunger that made me weak.

Conall snarled into my vulnerable flesh and I shuddered, blinking up at the sun, my smile faltering. *Damn.* This was a trick. But it was a trick that felt *wonderful*, and a part of me considered giving in to the lovely push and plunder of his tongue inside of me. I could try again later. Could wrestle him in bed, get Laszlo and Hywel to help me, possibly play a game of keep Evanthia off Conall's cock until he couldn't stand it a second longer.

My hands stroked down through silky red locks, and Conall groaned against me, the sound victorious. I cupped the back of his neck and hiccuped a moan, rocking down onto his full and starving lips.

His skin under my fingers was burning up.

"No!" I gasped, and I tightened my hand, yanking him away from me, my body pulsing at the edge of release.

Conall glared up at me, green eyes wild and glowing with defeat. I did my best to answer that stare with one of my own.

"I want your *knot* and your *bite*," I snapped. Conall bared his teeth at me, lip curling back, but his hair was fisted in my grip. His claws nipped carefully at my hips, but he'd meant what he said—he would never want to hurt me. "If I can't have those, then I'll go find someone else."

It was cruel and probably not a threat I could follow through on, but it startled Conall enough that I managed to slip from his grip, practically falling off the branch I'd been on, catching my hands to slow my descent.

"Evanthia—Christ, be *careful*!" Conall cried out, following me with a leap from the branch he'd sat on.

We landed on the ground at the same time, him more gracefully than me, and before I could dart away his arms were around my waist.

"Evie, *wait*, please."

I wrestled against him, pushing his shoulders back even as I rubbed our hips together. His cock was hard, knot already swollen and eager to fit itself inside of me.

"Evie," he moaned, head falling back, hips canting forward.

I twisted in his arms, my ass making an easy nest for his body to press against, and Conall's voice died off with a choke. I grabbed his arms around my waist and tried to dive forward out of his grasp. We went down to the grass together, twigs snapping under our knees. I bit off the yelp of pain as my hands hit the dirt, not bothering to disguise the eager bucking motion back against Conall, half fighting to free myself, half tormenting him with the blatant offer.

Conall's snarl was heavy and dark in my ear, his chest bowing over my back, soft curls tickling my skin. "*Mo chroí*, if you don't stop moving, I'll—"

"*Fuck* me," I finished for him, clawing at the dirt to try and escape, even when it was the last thing I wanted to do.

Conall's growl started soundlessly, a vibration that burrowed over my back and down into my own chest, but it rose in my ear, his breath hot over my shoulder, panting, mouth wide. I froze as teeth braced over my skin, not biting but warning me to *stop* moving. One of Conall's arms pulled away, but the other only fastened tight, barely creating room between us for him to shift and poise his cock at my entrance, the tip tucking inside of me.

"Evie," he rasped, tongue barely scraping over the skin of my shoulder.

I whined and thrust myself onto his cock, his roar ringing through his teeth as they tightened on my shoulder. He bucked in answer, his fingers digging into my hair to pull my head to the side, the hand on my belly sliding down to rub at my sex.

The chasing, teasing, fighting, and wrestling had pushed me to the tipping point of a frenzy. I could fall one way into a panic, or another into ecstasy. I was tense, gritting my teeth, already fluttering on Conall's cock as it stroked inside of me.

"I love you," I gasped out, more for myself, to remind myself I was safe, and with Conall.

He bellowed as he bit down, twisted my hair as he dug his knot into my core. I came with a silent scream, the mark of his teeth on my shoulder and the squeeze of my cunt on his knot a perfect match. It *did* hurt, but that hurt was tied in harmony with the rush of relief and luxurious gust of release—a perfect balance made to ravage through us. I whimpered and surged through sensation, rocking into Conall, not caring about the pull of his teeth in my flesh or the dig of his knot lodged hard in my body. No, I *did* care. I reveled in them both.

Conall's tongue was hot, swiping against my torn skin and his merciless bite, his fingers refusing to stop their tirade on my clit, even as I whined and sagged. He snarled, dragging another wave through my blood and heart and lungs, leaning forward and lowering us both to the dubious cushion of tree roots and violets.

I trembled as he pet between my legs, rolling to his side, the endless pleading nudge of his knot dragging more soft cries from my lips. Slowly, as if it pained him to do so, Conall's jaw loosened and released my shoulder.

"See what you've done, *mo chroí?*" Conall murmured in my ear, licking my blood from the wound, a surprisingly soothing tingle following in the wake. He curled his body around mine, rocking his hips against my ass, an unsteady rhythm that promised me a reprieve before quickly changing its mind. "Wolves are ravenous, my darling. You have me where you wanted me. And I know I will take exactly what *I* want. Over and over again."

He shifted, and out of the corner of my drowsy, blinking eye, I saw him propped up, gazing down at me. I smiled and turned my head, and our expressions matched in the same perfect satisfaction that looped between our hearts. The bond.

"What *we* want, mate," I said, my eyes watering as I reveled in Conall's riotous joy. He was digging through me, reassuring himself of the bond and of my own happiness.

He purred, ducking as I lifted my chin, our lips sliding together at last, sighs exhaled in the laving, sipping kiss. Our union flowed between our bodies, through the bond, a steady current that I gave into gratefully.

42.
NIGHTMARE AND NÉKTAR

"Y ou made me wait a very long time."

A brittle moan escaped my lips, my hands scuffing over my eyes as if they could rip the darkness away from my vision.

I am in the meadow with Conall, I told myself.

But I was here too. Dreaming once more in his reach. Conall and I had dragged one pleasure after another from each other until we were both too weak to move, the bite on my shoulder warm and soft and perfect. Its reassuring pulse of sweet pain was missing here in this cold dark. So was any tug of the new bond, an infinitely more terrible absence.

"I grew quite impatient. I have plans, you see."

I tried to open my lips, but dozens of points of pain pulled and bit into my flesh and I cried out behind the stitches.

Hywel will come, I promised myself. We had been so careful for so long.

"I'm sure you can imagine my frustration when it was the Wyrm who caught on my hook, rather than the great Welsh King of Dreams."

An eerie glow bloomed in front of me, a greenish shade of gray that seemed too muted to illuminate. A shape writhed and twisted inside of the light, and I shivered, shrinking back from the sight, before I noticed the slight dull sheen of scales and the thick plates of an underbelly.

Rolant.

The coiling mass turned, and a silver eye blinked at me, tinged around the edges with red.

"A lesser coup, I'll admit, but the beast will serve his purpose."

A shadow crossed over the vision of Rolant, and the light dimmed.

"Anyway, things worked out better than I might've planned."

Birsha's chuckle was the edge of an icicle running down my back. "I imagined my revenge on that little bitch human well out of reach, only for her sphinx to walk right into my net."

I gasped and light flared anew, this time to my left. A hollow roar sounded, as if Amon's cry was hidden behind layers of glass, but his wings shimmered dully in the strange light, black chains pulled taut as he snarled and yanked in his trap. The light flickered away and then reappeared to the right of my vision.

I stilled at the shadow that built, two broad dark horns sprouting on either side of a large and beautiful bull's head.

"The minotaur too. Truth be told, divinity, I had not imagined being able to gather such a powerful set. Not with my recent...difficulties. I believe you've done me yet another favor."

I screamed Asterion's name behind my sewn lips, but unlike Amon, there was no sign of fight or life from my minotaur.

"All I need is to find a new witch," Birsha's voice mused, eerily close to my ear but without breath.

He isn't real. You're in the meadow, I assured myself, but I couldn't shake my belief in the horrors he presented me.

"I will make you a bargain," he hissed. "Leave these creatures to me. Wake, and lie to your lovers about what I showed you. If you do, I will abandon you. You will have peace at last, at least from me."

The horns swayed, and I refused to tear my gaze from them.

"Evanthia," Asterion called, low and gentle. A simple plea. "Don't—"

"But if you bring war to my doorstep, I will show no mercy. Not to your beasts. And not to you when you are—"

A thunderous roar broke through the darkness. I cried out as the light flickered out, reaching with nothing toward the vanished sight of Asterion's horns.

"Don't come, théa," Asterion called, voice growing stronger.

A wave of red and threads of opal, brilliant and blazing like streaks of lightning, cut across my path, and a brief storm of fury burned up from inside of me before—

I sat up, gasping for air, tangled in the arms and hands and legs of my lovers, the familiar golden and glittering haven of our nest surrounding me.

"He has Asterion!" I cried out.

Birsha had wanted me to lie. To save myself, save Hywel and Conall and Laszlo, in exchange for my minotaur. Asterion, noble beast that he was, wanted that too. It was the kind of bargain *Birsha* would take. The kind of bargain I might've been desperate enough to accept months ago.

It was disgusting, and I tossed the offer aside before I'd even fully reached consciousness.

"Evie, I'm sorry. I'm sorry," Conall rasped, wrapping arms around my shoulders, pulling me into his chest. His head bowed and his mouth grazed over my fresh mark. The skin was tender, and the touch stung a little. Birsha had robbed from me while I was sleeping again.

"Evanthia, look at me," Hywel said, voice sharp.

I searched the room for golden painted horns, as if Hywel might've stolen Asterion from the nightmare like he had stolen me. Long, cool fingers caught my face, forcing my gaze to meet Hywel's.

"He has Rolant, Amon, and Asterion," I whispered.

Laszlo's fingers combed through my hair, snagging on the little braided feathers he'd given me. "It may only be an illusion, dear one."

I shook my head and swallowed hard. "No. Or it doesn't matter. Not if it *might* be real. Think. A dragon, a sphinx, and the King of the Labyrinth," I said. "He hasn't *killed* them yet."

Hywel's lips pursed, and I let out a soft cry, so afraid of his refusal but too weak to fight my way out of their embrace.

"Did you see the others?" Hywel asked. "Hunter, Ronan, and Ezra?"

I shook my head, and Hywel's expression was grave as he glanced over my shoulder to Laszlo.

"You think it might be true?" Laszlo whispered.

"What better way to force our hand?" Hywel answered.

"I should never have—" Conall started.

"Don't," Hywel snapped at him. The dragon's shoulders sagged and he huffed out a breath, moving one of his hands from my cheek to Conall's. "There's no blame. And if Evanthia is right...if Birsha has Asterion and the others, we needed to know.

I've been horribly tempted to try and manipulate the connection, if I'm honest."

"It's better this way. Birsha thinks the control is in his hands," I said, swallowing down the bile in my throat, locking panic away to better focus on the problem.

Hywel nodded, not sparing me from the truth I'd already discovered.

"We have to tell Esther and the others," I whispered, my eyes filling, hands clawing through the sheets around my legs. "We have to go, and-and—"

Laszlo reached for me, drawing me out of the bed slowly. "Evanthia, we will tell the others. And we will do everything in our power to bring—"

"No," I gasped, even as the horrifying reality of my decision weighed like a boulder on my chest. I shook my head and squeezed my eyes shut, forcing back the tears. "No. Whatever we do, I am coming with you. Even if that means facing Birsha once more."

⚜

"Our bags are packed," Auguste announced, hurrying into Laszlo's study with a solemn Booker at his side.

"We don't even know where we're going next," the enormous and grimacing figure of Mr. Tanner said. He'd transformed from the shocked Dr. Underwood, roaring at my announcement and sweeping the sobbing Esther up into his embrace.

"I think we ought to wait for Hunter and—" Nireas started, speaking softly, as if he already knew the words would create more turmoil.

"Wait for them?!" Hazel cried up at him. "We don't even know if they're *alive*!"

"Don't say that, please," Esther said, shaking her head and wiping her damp cheeks with a handkerchief Laszlo had passed her. "Please, I can't—Oh, not again!"

Hazel paled and pressed her lips together, covering her mouth with one hand and turning into the shelter of Nireas and Constantine's offered embrace.

I stood by the open doors of the balcony, watching the chaos as if it were only a scene of a play, as if I wasn't partly responsible for the arguing and the tears.

"Everyone, please, pause for a moment," Conall called, voice raised in stern command. Perhaps it was his nature, but even Hywel looked up from the map he'd been studying with Jude. "We need to make a decision on what action we are taking."

A half-dozen voices raised together at once in a nonsensical flurry of orders, and it was Hywel who cut through the frenzy.

"Enough!"

A collective breath was taken, and Conall offered Hywel a brief nod of thanks before charging forward.

"I can track their scents to retrace their movements. See if I can figure out where they went and who they spoke to, so we can be certain of what happened," Conall said. My breath hitched, hands clenching together, and the bite on my throat throbbing in refusal. Conall looked over his shoulder at me, and a sudden brush of calm reached into my chest. My eyes widened, and he offered me a half smile.

"I don't think we should wait that long," Jude said from the desk.

Conall turned back to the room and nodded. "Nor do I, honestly, but I wanted to offer a cautious option. Another choice is that we've made sure to have teams of allies within close reach of every known temple and house in Birsha's network. Personally, I think it's time we used them. We have more allies to contact in London and Paris and Rome, enough that if we decide we're ready, we can send word across the world and move against him and his houses all at once."

There was a heavy silence in the room, but my ears rang in warning. What if we weren't ready? What if Birsha knew our plans, our allies, and his own army outnumbered ours? What if we were already too late?

"This is what you'd advise?" Hywel asked.

Conall nodded once. "It is. If we give Birsha time to create another temple—"

"No!" Esther shouted, but Conall carried on.

"—we'll never regain the upper hand. Asterion and Amun

have led the charge against Birsha from the first. We can't afford to abandon them."

Hazel rushed out a breath. "So glad you came to that decision, because I am leaving to find Hunter and Ronan regardless."

Esther's tears hiccuped with a snort and she nodded firmly. "I am sick to death of Birsha and his schemes and his cruelty. I want *war*."

"Esther," Mr. Tanner growled.

She growled back at him, and his lips twitched. "I know I am only human, and I know I'm not even very good at fighting, but you are not leaving me behind to worry, and wait, and—" Her voiced choked, and Mr. Tanner gathered her close into his chest, muffling her cries.

Conall stuffed his hands in his pockets, striding to where Hywel and Jude had been scouring over a map. "We don't know yet where Birsha is. Miss Reed, you and yours should go to Star Manor. Magdalena will scry and Khepri will rally the patrons. Miss Nix, to London. Tell Mr. Reddy to shut his doors and bring everyone who can be spared. We'll go to Grace House and spread the word as far and fast as we can."

"Is there time?" Hazel asked, frowning. "London is days away."

Conall stared back at her and shook his head. "I don't know, honestly. But if we don't do this right, we'll end up dead and what good was trying?"

I bit off the shout that clawed through my chest, swirling out of the open door and marching, stumbling, all but running to the banister of the balcony that overlooked the dreaming sea. Was it my imagination, or was it shallower than it'd been weeks ago?

Talons clicked against stone tile and I swayed back, waiting for Laszlo's arms to catch me, tug me into his chest, and surround us with the soft comfort of his wings.

"Stay here with me, dear one," Laszlo murmured in my ear. "Stay here, and I will keep you safe. Hywel will eat Birsha as if he were a canapé. He and Conall won't rest until that despicable man is gone and dead."

I turned my back to the sea, rested my cheek on Laszlo's

shoulder, and listened to the wind whistle through the grains of his feathers.

I want us to run as far away from here as we can and never look back.

I want to turn back time and demand Asterion stay in this sanctuary with us, keep us all here until the world stops turning.

I swallowed hard and lifted my face to whisper in Laszlo's ear. "I will carry Excalibur to the battle."

His sigh was heavy, body leaning into mine and taking as much comfort from me as I did from him.

We will have vengeance, pretty morsel. Hywel had promised me those words before he woke. And as much as I wanted to run, to hide, Birsha had Asterion.

And I would take my vengeance for that violation alone.

Laszlo turned his head to press a kiss into my hair. "Very well."

Before we could exchange a sweeter vow, a sudden burst of shouts and cries sounded from inside the study. Laszlo's arms around my waist spun us and propelled us closer, and I gasped at the sight of red wings through the mass of people surging by the study door.

"Is that Ronan?" I asked, running forward.

Bloodied, bandaged, with a torn wing and a limp, it *was* Ronan. And not just him. Ezra flickered in and out of view, slightly less worse off but haggard with exhaustion. On the floor in the circle of our crowd was a makeshift stretcher, where Hunter lay, so pale he was more gray than green. Hazel was grave at his side, her hands hovering over every patch of bandage and bleeding scratch.

"—didn't realize what was happening to the witch, that Birsha was *using* her to latch the trap around Amon and Asterion. Not until it was too late. I was too high, dealing with the harpy," Ronan explained, frowning at Hazel.

"They left Hunter for dead, and I had to wait to drag him out again," Ezra rasped. "Dunno if I waited too long. Sorry, lovey."

"He's not dead yet," Dr. Underwood said, kneeling by the prone orc. Apparently, Mr Tanner had relinquished the grip on their shared body for the time being, seeing more need for a doctor than himself.

A whisper of sweetness tugged in my belly and I frowned, glancing around the room. *Néktar? Now?* It hardly seemed an appropriate time for—

I whimpered as a stronger pull yanked in my chest, and my eyes widened as I realized the direction was *out*, not in.

"Evanthia?" Laszlo asked, his hands on my shoulders as I lurched forward.

Birsha had leeched from me during the nightmare, but I was too well fed now for him to drain me dry again. Before the nightmare, I'd been *bursting* with vitality. And now...

Now some of it was trying to find its way out of me, and toward...

"Hunter," I gasped, slipping free of Laszlo's hold, weaving between Conall and Hywel.

Hazel looked up at me, face stricken and coated in tears, trapped in a blank worry fueled by the inability to act. I understood her expression—it was my own ever since waking and knowing that Asterion was in danger and out of my reach.

"May I?" But I didn't wait for Hazel or Underwood to agree. I wedged myself between Hunter's side and Booker's close stance and sank down to my knees. *Néktar* left me in a steady rope, an unpleasant pull that made my breath short and my head dizzy.

It was life force, strength, *the food of the gods*, and it knew as well as I did that right now *Hunter* needed it more than I.

I sighed as I lifted his heavily bandaged hand in both of mine, the flow a little less pinching and abrasive when I was touching him.

Hazel frowned at me and licked her lips. "What are you—?"

On the cot, Hunter moaned, his brow furrowing. He coughed and grunted, and Dr. Underwood reached out to push me away.

"Leave her!" Ronan exclaimed. "He's been still as death for the past day and—"

"Haze—" Hunter rasped. A soft cry bubbled up from Hazel's lips as a faint berry-pink flush stained Hunter's cheeks and he breathed in, ragged but deep.

"It's the *néktar*," I said, closing my eyes, trying to focus on the thin current, to offer *more* rather than simply let it be dragged from me.

"Hazel," Hunter called.

"I'm here, you're—You're all right, my love. You'll be all right."

I opened my eyes as Dr. Underwood murmured out a curse. He peeled back a crusted wad of cotton from Hunter's chest to reveal a quickly closing wound, the cut deep enough to reveal bone but fading fast.

"*Blodyn bach*, did you know?" Hywel asked.

I shook my head and let my eyes fall shut again as the room spun and jostled in my vision. "But it wanted to go to him."

It wanted to go to Ronan and Ezra too, I suspected, and I wasn't sure how much they would need, how much I could spare. But Hazel sobbed out a praise of relief, reaching across Hunter to squeeze my shoulder in thanks. We needed every pair of hands and claws and wings we could find. So I would pour my strength out, if that was what it took.

"Easy does it, *mo chroí*," Conall whispered, brushing his thumb down the back of my neck as he settled himself on the floor behind me. "Can't pour from an empty bucket, darling."

"These bandages itch," Hunter groused on the floor, tugging his hand from mine. It was fine—the current had shrunk again almost to nothing. He was well enough not to need my help. I raised my hand up in the direction I'd last seen Ronan.

"Are you—are you sure?" the imp asked gently.

I stretched my other hand out to where Ezra sat, almost sleeping, in an armchair. "It's going to you anyway. It hurts less when we touch."

They'd both grasped my hand before I finished the sentence, and my breath hitched as the twin and opposing ropes of energy left me.

"Shit, it's like a snuff of cocaine," Ezra muttered.

"Was worried it'd make me *aroused*," Ronan joked, until Conall growled softly and the conversation turned in a more serious direction

The plans were laid out once more, Hunter apparently so

recovered he could contribute new orders and suggestions. My head was swimmy, and the words were getting soft. Ezra pulled away first with a kiss against my knuckles, and Conall was licking my bite mark on my throat, shivery wisps of offered *néktar* leaving me before they had a chance to soak in.

Hywel's voice broke through the haze, minutes or hours later. "That's enough."

"She's asleep, I think," Conall whispered, lifting me from the floor.

"She gave too much," Hywel muttered, taking me from Conall's arms.

"I know where to get more," I slurred out, winking one eye open only to find two identical Hywels frowning down at me.

Two heads. Two cocks. I snorted, and someone huffed behind me. I tried to twist to see who, but Hywel grunted and clutched me closer to keep me from diving out of his arms.

"Take care of her. Conall and I will ready our bags," Laszlo murmured.

Hywel sighed, and I bounced as we headed for the door. "Come along, my dear."

"What does Dr. Underwood order for my recovery?" I asked, laughing, when I was sure an hour ago nothing in the world had been funny.

Hywel chuckled though, so it must've been at least a little amusing. "Never mind him. I have a *very* comprehensive plan in place. My pretty morsel needs fed, and I myself am *very* hungry."

43.
THE PATH TO VENGEANCE

I stood on the staircase of Grace House, overlooking the busy activity in the grand room below, and wondered which had changed more—myself or this house of women, no longer silent but active and serious, earnest and eager to help.

Isabel still reigned as queen, ordering her troops with a calm confidence and a gentle tone that she now offered to the monsters who milled about as well.

"Marius is putting up a stink," Lillian whispered in my ear.

My lips twitched. Marius was, in fact, standing still and silent, glaring up at us as he waited for the others by the door.

"He doesn't want to fight?" I asked.

Lillian sighed and leaned against my shoulder. She was more affectionate than ever, and seeing her again was the one bright spot in an agonizingly tense and desperate series of days.

"He does. But he once left me alone to go and help fight, and I ended up in trouble. He swore never to do it again—intended on leaving the battles to Asterion and the rest, I think. But he has a nobler nature than he likes to admit," she said.

Noble, maybe, I thought. *Bloodthirsty was more likely.*

"He could stay here," I suggested. As far as I'd seen, no one had pressured Marius to come with us to the battle.

Lillian shrugged. "If he stays and no one comes to attack Grace House, he'll be very put out to have missed the fighting and glory."

Definitely bloodthirsty, I decided.

"I offered to come with you," she said and then grinned. "He

KATHRYN MOON

nearly had a fit. So he must know I'll be safer here. And I don't really want to be anywhere near fighting, if I can help it."

"You will be safer here," I said, squeezing the back of her hand with mine.

"You could stay." She turned her hand to link our fingers. "You deserve shelter as much as any of us here."

Hywel had said the same when we arrived the night before. Conall had repeated the suggestion this morning when we woke, all tangled together. My mates had taken every opportunity in the rushed traveling to fill me up with strength and *néktar* once more. I knew it was partly because they hated to see me tired and drained.

But I suspected the possibility of my being able to gift the *néktar* away again—I couldn't call it *healing* someone when I had so little to do with the actual effort—was weighing on all our minds.

Asterion might need me. And I needed to be strong and ready for him in that case.

"I don't look forward to...to being near Birsha again," I said. *Seeing him. Facing him. Speaking to him.* "But I do *need* to be there."

Lillian sighed and nodded. "Part of me is glad, just to know how far you've come."

The monsters we'd gathered were moving toward the door. I turned and gathered Lillian in a tight hug.

"We'll meet again in the future, and we'll have more to talk of than this war," I said in her ear, a version of the words she'd said to me herself months ago.

Lillian nodded against my shoulder. "Be...be careful. And remind Marius to do the same."

My men waited for me at the bottom of the stairs, their eyes searching my expression as I approached. They were waiting for me to balk, to turn tail, and in truth a part of me was waiting for that moment too.

"Hunter is waiting for us outside. They got word from Star Manor," Conall said.

My steps faltered, and Hywel caught me before I could go tumbling down the last few steps. He swung me around but didn't release me completely, just let my feet rest on the tiled floor and held me tight.

"Birsha has Asterion and the others at the mountain. Where we found Excalibur," Laszlo said, frowning. "We think he must still have Nimue. We don't know if he'll use her in that disgusting ceremony of his, or if he's trying to make her cast whatever spell it takes to keep the monsters he traps alive."

"But it's not far," I said, the only words that mattered to me in that moment. "That's not so far from here. Not *Persia*, at least."

"He must be trying to regain his foothold here. The edge of England and Wales would be close enough for a new London house," Conall said.

"I don't care what his plans *are*—I care about destroying them. When do we leave?" I asked.

"Stay here, *blodyn bach*," Hywel said.

I turned my glare on him but paused as I realized his eyes were glittering, lined with sleepless red. Conall had dark shadows under his eyes, and Laszlo's feathers were endlessly ruffled with anxiety. My mates had been laving attention upon me almost constantly, shoring up my strength. But they were tired, and they were worried.

"No," I said, as gently as I could.

Hywel let out a long sigh and nodded. "Very well. We leave now. Put this on."

It was a dark leather baldric, and Hywel didn't pass it to me so much as tenderly wrestle it over my head, drawing my arm through. Excalibur's jeweled hilt was already waiting, blade sheathed in a matching scabbard. It weighed me down, thumping against my hip as if to remind me what I'd just committed to. Facing Birsha once more. Fighting not for my freedom, but for Asterion's. My hand found its way to the hilt as if the metal called to my fingers, and my heart skipped unsteadily as I grabbed hold.

"We've already picked out three locations for safe camps," Conall said, grabbing onto my free hand. We marched to the door together in a small huddle, Hywel's hand resting at the back of my neck, Laszlo slipping my arm through his. "We'll have the mountain surrounded."

"Just get me to Asterion," I murmured.

"With our wings and claws, *blodyn bach*," Hywel vowed.

⚜

"I'M SORRY," I WHISPERED, VOICE CATCHING AND EYES squeezing shut.

"Shhh, dear one, it's all right," Laszlo murmured.

Our bodies were still fastened together, chests heaving in the wake of delicious wreckage. I tightened my arms around Laszlo's sweat dewed back to keep him from rolling off of me. I needed his weight, needed to hide beneath his wings until I regained control of my emotions.

His talons soothed through my damp hair, lips grazing over my brow back and forth in a steady brushing rhythm, muttering gentle words.

"We'll find him. We will, I promise."

I hiccuped out a sob and my weak legs slid down to the thin cot we'd set up earlier in our camp tent. I nodded against Laszlo's shoulder, but it was more for his sake than mine. I didn't know if I had faith that we'd reach Asterion in time, didn't know if I believed we'd defeat Birsha. Part of me was already wondering how quickly I would break in that man's grip once more if I was torn away from my mates.

"I should be confident," I breathed against Laszlo's skin.

He fell silent and still, and my heart bit and snarled in my chest, angry with myself for giving voice to my doubts. He turned us, one hand untangling from my hair to draw a sheet up over our cooling bodies, his arm wrapping around my back.

"Do you think I'd be offended that you're frightened?" Laszlo asked. My head was resting on his arm, one wing shrouded over us, and I forced my eyes to lift to his, my breath catching at the tender heat of his gaze. "Dear one, I am frightened too."

I puffed out a breath and a whimper escaped my throat, but Laszlo cuddled me close, his feathered cheek brushing over my temple.

"Conall and Hywel can think in odds and figures and maneuvers. I only know what is at risk, which is all that I hold precious and dear, all that matters to me."

I moaned, but the tight tremor that had seized me in the aftermath of relief softened and slipped away. I wasn't alone. I was understood. Somehow, Laszlo had *always* understood me.

"I love you," I said.

Laszlo's feathers caught my hair in their grip as he turned to plant a firm kiss to my head. "I love you. You are brave, even when you're frightened. You're *here*, my love, and you're not alone." I drew in a shuddering breath and nodded and Laszlo kissed me again, scooting down the cot to reach my cheek, my mouth. "The others are approaching."

My hands tightened on Laszlo's back, and I sucked in a deep breath, calling up calm. Hywel and Conall would worry and fuss and fill my ear with all their accomplishments and promises if I told them I was afraid. They would offer to chaperone me back to the castle. This moment needed to stay between Laszlo and I.

We were pecking and pressing at one another's lips when the canvas tent flap swatted open, boots crunching over grass.

"Don't hide the view," Hywel announced upon entry.

Laszlo kissed my nose and withdrew his wing, cuddling me to his bare chest. "Not everything is for your entertainment, love."

"Of course not," Conall agreed, smiling wickedly and combing his hair back from his face with clawed fingers. "But in this case, I'm inclined to agree with the dragon. The sheet's hiding too much."

They were whole, safe, and in good spirits.

But Asterion, a soft voice cried out in my thoughts. As if he could hear them, Laszlo slipped his fingers into my hair, soothing through my scalp. Conall's smile sobered too, noting my anxiety in our bond.

"Marius is out hunting," Hywel said, grinning with sharp teeth, tugging his shirt off over his head. "Picking off Birsha's sentries one by one."

"And Birsha?" Laszlo asked.

Hywel and Conall glanced at one another as they undressed, and worry prickled in my chest.

"There's no sign of him," Conall admitted.

I sat up, gasping. "He's not here?! But then—"

Conall lifted his hands, tossing his clothes aside and hurrying to the end of the cot. "Magdalena's been scrying and reading her cards and leaves every waking moment. All signs point to him being here. Asterion and the others almost certainly are. But it wouldn't be the first time he ran from a fight."

"And if he *does*?" I asked, trying not to scream.

"We are storming his temples at first light, putting the poor souls he has trapped out of their mercy. If Birsha runs, what will be left of him? A crumbling figure, weakened. We'll find him, *mo chroí*. And we'll make sure he doesn't get his claws into Asterion," Conall said, crawling up the cot. He ducked his head and kissed my breastbone, nuzzling his face between my breasts, beard prickling and tickling. "How are you feeling?"

"Feasted," I said, a little terse.

"Good," all three of my men said at once.

"The waiting is difficult," Laszlo said, catching Conall's eye. I tried to catch the silent conversation that passed between them, but I wasn't quick enough, and Hywel distracted me by sliding into the bed from my left, drawing my face to his for a kiss.

"In the morning, it begins," Hywel murmured, passing his lips over mine once more. "By evening, the houses will start to fall. Birsha's last hope will be making use of Asterion and the others. He won't run, but if he does, you and I will fly after him with Excalibur blazing in your beautiful hand. We will watch him fall, *blodyn bach*."

"Vengeance," I whispered.

Hywel nodded, nose brushing against mine. "Yes. And then peace."

44.
MORGANA
LE FAY

"There!"

The word was ripped from my lips as Hywel dove down to the ground, a streak of violent red in the sky, the cries from the ground warning one another of our approach. I tightened my legs in the strange saddle Laszlo had placed on Hywel, huge and broad, my feet tucked into stirrups and my knees bent around Hywel's neck. My left hand gripped hard at the reins and I pressed myself down against his ridged back, just barely able to view the battlefield below from around the hard scales and bright spikes of Hywel's body.

I winced and closed my eyes as Hywel scooped a boggard disguised as a giant black cat from the ground, the scream of the creature sharp in my ears.

I can smell your fear, **blodyn bach**, Hywel mused.

I huffed and braced my feet hard in the stirrups, gritting my teeth and raising Excalibur high as Hywel tossed back the boggard. I swung the sword, turning my face away from the spray of blood, and the defeated foe went crashing down to the ground, a cheer rising up from the orcs below us. They were friends of Hunter's and seemed to be relishing the day more than anyone else.

Your arousal too, Hywel chuckled.

"Rude of you to point it out," I said, scanning the ground below once more, searching for any ally who might be outnumbered. Any sign of a small, plain, unremarkable man running from the field. Any glint of gold horns.

Hedonism takes many forms. And you need your strength today, Hywel said.

I rubbed a hand over the largest scale at the back of Hywel's neck. He had a little feeling in them, and he purred in my head at the touch.

"They're not making progress on the mountain," I called, staring at the dark seething shape of battle that still blocked the entrance we'd used when hunting Excalibur.

Birsha conjured many ghouls and revenants for today. It's messy work, but they're not strong. Just plentiful. Come, we'll scorch them.

I bit my lip, swallowing the refusal. Hywel had burnt the field twice so far, and the power and blaze was difficult to withstand. Especially in the chainmail Laszlo had dressed me in during the wee hours of the morning.

My eyes paused on a smaller pocket of fighting, and I tugged on the reins to alert Hywel. "No, look! Southwest. Madame Mortimer's army is cornered."

Stone Eater, Hywel snarled, turning to where I directed.

The Stone Eater must've been the massive lizard-like beast that had pinned a collection of the marble butlers. They'd appeared at our camp the night before, led by the beautiful dark-haired woman, who absolutely everyone but me seemed to know. She claimed to be a witch, which I thought was odd, considering the incredible pulse of power that surrounded her, far exceeding any witch's aura. I found her difficult to look at directly, but she'd seemed friendly. Her butlers were dressed in tight black suits and carried an array of weapons, and at the moment, they were barely keeping the snapping jaws of the scaled beast away from themselves.

I sat back down in the saddle just as Hywel dove down to the ground. My hands grabbed onto horns that sprouted from either side of his long neck to brace myself against the blistering pace.

Leap from my back, run for the tent. I'll return.

"But—"

This will be difficult, and I don't want you caught by our claws, **blodyn bach**, Hywel growled in my head, a shudder running down my back.

I stood, forcing my eyes to remain open, in spite of the terrifying sight of the ground rising up to meet us too fast.

Now!

I jumped as Hywel stretched his jaw wide, snapping down on the Stone Eater's tail. Hywel twisted in the air, dragging the beast away from the stone men, and his tail caught me around the waist, easing my flight to the ground. The butlers charged toward me, circling defensively around my body as Hywel's tail unwound and I dropped the last few feet, thunking to the hard ground on my knees with my chainmail rattling.

"Our mistress and Miss Reed are looking for you." The stone man had a low and simple voice. He held out his hand to me, and I accepted his help in drawing me up from the grass. Whatever Magdalena Mortimer was, she had a fine eye for detail, and I appreciated the many variations of handsome faces currently surrounding me.

"Take me to them."

As we marched away from the battle to the small tent where those who needed medical or magical attention rested, I twisted to look up at the sky. Roars tore through the clouds, the sky cut open by blood-red wings. I fought the smile on my lips as I found Hywel playing with the Stone Eater like a cat that had caught a mouse. A gold streak swooped below the dragon, Laszlo moving from one part of the battlefield to another. Conall would be on the ground somewhere, barking orders to the packs of werewolves that had come to our aid.

Breathe, I reminded my tight and frozen chest.

We reached the tent quickly, and I heard Esther's voice from outside.

"But-But how could you have let Rooksgrave *fall?*"

I parted the curtain, immediately lowering my eyes at the strange and heavy aura of the woman standing central in the tent.

Magdalena Mortimer spoke softly, but her voice had too much weight in my ears. "It was in the cards. We all answer to fate, darling."

I cleared my throat, searching the beds around the edge of

the tent for familiar faces and sighing with relief to find there were only a few mild injuries being tended at the moment.

"Evanthia!"

I raised my gaze to Esther, wincing against the burn of Magdalena out of the corner of my eye. "You were looking for me?"

She was as pale as Auguste standing at her side, and the vampire was busy gaping at Magdalena. "But I've known you for...for—"

"Ages, yes," Magdalena said, nodding. "Far too long to be a simple hedge witch, don't you think?"

Auguste blinked, and Esther spared the woman another brief, startled glance before turning back to me.

"Sorry, we've just had a bit of a...shock," she said, shaking her head. "Hazel should be here in a moment too."

"Who else knows?" Auguste asked Magdalena.

"Khepri."

"And that's *all*?"

"Well, my sister, of course. And Hywel might have recognized me, but of course a dragon loves a good secret."

I startled at the mention of my dragon, but Magdalena was blazing now, an eerie, brilliant shadow glowing thick and opaque over her skin, and I closed my eyes, covering them with my hand.

"And you see, she can tell," Magdalena said.

"Evanthia?" Esther called.

"I'm sorry, it's just very *uncomfortable* to look at her," I said.

"Oh, yes, that would be the glamour," Magdalena murmured. "I'll take it off now, if you don't mind."

I turned my face away from the flash of lightning-bright magic, but Esther and Auguste both gasped as it faded away.

"Goodness, what was—Oh! Magdalena, is that *you*?"

I opened my eyes as Hazel ran to a stop at my side. Her hair was falling loose from its braid, one lock near her cheek was singed, and the sleeve of her shirt was torn and marked with a little blood, but the *néktar* stored in me didn't revolt, so she must've been safe. When I glanced reflexively to the center of the tent once more, I found a new version of the woman I'd been introduced to the day before, and this one didn't make my eyes water in refusal.

Magdalena Mortimer was fae, I realized, taking in the high point of her ears and the sharp edges of the teeth in her wide smile. She was still pale, her skin glowing and shimmering like a pearl, and the hair that coiled and braided down her back was as black and fathomless as ink. She was beautiful, with features so impossibly fine and delicate they defied age, and huge eyes that threatened to swallow your thoughts and soul if you held her gaze too long. I pulled mine away and hauled a sudden gulp of air into my starving lungs.

"Morgana Le Fay, at your service," she announced with a flourish of hands that were now much longer and more spindling than before. "Although, truth be told, that name is a little heavy-handed and I've grown quite fond of Magdalena, so don't trouble yourselves."

Auguste turned Esther's cheek toward him, breaking that hypnotic stare. "There's so much you could've done," he said, frowning and staring down at the ground. "You've been playing matchmaker in the country when you could've been stopping Birsha in his tracks."

"Perhaps," Magdalena answered, with a shrug. "I did what I would do and what was done."

"Riddling faes," Hazel said with a sigh.

"Why reveal yourself now?" I asked.

"Nimue is my sister," Magdalena said, the easy lightness in her voice hardening to obsidian. "Or something like it. We are two opposites of an identical soul."

"Oh, Magdalena, I'm sorry," Esther said softly. Her heart was too sweet, I thought, faltering in its anger so easily.

I licked my lips and considered what Magdalena had said already and what I knew of the myth of Morgana Le Fay. She was as twined into the stories of King Arthur and the Lady of the Lake as Nimue, and sometimes they were even the same person. Sometimes Morgana was the villain too, the womb from which Arthur's demise was born. But Auguste was right—both Nimue and Morgana should've been powerful enough to stand up to Birsha.

"Nimue is *letting* Birsha hold her captive," I said.

Magdalena clapped her hands together. "Aha, she has it!"

"What?! But *why*?" Esther cried out.

I glanced up and Magdalena's perfect brow was arched, waiting for me. I heaved a sigh and rolled my eyes. "Because it's what would happen and did happen and will happen," I started.

"Oh, dear," Hazel muttered.

"And because...hopefully, we need her there?" I guessed.

"Wisdom with age," Magdalena murmured approvingly. "Very good, my dear."

Esther's lips pursed, and I didn't blame her for her ire, but the fae were a law unto themselves, and their definitions of right and wrong had more to do with plotting the stars and getting their way than any human concept of morality.

"I can't get into the mountain—the roots can't reach that far," Hazel announced, arms crossing over her chest. "And even if I could, I'd be alone in there, and I don't like my odds."

"What can Nimue do for us?" Auguste pressed Magdalena, grinding his jaw.

"A great deal, I'm sure," Magdalena trilled.

"What *will* she do?" I asked instead.

"I've *always* liked divinities, you know," the fae woman purred at me.

My eyes narrowed. "I wonder if dragon ever *eat* fae.*"

Magdalena laughed and her head fell back on her neck too far, her throat disproportionately long. But she settled and softened before our eyes, clasping her hands in front of her. "Nimue will speak. She will be your mouthpiece. For *one* of you.*"

"Speak? That's all?" Hazel asked.

"We can't get into the cave, so we have to draw Birsha out," I said, shuddering and turning to pace the tent.

"Perhaps Hywel?" Auguste suggested.

"*No*." Magdalena's voice was stone once more. "No, Nimue will speak for a woman."

One of you.

Hazel watched my restless strides, her lips turning down. "I'd do it, but...I never even met him. I doubt I made that much of an impression."

I turned on my heel, aware of the stares on my face. I circled the tent, wishing I could growl like Conall, breathe fire like Hywel, spread my wings and fly away like Laszlo.

"Does he know I'm here?" I asked, glancing at Magdalena.

"No."

I paused and gaped at her. "Really?"

"Nimue cooperates as much as she wants. She shields *you*, her victor, her sword wielder," Magdalena said, eyeing Excalibur in its sheath with a flash of jealous green in her eyes.

"Then that means it should be me," Esther said, lifting her chin, meeting my eyes as I spun to face her. "And I think I have a plan for us."

45.
THE VICTOR

By evening, Birsha's forces were winning the battle. Marius had surrendered when caught up between too many allies and foes in close quarters, unable to use his stare against the trolls he fought without risking the safety of friends. Conall and Hunter had retreated to a tent, blood coating their white linen shirts. Laszlo and Mr. Tanner were missing entirely, presumed captured.

Hywel had dropped from the sky, nearly crushing a troop of orcs and falling into an eerie sleep.

And I stood a mile from the mountain and the turning tide of violence, with his slumbering body at my back. I was shrouded in Magdalena Mortimer's black velvet cape, with Hazel Nix at my side. Our hands were linked, and we stood in the orange glow of a sunset between two trees, the edge of a small circling family of yews that seemed to bow toward a bare field at their heart.

"Are you ready?" Magdalena asked Esther, who stood before her.

Esther licked her lips, her gaze only lifted as high as Magdalena's beautiful rosy purple lips. "It's time."

Magdalena's long fingers reached out to Esther. The young woman lifted her own hands, wincing as those gleaming bone-white hands grasped onto her, twining around her wrists. Hazel stepped closer to me, shoulder to shoulder, her steady strength absorbing the tremble that ran through me.

Magdalena nodded once, and Esther drew a breath.

"I bet you think you're winning," she called out, bright and loud and steady. I envied her voice, her surety. "I bet you think that I'll give up. That you'll have conquered me, just because you've taken one of my lovers."

There was a pause and Esther's face turned, eyes wide, an answer in her ear only she could hear.

"Hardly!" she snapped back, her cheeks flushing. "Take what you can today, but...Amon is no match for a dragon." Another pause, and she laughed. "You underestimate me. That's your weakness, I think. You don't really understand *love*. I'll make a whole flock of dragons fall in love with me if it means I can kill you in another year or two!"

Hazel's eyes widened, and mine narrowed. Was Esther threatening to...steal Hywel away from me? I didn't like that one bit, even if it was for the sake of foiling Birsha.

"I can hear the doubt in your voice," Esther said, bucking her chin up. "And so I have a bargain for you. My witch put the dragon to sleep. Bring me Amon, and you may have the King of Dreams instead."

I wanted to run forward, press my ear to Esther's to hear what she could, and Hazel's hands tightened around mine, her head shaking subtly as I took an instinctive step.

"If you want to risk it," Esther murmured after the answer in her head, and then a moment later she sagged, pulling her hands free of Magdalena's.

A bird cried out from one of the tree tops—the only sound that reigned in the quiet place we stood.

"Did it work?" Hazel whispered.

Esther and Magdalena glanced at one another. "He says he won't come," Esther said.

"But he's leaving the cavern," Magdalena answered, her gaze distant. "He won't bring Amon."

"He'll want to see that you have Hywel," I said, nodding and glancing back at the dragon. "He...he *will* wake, yes?"

"I'll release him from the fog," Magdalena said. Which was not quite a *yes* but would have to do. Hywel had promised me weeks ago that he had many years before another sleep. "I'll leave you three now. I have work on the field."

"I should wait in the trees," Hazel said as Magdalena strode out of the circle of yew, her steps carrying her faster than they ought to. Hazel turned to me, pausing and studying my face. "Will you be all right?"

A laugh cracked out of my chest, and my head shook. "No. But I'm ready for this to be over."

"We'll be with you," Esther said, joining us. "He's afraid of Hazel and me because we defeated him once already. After today, he'll realize he should've feared you too."

"After today, he'll be gone," Hazel said firmly. She kissed my cheek and then slipped away, leaning back against a yew, which welcomed her until she'd vanished completely.

"Do you trust the fae?" I whispered to Esther, as if Magdalena might hear us.

"I do," she said, staring out at the woods, her lips twisting. "Maybe I shouldn't, but in spite of the things I wish she had changed, I can't say the path she set me on hasn't been wonderful. Well, most of it."

I sighed and nodded, wrapping my arms around my middle. "With the little I know about fae, she does seem fairly generous in good tidings."

Esther hummed noncommittally. "You should get into the shadows. I don't know how long we'll have to wait, but we don't want him to see you."

She's so young, I thought, staring at this girl before me. A woman, yes, but so early in life. I hoped her lovers had a plan to keep her with them for many years to come. She would age well.

"Will you be all right?" I asked, echoing Hazel's question to me.

Esther smiled, brave and fearless and confident. "I will. I'm terrified, you know. But yes, I'll be all right."

I swept her up in a hug, recalling Laszlo's speech to me the night before, hoping and praying to all the gods whose names I knew that my mates would be safe, that this woman and Hazel and all the men they loved would survive.

"You're not alone," I whispered in her ear, and then I pulled away.

I waited, tucked into the curve of Hywel's front leg with Magdalena's cloak shielding me. Hywel's heat and his steady breaths offered shallow comfort. The sun set quickly, but the time seemed to drag, every slight shifting shade of color in the sky another moment that I waited for Birsha to appear. What if he didn't come? What if Magdalena—or Morgana—and Nimue betrayed us, or failed us and fled? What if *what was and would be* was Birsha's victory and our defeat?

No, my own voice echoed in my head. *No, I won't accept that. I won't surrender again. I will fight until I am free, even if that freedom is death. I do not belong to Birsha.*

Hywel rumbled in my ear, tail scratching over the ground restlessly, and up from the burning bud of the sun sinking from the horizon, a figure on a horse approached. For a moment, he was only a brilliant silhouette, remarkable solely by the setting, and still I shook in witness, wanting to scream, to *run*.

Then the sun burnt away, and his shape settled and grew larger.

His enchantments were starting to fail. The temples *were* falling, as Conall promised, and the man on the horse was old and plain and average. His hair was steel gray and black, lines of age carving down his face, over his heavy brow. He didn't look strong or stooped, tall or short. Had he always been unremarkable, or was that part of the figure he'd built himself into, like the legend of my sword fashioning it into Excalibur?

"You meant it," Birsha said, slightly awed as he slowed the horse outside of the circle of trees.

"You underestimate me," Esther answered.

His laugh was sharp. "I did once. Where is your witch?"

"I will give up the dragon, but not her," Esther answered, hands fisting at her side. She'd wanted a weapon, but we agreed it was too important he see her unarmed. "I'm *not* stupid."

"You will give up the dragon? And your allies?"

"I will give up the dragon and my allies *in exchange* for Amon. Who I see you haven't brought."

"I'm not stupid," Birsha mimicked, smirking.

He wasn't moving. My breath was rough and uneven in my chest, my body so tight I thought a nudge might send me shattering into a pile. He *had* to move.

"I am beginning to understand your true nature, Esther

Reed," Birsha announced, and I held my breath as he swung down from his saddle.

"I doubt that," Esther quipped, turning to the side, offering him less of her body in case he were to strike.

"I'd assumed you were nobler, more determined to do good. In truth, you are a survivor, like myself."

"You forget that I know exactly *how* you go about your survival. No, I'm not like you." Esther's bottom lip quivered, and I wondered if it was an act. No, her terror was real.

"Hmm, we'll see. You're in your youth yet. Decisions will be made when the time comes," he mused.

Esther spun her back to him, striding toward the edge of the circle of trees, facing me. Her chin was high but her eyes were wide now, darting around the canopy as she thought. "We'll see. Are you going to bring me my sphinx, or should I wake the dragon now? It will be quick, and when he sees you—"

The bluff was enough. He hadn't survived so long with empty risks. Birsha burst into action, marching across the grass to the center of the small field, his hand raised and a storm cloud turning his plain face ugly with hatred.

"Wait!" he cried.

He did not want to face Hywel awake, that much was clear. He hadn't lied. He wasn't stupid. He'd survived a *very* long time, in hiding, shielding himself with stronger creatures. And now we had him alone.

But he was right about something else. He always underestimated Esther Reed.

The ground burst beneath his feet, dark roots caging and capturing him. Hazel had been busy while we waited, and she'd kept her ear high just as she promised, she and the trees in perfect harmony when Birsha stepped onto his mark. He shouted out, thrashing, and tore through thin threads, but he couldn't break them all at once, and the trees were eager to please Hazel's command.

I stood from the shelter of Hywel, watching with parted lips and faint breaths. Esther edged out of the circle, her hands clutched over her chest as she watched Birsha curse and fight. Some roots withered and twisted away, Birsha's remaining siphoned power killing them off, but that too wasn't enough, and it only seemed to make the stronger corded living ones more aggressive, squeezing hard at his legs and squirming to capture his hands.

Hazel stumbled free of a tree trunk, dazed and searching the sky and earth for a moment before shaking herself and staring at Birsha in his struggles.

"Huh. You're not what I expected," she greeted.

"*Nymph*," Birsha snarled, eyes wide. "I should've known."

"Half-nymph," Hazel corrected. She turned and looked back toward where Esther and I were huddled together. "It's all right. The trees know their business. You can come closer."

"I will kill you both and take the dragon. I will eat the flesh off your mates until their screams match yours and their bodies will fuel me for—"

"Goodness, he is nasty," Hazel said, tipping her head. An fervent cluster of thin roots scurried up Birsha's chest, cutting off his speech as they twisted around his throat and tightened.

Calm rushed over me at the sudden gurgle of struggle that died away from his throat, and I placed my hand over my chest, closing my eyes and digging through my emotions until I found the small thread of worry and pride. *Conall.* The pride bloomed as I reached out to him, the signal he waited for. I found myself smiling as I opened my eyes once more.

Birsha was glaring at the ground near where I stood, writhing in the grip of the roots, but he stilled as I pushed the hood of Magdalena's cloak back. A brief glimmer of genuine shock slackened his contorted features, and his lips formed the word *you*.

A growl shook the leaves of the yew trees before I could answer, and the ground rumbled as Birsha paled, his eyes growing wide as Hywel rose from his slumber. Magdalena was true to her word after all.

Blodyn bach. *I will stay with you.*

I turned to face my dragon, craning my neck back far to stare up at him, and shook my head. "Go, the others need you. Get us into the mountain, Hywel."

His head dipped and I laughed as he butted his massive snout against my hips, puffing hot air around me, surrounding me in a large cloud of *nektar*.

"Not now, you mad beast," I murmured, rubbing my hand over the scales and horns in front of me. "I...I *will* be fine. This will be over soon."

Hywel grunted and eased away, turning and nearly sending me toppling to the ground as he beat his wings. Esther grabbed onto my arm, and we braced against one another as Hywel's flight swirled the air and knocked us about.

I stole a breath, and Esther caught my eye before we turned to face the yew trees once more. It was growing dark, and with Hywel's dreams gone—giving the illusion of our loss, hiding our friends safely away while Birsha's army fought against shadows—the battle would turn again quickly.

There was just one thing left to do.

"Let him speak," I said to Hazel.

"Are you sure?" she asked, wrinkling her nose.

I nodded and she sighed, loosening the grip of the roots on his throat.

But Birsha didn't speak, just stared at me. He was stripped of illusions, lured out of safety by a young human woman, trapped by the eager obedience of trees, facing down his once captive prize. He was old, far older than he ought to have been, and with every minute that passed, more lines dug into his face. If we kept him here like this, I thought he would wither away on his own, time catching up with him at last.

He cleared his throat and eyed me warily. "Why send the dragon away? What do you plan on doing with me?"

I reached up to the latch of the cape, unbuckling it from over my chest and letting the fabric slide to the ground. I wrapped my hand around the hilt of Excalibur and drew it slowly from its sheath, a cool satisfaction softening the ragged edges of fear that pleaded with me to run from this man, this moment.

He was frightened too.

"I plan on killing you," I said, the words strangely gentle.

He swallowed hard, eyes wide on mine. "The ceremony is already in place. Your minotaur is gone. Trapped. His strength is mine."

He ground his jaw, stretching his arms to prove his point, snapping roots but gasping as more took their place, binding him tighter than before.

"Amon," Esther whimpered.

"If you're alive, they're alive," I said to Birsha. "We know how your temples work."

"You can't save them. *I* can save them," he choked out.

I turned Excalibur in my hand, my palms sweating. Esther called my name behind me, but I shook my head. I knew this man. I knew his lies and his manipulations.

"No more bargains. No more leeching strength from me or anyone else," I said. I frowned at him, trying to find the creature that crawled through my nightmares, that pinned me behind stone walls and stared at me from shadows.

"They're no better than I am!" he cried out, swelling in the cage of the roots, his face turning red as his hair kept fading to white. "*I. Am. A. King!*"

I winced as he spat, shouting.

"You were," I said. "You were a king. And you hated the idea that any creature, man or monster, might be stronger than you, more powerful, *better*. So you clawed your way into their world and broke them down to sit under your boot. But you're a coward, and you're an old man, and you've never understood the first thing about power or people."

Birsha's breaths fell into pants, a grunt of pain sounding, and then a strangled cry as something in the tangle of roots snapped.

"You won't save them!" His eyes were wild, a slight foam of rage around his lips as his jowls sagged.

I took a deep breath and lifted my sword. "I helped keep you alive for long enough. I'll do my best for them too. But this is the end now, Birsha, king of nothing."

You might be condemning Asterion to death, a small hiss sounded in my head. But if I let Birsha live, if I gave him another chance to run, to rebuild himself, I would condemn so many more lives, so many women like me. I knew what Asterion would do, what *needed* to be done.

And I believed that I could save the man I loved.

"He underestimated you too," Hazel said from behind me.

Birsha's eyes flashed wide. "Wait—!"

"He did," I said, and then I slashed the blade in my quaking grip forward.

Excalibur was light and smooth in my hand, fashioned to be victorious. With temples and houses falling around the world, Birsha was already at his end and an easy meal for the ambitious blade.

I held the ancient gaze of the man I had never been able to see clearly before now. I stared into Birsha's eyes, even as they turned, as they fell in a tumble to the ground, as they grew pale and opaque, dusty and decaying, dissolving into ash.

"What if he was telling the truth about—" Esther's voice broke, and she stepped to my side as Excalibur grew heavy in my grip.

I swallowed hard. "Birsha doesn't know the first thing about Asterion's strength. It isn't a piece of his body to be *eaten*. They're alive."

Hazel gasped as the roots gobbled and tore through the remains before us, twisting and tangling and digging through the earth, new life growing up from the ground at a terrifying speed. They rolled over the ground like shallow waves on the seaside, pushing us back, sucking the dust and bone and ashes of Birsha into the dirt to feed their own growth.

"Yews like death," she murmured. "They'll be good guardians."

Evanthia!

I grunted at the shout in my head, stumbling away from the rioting growth. "Here! The others?!"

All fine. We're breaking into the mountain now. Come. Hywel landed in the open field, his body steaming with heat, nose puffing out fresh smoke. ***He's dead.***

"Yes. Yes—He—" I whined, my knees wobbling, salt dripping between my lips as my breath hiccuped. "Hywel," I pleaded.

Hywel's head ducked down as I reached for him. His hot, dry breath burnt away the tears on my face that had fallen without my noticing, and his tongue slipped out between his lips to lick away the ones that came after.

He's gone now, blodyn bach. No more nightmares.

Hywel nudged closer, and I climbed onto his snout, holding the horns on his face and weeping into his scales as my chest throbbed and tore and seamed itself back together.

Share the saddle. I'll fly you back, Hywel offered Hazel and Esther. ***Quickly, now.***

Hywel's flight back to the mountain was gentle, his scales shedding heat to fight off the chilly air of evening.

"I spent half my life in that man's grip," I whispered to Hywel, the fury of grief softening for a moment, turning my body limp and tired.

That will fraction again and again. In time. We have time now, **cariad.**

Did Asterion have time? Had I consigned him to death in my determination to rid myself of Birsha at last? Fresh tears rose and were ripped away by the wind as Hywel made our descent in careful starts and stops.

The ghouls are gone, withered the moment you killed Birsha. We are only cleaning up now, and the entrance to the caves is cleared.

"Conall and Laszlo?" I asked, rubbing my cheek against my shoulder to wipe away the last of the tears.

They wait below, with the others. Take heart, Evanthia. Asterion waited millenia for you. He will not have succumbed so quickly.

I bounced on Hywel's snout as we touched down and stiffened as bright cheers rose up from the gathered party of monsters. Celebration? For—

Oh.

Hywel crouched to the ground and figures rushed in, the sudden crowd's appearance making me flinch. A huge, hulking shape moved closer, but it was only Mr. Tanner, snatching Esther up in his arms. Nireas gathered Hazel too, and then I was dragged from Hywel by a dirty, blood and sweat-stained Conall.

"Oh, *mo chroí*, come here now. I thought I'd lose my mind," Conall breathed, squeezing me tight.

I sobbed once against his shoulder and then bit my tongue and held him just as tightly. Heat simmered and stirred the air behind us, Hywel shifting back to his smaller shape. Gold feathers beat and rustled out of the corner of my eye, and in spite of the struggle of battle, Laszlo still smelled sweet and clean as he joined our embrace.

"Our brave, beautiful mate." Laszlo pushed my hair aside, kissing the curve of my shoulder. "Are you injured?"

I shook my head. "It was..." *awful, a relief, satisfying,* "...easy," I admitted softly, although that wasn't quite true either. I shook my head, and Laszlo and Conall released me, each keeping an arm around my waist.

A tall, elegant figure wove through the crowd—Magdalena, gleaming like a star in the night sky, bright eyes fixed on the black cave entrance. "We need to get inside."

Esther and her own men were also gathering at the opening of the cave, torches in hand, including one that floated invisibly.

"Ezra's scouted some already," Conall told me as we marched for the entrance. "There's no sign of any of Birsha's allies, but..."

"But?" I asked.

Conall lowered his voice. "No sign of our minotaur, or the others either."

My heart froze in my chest, my tongue numb. Was this it? Had I lost Asterion, the man who'd saved me, who'd championed me and sheltered me and *loved* me?

Would vengeance be worth it if Asterion was gone? I already knew the answer, and it made me queasy and cold.

Hywel looked back over his shoulder, expression stern and eyes glowing. "Birsha is gone now, along with the last of his warlocks. We'll find them, Evanthia."

I nodded, feigning his confidence, but Laszlo slid his hand across my back and linked our fingers together, squeezing once. He knew my fears too well.

We entered at the cavern pool where we'd found Excalibur, but it was still and quiet, water barely moving as we waded around the edge to another shadowy opening. The deep void of the caves knew my fears too, narrow and silent, a heavy pressure muting even our steps.

"There were enchantments that made the temple feel impenetrable, made us feel alone in the dark," Esther murmured from ahead.

"This is not Birsha's magic now, darling," Magdalena said. "This is the mountain. She's older than all of us."

My own heartbeat drummed in my ears, and the passage shrank until Laszlo and Conall had to release me, one in front and one behind. Would we all vanish into the mountain too? Would she swallow the strange creatures who had crawled into her belly while she was sleeping? Is that where Asterion and Amon and the others had disappeared to? I wondered how long I might wander in the dark, with feathers under my fingertips guiding me deeper.

And then a soft pang in my chest snapped into place, *néktar* tugging hard and urgent.

"Oh!" I gasped, and my steps stumbled, Conall bumping into my back. "They're close. I need—Out of my way, please!"

There was hardly room to move, and I barely knew who I was squirming past, shoving out of my way, but it didn't matter. Deep in the dark, someone was dying, and I only had to follow the pleading rope of *néktar* to find them.

I chased the painful calling in my chest, breathless and weak. *Let it go to him*, I thought, begged. Asterion.

I tripped over stone and slid down a thin, steep hole of a passage, and behind me Hywel cried my name, telling me to slow, to wait. It was too late. I was falling, dragged along by gravity and my own strange power, scraping my arms against ragged walls, hitting my head on low rock.

The ground beneath me vanished, and I dropped with a scream, light blooming suddenly, strangely violet and dull. I landed on my back, breath snapped from my lungs by the impact, and for a moment I could only claw at my own chest, searching for air and resisting the rebellious flee of my strength. It split, threads unwinding, turning in four directions.

I flailed on the ground, rolling to the side, a scream silent in my frozen chest at the sight of the twisted figure, blood seeping onto the ground and nearly reaching my prone form. A beast, a dragon! Rolant!

I cried out and then hauled stagnant air into my lungs. Rolant, tangled and weak, turned in on himself, his scales torn away to reveal sore and open flesh. I pushed myself up onto my hands and knees and twisted to search the room.

It was unevenly round, and it looked as though it had been freshly dug, rubble still littering the ground. Leaned back against the far wall was a seated woman, her eyes on me, a gruesomely bloody smile turned in my direction. She was beautiful, hair pale in the strange light, skin gleaming.

"Victor," she greeted, and my brow furrowed for a moment before I realized what she meant. This was Nimue.

I groaned as she reached a hand out toward me, my body lurching in her direction by the force of the *néktar* she stole from me.

"No!" My strength was for Asterion, not her!

"Heal me, and I fix this," she said, dark blood bubbling up from her lips.

My body shook and threatened to fall limp as I ripped my stare from hers. Amon was to my right, pale and silent but blinking at me, his chest rising and falling. It took me a moment to spot his injury, but they were there in his lap, bloodied fingertips cut short, his claws stolen.

Which only left...

I yanked myself once more, fighting against Nimue's draw on my power, my knees scraping against the ground as I scrambled to turn and find—

"Asterion!" I cried out.

He was sprawled against the wall, legs spread, head back, and in the shadows and the hollow light it took me a moment to make him out properly. His head lolled, and my breath stopped short.

"Oh, my love," I whispered, digging my fingers into stone and dirt, forcing my way in his direction, ignoring the choking pull on my chest, my throat, even my eyes aching in my skull. Nimue would steal all the life I had in me before I could give any to my friends, to my mate.

"*Théa*," Asterion whispered, blinking.

His horns were broken, gold cut away, but he was there waiting for me, calling to me. I wept and crawled to him, one painful struggling movement at a time, until his hoof was under my hand. I moaned, and Nimue's force fractured as I touched Asterion. There was still *néktar* spilling out of me, my vision going hazy around the edges, but she didn't control me now. I kept one hand on Asterion at a time, scooting myself into his lap, eagerly searching his body for wounds I might seal shut.

His chest heaved with a deep breath as I fell against him, wrapping my arms over his shoulder, pressing my lips to his jaw.

"Birsha is dead," I whispered.

"Evanthia." Asterion's arms circled me. "You shouldn't have come, and yet I knew you would. My fearless little goddess."

Rocks fell from above, one striking me in the back, but the pain was dulled and faded, distant compared to the soft brush of Asterion's fur under my cheek.

"Evanthia!"

"I love you," I whispered, my lips almost numb as they buffed against Asterion's soft ear.

"Oh, Amon! Are you all right?!"

"She's healing them."

"Evanthia, that's enough now. Morgana will break the bindings." A hand grabbed for me, but I whimpered and tightened my arms around Asterion's shoulders.

"*Théa?*" His voice rumbled under my cheek, reassuring and growing stronger.

"Evanthia! How do we stop it? She's getting pale."

The world shook and darkened, but large, warm hands squeezed my waist. Asterion was alive. Birsha was dead. Somehow, it had all worked out the right way.

"Evanthia, darling. Darling, wake up!"

No more nightmares, my sweet victor.

442

46.
WHAT NEXT?

*S*oft fingers combed through my hair, a familiar spice on my tongue.
*A gentle voice hummed an old, merry melody. I was dreaming, of
course, but it was a dream I'd searched for, longed for, missed for
centuries. Golden hair like mine, a wicked, laughing smile, but this time
there were tears in her eyes, little diamond drops that clung to her beautiful cheeks. Tears of abandon and of elation.*

"Where were you?" I asked.

*She cleared in my vision, not a blurry figure but a crisp and recogniz-
able vision. I looked like her, except she was untamed perfection, and I
was flawed and real, baring scars and fine lines. She was made of delight
and wild exultation, and I was living, digging through sorrow and joy
and piecing them together into experience. Half of me was made of her,
but half of me touched the earth, whether that was gentle grass or brutal
stone.*

There are paths in life I cannot tread, daughter. You were out
of reach.

*She laughed, not cruel, but happy to have me back again. I wept as
she stroked my hair.*

"No, sweet *BLODYN BACH*. Don't cry, *CARIAD*. Wake, please
wake."

Feather soft kisses grazed over my cheeks and I hiccuped,
sucking in a lungful of Hywel's drowsy, smoky scent. And then I

laughed through the tears, squirming and finding myself stuffed, stretched and filled on two cocks.

"While I was sleeping?" I teased, opening my eyes and grinning through shaky, wet breaths to stare down at my dragon.

Hywel gasped, eyes lighting up, and then groaned and surged up into me, his mouth sealing over mine in a hungry, desperate kiss. I sighed and parted my lips for his tongue, rocked back into his thrusting hips. Our teeth bumped and our rhythm didn't match and the moment was messy and full of gratitude and reassurance. I gulped *nektar* down eagerly, aware of the hollow ache in my belly, the sore and paper-thin stretch of my tired skin.

"I couldn't find you," Hywel rasped, rolling us on the bed, pecking kisses over my jaw and groaning as he plunged inside of me. "I couldn't get into your dreams. I thought we'd lost you."

"Hywel, are we in the hoard?" I asked, glancing around us.

"*Blodyn bach*," Hywel growled, and then he kissed me once more, hitching my legs around his hips and shifting the angle until I was whining and clinging to him.

I laughed and tried to focus. "The others?"

"Will *wait*," Hywel snarled, taking my face in his hands. He licked into my mouth to stifle my objections, and I moaned as he claimed control of my body from head to toe.

He pulled away, glaring down at me as I cried out, "Hywel! But Asterion—"

"Evanthia, you are my *mate*, yes?"

My eyes fluttered shut on a long sigh as Hywel found a lovely, dizzying spot inside of me. "Yes," I breathed, although the word belonged in answer to his question *and* the height he was driving me to.

"And are you wearing my mark?"

"N-no?"

"No. You are not," he bit out and then groaned, his chest collapsing onto mine, mouth skimming damply against my cheek as he whispered raggedly, "You nearly died, *blodyn bach*."

The mark wouldn't have saved me, I thought, but decided it would be wiser not to say. I turned my cheek and found Hywel's mouth, his eager kiss, the soft broken sounds drawn up from his chest as his arms wrapped around my back. He was barely tucked inside my ass, more focused on grinding deep in my core, but the hot pull there made me shiver with every short stroke.

"Where will you bite?" I asked, tugging on his bottom lip with my teeth.

"You know where," he murmured.

I pulled from his kiss, arching to offer the left side of my throat that he had once claimed as his. Had Conall known to bite the right side, or was that simply luck?

"Do you love me, Evanthia?" Hywel asked, slowing, lifting his face. He arched his eyebrows as I startled and glanced up at him. "You haven't said."

Have you? I thought, but Hywel had *shown* me, had observed all the courting rituals of a dragon, had done all but bite.

I had no courting rituals, no ceremony. I could only offer one thing.

I stroked my hands over Hywel's lean, broad back, up his throat to cup his face. Scales glimmered under the surface of pale skin—a reminder of the true nature of the beast I lay beneath.

"I love you, King of Dreams. I love you, mate of my mate. I love you, Hywel. I will clean your scales and ride your cocks and kiss your lips, and I will share my heart with you, pieced back together as it is," I said, kissing his chin and then his mouth.

His eyes fell shut and he shuddered above me, inside of me.

"Even though you are incredibly wicked to keep me from the others. They must be frantic," I said.

He only grunted in answer. Which meant *yes*.

"Did you really doubt I loved you?" I asked, smoothing his hair through my fingers.

"No," Hywel said slowly, blinking his eyes open and smiling down at me. "But I am a greedy dragon. It's nice to hear the words. I love you, my pretty morsel."

He was right, it *was* nice. I smiled and squirmed beneath him, laughing against his lips as he returned to the steady, perfect pace inside of me, sighing as it stirred warmth in my veins.

"The others will be close," Hywel murmured, trailing his mouth to my shoulder. "They'll need you too."

"Did you leave them behind on the battlefield?" I asked, grinning and grinding my hips to his.

Hywel huffed and then licked my throat, and we fell into a wordless whisper, hands clutching and bodies begging. I didn't notice when he set his teeth to my throat, didn't feel the smooth razor bite. I was too busy falling, feeding, claiming Hywel in turn with the clasp of my flesh around his.

The curtain to the hoard bedroom was whipped aside as we kissed and shivered through the aftershocks.

"Hywel, you bastard!" Laszlo said, and if it weren't for how sated and soft I was, I would've been genuinely shocked at the declaration from my mild-mannered gryphon.

"Don't waste your breath, just get in the bed."

"Asterion," I sighed, and Hywel grunted as I twisted toward my minotaur.

I let out a soft cry, freezing in place, and Asterion, who'd been undressing, stiffened and stared back at me. He was bronze and rust, whole and hearty, but his horns were still ragged. He reached a hand up toward them, touching lightly over the stumps, and then dropped it away.

"They won't heal," Asterion said, lifting his jaw.

I bit my lip and mourned their loss privately, sliding from Hywel to the edge of the bed. My body was still weak, shaky, and I could vaguely recall the voices of my lovers in the cave as they fought to untether me from the vacuum of *néktar* pouring out of me. Conall and Laszlo were undressing, eyes studying me eagerly but wisely not interrupting. Later, I would ask if Rolant and Amon were safe. For now, I had more pressing needs.

My hand lifted, and Asterion bowed his head.

"Do they hurt?" I asked.

"No," he said.

"Good." His eyes looked up, and I fastened my grip around each shortened stem of broken bone, holding his gaze with mine. "I *missed* you."

Asterion groaned and fell hungrily into me with a tug of my grip on his horns. I tangled my arms and legs around my minotaur and shouted as he filled the hollow of my core that Hywel had just left. He paused, nuzzling my fresh wound, with me poised halfway down his cock and squirming for more.

"Laszlo," he called.

My gryphon rushed to the edge of the bed, drawing me back to his hips. "Thank you, *Asterion*."

"We must all learn to share," Asterion said, smiling at me and then arching his head back to accept the kisses I laid on his throat. His heartbeat was beautifully steady under my palm, and if he noticed the grateful tears that fell to his chest, he didn't mention them.

Conall lifted my face from Asterion's fur, crowding close and claiming my mouth, tongue plunging as Laszlo and Asterion nestled me between them.

"I've half a mind to throw you out of the room, dragon," Conall growled.

Hywel's lips quirked. They were probably equally aware that Conall would find that a challenge unless Hywel cooperated.

"I have a better idea, pup," Hywel purred, sliding up from the bed to cuddle against Conall's back and whisper in his ear.

I turned my cheek to rub it against Laszlo's jaws, accepting his nipping kisses, sighing as he and Asterion settled deep inside of me.

"Are you still weak, dear one?" Laszlo asked, licking along the shell of my ear. I shuddered as Asterion flexed his hips, his groan rising with a fresh wave of *néktar*.

"A little," I admitted. My legs were certainly shaky, trembling in Asterion's grip.

Laszlo breathed in my ear, bucking his hips, and I realized Conall and Hywel had found a new occupation.

I grinned and giggled. "But probably not for long," I said.

"Not if we have anything to say about it," Asterion growled, ducking his head to lick into my moaning mouth as four eager bodies surged in my direction.

THE CASTLE WAS AS BUSY AFTER THE BATTLE AS IT HAD BEEN before, although any shadows were firmly attached to the real feet that crossed the stone floors and carpets.

I paused in the kitchen at the sight of Auguste overseeing a small army of house elves, one tiny figure shooing away a few snooping orcs.

Busier, actually.

Laszlo shepherded us out of the frenzy and into the main corridor, and that too was active, full of familiar and unfamiliar figures passing.

"Evanthia! You're all right!"

I stiffened as a blur of red velvet and dark curls rushed toward me, gasping as Esther caught me in a fierce hug.

"Amon?" I asked.

"Fine! He's been wanting to see you," Esther said, pulling away, beaming and flushed. She leaned in and lowered her voice. "Sphinx are very particular about debts, so don't argue with him or he'll be unmanageable."

I blinked and opened my mouth, unsure of my answer, when another voice called my name.

"Rolant!" I called, unexpectedly pleased to see him.

The dragon appeared from a doorway. He was pale, more severe than we'd last seen him, and he bowed stiffly in my direction. At my side, Laszlo tightened his arm around my middle.

"I won't come closer. You've done more for me than you ought to as it is," Rolant said. He nodded to Laszlo. "I only wanted to offer my thanks before I left."

"So soon?" Laszlo asked.

"I have affairs to get in order," Rolant said.

"But you're all right?" I asked, frowning at the careful way he held himself.

"I'll finish healing soon enough."

If Laszlo and Rolant thought they were keeping my *néktar* in line by a few meters of distance, they hadn't really understood what had happened in the cavern, but Rolant must've been well enough healed because I didn't feel a tug in his direction, and he turned and strode away before I could say anything.

Esther's eyes narrowed. "But...he *didn't* really say 'thank you,' did he?"

I snorted, and Laszlo shook his head.

"He's rushing off before we call in his debt," Laszlo said, and we continued on our way to the main room.

448

"I don't need *debts*," I muttered, shaking my head. I would've tried to help Rolant anyway, but in truth, I hadn't really been in control of the matter.

We slowed to a stop as we reached the great hall. Conall and Asterion were strolling in from the upper rooms, and Hywel was standing at the center, flanked by three women. One, with glimmering hair and golden skin, turned and beamed at me, and I stiffened to a standstill.

Nimue.

"My victor!" she cried, her voice all lightness and cheer. "At last. I've been positively *desperate* to see you."

On Hywel's other side, Nimue's sister stood in brilliant shadow, smiling wryly at me and holding the hand of the third woman, a feline beauty with vast wings, her sphinx mate, Khepri. I decided then that of the two sisters, I preferred Morgana, or Magdalena, or whatever she wanted to be called. Nimue floated toward us, silver-blue gown billowing and fanning around her lithe frame with every step. She and Magdalena did have similar features aside from their coloring, but there was a kind of hunger in this fae that set me on edge, or perhaps I couldn't shake the gory vision of her in the cavern, clawing strength from me against my will.

I stepped forward, tugging Laszlo by the hand to stand behind me, and Nimue slowed, canny gaze narrowing.

I would've saved them, you know, a hiss in my head offered. Out loud, Nimue said to me, "You're quite unlike my other victors."

"I only meant to help the centicore," I said, frowning and remembering the way Excalibur had been pierced into the poor creature's side.

Nimue's smile flashed, bright and garish. "Small choices make grand changes in fate's wheel."

"Sister," Magdalena called, drawing the fae's attention away. "I leave for Star Manor. Why don't you join me? We're overdue a reunion."

Nimue laughed, and the sound was made of brittle bells. "Oh! What a clever thought. Why don't you let me play the part of one of your little human entertainments? I make a lovely whore!"

Magdalena winked at me briefly, and Khepri, the sphinx, gave

449

her a nervous glance. "I'll consult the cards," Magdalena said smoothly.

"The cards," Nimue giggled. "How droll."

The room took a collective sigh as the fae left out the broad front door of the castle.

"I feel as though someone should send along a warning to the girls in the manor," Esther murmured, frowning.

IT TOOK DAYS, BUT SLOWLY THE CASTLE SETTLED. VISITORS came and went, bringing news of Birsha's allies who'd been lost or caught, the refugees of his houses and where they now rested, and recovered allies who were now safely free. Gradually, more left than arrived. Some, like Marius, never even appeared. He'd sent word instead from London, already reunited with Lillian and assuring Asterion that Grace House was safe and continued in good keeping.

"Will you sell Grace House or keep it?" I asked Asterion. I was learning to appreciate the ragged ends of his horns. They were especially sensitive, and the more I touched them, the more at ease he seemed to be with the loss.

He smiled and tightened his arm around my waist. I'd interrupted his latest meeting and locked the door behind me, and he hadn't even protested or claimed there was more to do.

Someone else can manage the trouble for a few hours, he'd said, and then pulled me onto his lap.

"I may gift it. Isabel's not done with it, and there's another... interested party who'd like to make it their home, I think," Asterion said with a sly smile. He bent his head to mine for a kiss and huffed as a knock on the door interrupted us. "Who is it?"

"Me," Conall called. "Hazel and Hunter and the others are readying to leave."

"Oh!" I climbed off Asterion's lap, flushing and accepting his help in cleaning me up enough to say our farewells.

Esther and her family had left two days prior, with a shocking number of hugs and a promise to host us all in Egypt as soon as we wanted. Amon had placed himself in my debt, and I'd whispered my request in his ear before saying goodbye. I didn't know if it was possible, but he'd looked thoughtful and nodded, and I could be patient enough to see how it played out.

I hurried directly to Hazel when we reached the great hall, a strange thrill in my heart as our arms wrapped around one another in a fierce hug. My friends before Birsha had mostly been human, and all of them were gone now. But Hazel was barely aging, and Esther had mentioned she was considering becoming a vampire, and I'd be very much surprised if Marius hadn't already determined several methods of making sure his wife lived a longer than human life span.

I had mates I could live my years out with, and now friends too. I released Hazel slowly, blushing when I realized how tightly I'd held her.

"I've kept in touch with the yew trees. All's well. They're eating away at the corruption faster than I expected," she said softly.

"There's nothing to worry about?" I whispered back.

She shook her head, smiling. "Magda—Mor—" She rolled her eyes and waved her hand. "Magdalena says there was nothing there to resurrect him with, just a bit of nasty residue, and that's fading quickly."

I sighed and nodded. "Good."

"*Very* good. I...I hope you'll come to London soon. Come to the theater," she added, grinning. "You'll love that. A proper feast for you by the end of the first act."

Promises of visits were exchanged, more hugs—dozens of hugs, it seemed—and then Hazel and her men slowly peeled away, waving goodbye as we remained at the castle doors, watching them climb into their carriage.

I held my breath as they bumped along the road, under the cover of the woods. Warm shadows and gentle hands surrounded my back, that first real taste of the peace we'd been promising ourselves settling in the air.

"What next?" I whispered, blinking.

The others were quiet for a moment as we absorbed the shift. Birsha was gone. Our lives were our own again. But what did that mean?

"I was in the middle of a book before you arrived," Laszlo said. "I might finish it."

Conall groaned and stretched, turning back to the castle. "I could use a nap."

"It feels as though I haven't had a minute of leisure in decades," Asterion admitted. "Might just...go for a walk."

I smiled and turned to Hywel, whose gaze was distant and unfocused. His eyes slid slowly to mine, a sheepish blush on his cheeks. I tipped my head, waiting to hear his plans.

"I've received word from the puck," Hywel said slowly. Laszlo's breath hitched, and Hywel swallowed before continuing, "About a bit of treasure in Portugal."

I grinned and wheeled back to the road, staring at the horizon. "I've never been to Portugal," I said.

There was a pause, a ruffle of feathers, and an itchy excitement in my chest from Conall.

"I'll pack a bag," Asterion said.

I laughed, squealing as Conall hauled me up and spun me toward the castle. "An adventure is just what I was thinking of," he cried.

I glanced over his shoulder and sighed at the picture of Hywel's head slightly bent, his lips against Laszlo's. They parted softly, and Laszlo turned and granted me a wink.

"I'll read my book on the way."

EPILOGUE
MANY YEARS LATER

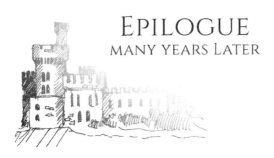

Asterion groaned as I pulled the hat from his head, revealing his horns at last. They'd grown slightly in the past century or so, starting to regain their curves at the corners, but they still irritated him under the disguises we used when traveling. He hitched me up off my tired feet and carried me as I combed my fingers through his dark curls.

"It's good to be home," Hywel sighed, the castle gates swinging shut behind us.

"You say that now. You'll be itching to go again in a month or so," I teased.

Asterion huffed, nostrils flaring. "I say we send Conall and Laszlo with him then. Have the place to ourselves."

I hummed. "Perhaps. Although I missed them this month. Perhaps our next adventure is a vacation?"

"Our life is a vacation, *blodyn bach*," Hywel laughed.

I grinned and shrugged. So it was. I had no complaints.

"But we do owe Amon and his little flock of vampires a visit," Hywel mused.

"You promised him no treasure hunting in Egypt," I reminded Hywel, whose lips twisted in annoyance. "You can't, Hywel. I'll miss Esther if I have to go thirty years without seeing her again."

"Oh, I promised and I meant it. But when it's for *sale* in a marketplace...?"

I ignored the question and gasped as bright golden wings

appeared in the opening door of the castle. Asterion let me down, and I took off like a shot, racing toward my gryphon.

Laszlo caught me in a firm embrace, both of us groaning as we filled our lungs with the scent of each other. "How was your flight?"

"Going through customs with Hywel is a nightmare, but planes are much smoother than travel by dragon," I murmured in his ear, and Laszlo laughed. "I brought you a present."

"You always bring me a present."

I scoffed and leaned back. "Are you saying you don't want it?"

Laszlo ducked his head. "I only want one thing from you at the moment, dear one."

I smiled and arched up for his kiss, sighing and softening in his embrace.

"I found it, *cariad! The Freewheelin'* with the missing tracks!" Hywel called. "I *told* you we should've gotten it when it came out."

Laszlo nipped my lips and then looked up at Hywel with an indulgent smile. "If we'd bought it at the time, you wouldn't have had half as much fun hunting it down later, would you?"

Hywel bent over my shoulder, including himself in our kiss. "True enough, my love. True enough. Where's our little silver wolf?"

"Here."

I squealed and squirmed out from between the two of them, racing inside to my mate. Conall growled and scooped me up. "Saved the best for last?" he asked.

"Oh, Hywel! I think there are new ones," I called, digging through Conall's locks in search of gray hairs.

"It's only a streak," Conall huffed, wrestling me away, but he eyed his reflection in a nearby mirror and frowned. "It ought to be more than that. I sometimes think your *néktar* is keeping me young."

"Maybe," I said. Or maybe the sphinx had managed to grant my request after all. I didn't care, as long as Conall got to grow old and ageless with the rest of us.

Conall blinked and turned back to me, scowling. "What are you doing over there? Get back in my arms, you little rascal."

I dove toward him, and Conall peppered my face with kisses, sighing as he tucked his cheek against my throat, sniffing the mark he'd made there that still shone like a fresh scar.

"Missed you, *mo chroí*," he whispered.

"Missed you, my mate."

"Laszlo's latest batch of kombucha is dreadful. Tell me you found him something new to obsess over."

"Coffee again, but this time they brew it cold," I answered, shrugging.

"As long as it isn't prone to explosion," Conall sighed. "Hunter texted. He and the others want to surprise Hazel with a visit here for her birthday."

"Oh, yes please!"

"Well, come on, everyone!" Hywel called, waving his latest treasure in the air. "I've waited this whole trip to listen."

"Where did you find it?" Conall asked, greeting Hywel with a kiss.

"An estate sale in Missouri, of all places," Hywel said, pulling the record from its sleeve and eyeing it greedily.

"He's more excited than he was about the moon rock," Asterion whispered to Conall.

The three of us exchanged wide-eyed glances. We didn't have the heart to mention to Hywel how *many* moon rocks existed in the world, and he was still the clumsiest of us when it came to using the internet.

"I like Dylan. In my opinion, this is a better find," Conall answered in a mutter.

I nudged them both to silence, and we trailed along together back to the large room that overlooked what was now merely a reasonably sized lake instead of a sea. On a warm day, we would fly down and go swimming. Hywel collected rare floaties, although I suspected it had less to do with their potential value and more to do with his personal amusement.

Laszlo patiently helped Hywel set up the record player, the pair of them smiling and exchanging small, welcoming touches.

"How was it?" Conall asked me.

"Fun, as usual. This is better, though," I said, curling up against his side.

"Mm. Next time, we'll all go," Conall said.

"Hywel wants to visit Amon."

Conall snorted. "Then we'll all *have* to go, or he'll get us into trouble again."

Hywel hurried back to sit at my side, drawing my legs up over his lap and patting them, his eyes bright with excitement. "Ready," he called, and Laszlo dropped the needle gently.

The truth was, I didn't really care about treasure, whether it was valuable or curious or mythical. I cared about these men. I cared about the life we chased after, fought for, celebrated in.

I returned Asterion's patience and generosity by always remaining at his side. I thanked Conall for the life and vigor he'd gifted me by thrusting it back at him with all the strength I had in me. I met Laszlo's study and diligence and refused to let him sink into stagnancy, constantly drawing change into his life, new curiosities to absorb him. I treasured Hywel, in all his greedy and never-ending hunger, because he matched me perfectly.

"Are you getting tired, my love?" I asked as Hywel yawned and stretched out on the couch.

He grinned, sharp and hungry. "Oh, *blodyn bach*, I have many centuries left before I rest," he said, rolling toward me, pinning me against a chuckling Conall. We caught the eye of Asterion and Laszlo, and my endless appetite stirred in satisfaction. I'd been patient, but it was time for a reunion of our little family.

"Good," I said, nipping at Hywel's lips. "Because I have plans for you. For all of us, as a matter of fact."

THE END.

AFTERWORD

"Nine inch will please a lady" featured in chapter 3 by our charming Red Wolf is a poem mostly likely by Robert Burns himself, or perhaps collected by him.

Thank you so much for reading this book and for reading the Tempting Monsters series! This series really changed my career over these past couple years, and it's sad and exciting and terrifying all at once to gently close the door on it now.

If you haven't read The Basilisk of Star Manor (Marius and Lillian's story) I highly recommend doing so. And if you'd be open to me writing more novellas in this universe, let me know! Birsha is now gone (huzzah!) and so the main arch of this series is over, but I have a few ideas for little side quests and smaller romances I'm interested in exploring.

Be sure to hang out in Kathryn's Moongazers on Facebook to keep up with the latest!

ACKNOWLEDGMENTS

Thank you to:

Jodie-Leigh, my incredible cover designer and delightful enabler.

Jess Whetsel my keen-eyed and word-wise editor. Meghan Leigh Daigle, my precise proofreader.

My amazing Moongazers who cheer on each and every kinky and playful step. TikTokers and Instagrammers who found this series and made it blow up well beyond a success I even knew how to imagine!

My writing pack, made up of the most amazing women a girl could be lucky enough to know and get to talk to regularly!

And finally, my amazing family and close friends who cheer for me so hard their arms must be super tired from waving the pompoms like that. I'm incredibly lucky to share my life and my work with so many amazing people!

ABOUT THE AUTHOR

USA Today Best Selling Author Kathryn Moon, is a country mouse who started dictating stories to her mother at an early age. The fascination with building new worlds and discovering the lives of the characters who grew in her head never faltered, and she graduated college with a fiction writing degree. She loves writing women who are strong in their vulnerability, romances that are as affectionate as they are challenging, and worlds that a reader sinks into and never wants to leave. When her hands aren't busy typing they're probably knitting sweaters or crimping pie crust in Ohio. She definitely believes in magic.

You can reach her on Facebook and at ohkathrynmoon@ gmail.com or you can sign up for her newsletter!

ALSO BY KATHRYN MOON

COMPLETE READS

The Librarian's Coven Series

Written

Warriors

Scrivens

Ancients

Standalones

Good Deeds

Command The Moon

Say Your Prayers - co-write with Crystal Ash

Secrets of Summerland

The Sweetverse

Baby + the Late Night Howlers

Lola & the Millionaires - Part One

Lola & the Millionaires - Part Two

Bad Alpha

Faith and the Dead End Devils

Sol & Lune

Book 1

Book 2

Inheritance of Hunger Trilogy

The Queen's Line

The Princess's Chosen

The Kingdom's Crown

SERIES IN PROGRESS

Sweet Pea Mysteries

The Baker's Guide To Risky Rituals

The Knitter's Guide to Banishing Boyfriends

Tempting Monsters

A Lady of Rooksgrave Manor

The Company of Fiends

Sanctuary with Kings

Novellas

The Basilisk of Star Manor

The Guardian of Grace House (coming...??)

Monster Smash Agency

Games with the Orc

Howl for the Gargoyle (coming 2023)

81798350R20277